P9-CMT-066

PRAISE FOR
PERRI O'SHAUGHNESSY'S BESTSELLING
NINA REILLY NOVELS

BREACH OF PROMISE

"A LEGAL MYSTERY FOR THOUGHTFUL
READERS . . . THE DIALOGUE IS CLEAN
AND SMART AND THE SURPRISE TWISTS
WONDERFULLY EFFECTIVE."
—*San Francisco Chronicle*

"LOTS OF UNEXPECTED TWISTS AND TURNS
. . . A SAVVY LEGAL THRILLER."
—*The Orlando Sentinel*

"GRIPPING COURTROOM DRAMA . . .
HEART-STOPPING . . . RIVETING."
—*Booklist*

OBSTRUCTION OF JUSTICE

"NINA REILLY IS ONE OF THE MOST
INTERESTING HEROINES IN LEGAL
THRILLERS TODAY."
—*San Jose Mercury News*

"A ROLLER-COASTER RIDE . . . A TALE
NOT TO BE MISSED."
—*Midwest Book Review*

"A CAPTIVATING MYSTERY . . . A
BEAUTIFULLY PLOTTED NOVEL."
—*Monterey County Herald*

Please turn the page for more extraordinary acclaim. . . .

ALSO BY PERRI O'SHAUGHNESSY

ACTS
OF
MALICE

PERRI
O'SHAUGHNESSY

Island Books
Published by
Dell Publishing
a division of
Random House, Inc.
1540 Broadway
New York, New York 10036

Dell® is a registered trademark of Random House, Inc.

ISBN 0-440-22581-7

Reprinted by arrangement with Delacorte Press

Manufactured in the United States of America

Published simultaneously in Canada

June 2000

10 9 8 7 6 5 4 3 2 1

OPM

Dedicated to the memory of Kathleen Miller O'Shaughnessy and to the Miller family

ACKNOWLEDGMENTS

We would like to express our grateful appreciation to the many people who helped us in writing this book. Patrick O'Shaughnessy, our brother and a partner in the Salinas law firm of Rucka, O'Boyle, Lombardo & McKenna, made a creative contribution to the ending and, as always, kept us aware of the masculine viewpoint. Even more, though, Pat's enthusiasm and sense of humor livened up our characters.

We thank Heather Mansoori of Walnut Creek, California, for her help in discussing some of the medical issues in the novel.

Maggie Crawford, our tactful editor at Delacorte Press, had a substantial role in strengthening various elements of the book. Her unflagging efforts compelled us to take it a level higher. We feel strongly supported by all the staff at Delacorte Press, especially its publisher, Carole Baron, and we would like to thank those in the art, marketing, publicity, and sales departments who add so much from behind the scenes.

Nancy Yost, our agent at Lowenstein Associates, Inc., was always available, always gracious, always savvy. She, too, has made creative suggestions that have improved the book.

We would like to thank our families for keeping us

grounded and happy throughout the writing process: Andy, Brad, Cory, June, and Connor.

Our cousin in Memphis, Helen Pearce, provided a funny Internet anagram that we enjoyed so much we put it in the book. And our cousin in Atascadero, Tim Tucker, a.k.a. Michael A, gave us the lyrics quoted in Chapter 13. The lyrics are from the song "Kevorkian Lips," © 1998 Walter Beeyt Project.

Finally, we thank the many readers who have sent e-mails to us, expressing enjoyment from reading our books. We feel very lucky to have their support and good wishes.

(*Excerpts from* THE STATE BAR OF CALIFORNIA
STANDING COMMITTEE ON PROFESSIONAL
RESPONSIBILITY AND CONDUCT
FORMAL OPINION NO. 1996-146)

Information about client misconduct imparted to a lawyer in the course of a lawyer-client relationship or which is involved in the representation of a client is subject to California Business and Professions Code section 6068 (e)1, which provides:

It is the duty of an attorney:

(e) To maintain inviolate the confidence, and at every peril to himself or herself to preserve the secrets, of his or her client.

ACTS
OF
MALICE

PROLOGUE

PRETENDING HE WAS still asleep, he felt his wife crawl out of bed.

Outside, he could hear birds. That meant last night's snowfall had stopped. He wondered if the sun had finally blasted through the layer of clouds that had cursed the sky the past several days.

Jim Strong didn't move, didn't even open his eyes. He followed the sounds as Heidi got ready in the bathroom, the ritual of every morning: splash water on her face, brush her teeth, search her face in the mirror until it was all back in place, her past, her present, her secrets.

She sprayed her hair and ran her fingers through it over and over. She squeezed sun block onto her hands and rubbed it on her pale skin. Every sound, so placid, so falsely suggestive of domestic peace, aroused a fresh wave of anger in him. She had no right to be so sure of anything. Not after what she had done.

He controlled his breathing as she came softly into the dim bedroom and paused at the foot of the bed. He felt her eyes landing on him, and stopping to prowl over his face. Then she turned away. He watched through slitted eyes as she slipped the long T-shirt off over her head, her long white back with the bumpy spine, the tight calves, and delicate feet that she was inserting quietly and carefully into her tights.

She was so very beautiful. After three years, he loved her more than ever. She had seemed so blunt, so honest, like he was, forceful, an athlete with her own code of honor.

He had always thought, if she ever cheats on me I'll —but now that she had, he didn't want to hurt her. He just wanted her to turn back toward him, where she belonged.

The ski bibs slid like satin over her body. Balancing on one leg, she pulled on her raglan socks, then tiptoed out of the room, carrying her boots and parka.

He opened his eyes. He could hear better with his eyes open. Now she drank a glass of milk greedily, down to the last drop. Now she stuffed her keys into her fanny pack, and shut it with a zip. Now she bumped into the fish tank, and now . . .

She was leaving.

Out on the street, she scraped snow off the windshield. Then the cold motor turned and started up. She didn't wait as long as usual for it to warm up. Forcing it into action, she took off.

He threw off the covers and jumped out of bed. Pulling up the shade, he saw what the new storm had brought: sunshine in a searing white blaze, and at least two feet of new snow, feathery and dry.

Was she going to meet her lover? He studied the heavily burdened trees, aware that for once in his life he didn't know what to do.

No matter. It would come to him.

At Paradise, both quad lifts were operating and the hill was jammed with skiers. Carrying his Rossignols

over his shoulder, Jim walked along the wall of the lodge
and examined the rows of skis.

No sign of Heidi's Kila. He would know, since he'd
watched her a hundred nights waxing them and fiddling
with the bindings, getting them perfect. He went into
the lodge restaurant.

"Seen Heidi?" he said to the day hostess, who
looked like Heidi, but was chunky and plainer. Gina
something, her name was. He had let her know when
she was hired that part of the job was to help him keep
tabs on the rest of the family.

"No, sir." That was good. He liked respect. He was
the boss. "I think she was in about half an hour ago. She
couldn't wait to get out on the powder."

"Who was she with?"

"Um, nobody. Your father's already in the back office, Mr. Strong."

"Okay." He didn't want to see his father right now.
"My brother show up?"

"Alex and Marianne just left," the girl went on.
"They were arguing. I think they separated."

"The gang's all here," Jim said. He chucked her under the chin. He knew she didn't like that, which made
him enjoy the gesture even more. He was angry at her
for looking like Heidi.

"Gangbuster day," she said with a bright phony
smile, and went back to work.

Pulling on his goggles to cut the glare, Jim trudged
outside. He wondered where Heidi might be skiing.
Off-trail somewhere, probably. Maybe somewhere with
Marianne. She was probably filling Heidi's head with
ideas about leaving him.

On the other hand, it was Marianne who had
warned him to watch Heidi in the first place, good

advice, as it turned out. He had watched and watched until Heidi screamed at him to stop spying. Then he had told her he knew.

With that half-defiant, half-scared look he was beginning to know so well, she had admitted it. She had said she was thinking of leaving him. She had told him who it was, cutting him off at the knees.

The sun burned into his face. He leaned against the outer wall of the lodge and slathered on sunscreen.

He could just ski, forget about her, and get in a few runs. From the top he could see most of the trails, though if she was off-trail in the trees he would never find her.

He decided to cruise down some of the black-diamond runs. Give her time to meet her lover, if she had the nerve. He would catch up to her sooner or later, and then . . . something would happen.

He skied all morning on the expert runs. The powder was so sensational he even forgot her now and then, although the anger in him still burned like hot lead in his stomach.

He had never been in such virgin powder. Once he came across Marianne snowboarding along the Ogre Trail, her black hair flying over red bibs. He flew by her, lifting one pole in a salute, but he doubted Marianne had even seen him.

He saw no sign of Heidi. He missed her, wanted her by his side.

Later, at the lodge, he ate lunch. As he spooned thin vegetable soup into his mouth, the hostess told him she thought his father had gone for the day. She reported no sightings of Alex or Heidi.

After eating, he went out again. He was hunting.

The day had deepened into a mellow afternoon, still crystal clear on the slopes, warmer.

He fell through light and shadow on white crystals, weightless, swerving and turning and falling endlessly, then riding back up to do it all over again.

No sign of her. He had a brainstorm. Maybe she was skiing the Cliff. She had talked about it often, but he thought she had never followed through. Today, with the snow so tempting, the conditions so perfect . . . maybe.

He took the Bald Eagle run halfway to an opening in the forest and dodged into it, pushing up his goggles as he ducked in because of the dark that closed around him. The faint downhill trail they usually followed was buried under the snow, and he had to look sharp to avoid trees and gullies.

In a clearing on the side of the mountain, steep and wooded, expert territory, the trail opened up.

Heidi wasn't there, but Alex was sitting in the snow, fixing one of his bindings.

Jim skied straight across to him.

"What are you doing here?" Alex asked sourly.

"What's the matter? Did you break it?"

"I don't like the fit on one of them. I spent an hour working on this fucking binding this morning and it still doesn't fit. I mean, I can ski, but I really hoped for what I paid I could get it so tight my foot would be screaming."

"Sit there." Jim planted his poles and herringboned over to Alex.

"Watch yourself. It's a long slide and the Cliff is dead ahead," Alex said. He stretched his leg out so Jim could have a look. The ski stuck straight up into the air.

"I remember." Jim took Alex's boot. "I can't fix it

with you sitting there. Get your lazy ass up and stand on it. What did you do to your eye?" He helped Alex up and gave him time to kick out a level platform and stand on the ski.

"Gene Malavoy came up to me in the parking lot last night and laid into me. I don't even know what it was about. I fought him off and he ran. Know anything about it?"

"I fired him yesterday. Can't imagine why he'd go after you, though."

"Fired him? What did you do that for?"

"Let's talk about it later. Step out of the binding now. Seen Heidi?" Jim pulled a glove off with his teeth and got to work on the ice-encrusted binding.

"She's off duty today, isn't she?"

"Yeah. She's up here somewhere."

"Maybe she's with Marianne."

"I saw Marianne. On the Ogre. Alone."

"Marianne likes that trail."

"You doing the Cliff?" Jim said.

"I'm doing the side of the Cliff," Alex said.

"Pretty extreme run."

Alex looked at him sideways, on the alert for a challenge. He was three years younger. He had never been able to keep up with Jim. "It's only for people with a death wish," he said. "We did it. Remember? I was, what? Thirteen? And you were sixteen."

"Yeah, but we were crazy then. I still don't know how you made it. Only thirteen years old. Jesus, Alex. You skied like a sonofabitch back then." He slapped an open buckle shut on Alex's boot, and noted a slight wince as the boot tightened over his ankle.

"You don't think I can still do it?" Alex asked.

"I never said that," said Jim, getting up, watching it

so he didn't start to slide. "Do it if you want. I don't give a shit."

"We could both go," Alex said, bending down to adjust his bib over his boot. "Straight down, then that last-minute turn before complete destruction. Remember?"

"Hotdogger's dream," Jim agreed. "It feels a lot tighter. Thanks."

"No problem."

"You haven't run down here since?"

"Not me," Jim said. "Thought about it a few times." He hadn't really, not after Alex had left and moved to Colorado with their mother and Kelly. "The snow's right. Deep powder, slows you down."

Alex kicked at the snow, testing the bindings. "So?"

"Why not? I feel stupid enough to do it."

"Let's do it."

He watched Alex methodically check his binding and boot buckles, watched him pull his long hair out of his eyes and look toward the edge, face eager and eyes on fire. He remembered the first time they had barreled toward the Cliff, making the turn just in time, going a thousand miles an hour, miraculously avoiding the trees. He remembered the look of fear on Alex's face, his own abject terror.

He also remembered his father's rage when Alex bragged about it later. "You are the older one, Jim. I hold you responsible . . ."

"So are we doin' it or not?" Alex was already dusting off the poles, going into his stance.

"Yeah," Jim said. Lining up next to his younger brother, he adjusted his goggles and looked up at the sky. Perfect conditions.

"Last one down is a rotten egg," Alex said, same as he had said the first time.

Down they plunged, playing to the fringes, moving on the edge of out of control instantly. The powder was so light it barely slowed them down. Knee-deep in it, they slid down the mountain. Jim fought to stay upright and avoid the trees. Alex, up ahead, laughed insanely.

Just that millisecond of watching Alex, and he almost went down! Jim flew on, gesturing like a madman, feeling like a madman, shrieking with laughter in the still air, hearing Alex's answering shriek down below, knowing it was coming up, the last moment, the moment of the turn, and he couldn't remember and he didn't care, was it go left or go right, left or right, right or left—

Alex turned left, so he went right—

Alex went left, but then he went into a skid so fast he blurred. He was skidding sideways straight down, fast, faster, straight toward the Cliff. Jim, bearing hard right, saw the whole thing, Alex getting the skis under him too late, going into a tuck, going for it—

Over. Alex went over the Cliff. No sound.

Jim thought he heard a bad noise below. Then he skied over a fallen limb and caught it on the edge.

He saw the tree. He crashed—

1

Through her office door, Nina Reilly heard the gentle guitar and coaxing voice of Carlos Botelho, singing that love is a paradox that disappears the moment you find it. Sandy Whitefeather, her secretary, had developed a fixation on this particular recording and had been playing it over and over for two weeks. In the outer office, Sandy hummed along with the tune, if that rasping monotone could be called a hum.

After a long morning in court, Nina had just had lunch, a spicy quesadilla from Margarita's Mexican Restaurant across Lake Tahoe Boulevard from the office. Her yellow silk blouse now sported a salsa stain on the front, right where it stuck out the most. Men didn't have this structural difficulty. Also, sometimes they had the advantage of those patterned ties, so useful for catching drips.

Naturally, the prospective client who had come to consult her was an attractive male, tieless but stainless, who had immediately noticed the blouse. He had noticed all of her very thoroughly before he sat down, and now he was looking around the office, getting his bearings.

A, amor . . .
Love takes its rhythm from the sea
Seeking and leaving eternally

Outside her window a light, dry snow fell, shot through with sunlight as the squall moved on across the Sierra into the high desert of the Carson Valley. It was only the beginning of November, and snow already capped the giant peaks that surrounded South Lake Tahoe. At over six thousand feet, Tahoe caught the cold currents of winter long before the valleys of the San Joaquin and the Pacific Coast.

Stretching out her legs under the desk to relieve the pressure on her stomach, she gazed past him toward that calming fall of snow, thinking, here it comes again, the change of weather, the new case, the trouble that falls endlessly through the door.

"You're gonna love this one," Sandy had told her the day before, handing her the phone message slip. This could mean anything: that Sandy approved of the client's political beliefs, family ties, or bank account.

Nina had written his name and address and phone number at the top of her legal pad: James Strong, Paradise Lodge Manager, care of Paradise Ski Resort, Stateline, Nevada. "Call me Jim," he had said as he looked her over, holding out a hand. He had taken off his red, white, and black Tommy Hilfiger parka and seated himself in one of the client chairs, but he didn't seem ready to talk yet.

She watched him check out the office with its fiddle-leaf fig in the sunny corner, the picture on her desk of Bob, looking not-too-thrilled at being caught on film by the school photographer, and the framed certificates on the walls. Nina Reilly, attorney-at-large. Graduate, Monterey College of Law. Admitted to practice before the Supreme Court of the State of California.

Hard-earned certificates. So hard earned, it had taken five years to pay off the student loans.

The low-key surroundings seemed to reassure him. Some prospective clients preferred ostentation. They went elsewhere. The Law Offices of Nina Reilly consisted of the front office where Sandy reigned and clients waited, the library and conference room next door where coffee was made and depositions were held, and Nina's small office in back, just big enough for the oversized desk and a couple of orange chairs given to her by her sister-in-law.

While Jim Strong looked around, she formed her own impression of him: blue eyes burning out of his face; brown hair, cropped close; powerful neck, finely honed features; a jock with brains. Skiing as a lifestyle had tanned his skin, beefed up his shoulders, and narrowed the rest of his profile. He was younger than Nina by a few years, in his late twenties. He wore a red sweater and jeans.

His physical presence was blinding. The ski bunnies must love him.

But it was his expression that her eyes lingered upon, the compressed lips that held things in, the furrow of skin between the thick brown eyebrows, the jaw that clenched and unclenched, working the muscles of his cheeks.

A man in the worst trouble of his life, she diagnosed, getting up to close the door that Sandy had left cracked open.

Slowly my love changes and becomes beautiful
Sending out sparks, and I catch fire—

She knew the Strong name from constant references in the *Tahoe Mirror*. Straddling Nevada and California, with runs in each state, Paradise was one of the oldest local businesses, a major employer at Tahoe, and one of the few ski resorts that was still run by a family and not a distant corporate conglomerate. Philip Strong, father and owner, also sat on the City Council, got loads of kudos for his philanthropy, and his fair share of respectful reverence for being among the area's founding fathers.

Also favoring the steady stream of publicity was the family's extraordinary athletic skill. Various members competed in world-class ski and snowboarding events that led to awards and exciting close races. It didn't hurt either that their physical good looks cried out for a Sunday photo spread. Nina suspected that they encouraged the coverage, which could only be good for a small resort struggling to wrestle patrons from the behemoths of Squaw and Heavenly.

But the most recent coverage, she remembered now, had been because of a tragedy.

She sat back down and swung her chair around to face him better. He focused on her face and she smiled.

"Any time," she said. "When you're ready."

"It's not easy, coming here." His voice was deeper and older than she had expected.

"I sure do agree with that. I have to come here every day."

A final hesitation, and then he came out with it.

"I think I'm going to be arrested."

She could smell his suntan lotion. Running a lodge

at a ski resort, he must need to use a lot of it. His wide hands were like mallets, so hard used they were cracked and earth colored. He obviously spent more time out- doors than in the lodge. He pushed himself back in his chair, compacting himself, as if trying to contain his energy.

"They're saying I killed my own brother." Opening his mouth, he held it that way for an instant, then snapped it shut, then began grinning in embarrassment and shaking his head. "Sorry. It sounds like such a bad joke. Kill my brother? Can you believe it?"

"Alex Strong was your brother? I read about his death in the paper. I'm very sorry." The front page of the *Mirror* had headlined, "Championship Skier Dies in Accident." She hadn't had time to read the rest, but there had been a large photograph . . . the face had looked like Jim's, the hair lighter and longer, the face younger but no less intense.

"Yes. Alex. First he dies on me, then all this. It's the worst week in my whole life. I'm licked. I can't handle it. I need help. I'm not too stupid to figure that out."

She allowed herself to feel a slight sympathy. He had lost his brother. She, too, had a brother. She had experi- enced grief, also, that lightless sea that rolls in, drowning everything.

But the truth was, almost every person who walked through the door and into her office had experienced misfortune. It was a given. Over the years she had had to become less sensitive to other people's pain and more attuned to her practical role in alleviating it.

"I want to hire you. How much do you need for a retainer?"

"We'll get to that. Tell me about your brother. What happened to him?"

"It was a ski accident last Sunday. Eight days ago. I've barely slept since then. I still can hardly believe he's gone." He swallowed.

"How did it happen?"

"I was with him. We were off-trail on the California side, hotdogging down a thirty-degree slope. The terrain was extreme, but if anybody could ski it, Alex could. We'd both been down that hill under worse conditions. It's a place that we called the Cliff. You head like a bat out of hell straight down, then you have to make a fast turn to avoid the drop-off. Alex was in front. I saw the Cliff coming up, dead ahead. I took a sharp turn to the right and Alex went left."

Nina nodded.

"We were laughing. I thought it was a riot."

Nina scratched a note on her pad and waited.

"Alex missed the turn. That's all. He couldn't get his skis around it. I don't know what happened—an ice patch, maybe. I looked back and saw it happening, how he kept trying to turn, getting closer and closer to the edge. I stopped paying attention to my own skiing and saw at the last second that I was heading flat out for a tree. I veered too sharply and crashed. Not a bad fall, but my left ski released. I wiped the snow off my goggles. I was about fifty feet away from the drop-off, not far at all. But I couldn't do anything to save him. I saw him go over." He paused, breathed deeply, and continued. "He did everything right, went into a tuck, pulled up the poles, went for it. I think he was yelling something, but I don't know what. I couldn't see his face, just the helmet.

"I lost sight of him."

He stopped. His hand went up to touch his forehead.

"What happened then?" Nina asked.

"I heard a sickening thud and I think I heard something, not a cry, more like a grunt, like he got the bejesus knocked out of him. I got my ski back on as fast as I could and rammed down through the trees along the side of the Cliff to him. I was yelling but I couldn't hear an answer.

"He was only out of my sight about ten minutes. Didn't take me long to find him. If it wasn't for the rocks, he would have been all right. He was a great skier. He could handle almost anything. He almost missed them. It was just damn bad luck."

Strong went on. "He'd landed on some granite jutting up through the snow." He stopped, cleared his throat. "Do you have any water?"

"Of course." Nina buzzed. Sandy opened the door and drifted in on a wave of samba music.

> I leave at dawn and walk around the city
> A spell like the mist still on me
> Like rain on me, and I am helpless

Until that moment, Nina had heard only the cheerful, relaxing side of the song, but the story Strong was telling colored the words in a way she had never noticed before. Now, embedded in the tender voice and those guitar chords that never quite resolved into majors or minors, she heard something new.

Sadness. And behind the sway of the rhythm, an evasiveness, a mystery.

Like the mystery behind the words of the skier in front of her.

"Water, please," she said, and Sandy disappeared without a word. Strong waited until the Dixie cup was placed in front of him, took a sip, and raised weary eyes.

"They think I killed him," he said again.

"Who thinks that?"

"Two detectives from the South Lake Tahoe Police Department came out to Paradise to talk to me yesterday. They said they were filling in some blanks for their report. I don't think they believed me. Something's going on."

"Why wouldn't they believe you?" The door was ajar again; Sandy was listening. Oh, well. Sometimes she offered up an astute comment or two after a client left.

"I don't know! I can't imagine why. It was an accident. He skied off a cliff, damn it!"

"You answered their questions?"

He nodded. "I told them everything I could think of. Alex was cremated. We just had the funeral three days ago. They don't give a shit that I've lost my brother. They asked me the same things over and over—how long was it before I got down to the rocks, what kind of shape was Alex in, what did I do to help him. Why didn't I save him. Christ."

They looked at each other. His eyes were dark pools, sunken into his head. His mouth twisted. Fear made people look that way. And just now, she was beginning to understand the fear better.

He was afraid for himself.

"All those questions. I told them everything. How we were yelling, screwing around. I was trying out a brand-new pair of Rossignols—"

"Were you racing?"

"They wanted me to say we were but we weren't. We were just trying to find the powder and have a good time."

"Okay."

"Not that we both don't ski fast," Strong said.

"Maybe too fast for the terrain. That's part of it. The risk."

"Did you tell them that?"

"Yeah. I admitted we were both going too fast. But you have to understand, there were eighteen inches of new snow up there on the mountain. We were up to our knees and still flying. Alex loved powder skiing. Do you ski?"

"Now and then. I'll never get past intermediate."

"My father put all of us kids on skis by the time we were three."

"All?"

"Me and Alex, and Kelly. My sister. She's a lot younger. I'm thirty. Kelly's only twenty-five. She's the only one of us who doesn't work at Paradise. She's one of those perennial students."

Nina wrote it down.

"Alex was twenty-seven. We closed Paradise, of course, and the whole crew came to the funeral. My father isn't taking it very well at all. He loved Alex."

"Philip Strong is your father, right?"

"Huh? Oh. Yeah." Strong looked away, seemed about to say something, but thought better of it.

"Was there an inquest?"

"Not that I know of. Just—an autopsy. The coroner confirmed it was an accident within forty-eight hours. There's supposed to be an autopsy report, but I haven't seen it. I don't want to see it."

"So," said Nina. "Maybe the police just want to clear up a question or two for the report. That's what they told you. Why not believe them, Jim?"

"Because I could see it in their eyes." He sounded convinced, but Nina still couldn't understand his concern.

Looking down at her legal pad she said, "When a family member dies, everything gets magnified. Your brother died suddenly, so more care would be taken with the reports. It's possible the police really were simply closing the books on the case."

She was giving him an opening. It was time for him to tell her the rest, the part that scared him the most. The police did not waste time on obvious accidents.

Right on cue, he said, "There's more." He finished the water and crumpled the paper cup.

"More?"

"It's my wife, Heidi. She took off the day after Alex died. I don't know where she is."

"She's been missing for a week?"

"That's right."

"That's a long time. She hasn't called you? You really have no idea where she might have gone?"

"No. We've been married three years." He said this tentatively, offering up the information as if no longer able to make a determination about which facts might be useful.

Was he afraid his wife's disappearance would convince people he was guilty of something? Nina didn't know him well enough to tell yet. He'd tell her in his own way, and she would have to be patient, allowing the facts to emerge.

Another silence. She made a note, looked expectant.

"She's a headstrong girl." Under his tan, he flushed and looked down at his tapping foot. "Heidi sicced them on me. She . . ." He played with his cup, opening it, crushing it again. "She went to the South Lake Tahoe police on the morning after Alex died, and she talked to the officer on duty, and signed some kind of written statement. I haven't seen it."

"Then how do you know—"

"That she did that? The detectives that came to the resort yesterday told me. And because of this, I didn't show it to them." Strong pulled from the pocket of his jeans a pink Post-it note that stuck to his fingers as he unfolded it with shaky hands. He handed it to Nina.

Heidi Strong's handwriting slanted right, the sign of an extrovert, Nina remembered vaguely. Strong's wife had pressed hard and written the first line in capitals. "**I KNOW WHAT YOU DID TO ALEX.**" Below that spooky lead followed some short lines. Nina read it all in a glance.

> **I KNOW WHAT YOU DID TO**
> **ALEX.**
> I'm leaving.
> I never want to see you again. I mean it,
> Jim.
> Don't even think about trying to find me.

That was it. No signature, no date, just a few words, sharp and direct, incised into the paper.

"Wow," Nina said. No other word seemed adequate. She turned it over and looked for something more but there was nothing.

"I found it stuck on the toilet lid that morning. Here I was, taking a whiz, just waking up, thinking about Alex, not even knowing anything's going on with her, and I see this note. I thought, I'm dreaming. But I wasn't. I searched the house. She was gone, all right. She'd taken our big suitcase and the roller one that fits under an airplane seat and her electronic keyboard. Her clothes, some books, CD's, her ski gear—everything she really cared about. She even took Freaky "

"Freaky?"

"Our cat. She drove off in the camper, a Tioga. Just big enough for the two of us and maybe a kid, if we ever had one . . ." He chewed on his thumbnail. "At first I thought she'd cool off, and, you know, realize she had totally overreacted. I waited for her to come home, or at least, to call. But it's been seven days and I haven't heard from her. I've called everyone I could think of. Marianne—"

"Who is that?"

"Alex's wife. She swears she doesn't know anything. I had to tell my father, too, but he doesn't have a clue. Then I talked to Heidi's friends on the Ski Patrol. She's a supervisor at Paradise. Nobody knows anything, or at least no one will tell me anything. She just took off without a word."

"Well, she left these words, Jim. What do you think she means?" Nina held up the note.

"Obviously, she blames me for Alex's death. When she got to Boulder Hospital that night, they were operating on Alex, trying to save him. I knew he wouldn't make it—" Strong exhaled in a short gust. "Just a minute," he said. Jumping out of the chair, he went to Nina's window, the one that looked toward Mount Tallac, one of the high mountains that ringed Tahoe.

The snow had cleared quickly, leaving a sparkling, already melting inch of white on the pane. Strong leaned close to the window, and from the side, through the slashing sunlight that forced its way between the dark layers of cloud hanging over the town, Nina could see the deep brown of his lashes and the glistening of his eyes as he stared out. She looked down at the Post-it. A ray of early-afternoon sun lit up the note like a laser. It looked like it might burst into flame at any second.

In the next room, Botelho sang,

> *Joy is green like a forest*
> *It burns and turns to ash, then grows again*

"I don't know what to do. I love Heidi," Jim said to the window. "She's—everything, you know? Who put this insane idea into her head?"

"The idea that—"

"I don't even want to say it. It's too bizarre for words. I keep thinking I'm gonna lose her for good. I couldn't stand that. I have to find her."

He came back to her desk, on her side, and leaned over it, putting his hands flat on the desk. "One of our employees, a woman named Jessica Sweet, told me to come and see you. She said you did a great job in an invasion of privacy case. She said you were unusual. That I could trust you."

"I remember Mrs. Sweet." Nina shifted in her seat. He was too close to her but seemed oblivious to the encroachment into her space. He had the nonchalance of an attractive man who was very comfortable with women. She caught the scent of the lotion on his skin again. Something tropical and warm smelling. Almonds?

With his head slightly cocked, he scrutinized her. "That's what I need. Someone I can relate to. Someone on my side."

"I agree that you need help. I'd like to try to help you."

"I like it that you're a woman. I feel good with you." Seeming satisfied for the moment, he went back to his chair.

"So Heidi blames you for your brother's death," Nina said. Might as well be blunt about it.

The twist of the mouth again. "So it seems."

"You have no idea why?"

"No idea."

"You've had some marital problems?"

"Just the usual."

Now she was sure he was evading her questions. "What happened at home the night before she left you?"

"We came home from the hospital. I was exhausted. She wouldn't talk. Not a word. I thought she was in shock. She's known Alex as long as she's known me. She went upstairs. I drank some tequila—a lot. I crawled into bed. She was there, sleeping. I woke her up. We talked and . . ." He cleared his throat, let her fill in the blanks. "Then it was morning, and she was gone."

Tenderly my love
Returns my caresses

"Brazilian music. Marianne plays that stuff all the time." He thumped the desk with one finger to the beat. "How can you hear yourself think?" Before Nina could answer, Sandy had turned off the CD. In the silence that followed, he pulled out his checkbook.

"Please. Find Heidi," he said. "And I also want you to get this mess about Alex straightened out. Can you do that?"

He clamped his lips shut before the question degraded into a plea, although she thought she could see the urgency of his need behind the hot eyes.

She pushed her chair slightly away from her desk and

from Strong. Did she want him as her client? She could tell him she had to think about it.

Once she was in, she would be all the way in.

She spent a moment mentally reviewing her other obligations and wondering where Strong might take her. He could have gone to anyone in town, to the loathsome Jeff Riesner, for instance. But he'd come to her. He could afford it, and his problems, ambiguous though they were right now, seemed comfortably within her zone of competence.

"Okay," she said after a moment. "I'll see if I can get a copy of Heidi's statement, and find out if the police really are continuing an investigation into Alex's death. Maybe they know where Heidi is. If they do, I'll try to put you in touch with her."

"Primo," he said. "Excellent," looking relieved and nodding his head. "How much do you want up front?"

"Ten thousand. I charge a hundred fifty an hour. If this gets resolved fast, you get the rest back."

He wrote out the check and handed it to her, saying, "You're cheap. Our business lawyer charges two fifty an hour."

"Yep. I've been called cheap. And a few other things."

"Gorgeous. I bet you've been called that, too." He smiled at her.

There was no heat in the smile. The heat was probably reserved for Heidi. Nina liked that. She smiled back and stood up. "I'll give you a call tomorrow. At Paradise?"

"If you find out where Heidi is, sure, call me at the resort. Otherwise—I'd prefer you called my home. I don't trust my reactions. You know?"

He got up too, and she noticed again that he was much taller than she was, long and lean with a trim waist. She could picture him turning gracefully between the tall trees, the even line of teeth as white as the snow all around him. . . .

"Jim," she said.

"What?"

"I'd better keep Heidi's note."

"Why?"

"So it doesn't get lost."

He hesitated. "Sure," he said. "I just want to hang on to it until tomorrow." Before she could protest, he gave her a half wave and she heard the door in the outer office slam.

Sandy came in, tapping her finger on her full lower lip. She sat down in a client chair, a sign that she wanted to say something.

After two years with Sandy, Nina had learned to interpret her signs. Sandy seldom smiled, almost never laughed. Her face remained composed whatever the crisis. But her crossed arms, or cocked eyebrows, or sudden studious attention to a speck of dirt on the floor spoke volumes.

A full-blood member of the Washoe Tribe, Sandy was a descendant of the people who had settled Tahoe and the Carson Valley long before the gold rush which had led California willy-nilly into statehood. She kept Nina's law practice operating.

Sometimes, she was the only thing propping Nina up.

Now she was giving her lower lip quite a workout, tapping it, massaging it, pulling it this way and that. She was really thinking hard.

Nina had long ago given up trying to outwait her. "I read about Alex Strong in the *Mirror*. Did you see it? The paper reported his death as an accident," she said. She put her stockinged feet up on the desk and her hands behind her head, stretching. "I have to stop eating quesadillas for lunch. I'm getting a stomachache hunching over the desk."

Sandy's lower lip released itself. It met the upper lip. The lips went in and out. Mesmerized, Nina watched words form. "A client that pays up front. That's already a change. We need more like him. After that last debacle . . ."

"That's all you have on your mind?"

Sandy found something to study on the ceiling. "That resort's pulling down big bucks. It's not as big as Squaw or Heavenly, but it brings in a lot of packages from out of the country. French, Germans, Japanese— all I'm saying is, he can pay his legal fees for the case."

"I hate to ruin your afternoon, but I don't think there will be a case," Nina said. "He's had a nasty week and he's lost all perspective and he's panicking."

"Hey! Wait a minute. We got a mountain. Don't go making a molehill out of it."

"Oh, I'll check this out for him," Nina said. "The cops, the autopsy—it was a violent death, Sandy. They have to be careful."

Now Sandy was all warmed up. "And why do people want to leave a warm house and go out and freeze and slide down a mountain of snow? It costs a fortune and then you break your leg or end up with a metal plate in your head." She was referring to another client, a tourist who had hit another skier and been badly injured the year before. "Like that Kennedy back East.

And Sonny Bono hitting a tree. Where's the fun in that?"

"It's exciting, Sandy. At Jim Strong's skiing level, it's thrilling. The danger is part of it. It appeals to intense people."

"I get my kicks just trying to pay the mortgage."

"None of this romantic nonsense for you. Is that what you're saying?"

"You've got that right."

In the outer office, the CD had started up again. "So what's with the love songs you've been playing all week?" Nina said. "I mean, talk about romantic. Makes me feel lonely. I'm starting to want to string up a hammock in the office and get in there with a boy or two and a bottle of rum."

What was this? Sandy was coloring, ever so slightly. Nina watched as the color mounted up her neck and bloomed into her smooth brown cheeks.

Sandy went into a full-blown blush.

"Why, Sandy," Nina said. "Something going on I should know about?"

Sandy heaved her substantial self out of the chair. "You've got that special setting in the Superior Court at three," she said over her shoulder, shutting the door decisively behind her.

Nina filled out her deposit slip to put Strong's check into the depleted trust account, looked at her watch, grabbed a file, and headed down the hall of the Starlake Building, toward her Bronco and the snowy outdoors.

The music followed her:

> Snow falls upon this dream of mine
> This dream we had together
> Oh why can't happiness endure

As she warmed up the truck she thought about Jim Strong. His brother was dead and his wife was missing. He had turned to her for help.

As simply as that, she had taken on his burden. They were lawyer and client, a relationship that sometimes becomes closer than wife and husband or sister and brother.

Had she jumped in too quickly? His problems had such blurry edges. . . .

Out here, clarity everywhere, the mountains sharp above the town, pines dripping, clouds in battalions marching across the new blue sky . . .

And back at the office, a brand-new file. "I know what you did to Alex," Nina repeated under her breath as the Bronco bumped out onto the boulevard.

2

At the courthouse, Nina put Jim Strong out of her mind.

Love the one you're with. It's a lesson lawyers learn early.

Her client was waiting with her husband, Mr. Geiger, in the hall outside the Superior Court main courtroom. Mrs. Geiger had hurt her back eighteen months before in a car accident caused by the other driver, but his insurance company didn't like the amount Nina requested as damages.

The problem was that Mrs. Geiger, a tiny lady who wasn't supposed to lift more than ten pounds due to her injury, had been videotaped by an insurance company investigator soon after the accident, carrying in groceries from the car, hauling trash bags out to the can, and lugging her toddler grandson around her modest yard out in King's Beach, all in a single disastrous afternoon.

This video had aroused such righteous indignation in the insurance company camp that not only was Nina's settlement offer rejected without a counteroffer, but the District Attorney's office was called in. Nina had arrived at her client's deposition a few months before to find Barbara Banning, the new deputy D.A. assigned to the Tahoe office, sitting in a chair next to the insurance lawyer, one perfect calf crossed above the other, on patrol for fraud.

For a few months, it had looked like Mrs. Geiger not only would lose her case, but might lose her liberty as well. This reflected badly on Nina, who had made the big damages claim, and it also seemed unfair to Mrs. Geiger, who really did have a bad back, although they all had to admit the video seemed to indicate otherwise.

Nina needed some new ammo. So, shortly before the time when all doctors' reports had to be completed, she visited the treating doctor again, bearing a copy of the video.

He hadn't liked having his professional judgment questioned or his patient ridiculed. He went through the video in slow motion, stopping now and then to look at Mrs. Geiger's movements frame by frame. He pointed at various frames and snapped things like, "Don't you see how she's grimacing in pain there? And there? See how she's compensating? She'll never be pain free again. She needs another MRI. I think I missed something. She's worse off than I thought."

So Nina called a last-minute follow-up deposition of this doc, and he muttered darkly about hip replacements and chronic pain syndrome down the road, which would probably necessitate expensive surgery. By the time he finished, opposing counsel was on the phone to his boss in some fifty-story building somewhere, whining for a bigger reserve.

On the third day before the trial was to begin, this lawyer made a reasonable offer, which Nina, biting her fingernails even as she spoke on the phone, rejected. An endless afternoon later, the lawyer called again and made a more than reasonable offer. Nina wrote the figure on a

piece of paper and pushed it across the desk to Mrs.
Geiger, who wrote, "Take it! Take it!"

But now, just at that tricky moment when the settlement offer was about to be confirmed in court, Mrs.
Geiger's husband, who previously hadn't shown any interest in the proceedings, had decided to butt in.

"I don't think it's enough," Mr. Geiger said. "I
could do better than this with these people." He
worked in the Personnel Department at Harvey's, so he
probably did know a lot about human nature, but what
he didn't know was that insurance claims adjustors don't
have human natures. They have Pentium processors.

"Then it's a good thing I'm the lawyer, because if it
were up to you, we'd be going to trial tomorrow. And
that wouldn't be smart. No offense," Nina added.

"Why not go for another fifty grand? These damn
insurance companies are sitting on all the money in
America."

"Mr. Geiger, you've seen the film. Now imagine
what the insurance company would have to say about
that at trial. Mrs. Geiger might lose. Then she would get
nothing. I don't think you should take that chance." To
make sure he understood, Nina went over the whole
thing again, but he brushed her counsel aside.

She thought she knew Mr. Geiger's real problem.
The door was closing; an amount certain must sound
paltry compared to the rank speculation in his mind.
The settlement amount must seem to Mr. Geiger to be
plucked from the air, as indeed it was, since damages for
pain and suffering in such cases were only loosely related
to the actual medical bills. If the company would give
this much, why not a fortune?

And he might also be thinking, as other clients

sometimes thought, that his guess was as good as that of this young woman with the long brown hair and expensive navy-blue blazer talking rapidly in front of him.

What he was brushing aside was the fact that Nina had fought dollar by dollar through this particular battle, and she knew from experience that there was no more money, not a quarter, not a plugged nickel.

Mr. Geiger began talking over her, his lecture segueing into a rant. He was going to have his say and her job was to listen like a good girl and then carry through with the deal.

Mrs. Geiger said not a word. She seemed remote from them, small, ineffectual.

Nina noticed a hot feeling incubating in her chest. He was another obstacle in the way of doing what was best for her client. She ought to soothe him, flatter him, placate him. It was her duty, for Mrs. Geiger's sake. Poor, meek Mrs. Geiger. What a home life she must have.

Lawyers, clients, and witnesses were walking back and forth down the hall, looking curiously at the small group of three huddled against the wall. Mr. Geiger continued to bluster. All he wanted was to bust her ass for a while longer, but they were plumb out of time.

To hell with him.

"It's not enough," he barked again.

Someone brushed by her and she looked up to see a face she hadn't seen for a long time.

"Collier!"

"Hey, Nina."

He was walking into the courtroom with Barbara Banning, who continued on her way without a glance. He stopped, taking in her situation.

"I'll give you a call," he said, and disappeared inside. Nina watched the door, her mouth slightly open.

"Well?" Mr. Geiger said. "Have I made my point?"

"Okay."

"Okay?"

"You win, Mr. Geiger. We'll reject the offer in open court. We'll go to trial tomorrow. Let's go on in and tell the judge."

A silence.

Nina turned around and pulled open the door. "After you," she said.

"B–But I thought—my wife had you accept the offer. I was just explaining how I thought—"

"You don't like my work; you want to overrule your wife's thinking on this; you think we'll do better at trial. Let's go to trial. Coming?"

"Ed?" Mrs. Geiger said in her tiny voice.

"Wait a minute! I'm not done yet—"

Mrs. Geiger reared up like a pony and banged her husband sharply with her wee purse.

"Shut up, Ed," she snarled. She turned to Nina. "Ignore him. You get in there and cancel that trial."

So to Mr. Geiger's secret relief they did that, and Nina filed some papers across the hall at the clerk's office, and by the time she had finished her errands the D.A.'s office was closed and it was getting dark. Bob would be waiting at home. She hauled herself up into the Bronco, slung the briefcase into the back seat, and drove down Pioneer Trail toward Kulow Street.

Winter was closing in so early! How high would the snow go this year? She looked at the snow wands lining the road, about eight feet high. On the other side of the lake, at the Donner Party memorial, there were trees the pioneers had sawed to make their huts in the snow—and the stumps were thirteen feet above the ground.

Well, she'd chosen to live in the Sierra. This winter she would get a really cool-looking pair of boots.

The day had been long and jumbled, like most of her days, a result of billing her work time in tenths of hours. She was really looking forward to the peace of home. Bits sloshed around in her brain—Jim Strong's weary blue eyes and restless body, Heidi Strong's note—she'd have to get on that autopsy report first thing tomorrow —and Mr. Geiger's face when Mrs. Geiger walloped him—she'd misjudged the Geiger marriage; Mrs. Geiger could take care of herself—and what was in the fridge to cook for supper and boy oh boy a glass of chilled Clos du Bois would really hit the spot as soon as she got the pantyhose off—if only Bob didn't have algebra homework . . .

And Collier Hallowell, back at work as if he'd never left, only a tall familiar impression in the hall, he had passed in such a hurry. She hadn't really expected ever to see him again. How long had it been? Ten, no, eleven months.

Where had he been? The last time she had seen him, just before he left town, he was so thoroughly screwed she had wondered how he could ever recover.

"Where's my boy?" she called as she burst into the cabin. All the lights in the place were on. No sign of Bob—he must be out with Hitchcock running around the neighborhood. She stripped down in the bedroom, hanging her clothes on a chair, pulled on jeans and her new sweater, a long apple-green number, then went in to make dinner.

Fifteen minutes later meatloaf and rice baked in the

oven. Nina sat on the rug in the living room in front of a bright fire sipping her glass of wine and watching the six o'clock news. Suddenly, with a bark and a slam, Bob and Hitchcock blasted in through the front door. Hitchcock, having the advantage of two extra legs, made it to her first. "Good boy," she said as she put her arms around his furry neck, but a dreadful putrid odor exuded from him and she jumped away, startling the dog, who knocked over her wine.

"My wine! What's that smell?" she cried. "Oh, no. My sweater!"

"Well, here's what happened," Bob said dramatically, spreading his hands toward the dog but not touching him. "He was nosing around in the bushes. It was dark, I couldn't see so well, but he wouldn't come, so I went back to look for him. Guess where I found him?"

"I have no idea," Nina said, dabbing at the wine with a napkin.

"Guess!"

"Why don't you just tell me," she snapped.

"I found him," he paused, setting up the punch line, "rolling in a dead chipmunk!"

"Ugh!" she said. "Get him out of here!" She leaped up and ran for the bathroom, tearing off her sweater as she went. Hitchcock took off after her, glued to her heels, anxious to show her his love. Changing direction abruptly, she ran outside, trapping the dog on the porch.

"I've got him!" Bob called, right behind her.

"Put the hose on him!"

"But it's freezing!"

"Put—the—hose—on—him!"

Human and animal screeches intermingled outside while she threw off her clothes and dove into the shower. A few minutes later she stepped out, wrapping a towel around her hair, and almost got run down by a soaking wet Bob, who ran past with a foul tail wind, heading into the bathroom. Hitchcock followed close behind, his stink unabated.

Nina, throwing towels on the floor and toward the bathroom, felt a sudden, sharp pang of alarm. The disaster was not over. Unconsciously, she had been registering the minutes ticking away; the meatloaf, baking, browning, wizening, blackening . . .

REEP! REEP! REEP! REEP!

She scrambled for the orange heavy machinery headphones she used to muffle noise, but she couldn't find them. Stumbling in the awful din, which now included shouting and howling magnified by the fine acoustics in the bathroom, she climbed a stool and reached for the smoke alarm, vividly remembering how her father, maddened by the noise, had once shot his off the wall.

The remainder of the evening, what there was of it, was calm. By ten o'clock, somehow, Bob was in bed, his algebra mostly done.

Month to month, like him, his room metamorphosed. The skateboarding and surfing posters on his bedroom walls had given way to Asian and African themes: Jackie Chan kickboxing his way out of a verdant rainforest and a couple of African masks he had found at a flea market. He had even bought himself a mosquito net at an import store to hang over his bed. Peering at her from under the milky swathe of material he looked like a creature from a fairy tale, not a thirteen-year-old boy whose shoulders and face grew squarer and more manly by the day.

"G'night, Mom."

"G'night, Handsome."

"Don't feel bad about the dinner, Mom. I like cold pizza."

"The pizza man didn't even have gloves. We're lucky he came at all with this snow coming down. Anyway, Hitchcock liked the meatloaf, so I guess it all worked out. We'll go out tomorrow night and bury the chipmunk to keep Hitchcock from doing this again. Why do dogs like to roll in dead things? It's disgusting."

Bob yawned. "Mom?"

"Yes, honey?"

"I *am* going to see my dad in Wiesbaden over Thanksgiving, aren't I?"

"Go to sleep now, Bob."

"You're not going to back out?"

"I said you could go and you're going."

"You always make it sound like I'm going away forever. It's just three weeks. Mom?"

"C'mon, Bob, it's late." He hated to end the day. He could drag it out forever, and she was very tired. "What?" She fought for patience. She ought to be grateful that he still wanted to tell her everything on his mind.

"Let's say there's a dance at school. And a girl asks me to go with her."

"Well," Nina said carefully, "that's big news." She strained to keep the cataclysmic impact this inquiry had on her from being noticed. "What's her name?"

"Nicole." Nicole. They were all named Ashley or Nicole or Ashley Nicole. A sultry temptress of thirteen was after poor innocent Bob who was still a child, although lately his voice had been getting deeper and she had noticed soft down on his cheeks where sideburns would one day appear. Nina ran her hand through her hair, wondering what to say

"Don't make a big deal out of it, okay? I just want to know—how can I turn her down? I don't want to be mean."

"You don't want to go with her?"

"I—I don't think so."

Oh, brother. She was in for it now.

"Maybe you should think about it. If she's a nice girl, maybe you should . . ."

"She likes Hanson. But she can skateboard."

"Hmm. Tell you what. Let's sleep on it, okay? This needs some thought."

"You're"—a big yawn—"avoiding the question."

"So I am."

She closed the door halfway, the way he liked it. After brushing her teeth, she climbed into bed with a couple of important files for the next day, but her eyes were closing. She would get up early and work.

As she sank into the mattress, her back and shoulders de-tensed in a way that was so pleasurable it hurt. She thought about the stunning thing Bob had said. He'd been asked out by a girl. He was going to go to a dance.

He was going to fall in love, take up cigar smoking, vote Republican, and leave her, and it would all be over in an eyeblink.

Jim Strong skied into her dreams. He schussed right into her living room, knocking over her wine, looking frantically for Heidi. He opened the cabinet door under the bathroom sink and disappeared into the secret house which could only be accessed by the trapdoor there.

She felt lonely after he left, but then she remembered she was marrying Carlos Botelho, who appeared with his guitar and sang to her under the coconut palms. He sang so tenderly to her, and she responded with all her heart. She waited to see his wonderful face. She knew it would be wonderful, even though she couldn't see it yet.

3

"YOU'LL HAVE TO talk to the D.A.'s office," the cop on duty at the desk of the South Lake Tahoe police station told Nina. "We wouldn't hand out a witness statement to a lawyer without an okay from them."

"Then let me talk to the officer who interviewed Mr. Strong last week."

The woman, who had the usual cop look, bored and vigilant at the same time, said, "He's off duty until Friday."

"Then let me talk to his supervisor."

"Out on a case. Leave a message."

At eight-thirty in the morning there was a blizzard outside, and a puddle of meltwater on the linoleum floor in front of the window where the cop was blowing her off. Nina filled out a message slip, marked it urgent, and went over to the county offices, which luckily were right across the courtyard.

Tahoe's permanent population of thirty thousand or so would be well served by the low redwood buildings clustered off Johnson Boulevard, which included the jail, police station, courthouse, and most county offices, if millions of tourists didn't also visit each year. During the off-season the county returned calls and conducted business with impressive efficiency. During the two tourist spells, ski season and summer fun-in-the-sun, you could hardly fight your way into the buildings.

The ski resorts did not usually open until Thanksgiving each year but even though it was still early in the season, Alpine Meadows, Sierra-at-Tahoe, Heavenly, and Paradise were already welcoming skiers. The tourists were clogging the main road through town in their four-wheel-drive vehicles, feasting on pizza and steaks in the restaurants, sliding into seats at the blackjack tables. The business owners were joyfully preparing for a long, nasty winter.

Nina usually felt the same anticipation at the coming of the fresh white stuff. She loved the holiday season. But this Thanksgiving, Bob wouldn't be with her. He would be in Germany visiting his father. Or going on dates.

Why can't he stay a kid a little longer? she said to herself as she shook snow off her hair and unbuttoned her coat in the hall of the county offices. Bob had become her companion as well as her kid since they had moved to Tahoe, and she knew it wasn't healthy for either of them to spend all their time together. She shouldn't be feeling this triste-French-movie kind of stuff just because he was taking a trip for a couple of weeks! Sternly, she told herself to get a grip.

The truth was, she had been happy wrapped in the cocoon of their house in the woods, but it all depended on Bob not changing. And he couldn't help doing that.

She knocked on the window of the Office of the District Attorney. "I'd like to talk to whoever is in charge of the investigation of the death of Alex Strong."

Looking even tougher than the cop, the receptionist was a foo dog who guarded the entrance to a place of power. She examined Nina's State Bar card, looked her up and down as though she'd never seen her before, and finally said, "Just a minute." The bulletproof window closed, leaving Nina in her usual mode of outsider.

As soon as she sat down in the hard metal chair against the wall, the door flew open. "You're up early," Collier Hallowell said. He seemed to move toward her as if to embrace her, but he stopped himself and held out a hand.

Gone were the rumpled suit and haggard eyes she remembered. Collier looked ten years younger. The haunted, insomniac look was gone too. He had grown a neat dark beard that went well with his tall build and the serious gray eyes. He dropped into the chair beside her, smiling.

Nina had known him as a man obsessed by the death of his wife, unable to move beyond it. He had left the D.A.'s office, where he was one of the most experienced and resourceful senior deputies, and dropped out of the race for county district attorney the year before, after making a serious mistake that had almost turned tragic.

Finally, he had just left town. His office called it a leave of absence, but no one had expected him back. Attorneys who run away and hide don't often return. To the town or even the profession. They open restaurants or become drunks. None of the ex-lawyers Nina had known had ever gone back to the pressure that had crushed them.

Collier, almost alone of all the lawyers in town, had tried to welcome her and befriend her when she had opened up her solo practice in the Starlake Building two years before. She had admired him. She had thought to herself, I can help him get over his wife. And she had been half in love with him. She had invited herself over to his apartment, but Collier hadn't been in any shape to do anything about her. She'd made a fool out of herself, going after a man who was incapable of caring. It still stung.

"How are you?" Nina said, also smiling, but wary.

"Same old shit." He always said that, but he didn't seem to mean the cynical phrase. "Been back for a week and a half. I was going to look you up. How have you been?"

"Hanging in there."

"Still haven't been able to get away from the criminal cases, I see, or you wouldn't be here."

"I gave up trying. You can't practice law in a small town and not do criminal work." She was talking to him in her brisk business voice as if he were a stranger. He did seem like a stranger. She realized that she had written him off in self-protection, because she'd never expected to see him again. "You look good," she said slowly. "Better."

"I can't take the credit," Collier said. "Time and nature did a job on me."

"No one seemed to know where you were."

"No one did. We'll talk about it sometime."

"Mr. Hallowell, line three." The receptionist was hovering in her window like a helicopter waiting for landing instructions.

"Put 'em on hold for a minute," Collier answered without looking back. He tucked his hands in his pockets and lounged with one arm on the back of her chair as if he had loads of time and no demands, and only Nina to consider.

"So," Nina said when the silence became uncomfortable.

"I thought about you a lot," he said. "But I didn't think I had any right to contact you."

This disturbed her. It sounded phony. She knew she hadn't meant anything to him, so why would he think about her? She said in a businesslike tone, "You didn't."

He looked down at his hands. She saw that he no longer wore the gold band that had linked him to his dead wife. His hand looked bare, vulnerable, without it.

"She's just a memory now," he said "Just a memory of a memory. I realized I might as well be dead, too, the way I was living. I started to recover when I realized that. And I realized I'd thrown my life away. Then I had something to work for, and I'm good at that."

"Something to work for?"

"To get it back," Collier said. "You can go home again. Here I am, living proof. I have a new place with a view of the lake. And the county gave me my job back."

"Another chance."

"Shocked the hell out of me, actually. I didn't deserve it, after what I did."

"They probably danced a jig when they heard from you. You were the best lawyer in the D.A.'s office."

He smiled again. "Let's see what I do with it."

"It's Judge Flaherty's clerk," the receptionist said, holding up the receiver. "What am I supposed to do?" They had both forgotten about the woman at the window.

"I'm in conference," Collier said. Then the eyes were on her again. "You wanted to see me, but I forget what for. Oh, right, the Alex Strong investigation. I'm looking into that death at the moment. I guess we'd better get to it. Who's your client?"

She turned her mind back to business. "His brother. Jim Strong."

"Oh ho. So he's gone and got himself a lawyer." Just like that, they were strangers again, opponents even. Collier removed his arm from the back of her chair.

"He's frantic to find his wife and to know why there seems to be this cloud of suspicion gathering around him. His brother's death seems like an obvious accident—"

"They sometimes do. At first."

"They?"

"Doc Clauson sent over an amended coroner's report yesterday. I'll have Roxanne make you a copy if you can wait a few minutes. Read it. Then we can talk some more tomorrow, if you want to."

"Thanks." He could hold her up for a few days on this, but Collier had never been that kind of lawyer. He had never guarded himself, never postured, never taken on that hard-bitten look. Sometimes, in the days before he had left, she had wished he protected himself better.

"Sorry. I'm going to have to go back in," he said. "Anything else?"

"I'd also like to see the statement Heidi Strong made. I understand your office knows where she is. She's apparently accused Jim of killing Alex. He's trying to find her, to talk to her."

"I can't give you her current address. She's afraid of him. She asked that her location be kept confidential. He ought to cool it or he may make it worse."

"Have you talked to her personally?"

"Not yet," Collier said. "I'm jumping through hoops as fast as I can, but we're really just getting started on this thing."

Nina didn't like the sound of that. For whatever reason, Alex Strong's death was getting urgent attention.

"Well, I need a copy of her statement right away," she said again, dogged.

"Mr. Hallowell?" the receptionist called. "Miss Banning is looking for you. The officers are waiting in your office."

"Tell you what," Collier said, glancing at the clock on the wall and getting up. "I have court in five minutes, but afterwards I'll have a look through the statement, black out anything that might indicate where the wife is, and . . . why don't you bring your client here tomorrow, about eleven. I'd like to ask him a few questions when I turn over the statement. I won't keep him long. Just looking into a few things."

"You mean, before we even get a chance to see the statement?"

"I'll produce it when we get together. Fair enough?"

Nina thought about it. He meant to question Jim about the statement before Jim had time to prepare any answers. She could prevent that. She'd read it first, and then she'd demand a couple of minutes outside and take ten, just to make sure Jim wasn't sideswiped. Exposing him to a surprise was risky, but Collier could hold up Heidi's statement for quite a while if they didn't offer something in trade.

Despite the eyes of the receptionist boring into his back, he waited patiently for Nina's answer, stroking his new beard, watching her.

"I'll mention it to him, see if he wants to," she said. "I'll call this afternoon."

"Right, then." Still he watched her, his eyes lighting on her in a warm way she didn't remember.

She thought she could feel the stream of his energy

pushing outward into the world again. His eyes, his posture, his manner, told her that he was finding the sight of her interesting.

She found herself smiling back at him. Standing up, she shouldered her briefcase. "I hope you'll forgive me saying this," she said. "But I'm almost sorry you came back. I always thought you were too good to be a D.A. I mean, I didn't think the work was good for you."

The receptionist sighed, gave up, and turned back to her complaining telephone.

Collier raised his eyebrows.

"It's none of my business," Nina said hastily.

"I'll take that as a compliment. The work isn't good for anybody, but it's our work."

She didn't know what to make of that statement, so she looked at her watch.

"How's Paul? You still work with him?" he asked.

"He's in Washington. He worked for a while with a private agency. Now he's involved in a temporary security job at the Senate building that keeps getting extended."

"Is that so? I never thought he'd put that kind of space between the two of you."

"Things didn't work out for us," she said.

"Too bad."

"Well, it's good to see you," she said. "You seem resurrected."

"Mis-ter Hallowell," said the voice from the window. "Miss Banning just called again."

"Be right there." He turned back to Nina. "Resurrected," he said. "I like that. The mummy walks again. Maybe a sorceress has called me back."

She drove through the white landscape to the Horizon Hotel and Casino for her breakfast, bringing the autopsy report into the restaurant with her. Hustling past the clang of the slots and the empty, shrouded blackjack tables, she picked a quiet spot in the great-smelling coffee shop that served breakfast skillets that would hold you all day for $1.99. Most diners spent quite a bit more than that as they walked through the casino on their way to eat, so breakfast was a loss leader.

A full-bearded prospector with a sunburned bald spot and a backpack beside him sat in one corner, sipping a mimosa. At the counter, a cowboy and his woman, coming off a night of partying, drooped over their coffee cups, skinny from smoking and glazed of eye, like Degas's absinthe drinkers.

Between mouthfuls of scrambled egg, she read over the report. Alexander Bradford Strong, age twenty-seven and three months and two days—his clock had stopped forever.

Alex Strong's body had lost its human significance. He had become a legal tool, transformed into words by an autopsy report. Now, she would autopsy the autopsy, dissect the words, look for things that were not right.

As she went through the dry medicalese, outrage boiled up inside her, energy she would need to beat Doc Clauson and the overpowering system behind him.

The report had been written, then amended two days later, the amendment consisting of a single page stapled at the end. She flipped to the back, and found things were far worse than she had expected.

She went back to the beginning and ran her eyes down the pages, forcing herself to review it all from start to finish.

A well-nourished male, five feet ten and 168 pounds,

muscular, fair-skinned, inclined to freckle. Alex Strong's eyes had been blue, his hair brown, the same as his brother Jim's, she remembered. His two front teeth were false, probably from a prior skiing accident.

When he died, he had been wearing a down parka, ski bibs, ski boots that had cut into his ankles but prevented any foot fractures, a black turtleneck cotton shirt, silk boxers, wool socks, a silver Piaget watch, and a gold chain around his neck. A small empty flask that had once contained cognac was found in a pocket of the parka.

No signs of vomitus in nostrils or mouth. No external evidence of disease.

Fingerprints and ID photos were taken at the scene. Clauson had gone up the mountain on skis to examine the scene.

Old injuries. A fully healed simple fracture of the left femur. Old arthroscopic surgery on the left knee. Old scar on the scalp just above the right ear. A recent black eye. A hotdogger's body.

External examination showed numerous contusions, abrasions, lacerations on the posterior—back—skin, from head to toe.

Internal examination. Head, some posterior endodermal bleeding consistent with a fall onto rocks. No skull fractures. Neck, respiratory tract, urinary tract . . . most body systems unremarkable. Slides and toxicological samples had been taken after the major organs were weighed. A preliminary blood alcohol test showed a .13 level, above the legal limit for driving but not stumbling drunk.

A fresh, simple fracture of the right tibia. The fall had broken his right leg this time.

Clauson had saved the abdominal area for last. Area

of severe contusion on the upper anterior —front—torso area, consistent with a crushing force. Internally, two lower ribs had fractured above the liver.

And the liver had been completely transected.

She remembered that the liver sat right in the middle of the body, protected partly by the lower ribs. But . . . transected? Nina thought back to a continuing ed course she'd taken in medical terminology. Transected meant split. Transected meant the liver had been torn in half by the force which had struck it.

She put her fork down gently and pushed her plate back, still reading.

Clauson's original findings and opinion were simple. Death was due to a fall of approximately fifteen feet onto granitic rock, which had resulted in transection of the liver. Strong had died within two hours from massive internal bleeding into the peritoneum, the lining of the abdominal cavity.

The last page contained Clauson's reconsidered findings. After a second trip to the incident site and further examination of the surrounding circumstances, Clauson had changed his opinion from accident to homicide.

Nina read this section several times, excitement and anger blurring the words. Clauson wrote as laconically as he spoke, and the import of his findings took time to understand.

Transected! she thought, and read on, to three new findings.

First, a statement obtained from Heidi Strong, the wife of the only witness to the fall, indicated that the witness, James Strong, had threatened to kill the decedent only a few weeks before.

Second, a reexamination of the front of the down

parka and the bibs revealed no traces of tearing or damage, even microscopically, in the area above the fatal injury. The overall damage to clothing and the pattern of abrasions and contusions on the subject indicated that the front of the subject had not come into contact with rocks before he landed on his back.

However, the front of the turtleneck shirt, which should have been protected under the bibs, showed slight tearing just above the fatal injury.

And third, Clauson now thought, based on photographs taken at the autopsy, that he could see faint patterning in the contused skin above the fatal injury.

She moved on to the conclusions. It was Clauson's reconsidered opinion that some severe blunt force trauma to the area above the liver had occurred after Alex Strong came to rest in the snow, alive and possibly conscious, on his back. Although Clauson did not rule out a blow with a large, heavy rock, he said that the rock would have to weigh more than a man could carry, and that no such rock had been found in the environs.

Clauson went into a discussion of something called foot-pounds, a measure of force. Then he came to his conclusion. It was his opinion that a party or parties unknown had come upon Alex Strong lying injured on his back, then opened the parka and pulled the bibs down, jumped on the midsection or possibly stomped the midsection with one foot, and then pulled the bibs back up and zipped up the parka in order to make the death look like an accident.

Sickened, Nina said it to herself minus the big words. Clauson was claiming that Jim Strong had jumped onto his injured brother's midsection, though Clauson hadn't used Jim's name. She imagined saying those brutal words to a jury, the scorn she would pour into that interpretation.

Fuming, she drank her coffee. Clauson had nothing! The parka hadn't been torn above the fatal injury—so what? Those things were made of a nylon blend so strong nothing could hurt them, and she would bet Alex Strong had worn the best parka available.

The fatal injury was in front. So Alex had hit something on the way down, or rolled! How could Clauson be so sure Alex had flown off the cliff and landed, simply and once, on his back? She would go up the mountain herself. There would be another explanation.

And Clauson was claiming that only a person in ski boots could have caused the injury, going way too far in his conclusions. He had a hypothesis, not a conclusion! And what about the "faint patterning"? Why hadn't he noticed it when he looked at the body the first time around?

She would get Ginger Hirabayashi in Sacramento on the forensics. Ginger would straighten it all out.

Heidi's statement—Nina wished she had it in hand. Clearly, Heidi was upset about something. Finding out what she was upset about and bringing that into focus would help to interpret her motive, maybe cast some doubt on her truthfulness. Or, they might convince her to recant. She had to be found right away. Whatever she had said in that statement, it couldn't be enough to convict a man of anything under such foggy circumstances. With his physical evidence so ambiguous, Clauson had no business even taking an angry wife's accusations into account.

Nina balled her fist, slamming it down onto the stapled pages. Clauson was a dangerous incompetent. He had done enough harm. This time, she would take him down.

Slowly, her breathing and heartbeats returned to normal. She could handle this report. If they arrested Jim, she might even get the case thrown out at the preliminary hearing stage. They had nothing but a bunch of medical gobbledygook which was wide-open to reinterpretation.

Nothing except for Heidi.

Outside, slow heavy clouds clumped low in the sky, threatening more snow. By December, they'd be swimming in it. As she drove along the gunmetal lake, Nina saw gulls listlessly riding the air currents above as though wondering where autumn had gone.

She remembered a description she had read of the Donner party, how the starving people built fires on the snow which melted and melted all night from the heat until they found themselves in the morning shivering in a wet pit of ice fifteen feet deep, with more snow below. The Sierra winters had been a harsh lesson to the pioneers, but soon enough the businessmen who followed had figured out a way to turn a profit from it, dressing it up with World Cup races, hot tubs, casino shows, and chalet ambience, at least on the Nevada side of the lake.

Sandy was on the phone when Nina gusted in on a blast of wind. No one was waiting, so Nina dropped her attaché on a client chair and trotted down the hall to brush her hair and finish calming down before returning.

"That was Mrs. Geiger," Sandy told her as she came back in. "She wants an appointment."

"For what? We're all set. All we need to do is wait for the check from the insurance company and deduct the medical bills so we can cut her a check for the rest. Does she have some questions?"

"No. It's a new matter."

"Oh, no. She didn't have another collision?"

"You might say that," Sandy said, her expression never wavering. "She wants a divorce. She knows personal injury money is separate property. She says she's gonna take the money and run."

"Really? A divorce? Now I feel guilty. I never dreamed she'd do that."

"She wanted me to be sure and tell you that you're the best thing that ever happened to her." Sandy delivered this news without a flicker of expression.

"And the worst thing that ever happened to her husband. Tell her we're blocked up. Make her wait at least a week, Sandy. She may change her mind. This may blow over."

"Or blow up." They were both thinking about Mr. Geiger. Sandy took a swig of diet Snapple. She had been drinking three or four bottles of the stuff every day, which must cut into her spending money, and where were the frosted Tastykakes that usually rested on the file cabinet?

Nina took a good look at her. Sandy was wearing lipstick, and not only that, she had had a really good haircut, a blunt cut on her coarse black hair that left it full and swinging around her shoulders. She looked younger, even in the voluminous denim skirt and hiking boots.

"Just sprucing up a little," she said when she noticed Nina's stare.

"Are you going to tell me what you're up to?"

"No." Sandy handed her a message slip. "Collier

Hallowell. He wants to meet at three-thirty in the afternoon instead of in the morning tomorrow. When did he show up in town again?"

"A couple of weeks ago. I ran into him at court. He's back in the D.A.'s office, back to felony prosecutions. Right in the thick of it."

"No kidding?"

"No kidding."

"I thought he was toast."

"Me, too. He seems to be over it."

"It?"

"His wife."

"Now what?"

"What do you mean, now what?"

"You know what. Him."

"What about him?"

"Can we get real? Can we please not avoid the question?" Sandy wagged her finger.

"If you want to know so badly, since my private affairs are open for your inspection, as opposed to yours . . ."

Sandy was immovable, a glacier filling a stenographic chair.

Nina said, "Burned there, done that. Okay? Call Jim Strong and ask him to come in here tomorrow before we go to the D.A.'s office. I have to talk to him. And call Collier and confirm that we'll see him at three-thirty."

"So we're gonna earn out that retainer. That's good, because the rent is due next week."

"Leave me to worry about that." Nina went into her office and closed the door. Music sailed up from underneath it on a balmy tropical breeze and she inhaled deeply.

4

By three o'clock snow occupied every crack left in town, dressing up the thrift shops and motels on the California side with another three inches of vanilla sugar. Bob would be catching the school bus about now, heading for Matt and Andrea's house and his cousins.

Nina lifted her head from the pile of folders on her desk, took a long yearning look out the window, and thought of snowmen, igloos, snow forts. Bob might be growing up in spite of her, but this afternoon he would be out with Troy and Brianna in the front yard under the snow-laden fir trees Matt loved so much, and the snowballs would be flying.

Jim Strong arrived early. Wearing the same boldly colored parka, he came in shedding snow from his shoulders like a buffalo and sat down. Tiny puddles on the rug followed in his footsteps.

"Whew! Hot in here!" he said. Standing up, he took off his parka, and her mind flashed back to the autopsy report matching him physically to his dead brother. He was a few inches taller than Alex had been, heavier, one eighty or so. Under the parka he wore a lightweight long-sleeved white sweater, thin enough to see the outline of the well-developed chest muscles underneath.

"We're opening every lift on the mountain," he told her. "The place is jam-packed. I had a hard time getting away. And then, of course, I wasn't exactly looking forward to this."

Standing across the desk from her his face looked resentful and alienated. He obviously was having a hard time.

"Have you heard any news about Heidi?" he asked.

She shook her head. She motioned to the chair, but he ignored her. "Still not a call, not even a rumor on my end," he said. As he had during their first meeting, he looked past her, to the mountain. "A big snow year's coming," he murmured.

"You must really watch the weather."

"Like everyone in the resort business. It's essential to our operation."

"How long have you worked at Paradise?" Nina wanted to know, but she also wanted to divert him from the session to come.

"Our family's owned the resort since 1935. We were the pioneers, before Heavenly or Squaw. I've worked there since I graduated. I love Paradise and I've never thought about working anywhere else. I studied geology and meteorology in college, and then for years, I groomed the mountains at Paradise every morning. I worked with the Ski Patrol on avalanche control, checking the snow depth, setting off explosives."

"Explosives?"

"To clear drifts and shaky terrain. To keep the slopes safe."

"Funny. I never thought about that. I guess the snow really piles up around here," said Nina.

"That's how I got to know Heidi. She was doing the

same thing. And then Alex came back from Colorado and he was around too."

When he began talking about Heidi, his expression hardened. "Somebody at Paradise must know where she is. She's worked there since she was in her teens. It's her whole life. You haven't heard anything at all?" He was trying to suppress his anger but his voice was acrimonious.

"Take it easy, Jim."

"It's damn hard."

"I can imagine."

"The problem is, people have somehow gotten the idea I'm going to be arrested. That makes them nervous about talking to me, know what I mean? It's self-protection. They don't want to get involved. I'm guessing, but that's how it seems to me."

"You may be right about that."

He was working himself up. "I can't sleep at night. I can hardly drag through the days. I can't stand the way everyone looks at me. What the hell am I supposed to have done? Why do I have to talk to the District Attorney?"

The autopsy report was right there in front of her. Like Heidi's Post-it, it seemed to burn with an inner fire.

Documents did sometimes come alive. They didn't always say what they meant. Language could only get so close to the truth; this paper, with all its scientific pretensions, was still written in symbols, rife with allusions, intimations, contexts. For as long as she was involved with Jim, she would have a hostile relationship with it.

She wished she could soften the blow, but it was time for him to understand his position.

"They want to talk with you because of this," she said, pointing at it. "It's the autopsy report. Listen carefully, Jim. The coroner filed an amendment concluding that Alex's death was a homicide."

His face drained of color. "So they do suspect me," he said so softly, he almost whispered. "I didn't really believe it. They think . . . My own brother . . . You're saying they might really arrest me. . . ."

When she tried to hand the report to him, his face clouded over and his eyes narrowed. "No!" he said, pushing it back to her, "I can't read it. I don't want to know what they found in his stomach, what he ate for lunch! Just tell me what you have to."

So she gave him the highlights, hardly daring to look up. She ran down what she had learned, what they would be doing at Collier's office, hurrying, getting it over with.

It must have felt like one long shock. She felt as though she were holding his finger in an electric plug the whole time.

When she finished, there was a lengthy silence. She wanted to reach out her hand, touch his, but she was afraid that at any contact he might jump up and run out.

"Listen. You're not alone in this. I'm good at what I do, Jim, and I'm on your side. I'm here to help you."

"They think I—I jumped on Alex? That's what they think?"

"The coroner up here doesn't know his ass from his scalpel. He's prosecution-oriented, and he makes mistakes. He should have retired long ago."

"That's what they think? That's it?"

"Yes. That's what they think. But I'm telling you, now that we know what's going on, we can turn this around."

He clutched his head with his hands and rocked in the chair. He seemed to be shocked speechless.

She couldn't blame him. Getting up from her chair, she turned her back to him and faced the window to give him time to recover, leaving the paperwork between them on the desk.

She remembered a painting that she hadn't thought of since college, depicting a strange, hideous, half-alive machine, doing things no one could understand. "The Elephant Celebes," the painting was called.

It reminded her of the system that Jim had been forced into. She tried to quell the tide of anger, at Clauson who just plain had it in for everybody, at Jim's wife for telling her tale and then running around the corner where she wouldn't get caught.

"Where's Heidi?" Jim cried behind her. "She must be so angry to do this to me. Why's she so mad? I feel like a damn moron! I thought I knew her."

"You have no idea at all where she might have gone?"

"I told you! None at all. That doesn't say much for our relationship, does it?" Now the words spilled out. "She's pulled away from me the last few months. She has her friends, you know, her job. She's outside, so I don't see her much. I work out of the lodge most of the time, keeping the administrative side going. It's hard work, and I'm trying harder to be good at this than I've ever tried to do anything."

"Who actually owns Paradise?" Nina asked.

"My father. My father is still the CEO of Paradise. Alex and I were the vice presidents."

"What exactly does Heidi do?"

"Supervises the Ski Patrol. She's been working the

mountain for twelve years. She trains the new guys, handles the big emergencies, checks out the mountain after each snowfall for avalanche danger. I met her when I started working at Paradise, straight out of college. She's—she loves to laugh, party, have a good time."

"Something must have led up to her leaving," Nina said, half to herself.

"When we were in bed—the night Alex died . . ." Jim said in a low voice. "She didn't want me. That hurt. I needed her."

"Well," Nina said, tapping the edges of the pages of the autopsy report on her desk to straighten them, "we'll learn more this afternoon. Here's what we're going to do. We're making a trade. You're going to go in and talk to Mr. Hallowell. I'll be right there with you, watching out for you. In return for that, he'll pass along a copy of Heidi's statement without giving us any hassle."

She went on for a few minutes, talking about questions to be careful about, warning that his statements could be used against him, making sure his story hadn't changed and that she understood it. Then she reached for her coat and they walked out together. "Why don't we go in my truck?" Nina said, pointing toward the faithful white Bronco not far from the door.

Jim hardly spoke on the short trip, just looked out the window. The snowplows ground through the streets around them.

The receptionist passed them through to the conference room and they waited a few minutes. The District Attorney's office consisted of a wide central area for support staff with several small offices coming off it for the lawyers, and a conference room at the far end.

A couple of uniformed officers were drinking coffee and chatting as she and Jim came in. Jim said, "Whussup, Charlie," to one of them.

"Sorry about Alex," said the one called Charlie, who obviously had no idea why Jim was there. "Awful. I watched him on the slalom run every year. He skied like a maniac, but he was so fast on his feet I never thought he'd crash so bad. He knew the hill like the back of his—"

Collier came in, bearing files. "Well. Take care," Charlie said. The two cops went out, and Nina introduced Jim. They sat down. Collier offered coffee.

In spite of the informality Nina was on high alert, acutely aware of being in the enemy camp. Each contact Jim had with law enforcement could bring disaster down on him; a careless statement or a discrepancy could be magnified into a lie, or made to look like guilt. It was how the Elephant Celebes operated.

Collier seemed ill at ease. He passed by her on his way around the conference table and brushed against her. She gathered her jacket around her as if he'd tried to tear it off.

"Sorry."

"No problem."

Coffee came. They all blew on it. Collier was thinking about something, his approach, maybe. Or maybe this was another witness technique they taught at D.A. training school. Make the witness sweat; that was it.

She caught him looking at her as she sat across from him, trying not to notice him. Was he thinking about her?

"Shall we start?" she said, her voice higher than she had intended.

The tape recorder started to whir. Collier identified the parties present and stated the date and time.

"Just for form's sake, I'm going to give Mr. Strong his Miranda warnings," he said, and took care of that technicality.

She decided to wrest what control she could immediately. "We're not here for some long inquisition," she said. "Mr. Strong has already talked to the police on two occasions. You know everything he knows. You mentioned that you had a few more questions. That shouldn't take more than fifteen minutes. And we would like to see the statement of Heidi Strong before we begin."

"I really don't know how much time we'll need," Collier said, but he took out a single copy and handed it over.

Without looking at it, Nina said, looking Collier in the eye, "We'd like to read this in private."

"Sure. I'll go make a phone call." He clicked off the recorder.

"There's a phone here. Feel free. We'll step outside."

They left. They walked past the busy secretaries through the buzzered door.

"You think he bugged his conference room?" Jim said.

"Maybe," Nina said. "You make a big production about turning off the tape on the desk, then you leave another one winding away in some closet. It's his bailiwick and we don't have much of an expectation of privacy in there."

"What about attorney-client privilege?"

"Keeps confidential statements out of court, but doesn't mean they won't listen when they can."

"Would you do that? Listen in on a conversation

between a lawyer and a client in your conference room?"

"No," Nina said. "But somebody else might. I have had some experience with bugs recently. You never know about these questions of ethics. Lawyers take an exam to prove we know legal ethics, but real life presents ethical dilemmas they never imagined at the good old Board of Bar Examiners."

They found a bench on the sunny side of the building, around to the side where they could get some privacy, and sat down very close together so that Nina could feel Jim's hard thigh pressed against hers. He seemed oblivious.

They read the statement.

It was in the form of a declaration, a statement under penalty of perjury:

I, Heidi Spottini Strong, declare as follows:

1. *I am over the age of twenty-one and a resident of the State of California, County of El Dorado. My address is 1225 Forest Road, South Lake Tahoe. I am married to James Philip Strong of the same address. I make this statement voluntarily.*

2. *I make this statement on condition that my current whereabouts be kept strictly confidential. I specifically request that no information whatever regarding my whereabouts be given to James Strong.*

"Somebody else wrote it," Jim said. "She would never write like this."

"She said something like it, and they wrote it up in

the proper jargon, and she signed it," Nina said. "It's the same thing."

3.   On or about October 5, my husband came home late from dinner with his family. He seemed angry and wouldn't speak to me for a long time. As we were preparing to go to bed I heard a crash in the bathroom where he was. I looked in and saw that he had smashed the mirrored cabinet door above the sink with a stone we use to hold soap. Half the glass had fallen out of the frame. He was holding his arm and staring at the frame.

4.   When I asked what had happened, he refused to answer me. I got a broom and swept up around him so he could step out of the bathroom without cutting his bare feet. While I was cleaning up, he sat down on the bed and didn't move.

5.   After a few minutes I turned out the lights and got into my side of the bed. Then my husband said, "The thing he loves most. I'll show him." I asked him what he meant and he said, "Alex is a dead man."

6.   I was frightened. Then my husband said, very clearly, "He's going to die because I'm going to kill him."

7.   I said words to the effect that he was talking crazy. He laughed and told me to shut up. After saying this, he lay down on his side of the bed and turned his back to me. I was so upset I got up and slept in the living room on the couch that night.

8.   The next day, and several days after that, I

asked my husband what he had meant by his behavior and statements, but he wouldn't add anything more. His manner became secretive and he seemed distant.

9. Then, on October 23rd, a Saturday, my husband left to go skiing. I did not know that he was planning to ski with Alex. At three o'clock Alex's wife, Marianne Strong, called me and told me there had been an accident involving Alex. I rushed to Boulder Hospital and saw my husband in the waiting room with Marianne and my father-in-law, Philip Strong. He told me Alex had been skiing out of control and skied off a cliff. I did not believe him.

10. The doctor came out and told us Alex had died in surgery. I left the hospital and went home with my husband, but I was becoming more and more afraid. I felt then, and I feel now, that my husband had something to do with Alex's death. The next morning I went to the South Lake Tahoe police station and spoke to the officer on duty, then made this statement. I have left my home because of this and wish to state again that my husband is not authorized to have any information as to my whereabouts.

I declare the above to be true and correct under the laws of the State of California. Executed this twenty-fourth day of October at South Lake Tahoe, County of El Dorado, California.

The statement concluded with Heidi Strong's signature, large and round, slanted to the right, just like the writing in the note she had left Jim. Nina moved over slightly on the bench and let him have the copy. He read it several times, as if he couldn't quite decipher it.

The statement was clear, convincing, disastrous. No vagueness here, no ambiguities, no grounds for misinterpretation that Nina could see, on this reading anyway.

Beside her, Jim crumpled up the statement and flung it onto the ground.

"Well," Nina said, looking at it, making no move to pick it up, "she tells a compelling story."

"This never happened. You have to believe me. Heidi's the one who broke the bathroom mirror by accident a few weeks ago—I don't remember the exact day—she was cleaning in there. She wove it into this story. That detail—it makes it sound so real. You don't believe this, do you?"

"We have to find Heidi and get this straightened out."

"No shit. What have I been telling you?"

Nina gave him a long look. "She's trying to put you in jail. This kind of hate doesn't come out of nowhere, Jim."

"I love her," Jim said. "I don't care what she said. And she loves me. She's confused is all. I—I'm sorry. I kept reading her note, and I couldn't stand for anyone else to see it. It was too humiliating. I tore it up."

"You *what*?" But something else even more important had struck her. "Wait a minute!" she said.

"What?"

"What's the matter with me? They can't use this!" Nina said. "She's your wife. She's repeating statements you made in the course of a private conversation with her."

"So?"

"Conversations between husbands and wives are privileged. Confidential. What do they think they're doing?"

"Privileged? What do you mean?"

"I mean this is garbage, legally speaking. You have a right to keep your conversations out of court."

Jim looked skeptical. "Really?" he said. "But she can still testify against me, can't she?"

"Nope. Same privilege. She can't testify about private conversations you had with her. I get it now. You talk about this, you try to explain it, you refute it or deny it or whatever, and Collier has an argument that you've waived the privilege. He must think I'm stupid." Angry and relieved at the same time, she jumped up.

"All right," she said. She dug round in her purse. "Take my car keys. Go right now and get in the Bronco. I'll be right back."

"I thought you said— Don't I have to go back in there?"

"Not anymore," Nina said. "Not until I understand all this better. It's too dangerous for you."

His face sagged with relief. He took the keys and bit his lip, saying, "Okay."

She returned to the conference room alone. Collier was waiting calmly in one of the beat-up chairs around the table, one ankle resting on the other knee, still drinking that godawful coffee. She noticed the "wanted" posters on the cheap wall paneling for the first time, full-face and profile shots of young, unshaven, but otherwise ordinary-looking men. It was like being in a suburb of the police station.

"It's not gonna happen, Collier. I can't let you have

him this afternoon," she said, looking at the posters so she wouldn't have to look at him.

"What? Where is he?" Collier half rose.

"Gone."

"We'll see about that." He picked up the phone.

"Think, Collier," Nina said. "You're not ready to arrest him yet, or you would have done it. He's under suspicion, and he's going to assert his right to remain silent. Heidi's statement isn't ever going to be seen by a judge or jury because he's asserting the marital privilege starting now. What else have you got? Doc Clauson? He's an embarrassment." She leaned against the door frame and closed her eyes. A wave of faintness washed over her. They had been reprieved.

"You tried to trick me," she said more quietly. "It's not like you."

"I never said it was hard evidence. You asked for it, I gave it to you. Am I supposed to go into a long lecture about its admissibility? Besides, I think it's the truth. That girl was scared. The detective who took the statement believed her."

"You wanted to get my client in here and trick him. And me. You've got a lot of nerve."

Collier came around the table, backing her into a corner. His eyes shone with anger. He said, "I'm not trying to trick you. I gave you the statement so you'd know what you're defending. You know enough now to see where this is going. It's early yet. You can still get out of it."

"Are you saying you threw this statement at me to make me get out of it? Am I hearing right?"

He put his arms out against the wall, pinning her in the corner.

"Listen to me," he said. "It's because I owe you. I'm

trying to help. I'm laying it out for you before the arrest so you don't commit to him blind. If you still want to represent him now, that's up to you."

"I don't want any favors! You make me feel like a two-year-old! Is that how you think of me?"

"Don't shout. If you'd rather, I'll leave you to make your own mistakes next time . . ."

His face was about six inches away. Nina's indignation was turning into something else. "I'm leaving now," she said, suddenly aware of a new feeling between them.

"No, you're not." She wished he wouldn't lean down like that. He had great eyes, but she couldn't bring herself to look at them. He stopped talking. Neither of them moved. His coat was gray gabardine, his tie red silk. She had the crazy desire to reach out and stroke it.

"Collier, move," she said, eyes downcast. "Please."

He leaned in and his eyes went blind and he planted his mouth on hers. She had been waiting for it. His lips felt warm, soft, right. She let him kiss her, let him feel how much she wanted it, but didn't kiss back. Relieved of all responsibility, she just stood there and took it like a woman.

The kiss lasted quite a while. Her mouth sent messages down her spine that stirred things up and she started trembling. His lips seemed to get hotter and hotter. He kissed her like he was searching for something, looking for her, only her. His hand went around her head and he held it buried in her hair so he could get just the angle he wanted. She was surprised to feel the soft bristles of his beard. This required investigation. Her arms came up to go around his neck—

"Collier?" Barbara Banning, the impeccable young

prosecutor, arms folded, said from the doorway. Collier stepped back, naked alarm in his eyes.

"I'll be seeing you," Nina said with as much dignity as she could muster. She walked past Barbara's fabulous perfume and curled lip, back into the pit where the secretaries labored, through the door, head held high, but in the hall she stopped, held her hand over her mouth, and said to herself, what the hell was that?

5

SANDY STOOD IN the just-plowed parking lot of the Starlake Building talking to a silver-haired Native American man in a leather jacket. Sandy often had visits from relatives and other tribe members. There was nothing extraordinary about this. The beat-up Chevy Cavalier with chains on the tires and the orange pennant flying from the antenna wasn't extraordinary, either.

What Nina found extraordinary was Sandy's posture: hands on hips, head thrown back. Though Nina could hardly believe her eyes, they insisted that Sandy was laughing. Also, even though the weather had turned menacing, Sandy was not wearing her usual shield, the heavy square purple coat she hung on the office hat rack with scrupulous care each day.

A few snowflakes swirled down in icy wind at the start of a snowstorm that would last into the night. The Bronco bucked over the frozen snow of the driveway and Nina pulled into her spot on the far end.

"Call me," Jim said, jumping out. He got into his truck, a late-model Toyota.

Although the Bronco was parked in plain view across the lot, Sandy and her friend didn't notice it. The man handed Sandy a small package, smiling at her, and then a mind-boggling event occurred: Sandy stood on her tiptoes and gave the fellow a peck on the cheek. She smiled again, a wide, unnerving smile that showed she had beautiful white teeth.

Then she saw Nina.

Jim's truck had just started up. He drove out and into the traffic.

The smile faded, the eyebrows grew together into a Frida Kahlo frown, and Sandy turned to watch Nina walk from the lot into the building.

Five minutes later she came in, still holding the package. Nina, on the phone in the inner office, gave her a wave through the open door. "Hmph," was the answer she got as Sandy sat down and turned to the computer, which had gone into a wait program Bob had installed, consisting of a dog chasing a cat endlessly around the monitor.

"Honestly," Nina said as soon as she got off the line. "I wasn't spying on you."

"Some people can't give other people a second of privacy." Sandy kept her back turned and didn't miss a keyboard stroke. Her bracelets jangled slightly.

"I know it's none of my business—"

"But you won't let that stand in your way—"

"Who is he?"

Sandy hunched her shoulders, indicating that she was vexed, a warning sign. Nina disregarded it.

"And what's in the package?"

"His name is Joseph."

"And?"

"He's Washoe."

"You looked pretty happy out there."

"You don't have to sound so accusing. Now, I have work to do. Isn't that what you hired me for?"

And not another word would she say.

Nina returned to her phone calls, thinking that Sandy had definitely lost her mind. If ever there was a woman who was done with men, it was Sandy. She wouldn't even discuss her ex, Wish's father. She was obstructive, stubborn, independent, and proud, not qualities that lent themselves to a love affair. Sandy, with her plain workmanlike talk and her dour expression. It couldn't be!

And yet, the Sandy picking up the ringing phone in the outer office seemed indefinably different from her former self.

Was Sandy in love? Why shouldn't she fall in love? And why did Nina feel this obscure disappointment, this sudden sense of insecurity? Had she thought, half-unconsciously, that she and Sandy had a pact: done with men, was that it? Was that why she felt betrayed?

Self-insight can be very deflating. Nina began feeling ridiculous. No question about it, she was a completely ridiculous person.

She could still feel Collier's lips pressed against hers.

She felt a very strong urge to know what Sandy was up to. Was Sandy seeing the man outside or was Nina completely misunderstanding the situation?

A buzz. "It's Ginger." Nina picked up and heard the breezy voice of Ginger Hirabayashi, an expert among experts in forensic pathology.

"How's business, Nina?"

"Oh, we're having a great time up here. How are you?"

"Cool. You have something for me?"

"If you're available. A skiing accident that's getting dressed up into a homicide. A young man, expert skier, my client's brother. Age twenty-seven. They were skiing together. The brother went over a cliff off-trail and landed on some rocks below."

"Is Doc Clauson still the coroner up there?"

"Yep. He reconsidered his original autopsy report and my client found out he was in trouble, after the cremation, unfortunately. Ginger, get this: Clauson's report concludes that the man died after the fall when somebody jumped on his torso in ski boots! Can you believe it? The trauma, whatever it was, transected the liver."

"Ouch," said Ginger. "Ski boots, hmm? Rigid, heavy plastic. Might leave a mark. Have they got your client's boots?"

"I—I don't think so."

"They will soon. They'll be trying to match up marks on the skin."

"Clauson did think he saw something he calls 'faint patterning' on the skin, but only from looking at the photos long after the body was cremated. You think there could be a pattern even through cloth?"

"Oh, yeah. Might be able to compare the boot bottoms and marks on the cloth itself. Do they have his ski bibs?"

"I guess so, because the bibs were checked. Not a mark in that area, or on the parka. But . . . the cotton pullover underneath apparently had some kind of minor damage. I don't have access to it. The report has this speculation in it that somebody pulled down the bibs and unzipped the parka before— My client hasn't been arrested yet."

"Intriguing. So where are they? The boots?"

"Well, I'm not sure. There's no mention in the autopsy report."

"Where's your brain, girl? Good thing you have me.

If they're still lying around in his closet, you could ship them to me. I'll give them up when they're demanded, of course, but meantime I could have a look."

"Good thought."

"Use gloves. Put 'em in a clean bag."

"I'll try to get them. And I'll send you Clauson's report."

"Fax it to this number." It was a San Francisco number. Ginger's office was in Sacramento.

"Where are you, Ginger?"

"Downtown in the Federal Building, waiting to testify and dressed like a dork to impress the jury. Have you got the photos of the body?"

"No, and I won't get anything else until after my client gets arrested. Which may happen soon."

"Bummer." Ginger mentioned her current hourly rate, which had increased, and Nina hung up.

"Sandy? I need a really good private investigator."

"You drove him away, remember?"

"There are others besides Paul."

"No. There aren't."

Nina didn't want to talk about Paul Van Wagoner. Exasperated, she said, "Why are you so mad at me? What did I do, except innocently drive into the parking lot of the building where I work?"

And see you with your guard down, she thought to herself, not expecting an answer. "Could you call around for me? I need to see somebody who's good at locating people right away."

"If you're gonna make me."

"And fax this to Ginger. Here's the number. Then see if you can get Jim Strong at Paradise. I need to talk to him right away."

"If I can get a word in, there's a Philip Strong on hold."

"Who?"

"Our client's daddy."

"Oh!" She picked up the other line.

"Miss Reilly? My name is Philip Strong. I'm Jim's father." He had a youthful-sounding voice for a man who must be in his fifties. Nina imagined an older Jim; tall, attractive, wearing a brand-name parka, holding the phone to his ear in the big lodge while he kept an eye on the skiers climbing onto the quad lift outside.

"I understand Jim came in to see you. I'd like to talk to you."

"I appreciate your concern. Unfortunately, I can't really talk about the case with anybody except Jim."

"Yes, yes. But *I* can talk to *you*, can't I? I have something to tell you. It's important."

"Certainly. Would you like to come to my office?"

"Actually, I was hoping I could invite you to have lunch with me at Paradise tomorrow. I promise I won't ask you questions."

"Does Jim know you're calling, Mr. Strong?"

A pause. "No, and I'd prefer he didn't," Strong said. "He might not want me getting involved at this juncture. Even so, I feel I have to."

Nina thought about that. If it would help Jim, she should go. "All right," she said. "About one o'clock?"

"Come to my office in the lodge."

"He's been around a long time," Sandy said later. They were turning off the lights, getting ready to leave. Sandy had gradually thawed into her usual cantankerous self.

"Who?"

"Phil Strong. He and my daddy were friends. They

used to hunt together when they were young. One time they hunted a bear. Illegal even back then, but they were both pretty wild, I hear."

Nina zipped up her parka and started gathering up her papers. "How long ago was that?"

"Oh, who knows. Thirty-odd years ago. That family started the ski industry at the lake. They've been here since people wore coonskin caps."

"And where's your father now?"

"Dead." Sandy said it with no emotion. "But he never did forgive that man. He almost stole my mother from him. That's what my daddy said, but my mother said she had more sense. I always wondered what the truth was."

"If he had, you'd be rich," Nina said, teasing.

"I am rich in everything that counts," Sandy said in her customarily severe manner. They went out together and Sandy climbed into her ancient sedan and skidded off onto the darkening icy street, leaving Nina to realize that Sandy looked downright happy.

Bob offered to make dinner when they got home. He was probably motivated by hunger and the certainty that Nina would not work her way around to his needs for quite some time yet. While she raced through her mail and picked up the living room, he rattled through the kitchen slamming drawers and opening cupboards, announcing a special dish he had in mind which combined a box of noodles, a few cans of soup, and a bag of frozen broccoli.

She didn't care what he made, she was so very grateful. She planned her praise in advance, and would say it, no matter what. That was how to raise a child that would cook.

They had lived in their A-frame cabin for over a year now, and although she couldn't remember ever shopping, somehow, over time, the place had gotten furnished and a few personal touches had begun to emerge. A soft rug defined the seating area by the large stone fireplace. Pictures of tropical palms, the ocean, and favorite art prints had somehow worked their way into frames on the walls.

The sun spent much of the day on the kitchen table, coming in at a slant through one set of windows in the morning and pouring through the large plate glass at the back of the cabin in the afternoon. The sunniness, the airiness of it, and her attic bedroom were what Nina loved about her new home.

Her main difficulty with home ownership, other than financial, was general maintenance. Her brother Matt had found her a handyman, a local man with arms like Popeye and a similarly half-cocked eye, and when things went wrong, if she remembered to call, he got around to making them right again eventually.

When she got involved in a case, she ignored everything else. She got up in the morning and ran out the door. Stacks of clothes, folded and unfolded, clean and dirty, began to pile up. Paperwork, especially junk mail, took up a larger and larger portion of the kitchen counter, and eventually oozed to the table until they had to push things over to set places.

Lately she had tried a new tack: no matter how tired she felt in the evening, she disciplined herself to spend at least fifteen minutes trying to establish some order before allowing herself the all-important glass of wine.

She was really bushed tonight. What she really wanted to do was fall into bed and have five minutes to think about Collier before sleep took her. Fifteen minutes, she chanted to herself, don't be lazy, go for it . . .

Pulling a throw pillow out from beneath a chair, she tossed it to the couch. It fell back to the floor. Sighing, she picked it up again. She knew that there was a philosophy behind this repetitive labor, something about being in the moment, something about enjoying whatever you did thoroughly, but housework had always bored her. She could hear her mother's voice even now, years after her death, saying, "Hustle, now, hustle."

She bent down and started picking up Hitchcock's sock shreds from the rug.

"Hey!" A muffled shout, and a pounding at the door flooded her with relief. Matt had come to interrupt.

"I'll get it!" she called out to Bob.

"Sis," he said when she opened the door, stamping the snow off his feet. "You do have a shovel, don't you?" He could barely see her over the snow-dusted logs he held in his arms.

She looked past him, observing the narrow footpath in the snow, the ice on the steps.

"Oops," she said. "I've been meaning to shovel that. Bob and I come in the back door when the snow's bad."

"What about other people?" Matt said, coming inside with his load.

"Other people? What's he mean, other people?" Nina closed the door on that problem.

"I'll shovel it for you before I leave."

"No, no, no, Matt. You've got your own walkways to shovel. Don't worry. We'll get to it."

Bob poked his head out of the kitchen to say hi. He held a wooden spoon which dripped thick red liquid on the floor.

"You'll get to it—in spring, right, Bob?" Matt said.

"I could do it this weekend," Bob said, "for a small remuneration."

"Nice talk," Matt said, sounding reproving.

"Yes, what kind of language are they teaching you at that school?" Nina said.

Bob laughed. "It's a word nobody but me can pronounce in this scene we're doing from *Love's Labour's Lost.*"

"How apropos to the moment at hand," Matt said, walking over to the empty metal stand that sat on one side of the fireplace. With a loud thump, he dropped the wood, raising a cloud of dirt mixed with snow. "Labor being lost, I mean."

"You're in a scene?" Nina asked Bob, coughing and waving her hand. "Are parents supposed to come to see the play?" She hated that it came out like that, so put-upon sounding, but making time for his school activities, in principle her first priority, somehow often ended up lingering somewhere at the bottom of the list.

Bob licked his spoon. "No, it's just for the class. We're going to critique each other. Will you listen tonight while I do my lines?"

"Sure," she said. "After we eat your delicious dinner."

He disappeared into the kitchen. "You let him cook?" Matt said, heading back toward the front door.

"Whatever it is, say good things about it, Matt." She checked her watch. Fifteen minutes were up. She had tried. Her heart had been in the right place. She had told herself to hustle. It wasn't her fault Matt had arrived. She sat down, put her legs on the coffee table, crossed them, and took a sip of the wine she had poured earlier. "Whew. What a day," she said. The wine tasted like summer, like Brazilian music, like Collier's mouth. . . .

Matt hovered meaningfully by the door.

"Gee, Matt. Thanks for bringing the wood. Why don't you have a seat. I'll see if we've got any beer."

"No," he said. "I've got more work to do."

She picked up the newspaper. He continued to hover.

Slapping it down on the table she said, "Okay. Tell me where you are going and what needs doing that obviously involves me."

"Out to the pickup to restock your woodpile."

"I guess we do need some." She rubbed her bare feet. She did not want to go out into the snow again, not even for the promise of many future warm fires.

"Andrea told me that you guys are almost out of wood. It's already winter, Nina. You need four cords per winter up here. This isn't the city. You can't just flip the thermostat to high and expect to get heat. Sometimes, the power goes out. In fact, it goes out several times every winter. When the power goes out, the ignition for your heating system doesn't work. It gets mighty chilly. Now. I brought you some wood." He threw her a pair of gloves. "But we're going to have to stack it under the porch."

"How much exactly are we talking about?"

"Half a cord."

"Oh, no," said Nina. "Not tonight. Not that I'm not grateful, but . . ."

He took her arm. "Up you go. Where are your boots?" He snuffled through the front closet, pulling out a pair of large Wellingtons. "Ah," he said. "Truffles."

After they stacked the wood to his satisfaction, so that it did not touch the house, so that it was covered with a tarp, so that the newest wood sat at the bottom of the pile, Matt consented to dine with them. Bob had made a casserole with tomato soup, cheese, and noodles, covered with crackers. The broccoli he boiled to a soggy gray separately, because Nina insisted on a vegetable, and because he preferred his ingredients pure, meaning, Nina had decided, untouched by anything that met current medical guidelines for nutritious food.

They ate every bite.

Bob ran upstairs to start his homework, leaving chaos in the kitchen. Nina began the cleanup by mopping up the now-dried red dribbles on the floor by the living room.

"Use some ammonia," Matt said, resting peacefully at the table.

"You know, the more confident and successful you get at your business, the bossier you get, Matt." Matt drove a tow truck in the winter and ran a parasailing franchise on the lake in summer.

He gave her a monkey grin.

She poured straight ammonia on the spots, reeling back from the smell. "I wish Mom could see you now," she went on. Matt had been their mother's angel, and he still had a deceptive boyish innocence about him even though he was in his early thirties now.

He had been through so much. While Nina had busied herself with law school and having an out-of-wedlock child, he had fomented his own revolution with drugs and dropping out. She never knew what had finally straightened him out. Maybe one of the rehabs their father had sponsored. Maybe the threat of prison.

Or possibly, he had grown up. It happened to everybody at twenty or thirty or fifty. Now, compared to her, he was exemplary, a doting father, prospering businessman, and faithful husband.

Matt said, "I hear you have a new client. The Strong family is pretty high profile up here. People enjoy gossiping about them. I hear a lot of stories."

"Oh?" She straightened up, feeling a crick in her back that told her that tomorrow even her cushy office chair would feel like a medieval rack.

"I heard something about Marianne Strong. Alex Strong's wife."

"What have you heard?"

"That would be gossiping. And I don't gossip," said Matt, too late.

"Do you wish to return home in one piece tonight?" Nina said.

"Okay, okay. Uh, she dated Jim Strong before she married Alex."

"That's all?"

"And she married Alex after Jim jilted her for Heidi. That was the story."

"And where did you hear this?"

"From a ski instructor who knows her. His pickup ran off the road yesterday and I went out with the tow truck. He was sitting in the cab with me while I towed the pickup to a gas station and we got to talking."

"Hmm." She stashed that factoid away in a safe place in the filing system in her brain.

"Is Jim Strong going to be charged with murder?"

Nina laid down the dish brush, wiped her hands, and walked to where she could see him better. "Can't talk about it," she said. "You know that."

He shook his head. "Why do you have to do criminal work? Why can't you do wills and trusts and appeals and stuff like that? You could still make a living, and you'd have more time to enjoy life. What's the attraction?"

"You promised to stop harping on this subject, Matt."

"Just remember what *you* promised. . . ."

"Right. No family involvement. I haven't forgotten."

Matt polished off his coffee and stood up. "Thank Bob for the astounding—I mean—outstanding dinner, will you?"

She laughed. "Sure."

But he didn't go. He leaned against the door. "I'll never understand you, Sis," he said.

"Oh, stop. I do it because it's real, Matt. I don't know how else to explain it. I'm a practical person. Criminal law isn't abstract or indirect, like drafting a bunch of papers that shift money around. Something real happens. It's a crisis point for my clients. People keep their liberty or lose it. I make a difference."

"But you're involved with people you might not even want to know, putting it all into saving them. I wish you could follow my lead for once. I decided a long time ago to channel my energies into keeping my own family safe and happy."

"And so far, you've succeeded magnificently. Really. I'm in awe sometimes, Matt."

He pulled on his wool hat and put his hand on the doorknob. "You have neatly changed the subject."

"Hush, Matt. Have a safe trip home." She gave him a quick hug. He went out, still shaking his head.

A hot bath helped, but even as she pulled on her nightgown in the bedroom, Hitchcock licking the water droplets off her legs, she knew she was stiffening up. She went back to the bathroom for some ibuprofen.

At last. Beautiful, wonderful bed. It was only nine-fifteen. Nine, ten hours of sleep stretched before her like a carpet of flowers. She curled up under the covers. Jim, Bob, Sandy, and Matt . . .

Collier.

Mrs. Geiger. Had the settlement really broken up the marriage? Was that good or bad? Was she somehow responsible? Should she take on Mrs. Geiger as a divorce client? Should she sink down gently through the layers of consciousness into a sweet swirling peace . . . ?

The phone on the bed stand rang. No, please, she really needed some sleep . . . It wouldn't stop.

She snaked out a hand and pulled the receiver off its hook, not moving from under the covers.

"They're searching my house!" Jim Strong said. "The police!"

"Okay. Let me think." It hurt, but she forced her mind back from its languor. "Did they show you a warrant?"

"Yes. Can they do this at night?"

"What time did they come?"

"Just before nine." It figured. Night search warrants required a much more detailed affidavit for the judge's review, but if the search was commenced one minute before nine o'clock, under California law it was still technically a day search. Collier, she thought again, but this time with a completely different emotion than that of a few moments before.

"They can," she told Jim.

"They're tearing the place apart!"

"I should have warned you it was likely to happen. Have you got anything there you shouldn't have? Contraband, guns?"

"No. We don't do drugs. I don't keep guns. There's nothing here. They're bagging up my ski gear."

"Damn it!" she said. "Excuse me, Jim. But have they got your boots? The ones you were wearing the night Alex died? It's really important. That's why I left a message at the lodge earlier today for you to call me."

"My boots? They're not here." As if someone might be within listening distance, he lowered his voice to a whisper. "My father went in the ambulance with Alex, and I followed in my father's Blazer. I left my boots in there."

"Where are they?"

"Why—I guess my father has them. I haven't felt like skiing since that day. They're probably still on the floor of the back seat."

"The Blazer's not at your place?"

"No—it's probably at his house at Marla Bay." He paused. "They're searching my car outside right now."

A gleeful, guilty thrill ran through her. Collier wouldn't have the boots tonight. Since Marla Bay was over the state line on the Nevada side of Lake Tahoe, it would take a while for the police to locate them, and longer to get a Nevada warrant.

"So they want my boots! I guess I should have thought of that."

"Jim, listen. It'll be all right. I'm going to go get the boots from your father tomorrow and send them to an expert in Sacramento. Don't try to get them yourself. Don't talk to your father about it. Understand?"

"Not really."

"Just do what I say. Okay?"

"Okay."

"Have they asked you any questions? They should know better than to do that without me there."

"They won't say anything to me."

"Well, if they do, tell them you spoke with me tonight and you are asserting your right to remain silent." He didn't have to be under arrest to assert that right, he just had to be under suspicion, and the search tonight confirmed that Jim was a suspect.

"Okay."

"Did the police ask you about the boots before?"

She could hear him expelling a deep breath. "Hmm. No, I don't think so."

And now she understood another reason why Collier had been so anxious to ask Jim just a few questions that day. He wanted to ask Jim where the boots were.

The cops had blown it. Now Jim had a lawyer and they would have to find the boots themselves. She would be glad to bring them right into Collier's office, as soon as Ginger had a crack at them.

She and Collier were embroiled in a subtle, dangerous game. She'd have to get sharper. She should have gotten the boots today. On the other hand, the police should have found them the minute they suspected a homicide.

"Aren't you coming out?" Jim asked.

"You don't need me, Jim. I can't stop the search. Just don't say anything and you'll be all right."

"Who has to clean all this up when they're done?"

"You, unfortunately. Do you have a Polaroid camera?"

"Yeah."

"Take pictures of the mess after they leave, just in

case. That's about all we can do." It probably wouldn't do any good but might make him feel better.

"Okay," Jim said again. Nina could hear slamming and banging in the background.

"I know how you feel," she said. "Violated. You can't believe a group of police can burst into your home and search into every private corner you've got. But that's how the system works. At least in this country you have to get a judge to approve it first. I'm sorry."

"I'm glad Heidi's not here. She'd—I don't know what she'd do. They're going through all the stuff she left too. I guess I'll go sit out in the car. I can leave the heater running. They're finished with the car. I'll wait until they're gone to go back inside."

"Good idea. Don't leave the property. Let them know where you are. Don't force any issues."

"I won't. Thanks for— I'm glad I went to see you. I couldn't go through this without your help."

"I'll talk to you tomorrow." She hung up with a clatter and sank back against the pillow, her mind buzzing with mental lists, details, strategic revisions.

6

POTENT SUN REFLECTING off virginal snowfields, and, filling a mighty fault line between high mountains, an oval of aching blue seventy-two miles around and sixteen hundred feet deep: Lake Tahoe.

Through this oval, running north-south, the California-Nevada state line splits the lake lengthwise, but the settlers of the nineteenth century ignored such political niceties. Instead of building their towns on the west and east sides, which would have placed them comfortably within one state or the other, they settled on the North Shore and South Shore with the state line running through the most populous areas.

On the South Shore, the line between the states is obvious. As the California town of South Lake Tahoe meets the Nevada town of Stateline, certain things change; the snowplows plow better, the sleepy motels become glitzy casino-hotels, and the party starts.

Or so Nina reflected as she drove across the state line into Nevada and into heavy traffic on Friday at noon. As Calcutta children pour into the thirsty street at the first moment the monsoon rain falls from heaven, so the gamblers, the skiers, the purse snatchers, the weirdos, the adulterers, and the party people were pouring into town to celebrate the early snow.

Once landed, some never left the casinos; some never left the slopes. A few never left their rooms. They were shoveled out in the morning with the empty whiskey bottles and Domino's Pizza boxes.

Just ahead, the sidewalks swarmed with bedazzled visitors making their way from one gaming establishment to the next. The locals looked seedy in their vests and jeans next to the bright spandex and nifty headgear of the tourists.

At Caesars, where Clint Black was appearing, the valets couldn't keep up with the demand and the cars stretched out into the street, blocking traffic. Vegas-style neon, tacky in the healthy glow of day, announced the weekend's other pleasures, a show called "Phantasy II" at the Horizon and a circus at Prize's.

While the Bronco idled in the traffic, waiting with the other sports utility vehicles for a break in the pedestrian flow, Nina watched the ivory mountain bordering the town on the right, also split between two states. Bright dots streaked down the ski trails of Heavenly. On the far side of the mountain, mostly inside Nevada, she thought she could just make out the lodge at Paradise.

Alex and Jim had been skiing that mountain, just inside the California line.

Ten more minutes brought her to the Paradise parking lot and its mud-spattered chartered buses. She traded her heels for a pair of ankle-high boots. Stepping out onto the slush over the asphalt, she buttoned her coat and dropped her head against the chilly breeze, hurrying to the lodge.

In the oak-paneled lobby with its antlered wall trophy, she ran into Jessica Sweet, Paradise's accountant. Mrs. Sweet looked just as hale and tan as the last time Nina had seen her, but not so combative. She had lost her daughter a long time before and in a way Nina had helped her find out what had happened to her.

"So he did go to see you," Mrs. Sweet said, wasting no time.

"Thanks for recommending me."

"You're the best of the local lot, I suppose."

"I'll do my best."

"He's a charming boy. A fantastic skier. It's bad for the resort, all these rumors." She told Nina how to get to Philip Strong's office.

Noisy families eating lunch filled the long trestle tables of the lodge cafeteria. Dripping skis lined the wall. Through the picture window, the beginners on the bunny slopes gave the diners something to laugh at.

Solemn as a mortician in her court clothes, Nina made her way through the skiers, ignoring the stares. There were probably only ten other suits in the whole town and eight of them were currently arguing with each other down at the courthouse. As she went down the hall toward Strong's office, the door opened and she heard a man say, "He just died! I don't want to talk about it!"

"Then I'll sell the shares to Jim," a girl's hoarse voice said. The girl, dark, in ski gear, came rushing out and brushed by Nina.

Philip Strong's office smelled like cedar. The chairs were upholstered in bright Marimekko fabric. Books and photographs lined the walls. He met her at the door and shook her hand firmly, a sinewy man in a skintight blue ski suit. No smile. He was upset about the conversation that had just ended, that was clear. She wondered who the girl skier was.

The first thing Nina noticed about the elder Strong

was that he was bald. Not totally bald in a way that makes a statement, but half bald, his dark hair curling around the bottom half of his skull, but then leaving off suddenly, nuked by a bad gene, unable to climb the slippery dome. It gave him a clownish look, though the rest of his face, lined deeply from nose to mouth, was sensitive, sorrowful.

"Sit down." He waved toward a leather chair. Nina sat down and set her briefcase with the large empty plastic Nordstrom's bag in it on the carpet.

"Where's Jim today?"

"In Reno checking on some equipment."

So much for introductions. Cautious, Nina waited for Jim's father to make clear his attitude and agenda. She meditated on how hungry she was. Hot soup would hit the spot. Would they be eating at the lodge?

A display case on the wall was crammed with skiing trophies and photographs. Philip had his trophies, but there were quite a few for Jim and Alex up there, too. The *Mirror* hadn't broken the news about the amendment to the autopsy report. When that time came, she was sure it would be front-page news again. The family was too prominent in Tahoe to expect much privacy.

"I'm very sorry about your son," Nina said.

He rubbed his forehead with his fingertips and his face lengthened. "Alex? Or Jim?" he said. He looked down at photographs spread in front of him on the desk. "I'm trying to keep busy." He motioned toward a cardboard layout for a brochure he had tacked to the wall. "Ski Paradise!" shouted the headline. Another version next to it said, "Paradise—come and get it."

They both watched out the window as, in the distance, a skier jumped a mogul, turned his body one hundred and eighty degrees in the air, and landed inches from the crags of a boulder. Nina held her breath until he scooted smoothly past.

To break the deadlock, she said, "I understand you were able to get to Alex just after the accident."

"Not soon enough."

"There was nothing you could have done."

"At least I could have said good-bye to him. But he was already unconscious. Mrs. Sweet picked up the call on the radio in the cafeteria and called me. I was up on the Ogre looking at a possible avalanche area."

"Alone?"

"What do you care? I met the Ski Patrol at the foot of the hill and climbed up with them to the bottom of the Cliff."

"Sounds like you had been there before."

"Only once. It was barely skiable. Too dangerous, with that drop-off. I told the boys long ago to stay away from there, but nobody listens. Have you noticed that? Nobody listens."

The phone rang and Strong picked it up. Staring at the wall, he spoke in a monotone. When he hung up, he still sat there staring at nothing. He was functioning, but only barely.

"That call was something I have to take care of. Want to walk along with me?"

"Sure."

She heaved herself back out of the cushiony chair and put her coat back on. He put on a baseball cap with his jacket and instantly turned into another person, younger and better looking. She could see Jim in him now, in the high color of his cheeks and the square chin. Now he looked forty, though he had to be much older, in his late fifties probably. She thought of Sandy's story about her mother.

The trail they took followed the flat groomed snowpack toward a weathered cabana. Next to it, a double lift rocked gently under its steel-supporting scaffold, its cables stretched out of sight up the mountain. Even through sunglasses, the snow was dazzling. The breeze had freshened into a frank wind.

"You know why people like to ski?" Strong was saying as she trotted along beside him trying to keep up. "Because it's just like flying. It's freedom from gravity. It's being a bird."

"Hey, Phil, how ya doing?" said a skier passing them, and Strong waved without looking.

"Alex was like that," he went on. "A bird. Flying high on the wind. But now he's gone." Still walking fast, he lifted a fist, then opened it and blew on it. "Poof," he said into a blast of cold air. "Gone."

They reached the cabana. The chairlift seemed to be broken. Skiers lined up, grumbled and complained, watched for movement, then, disgusted, pushed off again.

"Give us just a coupla minutes, folks!" Strong shouted to their backs, marching over to talk to a young man in a Paradise jacket. While they talked, Nina stood off to one side and watched the skiers.

These people seemed not to have a care in the world beyond a lost glove or broken ski pole. Their expensive duds made them all look rich. In her dark clothes and idiotic nylons, she felt very incongruous out here. She shivered. Dense clouds showed themselves behind the mountain, climbing onto the sunny backdrop.

Strong and the operator pointed through a door at the lift machinery, waggling their fingers as they discussed some mechanical glitch. "Chuck, you know the drill!'' Strong said, voice raised, annoyed out of proportion to the problem. Perhaps recognizing this, he took a breath and lowered his voice. "C'mon. Let's go over it one more time." They disappeared through the door.

Nina stamped her feet and crammed her hands into her pockets, remembering that she'd skipped breakfast because Bob had missed the bus. She had left in a rush to drive him to school. She was getting irritated. Did Strong really have something to tell her? After an interminable time, with a clank and a long, slow shudder, the lift shook back into action. Strong and the attendant came out, Strong's arm resting on the young man's shoulder.

A line formed instantly. Nina leaned against one of the supports and watched the attendant catch each chair as it came rolling in, slowing it for the skiers who stood with their heads craned back and knees bent. The seat caught two collegiate types at the back of the thighs and they sat down hard, then went swinging up, skis waving, whooping.

"I have to supervise here for a while," Strong said, adjusting his dark glasses. "So I guess we'd better get to it." He cocked his head, gauging the ski lift operation.

"Good plan."

"Why did Jim hire you?"

"Come on, Mr. Strong. You understand I can't answer that. No questions."

"It was an accident, wasn't it? Tell me! I have a right to know!" He was still looking toward the lift. She understood that this was such an important question that he couldn't look at her.

Nina didn't know how to answer. She shouldn't talk about the case, but it seemed wrong to leave him full of torment. "Jim assures me it was an accident," she said finally.

"Then why did he hire a lawyer?"

"My chin's numb, my feet are frozen stumps, I'm hungry, I came up here because you wanted to tell me something. Remember? So tell me. I'm waiting. For another thirty seconds."

"You're a tough little—"

"You try hanging around in this wind dressed like I am for half an hour, Mr. Strong. Then you can call me names."

He let out a surprised sound that almost resembled a laugh. "Sorry," he said. "All right. Jim and I haven't spoken since—since the accident. A friend of mine tells me Jim's been somehow implicated in Alex's death. That's impossible. It was an obvious accident and a criminal investigation is beyond belief. Meanwhile, Heidi—Jim's wife—hasn't come to work for several days. I was lying down in the office yesterday morning when the phone rang. It was Heidi."

"Keep going."

"I know where she is. She's worked here for a long time and she didn't want to just walk out. So she called me."

"What did she tell you?"

"She said that Jim threatened to kill Alex. She said she couldn't stand to stay."

"So," Nina said, "tell me, Mr. Strong. How credible is Heidi?"

"I don't know. She and Jim are having some problems."

"What kind of problems?"

"Nothing to do with Alex."

"Then let me get more to the point. Do you believe what she said?" Nina asked.

"Of course not," Strong answered. "Besides the fact that I find the whole idea insane, Jim had no reason to hurt Alex. Alex was—Alex didn't tangle with Jim. He looked up to him."

"Why aren't you and Jim talking? It would seem to me you would be drawn together at a time like this."

"Jim and I have some problems at the moment," Strong said. "I don't want to go into it. It has nothing to do with Alex."

"That's the second time you've said that. It has nothing to do with Alex." She rubbed her arms with her bare hands, trying to create warmth through friction.

"So? If it has nothing to do with Alex, it's none of your business. Heidi is having a hard time and has let her imagination take over. I can't believe her. But then, I don't believe anything," he said thoughtfully. "I don't actually believe Alex is dead. He's wandering around, still alive in some fashion. Look behind that tree over there. See that shadow?"

She knew better, but she looked. Nothing.

"Or maybe he moved behind the boulder," Strong went on drearily. "I thought I saw him yesterday, out by the cave he used to play in with Jim. It's gotten so I'm afraid to go to sleep. He comes to the foot of my bed and it's a tremendous effort for him, he's come from a very far place, but he keeps coming back. He's lost, I think. I'm afraid of him now. I love what he was, but not what he is now."

"I don't think I'd care to know a whole lot more about that," said Nina.

Strong grasped her arm. "I'm quite sure the spirit stays around for a while," he said. "I had a dog once who died after twelve years with me. He always used to push open my bedroom door at night with his paw and come in and lie down in the corner. He'd make this scratching sound with his claws as he pushed on the door. Well, a week after he died, in the middle of the night, I woke up to a scratching sound. Something dark and low came in, went to the corner, and lay down. I was terrified. You see, it wasn't my dog anymore. Think I'm nuts?" His mouth moved into a grimace like a smile.

"No. Just—"

"Yeah. I am nuts. Nuts with wanting my son back." His voice thickened. "Alex was so young. So talented. He should have had fifty more years."

"I understand," Nina said softly. "But I know Jim still matters."

"Jim? There's one problem with Jim."

"What's that, Mr. Strong?"

"He's not Alex," Strong said. Nina had an odd sensation as he said this, as if she was looking down into an abyss, the abyss Alex had left in his father's heart, maybe. She didn't like hearing these unguarded, painful things. She didn't want to be affected by them. But she wondered about the three of them, the father and his sons, and Philip Strong seemed to want to talk.

"No, he's not Alex," she said.

"If only Alex hadn't come back from Colorado. He'd still be alive. Alex probably dared Jim to ski the Cliff hill. He was still trying to catch up with Jim. When they were small boys, he'd toddle around after Jim, getting hurt because he wasn't big enough to do the same things."

"That's how it is with younger brothers sometimes."

"The little brother grew up," Strong said. "He

didn't quite know it, but he was Jim's equal in every way."

"You seem to be angry at Jim right now," Nina said. "I can't understand why."

"Angry? I'm angry at myself."

"For what?"

"For my mistakes. Some of them are irrevocable." His eyes, which had held a faraway look, came back to her. He frowned. "Forget it. I'm blabbering."

"What about Jim?"

"I don't have anything to spare for Jim right now. You clean up whatever the problem is."

She said matter-of-factly, "I'll do that. Where is Heidi? That's what you wanted to tell me, right?"

Happy shouts filtered down the hill. Strong was standing stock-still, struggling with himself. He seemed to be so busy experiencing his angry grief that the outer world couldn't get through to him very well. He had a living son in trouble, but he hardly seemed to notice.

"Heidi is hiding in a hidey-hole," he said eventually. "And she wants to talk to you. On one condition."

"Let me guess. That I don't tell Jim?"

"Right. You come alone. And don't tell him that you're meeting her."

"Why? Why won't she at least call Jim? He's suffering. He's sure if he could just reach her he could persuade her to come home. He loves her." She felt as though she was arguing to a blank TV screen. Strong had absented himself again. "Can you ask her to reconsider?"

"I've said what I promised her I would say," he said. "Talk to her yourself."

She thought about it.

"All right, then. If that's the only way."

A nod.

"But why does she want to talk to me?" Nina said. "If she's hiding from Jim, why talk to his lawyer?"

He shrugged. "Maybe she wants to tell him something without having to face him? I don't know. I'm just trying to do what she asked me to do." He reached into his shirt pocket and pulled out a piece of paper. "She'll be there between three and four."

Nina read it. Jake's in Tahoe City, all the way around the lake practically to the North Shore, over an hour of hard driving away. Heidi wanted to meet at a public place, and she didn't want to get too close.

"You know Jake's?" Strong asked.

"Mmm-hmm. What does Heidi look like?"

"Oh, tall. Buff. Blond."

"Like everybody around here. One more thing," she said, trying to sound casual. "I need the ski boots Jim was wearing on the day of Alex's accident."

"Why?"

Good. He hadn't heard about Clauson's report. "He asked me to get them from you," she said.

He thought for a moment, then said, "I suppose they're still in the back of my Blazer, out in the parking lot. Alex had borrowed the Blazer the night before—the accident—for some errands. Jim drove it to the hospital, and I picked it up there. Jim dumped his boots in the back with some other things."

"Has anyone been in your truck besides you since—"

"No, nobody. I haven't looked, but I suppose they're still there."

Lucked out again, Nina told herself, greatly relieved. She asked Strong to take her out to his truck. He sped down to the parking lot as if daring her to keep up. She wondered if he still skied, then thought, well, of course he did.

Then, on the wooded side of the lot, she saw a man who looked a lot like Jim moving rapidly between one tree and another. Alex? She blinked, refocused her eyes, saw only the usual patterns of shade and sunlight.

On the muddy carpet of the back seat, the red Tecnica boots were upright, stowed carefully along with some dirty clothes. Using a handkerchief, Nina gingerly guided the boots into her plastic bag.

They were heavy, enormous. She wondered how people could feel like they were flying while wearing such clumsy gear. Her idea of flying would be to take off her clothes and dive into a warm ocean.

"Did you ever wear Jim's boots, Mr. Strong?" she asked.

"No." He seemed to have no curiosity about her question, which must have sounded pretty odd. He stood off to the side of the car, hands in his pockets, watching a young couple unload skis from a rack on the back of a new red Volkswagen Bug.

He just didn't give a fuck about Jim, that was obvious. She felt a stirring of contempt. He should make himself care. He should help. He was the father. He should be strong and do his duty no matter what he was going through personally.

"Go home, Mr. Strong," she said, straightening up, struggling with the bag and the briefcase. "Get some rest."

He shrugged. "I can't leave Paradise."

The phrase struck her. All this joy around, and none for him. "You should rest. Get some sleep."

"Oh, no. See now, that's the mistake people make. They mistake sleep with rest. If you want rest, it's best to stay busy. Move fast and you keep the demons off your heels."

Demons? she thought. He was grieving, yes, but there was something more complicated going on that she could not understand.

She wondered whether he loved Jim at all, when he wasn't grieving about Alex.

"Well." Tilting his hand at his forehead, he gave her a kind of salute, turned, and walked away.

She drove west, back across the state line, along the string of motels, shops, and ski rental places which stretched for miles. At Highway 89, which bordered the west side of the lake, she turned north. Her watch said one o'clock. She would be very early. She could eat at Jake's before Heidi got there.

Hot sun had melted the snow on the asphalt, so she didn't have to worry about the road. On the lake, a couple of cruisers were moving north toward the marinas on the other side of the lake, twenty-two miles away. Even the forest seemed luminous today, as if the snow on the mountains reflected enough light to light up even Tahoe's darkest places. Most of the time, she had the road to herself.

As she drove on, clouds passed over the sun, casting long shadows with irregular borders. Her mood also darkened.

The highway passed personal landmarks. First she came to the turnoff to Fallen Leaf Lake and the Angora Ridge trail. She remembered a terrifying night when she had driven up there sick with fear, searching for Bob. Then the twists and turns above Cascade Lake came into view, and on her right she saw the thousand-foot drop to Emerald Bay with its jewel-like island. An orange kayak anchored off the island reminded her of Paul and the Markov case.

After that case, Paul had accepted a temporary position on the East Coast. It couldn't be good for his agency in Carmel for him to be gone for several months. His move had been a decision to put distance between them. He had been a friend, an occasional lover, and a very good private detective. She could have gone on forever with their on-again, off-again relationship, but he had gotten tired of waiting for more.

She had pushed him away, justifying her behavior to herself by saying that Paul was a wild card. He'd been a homicide detective before he started up his agency in Carmel. Brilliant and exciting he might be, but he went too far, regularly, with everything he did. Swinging around a curve she gave the steering wheel a slap. She had handled it badly and left hurt feelings.

The cell phone rang, and she answered quickly, thankful for the intrusion.

"It's me."

"Hello, Sandy."

"Mind telling me when you plan to show up at the office?"

"Oh, boy, I'm sorry, Sandy. I meant to call. I've got to go to Tahoe City this afternoon." She held the phone away from her ear to muffle the recriminations she richly deserved. When the tide receded, she put it back to her ear, saying, "Those are strong sentiments, Sandy. But I'm sure you can reschedule. See you tomorrow." She hung up, returning to her solitude.

Philip Strong had put her into a peculiar frame of mind. Alex's death had come as a terrible shock to his father. How did people go on when someone they dearly loved died? How had she survived her mother's death? There was no preparation for such endings.

She ought to be thinking about Jim, not Philip or her mother or Paul, but her mind, like Philip Strong's, U-turned back to Alex.

Who could say? Maybe somewhere out there, as Philip seemed to imagine, Alex lingered. Many religions told of a limbo, a bardo, an interim state in which contact could still be made. Maybe Alex really did visit his father in dreams. Maybe he hung out in the Paradise parking lot, for that matter.

Her mother had died when she was twenty-five. There were vivid dreams, so real, but gradually, they faded away.

Poof, gone. She felt the old desolation.

She drove slowly in her narrow lane halfway up a cliff some two thousand feet high, which topped out in white mountain and fell below to the lake. Where was the traffic? She was quite alone on the road. This part of the highway regularly fell into the lake in winter and it took most of the spring to prop it up again. The grid of metal supporting it didn't look particularly secure, and she thought for a moment, what if the sun decides to melt that cornice up there? Nina Reilly, *finito* in a brief cloud of snow, gone so quickly she wouldn't even notice.

Her death could come at any minute. Look what had happened to Alex.

"We were laughing," Jim had said. Life was so damn short.

The phone rang again. She didn't answer. It rang again. She answered impatiently.

"This is Collier."

"How'd you get this number?"

"I'm a D.A., remember? Sounds like you're driving. Can we talk a minute? And not about the case."

"About what then? If not the case?"

"About the kiss."

"Oh, that."

"Did you like it? Or do you hate me? I have to know, right now."

Several recent memories flashed through her mind: the kiss in the dingy conference room, Collier's check, how she had wanted to press right up against him and forget where they were; Sandy laughing in the parking lot with a man named Joseph; Bob growing up and leaving her; Alex Strong, dead at twenty-seven.

A whisper of that first memory touched her lips.

"I liked it."

"Good." He hung up, leaving her gaping at the receiver. She felt just like he had taken her by the shoulders and shaken her so hard her insides were rearranged.

A few minutes later, she passed Granlibakken with its bantam ski runs and lift, busy with a weekday family crowd. Roads off to the left disappeared into the forests. Blue and brown roofs of the big ski chalets that groups rented each winter flickered by between the trees. The road had returned to lake level. Here, the water that was so close to pure light lapped along the road beside her.

She was getting close to Tahoe City. She pushed the strange mood away, making her mind shipshape, then moved to the question of Heidi Strong.

7

HEIDI STRONG ARRIVED at Jake's after four o'clock, when Nina had just about given up on her. Jim's wife was too tall and attractive to be alone, so she drew some attention as she scanned the crowd. Possibly tipped off by the three empty latte glasses and the big empty soup bowl cluttering the table in the corner, she came directly toward Nina, clutching a gray purse on a long strap.

The waitress came over to them, pad and pencil ready. Heidi ordered the veggie burger and green tea, then licked her already moist lips, saying, "You don't look all that mean. In the pictures in the paper you always look mean."

"I am mean," Nina said. "You don't look like a liar, either, but I don't go by looks, do you?"

"I'm not a liar, but I don't give a damn if you believe me or not. You're paid not to believe me." Her tea came in a handleless cup, and she picked it up with large, capable hands. She wore only a man's diver's watch on her wrist and a thickly chased gold wedding ring.

She was in the best shape of any woman Nina had ever seen. Even her face muscles were sharp and defined. Only a face like that could get away with the short platinum hair.

Her hands stayed steady. Not a woman who scared easily. But under the aggressive attitude, Nina believed she was scared.

"You didn't tell him, did you?" Heidi asked.

"No. But he really wants to talk to you."

"Yeah. I left my home and my job and lost my whole life just to turn around and come back because he crooks a finger. I don't think so."

"Is there any way I can convince you to talk to him?"

"No. So don't bother to try."

"Well, then, do you mind telling me what's going on? This is your husband we're talking about. He's in a bad state. Don't you care?"

Heidi reached for a packet of aspartame, tore off the top, and dumped it into her tea. Her teaspoon clinked against the side.

"No," she said again.

"Well, you ought to care," Nina said. "You still wear the ring, I see."

"I like the ring, that's all. I picked out the design. Don't get moral on me. Who do you think you are?"

This counterattack was quite effective. Nina didn't want Heidi to leave. She put a clamp on her tongue. "Okay, Heidi. I'm not here to judge."

"I don't owe him anything anymore."

"There's got to be a way to work things out."

"There's no way."

"You can't avoid him forever."

"Maybe not. That's why I agreed to talk to you. I'm counting on you to make sure Jim leaves me alone. And one other thing. Draw up divorce papers for us. I don't have the money to hire a lawyer. Let him pay for it."

What a shame. Nina had hoped to act as an emissary of goodwill. Jim really needed somebody on his side, and with Heidi refusing even to talk with him, and his father so strangely detached, neither one appeared to be a strong candidate for the position. She felt very sad for him. He was all alone, with no one to stand behind him, no one to believe in him except the hired help.

"So what do you say?"

"He doesn't want a divorce," Nina said. "If you could see him, the sadness in his eyes, the love in his voice when he talks about you—he doesn't want to blame you for anything. Alex's death was a shock. People have strange reactions sometimes. Maybe that's what has happened to you."

"Why, I do believe Jim's got you conned. Maybe you'll get him off after all. What he did to Alex he'd do to me. I'm not staying around to be Accident Number Two."

"All right, then. But—"

"But what?"

"If you don't love him, okay. If you hate him, okay. If you want a divorce, well, Jim can't prevent it. But the story you're telling—that goes beyond revenge."

"You think I'm pretty harsh. Well, you would be too, if your husband smashed up the bathroom one night and said he was gonna kill his brother and then did it! I'm gonna tell the truth. For Alex. Let's not forget Alex."

"Who knows what the truth about anything is?" Nina said. "You say you heard Jim say something idiotic about Alex one night, maybe a month ago, maybe a year ago. Brothers get mad at each other. But the day he died, Alex was doing extreme skiing off-trail. His luck ran out. You were upset and you connected those two things in your mind, very naturally. The police made you get specific about things you don't really remember, and now they're turning your vague recollection into an accusation."

"It wasn't like that." Her voice shook.

Did Heidi have some idea that involving Jim in something so dire might make getting a divorce from him easier? "You do realize, you can't testify against your husband about any conversations you may have had?" Nina said.

"What? Why not?"

"It's called the marital privilege. It'll keep your statement out of court too."

"The police never said a thing about that. I don't believe you." The waitress set down a thick soy patty on a bun, exotically dressed in sprouts and tahini. Heidi looked at it vacantly, then returned her gaze to Nina's. "If it's so worthless, why are you here?"

"Well, your statement has been read by the police, by the coroner. It's having an impact on the investigation. Because of you, the police suspect Jim of murdering Alex. I came because I hoped you would reconsider your statement."

"I won't." She said this calmly.

"Then could you just talk to Jim? In my conference room, somewhere neutral. You were married three years. Shouldn't he have a chance to explain?"

"No. Now, stop trying to persuade me. I'm not talking to him, and I'm not going back to him. I'm going as far away from him as I can."

"But why—"

"Tell him I want a divorce! Get it?" She spoke loudly.

"I get it. I get it."

"Call Philip when the papers are ready for me to sign. He'll make sure I get them." She wrapped up the burger in her napkin as she spoke. "I'm too upset to eat with you. But I'm low on cash, so let's let Jim pay for this."

Nina wasn't getting anywhere, and Heidi was about to take off. She tried to think—what more could she learn? "Listen, I'd just like to know, Heidi. Why? Why do you think Jim would want to kill his brother?"

"You make him tell you that. He knows why. I don't."

"Wait! Don't go yet. I need to ask you some more questions about your statement."

But Heidi was already turning to go, stuffing the food into her shoulder bag. "You think I'm not sorry about all this? I've lost everything!"

"Stay a little longer, please. Convince me you're telling the truth."

Heidi said over her shoulder, "You want convincing? Have you checked out Jim's arm?"

She was gone, leaving Nina to wonder what she had meant.

The waitress came by with the check, and Nina remembered that the cupboard at home was bare.

"Two Tostada Grandes to go," she said. "Hold the sour cream. And a cheeseburger." Hitchcock liked cheeseburgers.

Her watch said four-thirty. She headed home, depressed at Heidi's intransigence, looking across the big emptiness of the lake. She wasn't looking forward to relaying the conversation to Jim.

Heidi wasn't going to go back to him. The marriage was over. The statement would continue to cast its shadow on Jim, whether it ever came into court as evidence or not, and she had failed.

It was only to be expected. Nobody stayed together any more. Women and men walked alone now, skittish rhinoceroses, suspicious and red-eyed and afraid of each other.

She turned on the radio, but the mishmash of ads and traffic announcements and Mariah Carey and ministers hairsplitting Bible verses made her feel worse, so she clicked it off again. She was alone on the road.

In fact she was more than alone, she was lonely. She wanted to call someone, but Andrea was at work, Paul was in Washington . . .

This feeling of loneliness was like a key turning the lock and releasing more emotions she really didn't want to face right now. Maybe it was Philip Strong's colossal grief, or the vulnerability she had felt in Heidi Strong behind the girl's pugnaciousness.

She began to fill with wanting, or maybe the wanting had been there a long time, kept somewhere dark because it made her feel so cold. Like a chilly river it flowed now into every part of her body.

Death was in that cold river, dark and low. The Strong case was spooking her, drawing out old feelings of abandonment and loss. Like Jim, she was all alone in the world, or that was how she felt at that moment. It was unbearable to be so alone.

She'd done it to herself. I'm a fool who pushes away everyone who could love me, she thought. A proud, arrogant, lonely fool.

Shaking and miserable, she pulled to a stop and pressed the buttons on her phone.

He answered immediately.

"I think—that is, I seem to really—"

"Tell me where you are."

"About ten minutes south of Tahoe City, by the side of the highway."

"Wait for me." The phone went dead.

She got out of the truck and sat down on a log on the rocky beach, looking out across the lake.

Iciness seeped into her jacket. Shoes flung aside, she kneaded her toes in the cold sand below the log. Time passed.

She heard the car drive up and didn't turn around, still in the grip of a puzzling distress.

Collier stood beside her. She didn't look up.

"Ah," he said. "I knew I'd find you."

He reached down and took her hand. "You're cold! C'mere. The car's warm." He led her to a pickup with a camper shell. Without letting go of her, he raised the back hatch. Warmth rushed out.

She climbed in. Pulling off his tie, he sat next to her on her left. The tie was flung aside. Reaching behind her into the empty cab, he found a sleeping bag to spread over them.

They huddled together. It was enough, almost too much, having him beside her. He was warm. He sent death skulking back out.

For a few minutes they just lay there, neither making a move toward the other. Nina couldn't believe he'd dropped everything and come to her. She had needed him, but she hadn't expected it.

And now she didn't say a word, and neither did he,

as though they both felt words would destroy everything.

They didn't need words. Everywhere their bodies touched, he communicated with her. A delicate silence stretched between them.

Her desperation and longing seemed to reach out and meet the same feelings in him. She shifted and her hair brushed his cheek and he drew in the scent of it. She listened to his breathing. His restraint, his hard body just barely touching hers, was arousing her, heating her.

No sounds, no blare, as quiet as a prayer. The highway empty. Out on the lake two gulls floated, beaks down, scanning for fish. They were utterly alone, as if the towns ringing the lake and two hundred years of history had fallen away.

When it became unbearable, when something had to give, he seemed to know it. He settled his arm around her, ducked in shyly, and gave her a fleeting kiss. Then again and again. Their lips meshed, locked. She glanced up. Pierced by his hot gaze, she lowered her eyes again.

"I was dying to see you," he said, pulling away, his voice rough. He reached out his free hand and slid it into her silk blouse, familiarly, as if he had done it many times, leaving her gasping, and then he unbuttoned it all the way and took it off her.

"The bra, too," he said, and she let him take it off. She let him stroke and fondle and kiss her for a long time.

Her hands came up to rub his chest, open his shirt, move down and pull open the belt and unzip the fly.

She touched him and he jerked. His mouth opened slightly and his breathing came harder.

She rubbed him and he caressed her until they were both half-deranged. Then he fell on her like a starving man at a feast. She tried to push her way into him as he was pushing his way into her, to become part of him. His body felt as hot as life itself, transmuting the loneliness she had felt into something almost joyful.

He didn't want to leave her. He pulled up the sleeping bag and lay next to her, nuzzling her hair, talking. He told her he needed her and she wouldn't get away again. He said that he couldn't believe his luck and nothing, nothing would come between them.

A car whizzed by. The wind began a fitful blowing through the trees and rocked the camper shell so that it creaked back and forth. Gradually they became themselves again. Nina sat up and reached over for her underclothes and put them on under the sleeping bag, suddenly modest. Collier buttoned his shirt.

They looked at each other in wonder and embarrassment.

One of them ought to make a smart, cynical comment now. Nina opened her mouth to try to say something funny but it just wouldn't come out. She put her hand on his arm. "I've got to go," she said.

He nodded. "I'll call you." They got out and he climbed into the cab. He didn't honk or wave, just turned around and headed back toward town. She sat in the Bronco, watching. Her face in the mirror was a wreck, the makeup gone, her lips swollen, her cheeks abraded by his beard.

> *A spell like the mist still on me*
> *Like rain on me, and I am helpless*

Friday night. Real life ran at her at the house, and she fell into the ordinary routine as though something extraordinary had not just happened. The mood that had frightened her so much had completely dissolved. She took a bath, changed into jeans, combed her hair.

Bob needed a haircut. Arguing all the way, they made it to Supercuts just before closing, gas tank on empty. Before going in, she locked the Bronco carefully, mindful of the Tecnicas still in the bag in back.

Bob wore his new clothes, which he had picked out at a military surplus store and which he carefully folded and put away each night: black cargo pants with pockets all over, black T-shirt with a Jackie Chan logo. He wanted a navy pea coat, but Nina had insisted on a red parka so he wouldn't look like a black hole in space.

Like clockwork, they had begun to bicker the moment he turned thirteen. Tonight was their first hair argument. Bob wanted to cut his hair short. Nina objected. "You have the most beautiful hair," she kept saying. He had been parting it in the middle lately so that it fell in two dark silky wings around his face.

Right now, standing in front of the reception counter waiting to be called, that face had assumed an obdurate expression that looked suspiciously like the one she saw in her own mirror from time to time.

"Short," he said. "It's my hair. The bowl cut is for kids."

"I'm the one that has to look at it."

"I'm the one that has to wash it and push it out of my eyes."

She resigned herself. At least he didn't want to dye it crimson like Taylor Nordholm's. Yet. "So long as you keep something around your ears. I can't stand it when they cut the sideburns off."

Bob's name was called and he went into the linoleumed pit to his assigned hair station, where a young lady with a golden stud in her eyebrow bent over him. They consulted. Bob didn't look Nina's way.

It's the invitation to the dance, Nina thought. It's Germany. He wants to look more grown-up. She didn't want that at all. Sitting down on the bench, she buried her nose in *Elle* magazine, but the rest of her went back to Collier and the lake.

After a long time Bob came to her, beaming. He looked like an underage Marine recruit. All traces of sideburns had been buzzed away. On top of his skull some hair had been retained to lead an uneasy existence, standing at attention at this and that angle. His chin seemed to have lengthened an inch or two.

She reached out a wondering hand and felt the stiff spikes. He had been moussed.

He was ecstatic.

"Oh, Bob," she said.

They went on to Matt and Andrea's to watch a kung-fu flick. The cousins and Matt assembled in the darkened living room in front of the fire and sounds of grunting and banging started up. While Nina heated the limp tostadas in the kitchen microwave, Andrea handed her some iced tea. "Come on, cheer up. He looks good," she said. *"Très chic."*

"If you're modeling for *Soldier of Fortune*. Next he'll join a vigilante group and start hoarding guns."

"Don't be such a mom. He just wants to try something new. It's natural. He's thirteen. Ride with it."

"Your turn will come, Andrea. Troy's not that far behind." She took a tostada out and set it on a paper plate. "How's it going at the shelter?" Andrea managed the Tahoe Women's Shelter, which had twenty-two beds and a new backyard playground, thanks to one of Nina's old clients, Lindy Markov.

"Calmer than usual. The husbands and boyfriends are too exhausted laying in wood for winter, finding their tire chains and shoveling snow to cause trouble. Plenty of jobs since the ski resorts are all opening early. So the domestic violence quotient is way down. We have six women and their kids right now getting themselves together. Manageable."

Cantonese expletives and savage thrashing sounds came from the living room. "We could adjourn to the hot tub," Andrea said, inclining her head toward the back door.

"A capital idea." Nina called to Bob to pick up his plate, and she and Andrea went to the icy patio. They pulled the lid off the wooden tub. Steam geysered up.

"Oh, yes," Andrea moaned, dribbling her fingers in the water. They got naked and hopped in.

Pure return-to-the-womb physical bliss. They lay there, the hot water tickling their chins, legs floating, spread out and justified, women under the stars taking their ease.

"So how's your love life?" Andrea said lazily.

Startled, Nina fell into a rigorous examination of her toes, which jutted like tiny icebergs into the mist. At least no *Titanic* was in sight yet.

"Heard from Paul?" Andrea said, on the scent now.

"Not for a while."

"Enjoying the serenity of the cloister?" A clump of snow fell from the pine overhead into the water, sizzling and dying instantly.

"Not exactly. There I go again," Nina said. "Love puts a spell on me and I'm helpless. Lines from a song Sandy plays over and over."

"Sandy? Our Sandy?"

"Yes. Something's going on with that woman."

"What?"

"I don't know. Yet."

They soaked quietly for a while. Nina began drifting into a reverie featuring the failed relationships of her past.

"Nothing but grief, every doggone time," she said. "Why can't I just live alone and be happy and content, Andrea? Why do I have to be tortured with loneliness and driven right back into it?"

"Aw, there you go again," Andrea said. "Self-pity puts a spell on you and you're helpless."

They both laughed.

"So who is he?" Andrea said. "Tell dear old Auntie Andrea." She put her arms behind her head and twisted her auburn hair into a knot, somehow tucking it so it stayed put without benefit of a rubber band. The cross she wore floated above her freckled chest.

"I can't talk about it. It's too soon." Nina really wanted to spill it, but she couldn't. She didn't know what had happened yet, so how could she describe it?

"He must be goooood," Andrea said, pleased at hitting pay dirt. "Judging by that flustered look on your face."

Nina turned onto her stomach and stretched out, arching her back to take out more crinks from the wood-stacking of the day before. "If I ever get married again, it's going to be a rational decision. I'll do like the French. Marry for money, stability . . . companionship."

"Sure," said Andrea. "Marry an accountant with agoraphobia. He'll never leave ya."

"It never lasts," Nina said. "You know it doesn't. Look at the women at the shelter. They were all in love once. Some of them still are."

"I got lucky. I got your brother. It lasted. You know, Paul really did love you."

"I know. And I owe him so much. He saved my life up there on Angora Ridge. But we never should have gotten involved. I had to think about real life. Like—he doesn't like kids. He and Bob didn't hit it off. And he wouldn't leave Carmel. And I won't leave Tahoe."

"And he got on your nerves."

"He was out of control, you know that, Andrea. He's—he's unpredictable and wild. I told you what he did to Jeff Riesner."

"But you miss him?"

"Sure," Nina said. "All the excitement. Anyway, it's over." They meditated on this for some time, eyes closed, floating.

Then Andrea said in a sprightly voice, "But love springs eternal."

"Oh, Andrea. How can you spout romanticisms with the work you do every day?"

"You're still young. You can fight all you want, but Nature's gonna have her way with you."

"She already did," Nina mumbled, sinking deeper into the water.

Andrea laughed again.

They stayed in the water for a long time, talking. It was one of those rare occasions when their children were near and taken care of, and neither had something urgent to do. They covered a lot of ground. Eventually, Andrea started in on codes of honor. She thought every woman should figure out her own. She was leading discussions at the shelter about it, and writing an article about it for the social worker's journal.

"I tell them, your mother taught it to you, even

though you may not realize it. It comes from your spirit, not your brain. It's your source of dignity."

"What's your code of honor, then?" Nina asked.

"Family first. Alleviate the suffering, don't add to it. Look 'em right in the eye, and let 'em have it if you have to." Andrea pantomimed a bomb exploding through the steam.

"You're a wise old crone, even if you are only thirty-two."

"That's my ambition. To be an old grandma with lots of grandkids playing on the stoop while I cook up a kettle of borscht in the kitchen. I can't wait till my seventies."

"No. Really?"

"Yeah. That'll be my prime."

Driving home through the dark snow-lined streets, Nina had to concentrate to keep from falling asleep. The spike-haired commando next to her drowsed into the headrest. Few other cars disturbed them. The heater blasted but she didn't need it because she was warm from the core. Her wet hair sent rivulets down her neck.

She had checked when she got in, and the Tecnicas hadn't gotten up and tramped away yet. Tomorrow morning she would deal with them.

Hitchcock met them at the door and she let him run around the yard for a few minutes. When he whimpered outside she opened the door, towel ready, and he came running in, white-muzzled, frosty-breathed. She wiped his feet and jaws and he trotted to his blanket-covered beanbag beside her tall pine bed as she climbed between the sheets. Bob had already gone to sleep downstairs.

She began thinking about Heidi's parting words—

something about Jim's arm, and the thinking imperceptibly melted into dreaming. This time Jim was skiing
down a steep run waving his Popeye forearms and she
was trying to ski alongside and have a look, but she
looked down to find flip flops on her feet instead of skis
and she began somersaulting backward, head over heels
down a cliff, a girl named Misty beside her. . . . The
phone rang, and she struggled for it.

"It's me." Collier's voice was hoarse.

She found that tremendously interesting. "I'm here."

"I know it's late but I couldn't sleep until I talked to
you. You better shut me down right now. You regret it,
don't you? You've decided it was a mistake, right?"

"Tomorrow afternoon about three?" Nina said. "I
couldn't stay long. We could have coffee."

"I'd like to come over there right now." These half-
growled words brought on a blast of sexual heat.

"God, Collier," Nina said, kicking off the covers.

"Shall I?"

"No. No, my son's here."

"Tell me you want me to, though."

"I—I want you to. But don't come."

"All right. Could you pick me up at my place? I'm
closer to town. Here's the address." He told her the
address, and she didn't bother to write it down, even in
her sleep-addled state.

She wasn't going to forget it.

8

SATURDAY. A nasty thought rocketed her up from her dream launch pad. Sunlight streamed onto her comforter from the window that looked onto the street, the one with the blinds she had forgotten to pull. Sweating and gasping, she rolled out, found her slippers, glanced at her watch—too early, far too early—and turned the spigots on the shower in the bathroom to which she had half-consciously staggered.

The Tecnicas! Flaming red and vulnerable in the back seat! Had she even locked the Bronco out there in the driveway? How could she have gone through the whole evening and never once checked out the bottoms of those things? What if they were striped, or diamond-shaped, or had some clear incised pattern that was repeated on Alex Strong's body? She still hadn't seen the autopsy pictures, and the report had been vague. Doc Clauson was keeping his options open.

Warm water ran into her mouth as she caught her breath again. What if there was a clear correspondence between boots and skin? What if these particular boots could actually be linked forensically to the injury?

Then it would be a murder. Then the case would be at an end, not at the beginning. Maybe Clinton's

lawyers could dream up a defense; Nina didn't think she
could.

She caught the upsetting thought that had awakened
her, that Jim might be guilty. She hadn't consciously
considered that before—the whole idea was bizarre! He
couldn't be! He couldn't have been lying in her office
that day. No one could lie that well.

The anxious feeling grew. She became convinced
that the boots wouldn't be in the Bronco. They glowed
in her mind like plutonium. She pulled on her robe
and ran outside in the snow, tugged at the back door—
locked, but she could see the Nordstrom's bag in back.
A moment later she had the key in the door and was
pulling a boot out of the bag, using a corner of the
robe to keep her fingerprints away, turning it over
and—

Gray metal with a heel plate and treads regularly
spaced, set horizontally, chevron-shaped. Imagine
someone designing the bottom of a boot with such
care and deliberation, setting specifications for a
mold . . . She pulled out the other one. A matching
set. You didn't have to be a lab tech to see those
grooves, she thought. They might show up on the
body after all—

No body! Alex had been cremated. So all they had
were photographs, and Doc Clauson opining on the
witness stand.

If it showed on the photos of the body, then. Collier would have those autopsy photos blown up to
Imax size, and . . .

No, there would be no need for blowups. If the
patterning matched, she would be over at the D.A.'s
office pleading for Jim's life.

On the other hand, there might not be a mark, she thought. I'm just considering all the possibilities that the police are considering. Fair enough. What's the matter, really? What's frightening me so much?

She thought again to herself, it's spooking me, everything in this case. Heidi, that terrible word, "transection," in the autopsy report, Philip Strong's indifference and talk about Alex's ghost, the actuality of the big red boots that would have crushed anything under them . . .

She went back inside the house where her son and her dog still slept and put the boots on the kitchen table. While she made coffee, she thought about it some more.

She was being irrational, panicking over shadows. If no corresponding pattern showed up on the photos, the seams on the bottom of the boots could also prove Jim's innocence. And what jury would ever believe a man would undress his brother and cold-bloodedly do that to him?

She needed the autopsy photos for Ginger, and she didn't have them, and she couldn't get them. All Ginger would have was the boots, if Collier didn't show up with a search warrant for her house and find them in the next half hour. Was he capable of that? Of course he was.

She got on the phone to a courier, who promised to come right over to pick up the package. The boots went into a box marked "Personal and Confidential" with Ginger's home address in Sacramento on it.

Ten minutes later she heard the knock on her door, and a girl from the licensed and bonded company she used took the box away, promising Ginger would have it by noon.

Then she called Sandy to ask her if she could reach Marianne Strong. Alex's wife could help her picture the family better, maybe give her some facts to defuse the police investigation.

Bob sat in the kitchen munching on his cereal, sleep-dazed. She went onto the back deck and looked out at the forest. The heavy-laden trees sent a fine drizzle down as the snow melted on the branches. The top layer of snow in the backyard had liquefied, but they wouldn't be seeing the ground again until March.

Her thoughts turned once more to the Donner Party, as they so often did when the snow began to fall. For months the eighty pioneers had starved in the woods near the North Shore during the late fall and winter of 1846, too inexperienced to find food. Many had died by the time the first party of rescuers arrived in the early spring of 1847, and what they found astonished them.

The starving pioneers were lying out in the snow enjoying a sunbath on a glorious sunny day, the surviving children playing at some game, ignoring the corpses of the dead strewn here and there.

In the worst extremity, the grotesque begins to feel normal, she thought.

She had been making love, relaxing in a hot tub, eating dinner, while all along Alex Strong lay broken in her mind, a corpse in the snow. The notion that the police were investigating whether Jim Strong had jumped on his injured brother with those heavy red boots meant for joy and fun was impossibly savage and ugly, but she was about to get dressed and throw a load of laundry in the washer anyway.

She and Bob would go out and play, take the sled and climb the neighborhood sledding hill. They would eat pizza at Brown Bear Pizza.

Part of her, the mother part, would be there.

Before three, Bob settled down with his homework in his room. Nina went into her bedroom and called the number Collier had given her the night before. "Yes?" he said on the first ring.

"I can't come."

"Oh. I'm disappointed. I've been sitting here thinking about you. I really want to see you."

"I've sort of come to my senses."

"Couldn't we wait on that? Before we start analyzing?"

"I've got a client you're looking at for a homicide. How can we see each other while that's going on?"

Collier said, "I just think we're two lonely people who got an unexpected gift. Let me see you. I can't talk about this on the phone."

"I don't know what I was thinking. Bob's doing his homework."

"You told me once we can look for happiness even in the middle of the work we do. You even made a pass at me."

"I remember. You were so exhausted that you fell asleep in the middle of a clinch. It was probably a wise move."

"I'm not asleep any more. Did you notice? At Homewood yesterday?" He had her smiling a little.

"What do you want, Collier?" she said. "I can't see you. I'm sorry."

"Where do you live?" he said. "Let me stop by later. Just for a few minutes. Just to talk."

"Just to talk? Nothing more? Get this cleared up?" Nina said.

"I promise."

"Okay, then. About eight?" She told him where she lived and hung up the phone.

She felt immediately that she had made a mistake inviting him to come over. She couldn't help it though. The phone call had made her hungry to see him, even if it was only for a minute.

It wasn't so odd that she would turn to him. Of all people, she and Collier could understand each other. She wished she could pour out her worries to him.

Longing and desperation, she thought. He would know how she felt because he worked under even worse conditions, with more criminal cases and more court work. Above all, he would understand what she had just been thinking, that when you're committed to dealing all day with the consequences of hatred, greed, and vengefulness, you begin to realize how grotesque it is to act normally, to brush your teeth and comb your hair.

You ought to be crying, tearing your hair out, gnashing your teeth like some biblical mourner, fighting every second . . .

Then the sun comes out and you're out there taking a sunbath in the snow, soaking up the rays and napping amid the corpses.

"You okay, Bob?" she called, opening the bedroom door.

"Are you gonna help me with my algebra?"

"In five minutes. Just one more call." She closed the door again and told herself that it couldn't wait another day. She should have called the night before.

"Ah, damn it, the day's shot anyway," she said to

that very reluctant part of her that was resisting picking up the phone.

Jim was home. "How are you?" she said.

He sounded faint, far away at first. "It's good to hear from you," he said. "I've been jumping out of my skin. The only thing that seems to help is cleaning up the mess the police made. What's going on? Did you find out anything about Heidi? Or about what the police are going to do?"

"That's why I'm calling," Nina said. "To check in."

"Thanks. You called me on a weekend. You knew I was worried. I appreciate that."

"I got your ski boots from your father's car."

"You talked to my father?"

"Yes. I shipped the boots off for some tests." She explained. Jim listened carefully.

"I'd laugh if I wasn't so angry about all this," he said. "You won't let them railroad me, will you, Nina? Find something in those photographs that isn't there?"

"Here's what I think will happen. We'll turn the boots over as soon as they ask me for them. The boots could exonerate you. The coroner has to have some reason for this suspicion he's developed. There may be some kind of mark on Alex that's inconsistent with the fall, or at least Clauson thinks it is. But if the boots don't match the mark, that will be the end of it."

She heard a groan on the other end of the line.

"I'm sorry," Nina said. "It's not easy to listen to this stuff."

"It's monstrous. You should see the way the people at the lodge look at me now. The way my own father looks at me."

Nina thought again of Philip Strong, of the look in his eyes. Had it been doubt?

"He doesn't give a shit about me. It's always been Alex. He favored my brother. Of course," he said, suddenly thoughtful, "Alex was a fantastic guy. I wish you could have known him."

"I talked to Heidi, Jim."

"You what? Where is she?"

"Listen. Here's what happened." She gave a full account of her talk with Philip Strong, of her meeting at Jake's with Heidi, trying to take it easy on him. But how could you minimize a demand for a divorce?

When she had said all she wanted to say without a single interruption, Jim still didn't say anything.

"Jim? Are you there?"

"Let me get this straight," Jim said. "I asked you to help me find my wife so I could talk to her. That's really all I wanted. It was the main thing."

"That was part—"

"It was the main thing. The main thing. This other stuff, this crap about Alex. It may not come to anything. But talking to Heidi, that's the main thing. So my father"—he spat out the word—"tells you where to meet Heidi, and do you call me and tell me? No. You wait until Heidi's long gone. You go talk to her yourself, without consulting me. You keep it from me."

"It was the only way I could see her, Jim. I had to promise—"

"So promise. Then call me. You act like my father hired you, or Heidi, not me."

"I gave my word."

"Your word! Who are you, Mother Teresa? Your word!" He sounded furious.

"I'm sorry. I really am. I really tried with Heidi, to get her to call you. She's adamant."

"You gave your word to me, didn't you?" Jim said. "You're my lawyer, aren't you? So why did you do this to me? Not tell me, not let me go?"

"Jim, I . . ."

She took the receiver away, looked at it in astonishment.

He had hung up on her.

"Mom! How much longer?" Bob called from downstairs.

"Be right there!" She took a few breaths, rubbed her temples, wondered if Jim was right. She didn't know. She'd had to act and she'd done what seemed like the right thing to do. She'd given her word.

She went downstairs, grateful that middle-school algebra always had an indisputable right answer.

At eight o'clock, she and Bob were climbing the freshly shoveled steps up to the front porch after their walk, Hitchcock already barking at the door, when Collier pulled up. He came down the driveway rapidly, and she had the insane impulse to run to him and bury her face in his chest, but what would Bob think of that? And what about her resolution?

He stopped awkwardly at the foot of the steps. "Hi," he said. "Sorry I'm late."

"Sure. Uh, Bob, I'd like you to meet a friend of mine. Mr. Hallowell."

Bob stuck out his hand like the well-mannered kid he sometimes was, and they shook hands, Collier saying, "Call me Collier," and taking a good look at him. They all stood on the porch for a moment. Then Nina said, "Would you like to come in for a minute?" Since he'd just driven across town to do exactly that, the invitation sounded moronic, but now they were acting for Bob's benefit.

"Sounds good." They all wiped their feet and clomped inside. Collier looked around at the new Danish rug and the fire in the free-standing fireplace, nodding. He seemed nervous. "Very—very well done," he said. He was wearing a thick gray sweater and corduroy pants, his hands in the pockets.

"Bob, don't you need to go take your shower?" Nina said. She had had the sudden thought, we can't talk here.

"As a matter of fact, Collier and I have a short errand to run," she went on. "Work stuff. You go ahead and get ready for bed, and I'll be back in half an hour."

They both looked surprised to hear this, but Bob went off obediently enough and Nina said, "Well?" and Collier held the door open as she went back out into the star-flung night.

They got into his car, and Collier started up the motor. Nina put her hand on his warm thigh and felt the tightness of it through the corduroy as he started up and guided the car down the road. "I just had to leave," she said. "Just for a minute." Her hand stayed on his leg.

"No need to explain." He drove through the neighborhood to Jicarilla, a dead-end street with a turn-around shielded from the nearest houses by the trees. The night was silent, crystalline beyond the windshield.

"Collier," Nina murmured, "Hold me?"

He already was holding her. He opened her mouth gently with his mouth. She held onto him.

There was only the breathing and the motor running and the heater sending out its warmth as he moved over on the seat and she moved onto his lap, still mouth to mouth, never losing that connection while they struggled with their clothing.

And finally they were one again, where they belonged, connected at mouth and groin and chest. They began moving in the ancient, primitive, deeply comforting rhythm. For that timeless time she was only a woman. With him it was simple and joyful and good, better than good, much, much better than good.

9

NINA SNEAKED INTO work on Monday morning, ashamed. She was ashamed because she was in love.

In love. Not the exasperated playful love she still felt for Paul, in which so great a part of her remained unaffected. Not the practical kind of love she had felt for her ex-husband, Jack. With Bob so young and her career just starting, her union with Jack had felt like two oxen yoking together to pull the heavy load. Not the nostalgic affection she still felt for Kurt, Bob's father, whom she had loved so long ago.

She had diagnosed herself. It was crazy fool love, exactly what she had feared and prepared against during the soul-searching months following her divorce.

For two years she had been mother and lawyer, challenges enough. She had bought a house and her own bed where she could sleep diagonally if she chose, rip off the covers if she got hot, snore if she had a cold. She made fruit smoothies for dinner in the summer and soup in the winter, with no stubbly male presence to give it a dubious look and send her back into the kitchen for meat. She put up pictures she liked and spent her spare money on Italian shoes, without having to answer to anyone.

She had made her own plans for the future, timidly

at first. And she had enjoyed doing the driving. Her power wasn't absolute—she lived with a temperamental young prince—but making her own decisions was habit forming. Once she had made the decision not to fall in love anymore, she had experienced a huge relief.

Besides, who would want her, want all of her, a struggling lawyer in her mid-thirties whose idea of a really hot time was reading in bed, glasses on, at two A.M.?

But as the months went by, in spite of herself she had found herself clumsily reaching out. One hand reached out, the other slapped it down.

Why couldn't she stay in her sere and serene solitary state? She could support herself, Bob was fine, she'd had her child, and she was, as she knew quite well, hard to live with. Not worth it, she reminded herself firmly. Burned there, done that.

And yet, from deep in the brain stem, from the pea-sized pituitary, a stream of hormones furtively flooded her castle, bringing that longing to fall deliriously from the ramparts. She had slept with Paul, that epitome of hyper-masculinity, and had felt herself on the brink of falling in love with him. With all the strength she had left, she had pushed him into leaving her.

And now Collier had come back to Tahoe, slipping quietly into town, no fanfare, the one who could really understand her, the one with eyes she could hardly wait to lose herself in.

Tenderly my love
Returns my caresses . . .

A fallen woman she was, foolish, absurd, an object of pity, no sleep, lust burning through her underwear.

She kicked herself for her weakness and wondered how soon she could see him again.

Taking off the wool beret, she fluffed her hair and opened the door to the office, decorous, briefcase reassuringly heavy in her hand. Clients, crimes, injuries, divorces, all manner of unpleasantries waited therein. She was looking forward to flipping her mind back into its accustomed dry and analytical mode.

Warmth. Bright colors. Music. Brazilian, sensuous. Sandy, in complete dereliction of duty, sat next to the silver-haired Native American from the parking lot. She was holding hands with this fellow, whispering something in his ear. He was smiling. As Nina came in, the hands sprung guiltily apart. Moving faster than Nina had ever seen, Sandy glided to her desk.

Nobody spoke for a minute. Finally, in a tight schoolmarmish voice, Nina heard herself saying, "Good morning," meaning, It's Monday morning; there's work to do, what's *he* doing here?

He put on his cowboy hat, stood up. He wore jeans with a thick leather belt and a silver buckle. His brown face with its big nose was seamed by the sun. He looked down, nodded at the floor several times, and looked back up at Sandy.

"I was just leaving," he said. "So long." He took his grizzled leather jacket from the rack.

"So long," Sandy said, barely visible behind a vase full of carnations and snapdragons on her desk.

The door closed.

"I really don't think it's the time or place to be necking, Sandy," Nina said. She knew it was herself she was talking to, but she couldn't seem to control her tongue.

The mood drained away. The office became just an

office, plants, Sandy's desk, comfortable chairs for uncomfortable people, an Indian basket filled with magazines on the coffee table in front of the chairs.

Sandy didn't answer. She held out the usual sheaf of
messages, but only part of the way, forcing Nina to
reach past the flowers for them.

Sandy looked very smug and a faint smell of bay rum
hung in the air. These things annoyed Nina further.
Here she was, trying to lecture herself back to sobriety,
and Sandy was undermining her efforts behind her
back. At the very least, Sandy should try to look
ashamed of herself after this garish display of affection.
Affection in a law office! An oxymoron!

"Nice flowers," Nina went on, still in the grip of her
inner schoolmarm. "But not appropriate. I mean, this is
a business. I can hardly see you back there." She began
looking through the messages, conspicuously dropping
the entire sordid matter, but noticing from the corner of
her eye that Sandy's face was turning that florid color
again.

"Not as nice as the ones on your desk," Sandy said.
Her tone was flat-out malicious.

Their eyes met. Nina looked away first.

"If you want to talk about appropriate . . ." Sandy
said.

Orchids. Extravagantly beautiful. The card said,
"Run away with me for the weekend." Underneath
that, a poem in Collier's printing:

> Do you believe that we have lived before
> Passed together through some ancient door
> Maybe our spirits can intertwine

Til there's no more of yours and no more of
mine

Nina ran her fingers along the underside of one of the white and pink orchids, which bent along with the movement, preening at her attentions.

The phone buzzed. "It's Paul," Sandy said. "And you're supposed to be in Zephyr Cove at ten. I got hold of her over the weekend like you said. Don't forget. Marianne Strong."

"Hey," Paul said. "How's it going, Boss?"

"Hey, Paul. How are you? How's Washington?"

"Corrupt and scandal-ridden. Oh, you mean Washington? It's fine. It's drizzling today. I can see the Washington Monument from my office. It's a big one. Freud must have laughed his head off."

"Uh huh."

"Keeping safe? The kid okay?"

"All's well, here. Thanks for thinking about us."

"Good, good," said Paul. "Heard you're having a huge snow month."

"That's right. We're up to our eyeballs."

"What else are you up to?"

"Oh, not much. The usual."

"Interesting," said Paul, and Nina thought, what, has he got e.s.p. now? She was damned if she was going to say anything about Collier. Paul would have too many opinions.

"Well, great to hear from you," she said.

Paul ignored this cue.

"You were wondering how I am," he said. "After I finished up the big security project, I started guarding this old Senator that everybody likes. We play tennis and

I let him win, and then we drink scotch and get even more relaxed."

He waited for her to say something. When she didn't, he said, "I miss the trouble you always get me into."

"Uh huh."

"You wouldn't be in any trouble?"

"Certainly not," Nina said, momentarily startled out of her daze.

"Now I know you're not listening," Paul said. "There's always something. In fact I heard you took a homicide case. Who's your investigator?"

"Tony Ramirez. Jeez, Paul. I really have to do something about Sandy. For some reason, with you she gets a major case of loose lips."

"I'm the only one she would tell. Because she knows I'll be there to take care of it if you need me."   .

Again he waited. She couldn't take her eyes off the flowers. So many gradations of color. So subtle.

"In spite of the fact that I'm in Washington, I've been thinking," Paul was saying. "You know—"

She interrupted briskly. "All's well in the mountains. I'm glad to hear things are going well for you, too."

"Ah, Nina." It sounded like a sigh.

"What?"

"Nothing. Watch out for yourself. I'll check in again."

"Super. Great to hear from you." She hung up, forgetting about the conversation immediately. Her finger went back to caressing the orchid petal.

Sandy appeared in the doorway. She appeared to be preparing to deliver a lecture.

"Sorry, Sandy. I overreacted," Nina said. "Some personal issues I was having this morning."

"This is America. I thought. Right of free association. I thought. Or maybe that doesn't apply to us—"

"Oh, for crying out loud. I said I was sorry. I was acting like a jerk. I'm sorry. Really."

"You know which Constitutional Amendment that is?"

"The First. Now, please, give me a break."

"If you tell me who sent the flowers."

"Collier."

"Ah hah!"

"Okay," Nina said "Since you've raised the topic. Let's discuss ah hahs. That man, for example, the one— sitting with you when I came in. Joseph."

Sandy disregarded this. "You ever find out where Hallowell spent the last year?" she said.

"No, we haven't talked about it."

"What happens now?"

"I have no idea," Nina said with feeling. "What about you? What's happening there?"

Sandy's lips worked a while. "It's bad," she said finally.

"How bad?"

"Bad enough that he's moving in next week."

Nina said, shocked, "I thought I was in trouble. When's the last time you lived with a man?"

"1986," said Sandy, "which is when he left me."

Another six inches of fresh powdery snow coated the streets. Hot sun burned through the trees, flattening the lake into glass. Nina floated through wonderland in four-wheel drive, past the casinos, around the lake to the Nevada side. She was going to see Marianne Strong.

The community of Zephyr Cove consisted of a pinestudded sandy beach, a barnlike restaurant, cabins and snowmobiles for rent across the highway in the woods, and quite a few discreet expensive homes tucked here and there.

Number 273 Granite Springs Drive was built in the contemporary mountain style, of cedar and glass, high up the hill to catch rays and lake views.

Wiping her boots on the mat, she rang the bell. The intercom next to it came to life. "Yes?"

"It's Nina Reilly."

"Come in and wait, okay? I'll be down in a couple of minutes." The woman's voice was husky. Nina pushed open the heavy door at the buzzer and found herself in a polished entryway with tiled floors and a chandelier. As she entered the high-ceilinged living room, Nina saw that Marianne and Alex had both taste and money, or at least a taste for money. The walls had that sponged look, with recessed lights and casement windows looking out upon a terrace. Several important-looking bronze sculptures controlled the corners and a Calderlike red and blue mobile hung from the ceiling. All was beige, cool, and minimalist.

She sat down at the glass-topped dining table and looked around, scanning for signs of despair, tragedy, loss, finding nothing. No black-wreathed silver picture frame with Alex's photo, nothing melancholy at all. No reading material except for a couple of *Paris Match* magazines tossed on the coffee table. A trophy case full of gleaming tokens of Alex and Marianne's success.

Marianne was taking her time. Not a peep came from upstairs, and Nina couldn't sit still and behave any longer. Her eye caught a writing desk in the corner with a few papers and she crossed the kilim rug to it. A hasty glance at the staircase showed no shadow, so she bent to the papers and immediately saw a document stapled to a blue backing on the bottom. In California, that usually meant a will. Another quick look at the empty stairs. It was in her hand. She went straight to the third page, where the action usually starts, and scanned it swiftly, then reinserted it at the bottom of the pile of bills.

When the legs appeared at the top of the stairs, Nina was looking at the mobile.

Marianne Strong made her entrance count. She came down a few steps very slowly, smiling, her large lustrous eyes raking the room. Then she seemed to bound the rest of the way.

Nina already knew her. She was the girl who had rushed out of Philip Strong's office, practically knocking her over. She wore black tights and a long black sweater that showed off a compact gymnast's body. She was smaller than Nina had expected, in her early twenties, with coffee-colored skin and fashionably cut shoulder-length wavy black hair.

"Isn't Jim coming?" she asked in that scratchy deep voice, coming over to Nina. "Why did you come without him?"

The perfume, the voice with its faint accent, the whole effect was European. Nina remembered Jim telling her that Marianne was a Brazilian who had been brought up from early childhood in France.

"No, that wasn't the idea," Nina said. "Sorry if there was a misunderstanding."

"He's avoiding me. What did I do? You know, he didn't say one word to me at the funeral. Has he talked to you about me? The bastard! I'm really getting mad at him now. Tell him I said that, all right?" She sat down and lit a Sherman's cigarette from the box on the side table, letting herself take a long calming drag. "Well, sit down. I can't believe it. I spent two hours getting fixed up for this meeting. Bastard!"

Nina sat down in a chrome and leather chair that she hoped was only a knockoff of Breuer's famous Wassily number.

Marianne laughed. "I'm not really mad. Listen. Don't tell him what I said. You want something to drink? A soda?"

"No, thanks."

Marianne slumped down on the couch, taking quick puffs from her cigarette, thinking about something else. "I don't know what my secretary told you—" Nina added.

"I know all about it. Everybody on Ski Patrol is talking about it. God, what a circus. Alex would be so disgusted. He died doing what he loved to do. It's very simple." She went on about the newspapers and the complications, starting up another cigarette when the first was half smoked.

"I'm sorry about your husband," Nina said when Marianne wound down.

"Oh, yes, we all are. My poor Alex. I'm desolate."

She did not look desolate. But of course, Nina reminded herself, grief takes many forms. "How is Jim?" Marianne went on.

"He's getting along. I believe my secretary told you I had a few questions about Alex."

"Yes, she did. I know all about you. Jim has asked you to help the family sort out some details. I understand that the coroner has made an awful mistake," Marianne said almost gaily. "So please, fire away." She seemed to be enjoying the attention. Her moods shifted faster than Nina could keep up with them.

"The coroner has filed a report which concludes that Alex was murdered," Nina said. "Essentially."

"What an asshole. Honestly. For chrissake, Alex never held back on the snow. He'd broken half the bones in his body already. He always went for it. I hate to say it," her voice lowered to a whisper, "but it was going to happen someday, you know?"

"There's a chance that Jim will be arrested."

"Oh, it's all so stupid. Jim's got his problems, but kill Alex? Never," Marianne said. "Alex was his double, his shadow. No way."

"What problems are we talking about, Marianne?" Nina said, leaning forward in her chair.

"What did I say? Problems? Oh, no, I'm not going to get myself in more trouble with Jim. I was only trying to help, but he's holding it against me. It's infuriating! Would you talk to him? Explain that I deserve a little sympathy? My husband is dead and he won't even come over and comfort me!"

"Maybe if you explained a little more to me, Marianne—about Jim, and why he's angry—maybe I could talk to him."

"He hasn't talked about me? Not at all?"

"Yes, he has."

"What did he say?" the girl asked eagerly.

"Well, he told me about your being from France—"

"Chamonix. My father was a ski instructor there. My mother is from Rio. She couldn't stand the winters. She couldn't even stand up on skis. She left us when I was six. What else did he say?"

"He said you are a champion snowboarder."

This brought a self-satisfied smile. Gesturing at the trophy case, Marianne said, "Actually, I met Jim before

Alex. We met four years ago at the United States Extreme Championships at Crested Butte. I took fourth in the Women's. But downhill isn't my event. Really. It's for maniacs, let's be honest. Let the crazy local girls break their legs and tear their tendons. I don't do that anymore. I do freestyle. You know, tricks. It's safer in a lot of ways. You don't have to go so fast that you'll certainly break something if you go out of control. One, two, three tricks and you're done. It's over. I'll be performing at Paradise two weeks from next Friday at the Festival of Lights. Come and see me."

"Sounds good. You were saying?"

"Oh, yes, Jim invited me to California for a weekend and I stayed and became the snowboarding instructor at Paradise." She tossed her head and said, "We were together for six months, then we had a big fight and he started seeing Heidi. Alex and I began going out, and we married. That was two years ago."

She was looking at Nina's chest in a frank, not really offensive manner. She was one of those women who compares herself physically to every other woman she meets.

"So you're a lawyer," she said. "Does that mean Jim has to tell you all his secrets? You must get very close to your clients."

"Not that close," Nina said. Marianne laughed again.

"I have a dirty mind," she said.

"So Jim's mad at you?"

"Obviously. And I was only trying to help."

"Why?"

"Because Heidi was screwing around, and I told him. He's mad at the messenger, that's all." She put out the latest cigarette and got up. Walking over to the mobile, she gave it a push and it began to spin. "Pretty, isn't it?" Marianne said. "It cost enough. So. What do you think? Should I have kept my mouth closed?"

"I guess I'd need a few more details to be able to answer that."

"I heard her a couple of weeks ago on the phone in the equipment room, talking to her lover. She was afraid Jim might find out. I don't know who her lover was. She knew a lot of men."

Nina tried to look skeptical.

"She was really involved with this guy," Marianne said, her tone insistent. "It was clear from the way she talked to him."

"How well do you know her? Heidi?"

"Oh. I know her very well. But we don't get along. She thinks snowboarders are stupid. That's because she's too big to be good at it. She's a big cow with muscles like a man's. Just a minute." She left and came back with a couple of bottles of Evian water. Nina unscrewed the cap and drank the pure water thirstily.

"Please don't tell Jim I called Heidi a cow. It's just between us," Marianne said. "He still loves her, but he's bound to get over that soon enough now that she's left him. Oh, did you think that was a secret? Everybody knows she accused him of killing Alex and took off. She's probably with the other man right now." Her eyes glittered.

"So you told Jim about this conversation Heidi had?"

"Of course. Out of respect for him. Out of friendship. So he wouldn't go around with the horns on. You should have seen his face." She gave the mobile another spin. "Americans don't take this sort of thing very well.

He should thank me. He's treating me like shit instead. Would you tell him that?"

"Oh, yes, I'll definitely take it up with him," Nina said. "Did you tell the police that you had told Jim about his wife's affair?"

"I didn't volunteer, if that's what you mean. An officer came and asked me questions. I had to answer, naturally."

"Naturally," Nina said. "So tell me. Where were you the day Alex died? Just for my records."

"I didn't kill my husband. How ridiculous! It was an accident!"

"Then you won't mind answering my question."

"I was snowboarding, but a long way away from them. I knew Alex would go off-piste. Off the groomed trail, you know. I play it safe. I'm only a daredevil when somebody pays me. So, the accident happened when I was on the other side of the mountain. It was a beautiful day, how it gets after a fine thick snowfall in the night."

"You were with friends?"

"I'm too good for my friends," Marianne said. "Remember, I am a pro."

"Who might have seen you out there?"

"I saw Jim on the Ogre. That was some time before the accident. I carried my beeper and when I got buzzed I went down to the lodge and checked in. Alex was already on his way to the hospital with Philip and Jim. Heidi was still on the mountain somewhere. My— The night host took me there. It was such a hideous shock."

Nina was watching her closely, looking for signs of genuine sorrow on that hard handsome face. She saw none.

"Les jours s'en vont, je demeure," Marianne said,

shrugging. "We had a lot of fun together." That seemed to be her final word on the subject of her husband's death. She was still standing a few feet from Nina, a black clad gamine made of steel.

"I'm getting too old to keep up with these sixteen-year-olds. I am going to retire, I think." Marianne went on firmly. "In fact, I'm quite sure of it. Maybe I'll go home to France and leave your big messy country. I'd like to get Jim's advice about it."

"I suppose there was some insurance. And Alex's share in the resort. You'll be able to afford it," Nina said.

"My money is my private business," Marianne said. "Look, I have places to go."

"Sure," Nina said. "Absolutely. But there's just one more thing I'd like to ask."

"Yes?"

"Was Heidi's lover your husband? Was it Alex?"

Marianne's face went red. "Stupid, stupid question," she said. "You think I would stand for that? Talk about him this way? Of course not! Alex was very much in love with me! With Heidi? I don't think so!"

"You have no idea who it is?"

"If I did, I would have told Jim!"

"Just asking," Nina said. She shouldered her bag. "I'll show myself out."

"Wait!" Marianne grabbed Nina's arm and squeezed it. "Look. I've helped him by talking to you. I'm on his side. He owes me— you're putting me off—I need to talk to him—"

For just a second, experiencing the strength of the glowing young athlete in front of her, she was ready to believe many things about Marianne.

"Take your hand off me," Nina said grimly.

"You need to lift weights," Marianne said. "Your

muscle tone is really bad." She let go. Nina went outside and Marianne slammed the door behind her.

As she came out onto the steps, breathing hard, angry, Nina saw a dirty pair of ski boots off to the left by a supply closet, still dripping wet. She didn't give a shit what Marianne thought, if she was watching. She went over and picked up a boot.

They weren't Tecnicas. They also weren't Marianne's. They were men's boots, an unfamiliar brand called Dalbello, much bigger than Marianne would wear. She looked at the metal sole. A different pattern, but a pattern.

Whose boots were they?

10

No one wanted to be snatched from Tahoe's sunshine and squashed into the poorly lit squad room on that Monday afternoon. Not Doc Clauson, the coroner for the County of El Dorado, Tahoe Division. Not Officer Floyd Drummond, who had taken Heidi Strong's statement the week before. Not the pudgy D.A.'s investigator, Sean Voorhies, and not the two deputy D.A.'s.

Barbara Banning, the Tahoe D.A.'s office's newest deputy, was inspecting her nails, and the entire roomful of men was watching her do it.

Collier watched her watching them watch her.

Barbara would go far. She had a quick mind, middle-class sex appeal, and an inexorableness that reduced most of her defendants to road kill. Today, Henry McFarland, their boss, had assigned Barbara to "help" decide what to do about the Alex Strong investigation. McFarland didn't quite trust Collier.

Fair enough.

Collier looked down at his notes one more time. He didn't want to be there either—because he didn't need a loser case in his first month back.

"Okay," he said. "Let's get started. We're here to look at the Strong situation. It's been over two weeks since the guy skied off the cliff. We have to arrest the brother for something or back down on the amended autopsy report, one or the other. Sean, you've been on it a week. Summarize the results of the search of Jim Strong's house and car last week."

"That's easy," Sean said. A portly mountain boy with a deceptively easy manner, Sean loved a conviction. He didn't look too sure of himself today. "We found nada," he said. "Except we grabbed all the ski gear in the house. Not including the boots, as you know from my report there."

"So where the fuck are the boots?" Barbara said. Several of the men in the room looked jolted at hearing such hard language passing through such soft lips.

"Located. I found them over the weekend," Sean answered. "At least, I found out where they were. The father had 'em in his car at his house in Marla Bay. That's why the search of Jim's place didn't turn them up. But the father gave them up."

"Gave them up?" Collier asked.

"To Jim's lawyer, Nina Reilly."

Heads shook at this news. Collier shook his head too, unhappy that he hadn't thought of it. Nina could be very crafty. She had a knack for getting to things first.

"The FedEx gal on Reilly's route?" Sean went on. "She's a mighty sweet young thing. Didn't mind letting me sneak a peek at the Send To addresses for the week. There it was. A big package from the law office for a Doctor Hirabayashi in Sac."

"Shit," said Doc Clauson. "Ginger's looking at them. That's the boots all right."

"Reilly's interfering with a police investigation," Barbara Banning said. "Maybe we should teach her a lesson. What do you think, Collier?"

"I think we'd end up wallowing in technicalities when we ought to be getting the evidence back," Collier said. Sean let out a strange sound that might have been a snigger.

"My information about her is that she has a fascinating social life," he said, looking at Collier.

"I don't give a shit about her social life. I want to know if your office is going to back up my report," Doc Clauson said, fingering a packet of matches. He wasn't smoking anymore, but unfortunately he wasn't smoking any less. He had quit a dozen times since Collier had known him. Collier saw that the usual Camels had found their way back into his shirt pocket.

Clauson had stuck through thirty years of autopsies, forensics investigations, and courtrooms. He was good with bodies, but he had recently been getting his ass chewed by the local defense lawyers. He was getting sloppy, or the defense lawyers were getting better, Collier didn't know which, but he was fond of the old guy and he still respected him.

"Now look here," Clauson went on. "If my report gets tossed, there's going to be a criminal walking around free. Patterns on the kid's skin. Stomped to death. I'm sure of it. Everybody see these pictures?"

"Nasty. The ones of the liver are the worst," said Sean.

"But Doc," Collier said. "You thought at first—"

"Missed it. I did. I admit it. So many contusions, broken bones, hemorrhaging, obvious accidental circumstances. Anybody could have missed it the first time around. I asked for all police reports so I could be aware of the surrounding circumstances. I don't just look at the body. If I'd had the goddamn witness statement—"

"Don't look at me," said Officer Drummond. "I

turned it in. I went through channels like I was supposed to. The world is full of flakes. Heidi Strong was
flaky too. But I took the statement—"

"How is it that it took three days for the statement to
get to the coroner, Officer?" Barbara asked in a sharp
voice.

"Well, ma'am, the lieutenant was out sick. There's a
flu going around. It's the change of seasons. The secretary types it up, she passes it back, the girl signs it, I put
it in the lieutenant's in-box. The sergeant's supposed to
check it, but he calls in next morning and he's sick too.
The rest of us are dealing with that bomb threat at Harrah's last week—"

"And meantime, the family's hassling us at the
morgue," said Clauson. "They want the body. It's now
four days since the kid died. I give it up and he's ashes
about eight hours later."

"So now no second opinion is possible with regard
to the markings you saw on the body," Collier said.

"Well, I saw 'em. And we have the pictures."

"The pictures suck," Barbara said. "I think Mr. Hallowell and I are in agreement on that. There are marks,
sure, but the man went over a fifteen-foot drop and
landed on rocks. A jury would look at the pictures and
feel that there was doubt."

"I'll testify," Clauson said. He straightened up and
firmed his jaw.

"Big deal," Barbara said, tapping an eraser impatiently on a yellow pad. She flipped it, picked it up,
flipped it again. "You're compromised."

"Collier? You tell that woman I know what I'm talking about," Clauson said, clamping his lips together into
a thin line.

"Let's all calm down," Collier said. "Let's look at

what else we do have. Clothes of the victim that show the bigger picture. We've got Strong's wife telling us about a threat, though the statement doesn't really specify a motive —"

"Sorry to rain on your parade," Sean interjected, "but we ain't got Strong's wife anymore. I went to the motel where she was staying on North Shore yesterday and the manager said she blew."

The room erupted.

Collier put up a hand to quiet the noise. "I thought you said she was cooperative and reliable, Sean," Collier said.

"She was. We were getting to be friendly. Guess she had second thoughts. At least we got her statement."

"Her statement's not admissible, you turkey," Barbara said. "And you didn't even get it to the coroner in time. Now you've lost her. Even if she can't testify directly, she can lead us to crucial admissible evidence. Jesus!"

"She'll be back," Sean said. "She lives here."

"What's the father say? Philip Strong?" asked Collier.

"He says we better remember he's one of the big employers up here, or words to that effect," Sean said.

"How about the widder?" Clauson asked.

"The widow," Collier said, for the benefit of those who might need an interpretation. "That would be Marianne Strong."

Sean said, "Sexy girl. Frenchie. You know."

"No, why don't you explain that, Sean," said Barbara, shifting her attention from the eraser in front of her back to the investigator. "I'd be interested to hear your views on the sexiness of French people. Since we seem not to have any actual facts to discuss."

Sean took up his notes, detouring quickly away from another lashing. "She's a competitive athlete, a snowboarder. Took a first and third in state competitions last year. Very full of herself. Hard to imagine her married, in fact, because she's not the type that has room in her boudoir mirror for more than one face," Sean said, pronouncing the French word with careful, satirical correctness. "In my opinion."

"Go on," Collier said. He liked Sean, knew he was smart and good at his job, and hated to see Barbara humiliate the boy, but he, too, felt frustrated by the lack of sound physical evidence.

"Said she thought his wife, Heidi, was having an affair. Said she hinted about it to him."

"Ha! There's your motive! Jim Strong killed his brother 'cause young Alex was playing around with his wife," Officer Drummond said. "Case closed."

"She seems positive it wasn't Alex that Heidi was sleeping with," Sean went stolidly on, "although it's a possibility, considering her attitude toward her husband, which seemed pretty cool, if you ask me."

"She could be lying."

"In fact, I get the idea she's carrying a torch for Jim."

"Then she could be lying to protect him," Collier said.

"She could have done it herself," Sean said. "She was on the mountain, alone." Groans all around.

"That's all we need," Drummond said. "Another suspect. Listen, you think Jim Strong wouldn't have seen or heard somebody down there with his brother? He might have been out of sight, but he would have heard something. He'd have said something to clear himself."

"What about tracks?" Collier asked.

"Are you kidding? After the emergency people got done up there? Forget about it."

"You don't have to prove a motive to get a murder conviction," Barbara said abruptly. "If we get more on an affair between Jim Strong's wife and the victim, dynamite. But what do we have in the way of direct evidence?"

"All right. One more time," said the Doc. "Contusions and lacerations all over his back, back of the head, legs. Get it? He landed on his *back*, one leg under him, the one that broke. Now. Damage to the *front* of the turtleneck just over the skin patterning and major contusion, which is just over broken ribs and transected liver. In front, get it? He was stomped in front."

Barbara said, "You said you don't *think* the fall would have caused such an injury. How sure are you, exactly?"

"I looked at the cliff. I looked at the snow. I don't think he hit anything else on his way down. He fell on a flat area. I don't think he rolled. He would have had contusions all over, and he only had 'em on the back. The fronts of the parka and bibs weren't damaged," Clauson said. "I've been around a long time. And it doesn't sit right."

"The fact remains that your original opinion was quite different." Barbara gave him a look that said things about the twenty-five-year age difference between them. She obviously didn't trust Clauson, and Clauson didn't like her either.

She went on, "As to the rest of it, the defense will raise holy hell at you for releasing the body for cremation. There's no opportunity for an independent examination, not to mention you missing the markings the first time around."

"Just get me the boots," Clauson said, turning to Collier. "We'll bury him with his boots."

"I'll get them," Collier said. "Floyd, you're assigned to this matter for a couple of days. Go back up in the snow with a photographer and search the area again. Commandeer whatever equipment you need from Paradise. I'll call Philip Strong about it. Sean, you know what you have to do. Find Heidi Strong. And go talk to Kelly Strong in Incline Village. Maybe she can help with the motive question. See if she knows whether there was an affair between the victim and Heidi Strong. And ask her this: Was Jim Strong capable of doing this kind of violence to his brother?"

"Okay, let's go." They all filed out, except for Doc Clauson and Collier.

Clauson was drooping. Beads of sweat stood out on his forehead. Collier thought, he doesn't look good.

"Hey," Clauson said. "Just have to say one more thing. Always thought you were good, Collier. Solid. Smart. I ever let you down?"

"You've always done your best, Doc," Collier said.

"Well, listen to me now. This is a vicious crime. Have to be depraved to do it when the vic's lying there moaning for help. Can't let him get away with it. Trust me. This is a homicide. Can't understand how I missed it the first time around. Sorry about that."

"I'll get you the boots," Collier said again. "You blow up those photos, show me they match the soles of the boots. And I'll put him away for you."

"That a boy. That's right. See you."

"Doc?"

"Yeah?"

"Take care of yourself."

"It's just a cold or something."

Back in the office, Barbara was waiting, posed to maximum advantage on the edge of Collier's desk. She was allowing herself to look slightly disturbed. "Could I have just a minute?" she said.

"Sure." She really was a good-looking girl, with her smooth dark pageboy and the remote Catherine Deneuve face. That kind of girl was too cold for him, though.

"I thought you might like to hear my considered opinion regarding whether we should file some sort of charge against Jim Strong."

"Yeah, of course, Barb. What is it?" He sat down at his desk, wishing she had given him more time to digest the meeting.

"Dump this piece of shit."

He smiled. "I know. Keystone Kops," he said. "It's too weak to go forward at this point, I agree. But I've worked with Clauson a long time. I want to keep it open until we see what happens with the boots."

Barbara didn't like hearing this. She came around the desk, began massaging his back. "God, you're stiff," she said. "Collier. I'm speaking as a friend. The word around the office is that you've lost the edge since you got back. You're acting like a wuss. Clauson fucked up. Dump it."

Collier gently reached back and patted her hand. "What is it?"

"I used to look up to you. Last year, before you left. I came up to Tahoe after a few years of sitting in a private firm's law library. I didn't know a thing, you taught me, you watched over me. I thought you were— I thought you were—interested—"

"I'm not."

"No. You're not. Anymore."

"I'm sorry."

"I don't want you to be sorry!"

"Is it Nina?" Collier asked. It was Nina, and he was tired of dancing around it.

Barbara froze. Slowly, she removed her hands from his shoulders. "You know, if you go forward on the Strong case, you're going to have a conflict of interest with her representing the defendant. Have you thought about that?"

"I'll deal with that if and when I have to."

"If you don't go ahead, it'll look like you caved in to her."

"Barb, it's late."

"I can't believe you'd prefer her to me. Well. Your loss."

"I'm sorry. I really am."

"They're all dirtbags, you know it. Defending the guilty. How could you?"

"Good night, Barb." He closed the door. The outer office had emptied fast. Six o'clock.

On the way home, Collier stopped at a florist shop near the Swiss Chalet Restaurant, not far from Nina's office, and bought ten plants to set around his place. That ought to wow Nina. He expected them to stay alive for at least a week. When they went he would buy some more. She loved plants.

Turning off the highway at the Smart 'n Final, he came to Glenwood Way and the small green-trimmed apartment house he'd decided to call home.

The apartment looked much better when he had set the plants around. He undressed, tossing his dirty clothes into the pile in the closet, and let the water wash all the crap off him from the day. With his eyes closed against the spray, he sang an old tune from a musical, *The Desert Song*. My desert is waiting, dear, come there with me . . .

He plucked a thick clean towel from the rack and rubbed his chest. He was happy. He hadn't been this happy in years. He had his job back, and the woman he had decided he wanted was coming to see him.

Dressed again, he turned his attention to the kitchenette. The house cleaner had washed the dishes and wiped the counters. Alles in Ordnung. He opened the fridge, got out the frozen shrimp, and set it under running water to defrost.

Music! There ought to be music.

In his closet he found an old boom box. The public radio station had a classical music concert going, Bruckner's Third. It sounded like a movie from the forties and fit his mood. He made shrimp cocktails with a lot of horseradish, listening to the music and sipping from time to time on the shot glass of Jack Daniel's he'd poured. He kept looking out the window for her, but she would be late. She was always rushing into court at the last minute.

He imagined her in court in her sober suit and foolish high heels, the long hair always a little wild, the fresh cheeks and full lips. To think he had let her go last year!

Now. What else? He basted the steaks with teriyaki and stuck them under the broiler. Salad. She'd like a salad. His luck held. He had remembered to buy a presorted bag of fresh spinach. He made a piece of toast, buttered and spiced it, chopped it into croutons, dumped it with spinach in a wooden bowl and poured dressing on the concoction, tossing it with a couple of forks. Done.

She was late. He wondered if she would like the

place, see how he had changed. He walked around, making an inspection. Alles in— The sheets! The sheets hadn't been changed since he'd moved in.

He ran to the closet and rummaged around, coming up with the spares. He began making the bed.

"Hi," Nina said in the doorway. "The door was open. I took the steaks out of the oven so they wouldn't burn."

"Hi," Collier said, the sheet hanging conspicuously from his hand.

Glancing at it, then at the half-made bed, Nina came toward him. "I like your apartment," she said. "So much more cheerful than the one you used to have. Here. Why don't you let me help you with that chore?" Smelling like roses, completely at ease, she tucked in a couple of corners, nice and neat.

"Let's have a drink," Collier said. In the kitchen he made her a Jack Daniel's on the rocks while she exclaimed over the fern he had stuck on the counter.

"What kind of day did you have?" she said.

"It's great, now."

"I feel the same way." She puttered around setting the table and he watched her. She looked luscious, but it wasn't just that, she looked right. She looked right in his kitchen, just like she felt right in his arms. She walked around, talking and laughing, hot and cozy as a fire, and made the place home.

She was right. He knew it.

He watched her, thinking about all the grief and all the long days and lonely nights of his life in the past few years. She was hope to him, a chance for a second life. He tried to act casual so she wouldn't be embarrassed at the intensity of his feelings.

"Shrimp cocktails!" she said, when he took them

out of the fridge. "I love them!" They sat at the table—he'd forgotten a candle but so what—and ate. Then he gave her the Delta Airlines ticket to Honolulu and watched her eyes light up.

"So that's what you meant with your note in the orchid," she said.

"It's only a weekend. Three days, if you can get Friday off."

"I will get Friday off."

"Great."

Then Nina said, "I brought you a present too. Nothing much." It was a CD of samba music.

They turned off the lights and danced, not really dancing, more swaying to the music, holding each other tight.

When there didn't seem to be much point in standing up any more, they went to bed.

Her skin was unbelievably smooth, the curve of her hip maddening. He smoothed her hair, muttered things, kissed her everywhere. They made love, and talked until eleven about Bob and her dog and the early snow, and then she had to go.

He felt like he was fourteen years old, with that same sense of wonder and discovery. He watched her go from the kitchen window, the moon sending glints of snow all around her, smirking like a fool, thinking, she's the right one, how could I get so lucky twice in one life. The music was still playing in the living room, and he went in and looked at the English translations on the liner notes.

> *Joy is green like a forest*
> *It burns and turns to ash, then grows again*

He knew that. He'd learned it all the hard way.

It burns and grows again. That was love, too. He was going to make every second of the rest of his life count.

He hadn't asked her about Strong's boots. Unwritten rules had already grown up between them, and the first one was: don't talk about work except at work.

He would send Drummond down to Sac for them in the morning.

On Tuesday at noon, another brilliant day, Nina was just climbing into the Bronco in the courthouse parking lot when who should appear but Doctor Ginger Hirabayashi, forensic pathologist, looking like a reindeer.

At least, her red nose did. The rest of her was black: black watchcap, black leather jacket, baggy black slacks, and a big black muffler. Above the nose she wore a big pair of black Ray Bans. She looked like a gangster or a Japanese hip-hopper. Her hands were plunged in her pockets.

"Sandy said you'd show up here. Jump into my car. Let's go somewhere warm. Get something to eat."

"What are you doing up here?"

"Eating lunch. Come on. How much time have we got?"

"I have to be back in court at one-thirty."

Locking up the Bronco again, Nina crunched through the snow and got into the black BMW with the tinted windows and the full ski rack. A girl sat in the back seat.

"Meet Caroline," Ginger said. "She offered to keep me company."

"Hi," said purple-haired Caroline.

"Eagle's Nest okay?" said Ginger.

"Sure. You know your way around here, Ginger."

"I ought to. I own a condo here. As long as I had to come up, I thought we ought to get some skiing in."

Ginger drove them smoothly to Kingsbury Grade, the steep road that leaves the Tahoe basin and drops in a few miles two thousand feet to Carson Valley. The road she turned on led to a startling sight—a small city of condominiums built for skiers around the foot of the Heavenly Resort, on the Nevada side. Most amazing of all was an enormous complex high on a hill of hundreds of condos called The Ridge Tahoe. "That's where my place is," Ginger said, pointing toward it.

The Eagle's Nest had a broad back deck with a vista, filtered through the trees, of one of the Heavenly runs. Just a hundred feet away, people were zooming past.

They ordered hot ham sandwiches, milk, and coffee. Heat lamps had been set up and the decking was swept clear of snow, but even so, most of the diners had chosen to eat indoors by the fireplace.

"Take a hike, baby," Ginger said to Caroline.

The girl stood up and stretched. "I'll check out the view from the bar," she said, and went in.

"She knows I have to talk to you in private. This isn't for phone lines or e-mail." Ginger took off her leather driving gloves and tossed them onto the table.

"You're scaring me, Ginger."

"Paranoia strikes deep," Ginger said. "Murder cases are like that."

"It's the boots, right?"

"It's the boots. First of all, I had visitors at the lab this morning. A South Lake Tahoe cop, accompanied by Sacramento County deputy sheriff. They took the boots and made a number of caustic remarks regarding obstructing a police investigation. Big words, unpleasant noises. You can picture it, I'm sure."

"I'll cover you, Ginger. Don't worry about it. I knew the boots would be located eventually. I'm surprised the D.A.'s office didn't just ask me to produce them. I was prepared to do that."

So Collier hadn't chosen to mention sending his errand boys to nip at Ginger. Fine, she told herself. She had pulled a fast one on him sending the boots down there. He had only responded in kind. It was part of the job.

"They also took my samples and records. Under subpoena, of course. They even took my computer."

A gust of cold wind made Nina shiver. She moved her chair closer to the heater. "I'll get the computer back for you. Are you saying you found something?" she asked.

"I finally got on the boots this weekend. Here's a photo I totally accidentally forgot to hand to the cops. Of the soles."

Nina stared at the distinctive pattern of short parallel lines on the upper and lower soles, and in the middle, the chevron design with a logo showed that as much care had been taken in designing the bottom of these boots as the maker took with the tops. "Nice shot," she said. "We need those autopsy pictures to see if this pattern matches the marks on the body. I wish I could have gotten them for you."

"I wish you could have gotten the body for me."

"So—we don't know yet. Whether there's really a pattern on the skin, or if there is, whether they can make a match. If they arrest Jim, you'll get the pictures. We're still in the game."

"True, as far as the patterning." Ginger took off her Ray Bans and wiped the lenses on her napkin.

"Uh, oh."

"I took a small sample of detritus from between the grooves on the sole. A very small sample. There's plenty more dirt left that Clauson can collect, and besides they copped my lab notes, including the computer file. They know by now that I examined this sample on Sunday afternoon."

"Don't stop now."

"I found something."

"What?"

"Brace yourself, Nina."

"Just get on with it!"

"Two black cotton fibers." Nina made the connections. For a minute she couldn't say anything.

"Alex's turtleneck?" she finally whispered.

"The autopsy report said he was wearing a black cotton turtleneck with some damage. I don't have the turtleneck. They do. All I can say is, two black cotton fibers. If I found two with a minuscule sample, there will be more, probably all over both soles."

Nina put her head in her hands. "I can't believe it. Jim would have had to—"

"Yeah, jump on him and then really grind those soles on the shirt—with the victim in it. It's not a pretty thought. I had another stomping case a few years ago, a couple of rednecks who stomped an unconscious drunk lying in a gutter, for kicks. It's an opportunistic kind of thing. It does happen."

"There has to be some other explanation!"

"What are you going to do?"

"Ask Jim."

"I hope he tells you the truth," Ginger said. "Save the State of California and you a lot of stress and time."

"I just don't believe it, Ginger." She was fighting not

to believe it. Now there was physical evidence to add to all the bits she had been trying not to register.

She told herself, it's not proof beyond a reasonable doubt. There were still ways out. If it was murder, maybe someone else had done the murder. There had been ten minutes to do it, and everything Jim had told her would still be true. She tried to think about these things, to erase the pernicious flood of doubt that would kill her effectiveness as an advocate.

Ginger looked toward the deck door, where Caroline was just coming toward them. "They're mostly guilty," she said. "You can still make sure he gets fair treatment all the way down the line."

Nina managed to call the lodge at Paradise before she had to go back into the courtroom. Yes, Jim stayed around until about nine most nights, the hostess told her.

She went back to her civil case. Love the one you're with. But when court adjourned at four, she narrowly avoided knocking her client to the ground in the swiftness of her exit.

As usual, the lodge was thronged with skiers. She plowed through them without paying any attention. Jim's office door was open and she marched in. Judging by the trophies and photographs on the walls devoted just to him, he was one hell of a skier.

He had the phone pressed to his ear, but when he saw her, he said good-bye and hung up. He read her expression instantly. "Nina? What's happened?"

"Not here," she said. "Outside." Ginger's paranoia had struck deep all right. Jim put on his parka and followed her out to the bunny hill, quiet now that the lifts had stopped for the day. The sun had slipped behind the crest of the mountain. The winds had stilled. Even the birds had silenced, maybe gone for the winter already. A cold twilight was settling over the Basin. Nina drew her coat around her and brought up the collar.

There was no point in making small talk, even if she had it in her to make small talk. "Dr. Hirabayashi—you remember her, she's the pathologist we sent the boots to —found some fibers in the grooves in the bottom of one of the boots," she said.

She waited for Jim to go through the same process she had, to forge the connections.

"Fibers?" Jim seemed confused.

"Black cotton fibers."

The news had no effect. Jim looked into her eyes, interested but unafraid.

"How did black cotton fibers get on the bottom of your boots, Jim?"

Now he got it. His mouth fell open. He almost sputtered. "What'm I supposed to say?"

"Your choice," said Nina. She took his arm. "Alex was wearing a black cotton shirt the day he died. You can tell me what you know about that, or not. Whatever you tell me, I'll never reveal to anyone."

"I have no idea! No idea!"

"Jim, I want you to know I can still help you, no matter what you may have done."

"Oh, no," Jim said. "This is unreal. Some fibers you can only see under a microscope have made you turn your back on me. You think I did it, don't you?"

"I can deal with it if you did." She tried to sound confident, nonjudgmental, to hide her disappointment. While she waited for him to speak again, she concentrated on his eyes, wanting to see inside to his naked soul.

He turned toward a stand of tall pines, placing his hands in the pockets of his parka. He stepped up and down on the snow in place, gently, as if lifting his feet was very, very painful, apparently unaware of the grotesque congruence of his actions with the accusation. His profile in the shadow of the evening revealed nothing except some confusion, and possibly some anger.

He was studying the matter, turning it over in his mind, and Nina had no idea what he was thinking. At the best of times, she would guess he was a very guarded person. And so, she realized, was she.

He turned back to face her. "You can't tell anyone anything I say unless I give you permission?" Jim asked. "Attorney-client privilege, right?"

Did this mean he was breaking the standoff? Was he about to tear down a wall and unload the real truth on her? She could not help experiencing a moment of personal fear—was she about to find out that at this very moment, she was standing on a darkening, desolate mountain with a vicious killer?

"That's right," she said, coughing slightly to give herself a moment to regain her composure. "It's a law. An attorney must hold the client's secrets inviolate at every peril to himself," she said, quoting the Business and Professions Code section which had been drummed into her in law school and which she considered the most important ethical rule of the profession.

She tried to think practical thoughts, preparing to offer him her best professional support. Surrender him, maybe get a psych report, bring in a lot of character witnesses at the sentencing—

"Then there's no point in lying. I'm not lying, Nina. I just don't have an explanation for those fibers, unless it's just some dumb thing like—we all buy our shirts at the same store, and my father happened to have one in his car when my boots got tossed in there or that, if Alex was in fact murdered in the moments before I got to him, the killer also decided to frame me and somehow set this whole thing up."

From the lodge, only a couple of hundred feet away, came the sound of clanking knives and forks, happy chatter.

"Please believe me," Jim said. "Please, I know I didn't do anything to Alex. And you tell me now that there's something on my boots that proves I did. Well, if that's so, someone else put it there. I didn't get down below the Cliff for almost ten minutes."

"What are you going to tell me if the soles of your boots have the same pattern as the marks on your brother's skin, Jim?" Nina said.

"Then—it's just awful. And if I ever find the bastard that did that to my brother, I'll take him out. Look, Nina. Those boots I wear are like— the Nikes of ski boots. There's nothing unusual about them. I suppose there was enough time Alex was out of sight for someone to hurt him like that, but it's foul to think about. And all I can tell you is, you've got to believe me because I didn't do it."

"I don't know how much time we have left," Nina said. "A few days, maybe, while the coroner goes over the boots and makes tests. Then a few days more while the district attorney's office reviews all this. But the fibers really back up Clauson's conclusion that Alex's death was a homicide, Jim. And the boots are yours. That's enough to charge you."

"Fuck," Jim said bitterly.

"One more question. I'm sorry but I have to ask it. Was Heidi seeing Alex—outside the marriage?"

"You mean, sleeping with him? God, no! Who said that?"

"It's just something I have to check out."

"Well, it's a lie."

"You're sure?"

"Positive!"

"You said one time that she'd drawn away from you—"

"My wife was not sleeping with my brother," Jim said very deliberately.

"Marianne mentioned to me that—"

"Marianne is a vicious little liar. She'd love it if Heidi and I split up. She thinks she's still in love with me. Is she spreading that lie?"

"Okay," Nina said. "I hear what you're saying. Now, I want you to go home and think about all this. We'll talk again later."

"I'm not lying! Tell me you believe me, Nina."

"I'm on your side, Jim. I'm not saying that I don't believe you. I'm going to think about what you said, keep looking into it. Now, we've hired an investigator, Tony Ramirez. He's looking for Heidi. Maybe we can find her and straighten this out."

"I trust you," Jim said.

"I have to go."

"Are you married, Nina?"

Involuntarily, she glanced at her ring finger with its faint crease. "Why do you ask?"

"Just that—"

"What?"

"Nothing. Thinking about Heidi, I guess."

"Here's something else you should do. You need to put together some money in case you need bail." She gave him the name of a good bail bondsman, just in case. "Can you get twenty-five thousand dollars in cash? I doubt the bail would be set higher than two hundred fifty thousand. You only have to put up a cash bond of ten percent. And your house."

"It's really going to happen, isn't it? I'm going to be charged." He sounded forlorn.

"Try not to worry. I do have to tell you—I'm going out of town this weekend, leaving on Thursday morning. I'll be back Monday night."

"Leaving? Where are you going?"

"It's a business trip. Sandy will be in touch with me if anything breaks."

Matt and Andrea said that Bob was welcome. The timing was bad, since he'd be leaving for his two weeks in Germany in three weeks, but she wanted to take this weekend with Collier more badly than anything she had wanted in a long time. Rising early and working late, she compressed the week's work into three days and on Thursday morning took Bob to school. Matt would pick him up.

"You're sure it's okay?" she said to him as he pulled his pack out of the truck and shouldered it.

"It's okay, Mom."

"Really?"

"You have to promise I get to go with you next time."

"Fair enough." She kissed him on the forehead. "To Matt's after school, don't forget!" she called after him.

He joined the group of students walking across the field of snow toward his first class. He looked so tall. When had he gotten so tall?

11

On Lanikai Beach. On the windward side of Oahu, away from the Waikiki scene, in a low white cottage built on sand. Benevolent gods and goddesses ruled from the fiery volcanoes, warmed the green sea, deposited the sand grain by grain onto the palm-fringed beach.

Collier had spent his healing time here.

She lay in his arms in the shade of a palm, snow and mountains and murder case forgotten, watching the cavalcade of walkers and joggers, silent for once. Implicit between them was their agreement: no talk of their work.

They swam through waves pleated with sun. The sea had an old calm. Underneath, in the shadowed shallows, a city of fish munching on the algae-covered coral, speckled, striped, translucent. She heard a crackling sound in the water when she dove down, as though the fish were talking to each other.

They came together way out from the beach, fitting as neatly together as two parts of a zipper. Nina swam away, laughing, and he followed her, toward the Mokoluas, the two wild islands in the distance.

Sunset. They sat at a table on the deck.

"So—what do you think happened to you last year? I

mean, how do you describe it to yourself?" Nina asked. She poured him another glass of wine. They were still in bathing suits.

Across the quiet sea, the Moks subsided into the twilight. The last kayakers set out from the tiny beach on the larger island, way out there, and headed back toward home.

"Oh, I'd been on the job too long, been alone too long, grieved for my wife too long," Collier said. "In our line, you have to have a life outside work, to keep it in perspective I went into a tailspin, but I had to keep going, you know? Get up and get over to the office and try cases and make deals and talk to victims.

"For a while it just took everything I had. That was all right, as long as I was still doing the job. The time came when I couldn't do the job, though, and that was the end, because the job was my life. I started obsessing even more about my wife. I stopped sleeping. Nothing like it had ever happened to me before."

"I think—that night on the roof of the casino—I think you were awfully close to death," Nina said. "I'll never forget it."

"Afterwards, I just wanted to hide," Collier said. "I was in touch with a professor from college who'd left academia and made it big in real estate in Honolulu. He and his wife own the big house next door. I called him. He offered to rent me this cottage. They only use it when their kids come to visit. I didn't even leave the cottage for two weeks, not even to go to the beach. I felt like I'd been in a fire. Like a burn victim. I lay on the bed and stared at the ceiling."

"I wish you'd called me."

"I didn't want to be found. But—later, when I

started getting better, I looked back at Tahoe and I realized it had all been there, work that I loved and people that cared about me. So I gave myself a goal. To get it back. I didn't think I deserved it, I wasn't sure it was possible, but I had to try."

"Did you ever talk to someone? A professional?"

"Just the local medico. He checked me out and told me to run on the beach and swim twice a day and to make some friends. And the main thing—you're going to laugh, but he was right—he told me not to read."

"Not to read anything?"

"Nothing. No newspapers, no magazines, no books. And no TV, no computer. He took away all the entertainments that made it possible for me to live in my head. He sent me outside like I was ten years old on a Saturday morning. I was desperate, so I took his advice. Mainly because I had decided I was the stupidest son of a bitch alive."

They smiled at each other. "Excuse me. I have to kiss you now," he said. They did that for a while.

Breaking away finally, Nina said, "I'd like to hear the rest of your story."

"Well, I did make some good friends here. Mark and Patty in the big house, and the kid that lives on the other side. Isaiah, his name is. He taught me the best snorkeling spots on the island. I'll always come back here now. Once or twice a year from now on, I'll set my work aside and go outside and live. You understand, don't you, my darling?"

"Oh, yes. You have things to teach me now," Nina said. "Collier? Have you ever thought—do you have a code of honor?"

He looked surprised. "I wouldn't call it that, but— once upon a time, I would have said, to try to right all the wrongs. But I couldn't begin to do that. I thought about that a lot last year. I decided on something more realistic."

"What was that?"

"To try to right some of the wrongs. Just some of them. Listen. Let's bring Bob next time. We'll take a boat out to the Moks."

She looked out to sea. Like the old Hawaiians said, everything was alive and moving: tinted clouds, sky exhaling trade winds, surf brushing shore, ti leaves and coconut palms trembling and waving, even the gullied cliffs behind them standing like leaf-skirted warriors against the sky, holding fast, watching the Pacific.

Dusk. The sky psychedelic. Collier cut up a mango and shared it with her. They sat outside and talked some more. Collier told her about his family and his childhood. She told him about Kurt, Bob's father, and Jack, the lawyer she had married and worked with during her San Francisco days. As she talked, she realized that her past had become simple. It was the past, that was all. Now only the present was real.

Night in their bed. "I don't want to go back," she cried. She buried her face in the pillow.

Collier stroked her hair. "Let's pretend this night never ends. Your hair is damp on the pillow. You are beautiful, and you are mine." He stopped for a moment, then said in a low voice, "Will you agree to that, Nina? To be mine?"

Nina got up on one elbow. Her hair fell across her face. He tucked it behind her ear. She wore white shell earrings he had bought her and nothing else.

"I agree," she said gravely.

"I'm in love with you, Nina."

"Oh, God. Are you sure?"

"Do you love me?"

"Oh, boy."

"Tongue-tied, eh? Why can't I do that to you in court?"

"It's nothing to laugh about. It's a very serious—"

"No, it's not. I just wondered. It's not a geometry test. You don't have to try to figure out the correct answer. You know, you have the most remarkably beautiful neck. I like how it sits on your shoulders. I like the slope of your shoulders, and especially your collarbones." He lay his head on her chest as if he wanted to have a private communication with her heart.

"I love you too," she whispered. Relief overcame her as the fortress within her opened its heavy armored gates.

"Let's go for a swim," he said a long time later. "We have all night. We won't go to sleep at all tonight."

"I don't want to swim. I don't like the dark water."

"We'll just wade." He took her hand and she followed, cut free from all other anchors.

The sea lapped against their waists as they faced the mainland three thousand miles away. Cassiopeia and the Pleiades glimmered overhead. On the shore the shorebreak and bushes protected them from the view of the houses. The moon cast its familiar line of silver along the water.

She knew what would happen.

Collier came up behind her and pressed himself to her so she could feel him hard against her. His hands gripped her hips through her suit as he pulled her even closer against him. She leaned her head back and reached her arms back and held his head.

He leaned her over and she felt his hand under the water, pulling her suit aside. Waves washed across them and they almost lost their balance. He entered her suddenly, as impersonal as a sea god, and she closed her eyes and let go, letting him keep them both afloat, cool everywhere except in the burning center where he was.

The call and response of breathing began, and her breathing became moans. The sea moaned with her while the wind caressed her face. She felt his breath in her ear.

They rocked in the shifting sea. The unknown in her met the unknown in him.

Straining, he pulled her to him one more time. He groaned.

He fell away and she slipped under a wave. When she came back up, wiping the water away from her eyes, she saw his dark head deeper out, swimming with long strokes away from her. She let him go and watched for a long time, waiting patiently for him to return to her.

They had showered and gone to bed.

"I want—I need our spirits to intertwine. So you never leave me again," Nina said.

"All right. We'll stay here forever."

"I'll become a lei maker," Nina said.

"I'll fish."

"That's good."

"We'll give Bob thirteen siblings, island princes and princesses, who drink coconut milk and play the ukelele . . ."

"And love to fend for themselves. Otherwise, we could never raise them."

"Nina?"

"Mmm-hmm."

"I would so love to have a child. I mean, I know I could love Bob. But, a baby."

"I know."

"What do you think about babies?"

Dawn.

The plane left from Honolulu Airport at ten. They barely made it.

"Nina?" She had been falling into a doze in spite of the noise of takeoff. His intensity had kept her awake all night.

"What?"

"Do we have to stay alone, live alone, stay lonely all our lives?" Collier asked. "Is that our fate?" He was sitting bolt upright beside her.

"It doesn't seem like a very good plan anymore," Nina answered drowsily. "What shall we do?"

"I'm not sure."

"There are so many considerations," Nina said.

"But none of them matter. Not really."

His tone, so definite, woke her fully. She became aware of everything—the slightly stale air, the engine noise, the smell of his shirt, the scratches on the window.

"I know we haven't known each other very long," he said.

"Two years," Nina answered. "I've sat opposite you in court many times, trying to understand what you were thinking, trying to figure you out. I know you very well. We think alike. We're both trying to do the job and be decent about it. I know how intelligent you are, how mature, how good . . ." She saw how this praise affected him. He had no idea how good he was. No one had loved him for so long.

They were landing. "I can't really be a lei maker," Nina said. "Can you live with that?"

Wheels bumped against tarmac. He nodded. He knew what she was explaining, that she wouldn't change her work. It was all she did well and the only way she could help, and she knew he felt exactly the same way about his work.

"We'll figure something out," he said.

"The only thing is—I wish I'd never met Jim Strong," Nina said. As soon as it was out, she wished she hadn't said it. What she meant was, I wish that investigation weren't between us right now, before we get a chance to figure out how to work in the same town. Collier might take it wrong and think—

But maybe he didn't know about the fibers yet. Clauson might not have filed his supplemental report by the time they had left.

She was sure about it when he answered lightly, in that new warm voice of his, "Who knows? Maybe it'll go away."

So she was still a step ahead of him. She knew that wasn't going to happen.

She talked to Bob about her feelings for Collier that night. After initially acting very blasé, then asking a question or two about Paul, he began talking about his father and she realized that he had been nursing some private fantasies. He said he would think about all this and get back to her, and retired to the phone in his bedroom, where he would seek advice from people like Uncle Matt.

Of course, he would need time to get to know Collier.

It was only nine, but she couldn't keep her eyes open. She climbed under the Hudson blanket in the cold attic room and set the alarm.

On Tuesday morning she had just taken her coat off and hung it on the rack at the office when Collier called, much sooner than she had expected.

"You have until close of business today to surrender Jim Strong into custody at the South Lake Tahoe Police Department," he said, his voice not brusque, not cold, just very different from the day before. "I'm telling you as a courtesy since he's represented."

She kept her voice as professional as his. "I appreciate that. What's the charge?"

"Murder. First degree."

"I'm going to insist on a preliminary hearing within ten days."

"Do what you have to do."

"We'll produce him."

12

SHE ACCOMPANIED JIM to the station and stood by him while two detectives read him his rights again and went after him with questions. On advice of counsel, Jim refused to answer. Eventually, he was led over to the jail for booking.

Barbet Schroeder, who wrote the courthouse stories for the newspaper, had somehow gotten wind of it. Her photographer managed to get a shot of Jim as he was escorted into the jail.

Tomorrow he would be arraigned. He had roots in the community, came from a prominent family, and had never been arrested for anything before this. Some sort of bail would be forthcoming, and he would be freed after spending just one night locked up, for now at least. But the morning paper would come out, too, and then he would be notorious.

Polite in their way, the jail deputies moved efficiently through the processes of turning Jim into an inmate. The smell of coffee, the TV with its commercials coming from somewhere within, and their relaxed manner helped. Jim went through it all fatalistically, shrugging his shoulders when she asked how he felt. Only at the last moment, as she was leaving so he could be issued his jail jumpsuit and go through all the other humiliations of being stripped of his liberty, did he turn to her and whisper, "Don't give up on me."

As it closed, the jail door sent out a puff of air, closing out all that was fresh and alive.

On Wednesday, at the one-thirty arraignments, Judge Flaherty set bail at $300,000 after a short argument by the attorneys. Collier was right there in court with her, and they both were very careful not to touch or say anything personal. Collier looked so tall and distinguished, and she was proud—no, she was indifferent.

Or was she indignant? What she was, was confused, and no time was available for confusion. In a few days, a preliminary hearing would determine if Jim would have to endure a full-scale murder trial.

After the hearing, Collier handed her an envelope marked with the coroner's address. He chose that moment to smile, and at that unpropitious moment Barbara Banning walked in, wearing a designer suit, her arms full of files for the hearings to come. She looked at Nina, then at Collier.

How did she know? How could she know? Had Collier told her? Barbara's eyes flitted back and forth at them. Her finely plucked eyebrows climbed toward her hairline and a cynical expression appeared.

Of course. They were so obvious, two smiling lawyers with matching sunburns, not the ski-goggle sunburn, either. They had been caught red-faced.

Now Nina saw how difficult their jobs might become. She did not look at the envelope; she didn't want to know yet what they had found on the boots. Besides, instant interpretation was out—her brain seemed to be tangled in kelp. She would study the material later, carefully, when the seaweed dispersed.

That afternoon, she left work early. She and Bob and Hitchcock took a long walk along the lakeshore, on the thin strand of sand left between snow and water.

"Get these away from me," Tony Ramirez said, pushing at the autopsy photos with his index finger. "I've seen enough." Crammed into Nina's office, Tony, Ginger, Sandy, Nina, and Sandy's son, Wish Whitefeather, had all found seats somewhere. On Nina's clean oak desk, the photos were defilements.

Outside, a few flakes of snow fluttered across the forest and marsh, obscuring the distant lake. They had been talking strategy for the last hour. The mantra of this case was to be: it was an accident. But, since the prosecution theory was murder, they were going to have to deal with that. The best bet seemed to be to find some more suspects.

Ginger took the photos, eight-by-ten glossies with excellent resolution, and stacked them back into a neat pile. "A shame they're so vivid," she said. She put the views of Alex Strong's stomach, the ones with the patternlike marks, on top. Next to the autopsy photos she placed another blowup of the bottoms of Jim's ski boots.

"See for yourself," she said. "I'll have them scanned into the computer and we'll play around to see if we can sharpen up the details even more. If we want to sharpen up the details."

"I don't see anything on the skin," Sandy said. "Just some marks."

Nina raised her head at this: If Sandy wasn't sure she saw a pattern, a jury might react similarly.

"Although they do seem to run in short stripes," Sandy added. "Like the boots." Nina's head sunk back on her chest.

"That's how they look to me too," agreed Wish. "Like, when I wear my belt buckle too tight and I go to take my pants off, I can see the outline of the whole buckle on my stomach, even the metal thing that you put in the hole in the belt . . ."

Wish was studying criminal justice at the community college. He had pulled his long hair into a ponytail that went halfway down his back, accentuating the high forehead and big ears and the innocent look on his face. If he got any taller he wouldn't fit into the conference room at all.

"I guess we ought to feel lucky that the logo isn't imprinted too," Nina said. "There's obviously some sort of pattern. Ginger, what can you do with this?"

"In two weeks? Here's the best bet. Have Tony here scrounge up half a dozen other pairs of ski boots with similar bottoms. Let me compare them to these faint markings. I'll let you know if I can testify that it's impossible to tell if it's Tecnicas."

"I saw a pair of men's boots at Marianne Strong's house. They weren't Alex's, because they were still wet. The maker was Dalbello. They were about a size eleven."

"Cool," said Ginger. "They're Italian boots. I'll test a pair of those first."

"Maybe she has a boyfriend," Tony said. "I'll look into that."

"But if the pattern is boot prints, it's definitely a homicide," Nina said. "How could— They didn't find any blood on the boot bottoms. How could that be?"

"Human skin is amazingly resilient in maintaining its integrity even when it's dealt a crushing trauma," Ginger explained. "The external skin doesn't seem to have shown much bruising. The initial hemorrhage was internal only. So I can't say that the lack of blood on the boots helps much."

"They did find some droplets on the black shirt," Nina said. "That might be important in considering the timing, since the parka would have had to be opened and the bibs pulled down long enough for the blood to trickle there from the face."

She saw Wish grimace. Wish and Sandy's reactions were important to her, since a jury might be expected to react to these forensic details in a similar manner. In his face, she could follow just how ugly the prosecution's scenario would look.

Wish noticed that she was watching him. "Don't worry, Nina," he said. "We'll find out what happened. We'll help him." He gave her a sunny smile. Gratefully, she smiled back.

"At least we can whack Clauson on some of the other findings," Ginger said. "Leave that to me." She wore all black again, but without her hat. "As to the thirty-five additional fibers they found on the Tecnica soles, I can't help. I'll go over to the police evidence locker today with some equipment and have a look, but we can assume they will be black cotton fibers, and we can be pretty damn sure they'll match the shirt. That's all science is likely to tell us."

"So what's the cockamamie story Jimmy told you about the shirt?" Sandy asked Nina.

"He seemed to be as shocked about the fibers as I was. After he thought about it, Jim said that everybody in town wears those shirts. They're from Miller's Outpost down at the Y. He reminded me that the Tecnicas were in his father's truck and asked if they could have

come into contact with a shirt there. He also said someone must be trying to frame him."

"Quick thinking," Sandy said dryly. "So, after
stomping Alex to death, the killer lifted some fibers off
the dead man, found the boots in the car and planted
evidence to frame Jim. I think a coo-coo bird got in
here."

Tony said, "Look. Let's get real." He was a local and
a friend of Sandy's with a P.I. license, shrewd and honest even if, at sixty-seven, he was a bit over the hill for
the more physical aspects of his work.

"We just don't know enough yet," Nina said.
"Philip Strong was on the mountain that day. So was
Marianne Strong. They both knew the area where the
brothers were skiing." Nina told them about Marianne's
continuing interest in Jim.

"I happened to get a look at Alex's will at the house.
He left everything to Marianne, but it's *what* he left that
I found interesting. The will stated that he was leaving
his interest in a one-sixth share of Paradise to Marianne,
and also the additional one-sixth share recently purchased from his sister Kelly. Jim holds one sixth, and
their father holds the remaining one half. So Marianne
now owns one third of the stock. That's a lot of stock."

"How much is it worth?"

"Jim thinks his share is worth half a million dollars,
so hers is worth a million now. Tony, we have to look
closely at this woman."

"Maybe she has her own ideas on how to use the
money," Sandy said. "I could think of a few."

"She sounds good. How about Heidi?" Wish asked.
"Was she skiing too?"

"Yes," Nina said. "And she's an expert skier too. All

of them are experts. A mountainful of athletes in ski boots."

"Expert skiers," Tony said with a snort. "Arrogant punks with money to play all day and party all night. Bet your client's real surprised to find himself knocked off his skis like this. Probably never had anything happen to him worse than a stubbed toe."

"I would like to mention that Philip Strong hands the Women's Shelter a big check every Christmas," said Sandy. "Not everyone with a little money in his pocket is an unproductive slacker."

She and Tony exchanged a sideways look, and Nina wondered where Tony fit into Sandy's life. Just about everyone she recommended was a member of her extended family.

Tony moved back to the question of whether someone else could have killed Alex.

"Even if other parties were hanging around with nefarious intentions, there was only a ten-minute window, assuming the client is telling the truth. Otherwise, the client would have seen somebody do something," he said.

"It's early yet," Nina said, stressing the words. "And we are assuming he is telling the truth. We're his support. His family seems to have abandoned him. I've just heard his father left town. He was really grief stricken when I talked to him."

"Judging from the fact that I'm sitting here, I figured the client wasn't planning to plead out," said Tony.

"He swears he didn't do it," Nina said.

Nobody said anything.

"So I'll see what I can find out about Marianne Strong," Tony finally said. "And I'll check out the

father. Any idea where he was the day of the accident?"
They were still calling it an accident.

Nina said, "He was at Paradise, maybe on the mountain, maybe at the lodge. Try to firm that up, Tony. But, honestly, I don't think Mr. Strong could kill his son. He's taking some time off, and according to Jim, he's staying with his daughter on the North Shore. Talk to Jessica Sweet, an employee there. She wants to help. Wish will be glad to help you. I'm going to have a look at the place where Alex died this afternoon. I may ask you to go up there tomorrow and take photos.

"Which brings us back to Heidi," Nina went on. "Marianne Strong claims that Heidi confessed to her that she was having an affair. But she wouldn't say with whom."

"I sincerely hope it wasn't with Alex," said Ginger.

"Big nail in Jim's coffin," Sandy agreed.

"I'll see what I can dredge up," Tony said. "All right, let's review the alternative killers."

"His father?" Wish said.

"Would a father kill his son like that, and try to hang it on his other son? What the hell?" Tony said.

"Yeah? What the hell?" Wish said, his eyes wide as he pondered this.

"Watch your mouth," Sandy told her son. "How about Marianne? If she killed her husband, she'd have a crack at Jim, if she also could get Heidi out of the picture. Which she did."

"But how could Marianne get Jim's Tecnicas and the turtleneck shirt together?" Wish asked. "I've got a shirt just like that. No wrinkles and they don't show the dirt. Everybody wears them because they're like sweats but kinda formal. Black is the best." He nodded approvingly at Ginger.

"Where did you get your shirt?" asked Ginger.

"At Miller's Outpost. Just like Jim said. Everybody wears them."

"Hmm. Now there's a tantalizing notion, dude," said Ginger. "I'm thinking I'll stop there on my way out of town and buy a few black turtlenecks."

"And compare the fibers, right?" Wish said, excited.

Ginger said, deadpan, "No, I'm gonna give 'em to the gamblers on the road out of town who lost their shirts."

"Oh, wow," said Wish, nodding.

At home, Nina dug out slightly mildewed ski bibs and fresh wool socks. In this weather, nineteen degrees and dropping, she wasn't looking forward to doing what she had to do next.

Jim waited at the door to Paradise Lodge. It was barely one o'clock, still snowing slightly, the top of the mountain bearded in cloud, but windless and bitterly cold.

"Back home safely?" Nina said. "No trouble with the bail?"

"Smooth as silk. Anything new?" Rose-tinted goggles covered half his face. He looked right at home in his blue ski suit, arms and legs straining at the material as if he were an action hero in a kid's TV program.

"No. Lots of things in progress," she answered. That about exhausted the conversation. Very likely he also dreaded this morbid field trip.

For a few minutes, they occupied themselves with the skis. Nina had trouble with the bindings, and Jim knelt at her feet to adjust them.

Outside again, they made their way over to the lifts. Not many skiers had come out to brave the white sky, so they had the big quad lift to themselves. As the ground slipped away under them, then became invisible, Nina clutched at the camera in her jacket. Still there, but what would be the use? Even if they found the spot where Alex had died the weather made good photos unlikely. Even with Jim along to help her find the way, could she ski well enough to track the path of an expert skier? The cold slithering into her bibs made her bones feel brittle, fragile.

From the top of the quad lift, at eighty-three hundred feet above sea level, they took another lift. On a clear day the lake would be shining below. Today, she could barely see Jim. The snow sped past lightly, stinging her face, small dry flakes that meant great weekend skiing.

"Maybe we should come back," she finally said as he helped her up after she spilled off the lift, losing a ski. "I'm not an expert—the weather makes it hard to take pictures and—"

"Let's get it over with. You're with an expert. I won't let anything happen to you. You have to see them —the rocks and the cliff. We're suited up now. I don't care if we can't get any pictures."

"I don't know."

"I'll carry you on my back if I have to. Just take it easy. The fresh snow will give us more traction—otherwise it might be too icy for you to manage."

She followed him carefully along a ridge which took them above a misty ridge and canyon, skiing glumly behind him on the narrow trail, her wool hat pulled low.

They went over the mountain, like the proverbial bear, but all that they could see was near whiteout. The tourists no doubt were down in the warm casinos, drinking Bloody Marys and watching their money disappear like magic.

"Wait a minute," Nina said. "I don't remember seeing this run on my map."

"It's not. We're off-piste."

"Off what?" She was pissed off all right, pissed that she'd agreed to do this, pissed to be so cold, pissed at the snow melting between her bibs and gloves, pissed at her mood, so unlike her, so apprehensive.

"Off-trail. Out of bounds," Jim said.

Nina remembered. Marianne had used the same term.

"Alex always liked to say he owned this mountain. We ski wherever we want, and this is where we skied that day. C'mon," he said. "The first part's easy." He disappeared over the edge.

"Oh, sure." Inching toward the edge, she saw a treeless slope and no trail, but not much of an angle. She bit her lip and stopped briefly to give herself a mental pep talk. Pushing off, she made her way cautiously down to the ledge where Jim was waiting. Now the slope was becoming much steeper.

"I'd love to show you how I really ski this, another time," Jim said. "But for now—see that tree off to the right about a hundred yards? Go there, as slowly as you can. I'll be right beside you." He stayed with her and she managed it, thrashing about like a small clumsy elephant next to his elegant antelope.

"Your turns need work," Jim said as she came to a stop, breathless with anxiety.

"No kidding."

"So. Now follow me very carefully down this snowfield. At the bottom is the cliff. You don't want to go off like—"

"Okay, okay. Just go slow."

"I've got you." He went ahead, walking sideways on the mountain in a herringbone pattern, in perfect control.

Go slow, she ordered herself. With exquisite caution she inched out onto the snowfield. Unexpectedly, the skis pushed down into the snow just enough to hold her, but not enough to trip her, which gave her the courage to continue. Down she went, imagining herself, a tiny dark speck in the white scheme of things.

When they were about twenty feet from the edge, Jim motioned to her to turn toward the right, where she could see that the slope resumed. Unfortunately, just as she turned, the skis chose to turn a slightly different way.

And she was off, sliding toward the cliff.

"Sit down!" Jim yelled, but the movement had its own life, and it was taking her along with it. Flashes of panic alternated with exhilaration—she had never skied so smoothly, so fast, sliding down this glassy slope into oblivion. She tried to turn toward the trees, but she was going to go off Alex's cliff, join him—

A hard body bowled her over backwards, falling onto her.

"Don't move," Jim said. She lay on her back, panting, looking up into his goggles. Her hat had fallen off. She couldn't have moved if she'd wanted to. She lay there, panting, his weight still on her.

She became aware that he wasn't moving, and made a tentative motion with her body, which only dug her deeper into the snow.

"Nina?" Jim said. "You feel good. Under me like this."

"What?" she said. "What did you say?" She started to push him off, but he didn't move.

"Don't worry. You weren't in any danger. There was plenty of time to take you down."

"I'm going back up. I've had enough." She pushed at him again, succeeding only in digging herself farther into the snow.

"Too steep," Jim said. "Better to traverse this stretch and go down the side. It gets easier from here."

"Get off me!"

He rolled away and she tried to get up, but she couldn't. "Here," he said, and held out a hand. He kept holding her arm as they moved carefully to the right side. As he had said, the slope became more gentle. "Here's the tree I nearly hit," he said. He pointed to a small fir with low-hanging branches. "Would have impaled me," he went on.

He seemed unaware that he'd just acted like a complete asshole. For a moment, he had made her feel helpless and frightened. She kept well away from him now. Had he really said what she thought she'd heard?

He had also quite possibly saved her life. Should she thank him or verbally lambaste him?

She really, really wanted this to be over soon.

"I don't appreciate the way you spoke to me just now," she said.

"Yeah, I was way out of line. Sorry. It just popped out. Stress, you know?"

"Don't do it again."

"Right."

A pause, and then Nina said, "But thanks for stopping me."

"Least I could do. Are we okay, then?"

"I guess so," Nina said, but her uneasiness lingered.

She took her camera out and took a few pictures of
Jim standing against the tree, showing where he had
nearly hit it, at the same moment he heard Alex strike
the rocks below. They were probably going to be useless
because she couldn't get any perspective into the scene.

"Did Marianne snowboard this run or is it too
steep?"

"Looking for suspects? Nothing's too steep for Marianne. I don't know about that day. She could have been
on either side. I just don't know."

Nina remembered Marianne denying that she ever
skied the Cliff. "Heidi?"

"She's fantastic on skis. A ballerina of the slopes."

"Did she know about this run?"

"Come on. Heidi kill Alex? Why?"

"And your father?"

"Ah, yes. My father. He was here within five minutes after I got down and told Jerry, the guy who runs
the Ogre lift, to radio the lodge. So he was close by."

"Somebody must have seen something," Nina said.
Jim said nothing.

In spite of everything, she knew that she had been
right to make the effort to come here. She could almost
see Alex now, flying toward the cliff, the two of them
laughing madly, see Jim pivot away just in time to hit
that tree, see Alex gone in an instant and hear the sickening thud. She had needed to see this place, inaccessi-
ble as it was.

"Ready for the last bit?" Jim said.

"As I'll ever be." They picked their way cautiously
down the side slope to the rocks below the cliff. It took
at least twenty minutes.

They were in an almost flat place. The rocks on the
left stuck up as much as five feet from the snow cover,

but most of the rest consisted of a sort of sloping shelf with a variation of only two or three inches from place to place, swept clear of snow by wind. She looked up. The cliff above this island of granite couldn't be more than twenty feet high. It was a rock wall, practically vertical, with a snowy unstable-looking overhang at the top. At the bottom of the wall ice and piles of snow were evidence that bits of the cornice must shear off from time to time.

She had narrowly avoided going over that thing. Alex hadn't been so lucky.

The wind was coming up. Sitting down on the broad granite shelf, Nina removed her skis, plunging them into the snow at the foot of the rocks so they couldn't slide away.

Torn police tape still fluttered here and there. Off in the bushes an empty Pepsi can lay crushed. The island of upthrust rocks was about thirty feet wide and twenty feet deep. On either side, clean snow had already covered the tracks of the emergency personnel and the police.

"Show me," she said. Jim skied up and stopped a few feet away. He took his skis and goggles off, too, and sat down beside her on the rocky ledge. She began taking photos.

"We're here. The visibility was better, and the wind stayed down that day," he said. "I found him right here." His hand caressed a flat area next to the sharp upthrust. "There was blood on these sharp rocks. I don't see it now. That's where he must have fallen first, then slipped to here. He was on his back, his leg twisted under him when I found him." In the absolute stillness, his voice sounded amplified.

"Did you see any other tracks? Before the rescue people arrived?"

"No. I was trying to help Alex. I wasn't looking."

She felt that if they shouted they would be heard miles away. "Were his eyes open?"

"No! But he was—moaning. I hate to think about it. I told you, he was still alive."

"How far is it to the bottom?"

"A few hundred feet. The paramedics climbed up. Harder that way, if you ask me. The Ski Patrol had no trouble skiing down like we did."

"So he was lying there, face up, moaning."

"He was bleeding. Here, now I can see it."

Brownish stains—she saw them now. "Where were the skis?"

"One still on. The other farther down the hill. I carried them down for him as we left. And the poles."

"What was the first thing you did?"

"I said, 'Hey, buddy . . .' He didn't answer. He was in shock. I—I was afraid to move him. You have to worry about a broken neck. I've had ski emergency training. I should have left him just like that and skied down the rest of the hill for help, but when I was actually in the situation, I couldn't just leave him. I was talking to him the whole time."

"Were his clothes torn?"

"I don't remember—let me think—I think his parka was open. Yeah, it was."

"He wouldn't wear it unzipped, would he?"

"Oh, he might've. Alex spent half the winter in T-shirts. He had a metabolism like a volcano—never needed a blanket at night."

"Well, give it your best shot. Zipped or unzipped?"

"The sun was out. It wasn't especially cold. He was wearing a medium-weight parka—I'd say it was open."

"So you could see the bibs? Alex's bibs?" she said, rubbing her mitten against the rough rock she sat on. She took off the mitten and cleaned off a small area of granite.

"The bibs? I suppose they had blood on them. I wasn't thinking too straight. I couldn't decide whether to stay and hope someone would come, or get going down the mountain. I sat beside him and I lifted his head, tried to brush off the blood. He was losing consciousness. I freaked and I was yelling, 'I'm going for help, I'll be right back . . .'

"I was patting his hand and yelling for help when his body gave a sort of jerk. His eyes went half closed, not moving. He seemed to stop breathing and I gave him mouth-to-mouth but it wasn't working.

"After some time I gave up. I skied down the hill and found Jerry. I was shouting, limping from my fall, raising the alarm."

"Did you listen to his chest?" She had to keep at it, get Jim's story, the one he was going to stick to . . . She scanned the rocks, cleared a tiny pocket of snow, listening with painful concentration because she really wanted to know, had to form a judgment before the prelim as to whether he was telling the truth.

If he was lying, his pretense of grief was diabolical as he described Alex's last moments in this voice full of stops and starts, full of pain.

He had to be innocent, had to be. But the agonized words that fell from his tongue were contradicted by an ever-increasing amount of evidence. A mountain of evidence, with slippery slopes . . .

Knowing that her face would betray how critically

she weighed his words, she didn't want to look at Jim. Instead, she looked down at the rock, rubbing angrily on it with her bare hand.

And cut her hand. "Ow!" she said. "What was that?" She bent and pushed up her goggles. Without that rimy layer obscuring her vision, she could see that the rock was not really gray, it was bicolored—dark, then light, then dark.

The light parts stuck out. "Wait," she said, holding up her hand to stop him from talking. "Look at this."

He got down on his knees in the snow so that his eyes were level with the rock and said, "What?"

"The rock. It's sort of striped in dark and light."

"Uh huh. Looks like thin veins of quartz in the granite. Not so unusual."

"But they're at a different height from the granite."

"Striations. They're a different hardness, so they don't erode at the same rate."

"Climb up there on the sharp rocks and see if the tops have the same kind of markings," she commanded. He stared at her for a moment, then jumped up and ran lightly along the rock shelf and leaned over the outcropping, tearing off his goggles and ski gloves as he went.

"It's the same up here!" he yelled. "Come on. I'll help you up!" In about two seconds they were both running their bare fingers up and down the irregular rocks and straining their eyes, looking for bloodstains.

"Here! And here!" Jim said. Within a few inches of an area with the staining, she could see it—striated rock, the quartz running in slender veins.

"It's all over," Nina said. "Everywhere! All you need to do is look." She thought of Doc Clauson's Coke-bottle glasses behind a pair of tinted goggles. All that magnification hadn't helped. He had missed it.

Jim was waiting for her to say something. He had bitten his lower lip so violently in his excitement, a drop of blood began to form and roll down. Breathing hard herself, she ran her fingers and her eyes over the raised striated areas. They were both kneeling on the rock now, their noses two inches away, like a pair of raccoons at a full garbage can.

"We might have something here," she said soberly, and sat back on her haunches.

"It might make a pattern, maybe?"

"It might make a reasonable doubt." Furrowing her brow, she got down to look again. The raised lines of quartz were still there.

What if what if Alex had hit the striated rock somewhere on his way down? Could it have left a faint pattern on his skin where it hurt him so terribly?

A jury might think so.

In that moment, she allowed the lineaments of the case to shift back in her mind to the most likely truth—that there had been a tragic accident. An accident, nothing more.

They looked at each other.

Nina said, "You need to bring Tony up here—can you take him tomorrow? We need an independent witness with a camera. Ginger! She'll come up too. Maybe she can rig up some sort of simple test. Maybe they can find some blood somewhere up here that the police missed, in addition to the obvious bloodstains. And we might send up a geologist or something before the prelim. I'll have this area cordoned off again."

"Sure. I'll take anybody. I'll do anything. I'll fall down on the rocks myself. Everything has changed, hasn't it? I thought I was in real trouble."

Nina said, "The police—the coroner—should have noticed this."

"Damn right!"

"Maybe it was an accident, just like you said."

"It was! Like I said all along!" His expression had already moved from relief to triumph.

He moved toward her as if he was going to hug her. Nina moved slightly away and he stopped.

"Can you talk to the district attorney and stop all this craziness without me having to have a hearing?" he said, dropping his smile.

"I don't know," Nina said. "I don't even know yet if I want to reveal this before the hearing. We're not obligated to tell anybody about this in advance. It will have a huge impact on the judge. I'll bring him right up here if I have to. We'll put on a defense and get the case dismissed formally. That's it. That's the easiest way—"

She babbled on, thinking out loud, and he hung on every word, until a pang of shame hit her. She could no longer allow her doubts about Jim's innocence to contaminate his defense.

Jim seemed to realize this at the same moment. She thought she read an accusation in his expression.

"I have to get back to the office and make some calls," she said.

"Listen, Nina—"

"We should hurry."

"You thought I did it. I'm sensitive to women. I notice things."

"I hadn't formed an opinion," she answered, weaseling in classic lawyer form.

"You almost let me down. But it's okay. No matter what you were thinking, you stuck with me. You're a loyal person, and that's everything to me. And you came up with these markings very fast. So don't worry about it."

Nina said, "Thanks, Jim." The snow that had melted above her wrists had hardened to an icy bracelet. "Let's go," she said, shivering, grabbing her poles and shaking snow out of her hat before replacing it on her head.

13

COLLIER TURNED ON the hot water and stepped into the shower, his razor and a pair of manicure scissors in one hand. Once he had slammed the door, he remembered his watch. Just in time, right before that arm went under the spray, he took it off, setting it on the top edge of the shower, praying it wouldn't fall off before he was finished. He was beat. He had just had a long jog after a long day at the office and he planned to sack out early.

To get the spray on his head he had to stoop. The bathroom of his apartment had been outfitted for a midget, but the spray fell hot on his shoulders and the tension oozed out of his body like a croc out of the mud. He turned to the guaranteed fogless mirror hanging over the shower wall and began trimming his beard.

The phone rang. It always did. He kept a cordless on the sink. He reached out the door and brought it into the shower, keeping it out of the spray.

"Hallowell."

"You don't know me, Mr. Hallowell."

"Then how did you get my number? Call my office." He was about to punch the button cutting her off when he heard the remote female voice at the other end of the line say, "I'm calling about the Strong case. I understand you're in charge."

"What about it?"

"I know something that might help."

"All right, give me your name and number." He wasn't exactly sitting at his desk, but if it was about Strong, he wanted to hear it.

"I can't do that. I'm sorry."

He turned off the shower and stood there dripping, clipping a few more wild hairs in the shaving mirror, pressing the phone between his shoulder and his ear.

"But I overheard a conversation between Jim Strong and his father. Philip Strong."

"I'm listening."

"This happened only two days before Alex died."

Collier noted the use of the first name. Someone who knew the family. A housekeeper, he thought, or one of the lodge employees?

"Mr. Strong had Jim in his office. He asked why Jim fired the night host—you know, the guy that greets and seats people at the restaurant."

"His name?"

"Gene Malavoy. He doesn't know about this conversation."

"And?"

"So Jim says, he says, I'm the manager at the lodge, so why don't you just let me do my job. Butt out of my business. And Mr. Strong gets all bent out of shape and says, don't forget I'm the managing partner of the resort. Gene's a hit with the customers. He needs the work. Marianne's not gonna like it. And Jim says something like, he's a loser and I want a girl for the job."

"So what did Mr. Strong say to that?"

"Then Mr. Strong says pretty calmly, but you can tell he means it, Jim, listen, I think it would be better if you let Alex take over for a while, the administration side isn't for you. So Jim laughs in a really nasty way and says, 'That's funny, 'cuz I had to give Gene a reason. So I told him Alex got him fired.' "

"Then what?"

"Mr. Strong says, you shouldn't have done that. And Jim says, but I did, and he laughs again. He says, 'It's always Alex. Well, not this time.' "

"And?"

"The phone rang and the door opened and that was it."

"I need to talk to you more about this," Collier said, trying to stay businesslike, hoping not to scare his caller off. "Let me talk to you, just briefly. Fill in a few blanks. How about I meet you at a coffee shop in town?"

"I just had to tell somebody," the girl's voice said. "I wondered if Jim did kill Alex 'cuz Alex was going to take over the lodge again." The line went dead. Collier hung it on the soap rack and returned to his beard.

In five minutes he was done, more or less dry, dressed in his old plaid flannel boxers, and on the phone again dialing Sean's beeper.

He padded into the kitchen and cracked a beer, then lay down on the living room couch. The fireplace still sent out plenty of heat, and he was beginning to feel luxuriously sleepy when the call came.

"Yo," said Sean.

Collier said, "We have a confidential informant in the Strong case, so confidential she wouldn't even give me her name. I need you to find her tomorrow and bring her and another witness in for me to talk to if you can."

"On a Saturday?"

"I'll be there all afternoon. First, a guy named Gene Malavoy. He was working at Paradise Lodge as a host, at least until October twenty-first. Second, a girl, probably works at Paradise, probably under the age of twenty-five, was in the vicinity of Philip Strong's office two days before the Alex Strong killing."

"Now how am I supposed to find the girl?"

"Well, get Gene Malavoy at least. Run with that, but keep it quiet. Don't let Philip or Jim Strong find out what you're doing, at least until I've talked to these people."

"Done."

"Call me as soon as you hit."

"You got it."

Collier hung up, got a pad of paper, wrote down exactly what the caller had said, dated and signed his note, went to the refrigerator and poured himself a celebratory second beer. Could be a break. Could be good.

No one could have been more cavalier than Bob as dance night rolled around. He had decided to go, not with the girl who had called him, of course, but alone, and Taylor Nordholm, his buddy, was supposed to meet him. Nina couldn't get him to tuck his shirt in or to wear his best sneakers. She had gathered from Bob's vague answers that contact would occur, but on an elaborately casual basis.

She still didn't know anything except the girl's name, Nicole. She was "some girl." All Nina could discover was that Nicole was a little older than Bob. When she pressed ever so delicately at the dinner table, he retaliated by bugging her about getting a laptop computer, which set them to bickering and effectively terminated the topic.

However, Nina had continued to think about this watershed event all week. The girl had set a challenge for Bob that he might not be ready to meet. Now that she had called him he wanted to go to the dance because her interest interested him, but because she had embarrassed him with her interest he intended to ignore her. He might never say a word to her all night but Nina bet he wouldn't miss a single move she made.

By Friday, Nina sympathized with the girl. Nicole was in for one of those nights Nina was not too old to recall in which the boys stand against the wall making disagreeable comments and acting obnoxious while the girls wait in vain for an invitation to dance.

"Promise me you'll ask her to dance at least once," she said to Bob, "or dance with her if she asks you."

"Nobody ever dances."

"What do you do at a dance, if you don't dance?"

"Eat. Play some of the games."

"You want her to like you, don't you?"

"She already likes me. She called me."

"But, sweetie. Don't you know that if you don't show that you like her, she might lose interest in you?"

"Fine," said Bob with the blithe brutality of a thirteen-year-old.

"You don't want to hurt her feelings, do you?"

"I won't hurt her feelings. Relax, Mom, okay? Don't get your undies in a twist." Snickering, he went off to dig through the laundry for his favorite, soiled, corduroy pants.

At quarter to eight, they arrived at the school. Bob jumped out of the Bronco, slamming the door before Hitchcock could follow. The gym, a stucco sixties relic like so many California school buildings, looked so decrepit that more snow might cave in the roof, but at least it was brightly lit. With nary a good-bye or a wave, Bob plunged his hands into his pockets and went to join the long line of middle-schoolers snaking toward the doors.

Some of his classmates were very tall, usually females, and some were very short, usually males. Some wore unusual hair colors and some wore clothes as bizarre as costumes. The majority dressed like Bob, in jeans and sweatshirts. A few smoked surreptitiously; a few shoved; a few complained at the shoving.

In the mild cold of the evening the generally under-dressed preteens and teens spewed out excited, rattled chatter that sounded vaguely dangerous to Nina, like neon crackling in a rainstorm. From inside, she heard, over drums and guitar, a cool, sardonic voice singing: "Your ultimate bliss—Will be my terminal kiss."

God, this isn't the way I imagined his first dance, she thought. She wanted to get him, take him home, break his legs and stuff him back into his crib. When she let him out again, she would make him wear an ascot like Prince William and attend only cotillions.

She drove by Collier's apartment. A faint light behind the shades seemed to indicate that he was home, and she pulled into a parking space, letting the faint stirrings of longing have their way. But no one answered the bell.

They were out of milk and laundry detergent. The Raley's was open and wouldn't be crowded. Better to hit the bigger Raley's grocery store by the casinos, because . . . because that made it so much easier to drive right by the Raley's and turn into the Harrah's parking lot because it was so easy to park there.

Although the space actually turned out to be some distance from there, she had her coat after all and her jar of quarters jingled merrily as she opened the glove compartment, which got her to thinking about how intensely mindless playing quarter slots is, you can forget the whole pressure cooker full of kids growing up as fast as weeds and clients in bad fixes and the mortgage payment on the cabin and not incidentally being in love with a prosecutor, and maybe you can sit on a red vinyl stool without working too hard and a bell will ring while it all comes pouring out, quarters and fame and love and beauty and art, and true to the usual pattern of events when she started feeding quarters to her favorite machine inside the hot, crowded, red-carpeted palace of greed she had somehow entered, it responded obediently and excitedly and gave her cherries and bar-bar-bars, so that she became convinced that she was special in this machine's life, she and the machine were soulmates at this exciting moment, so she started feeding in three quarters at a time, upon which a dry spell ensued, in fact it kept landing two sevens on her line with the third seven just above, tantalizingly out of reach of the jackpot, which made her aware that the machine had begun to tease her, and she in turn became stubborn, knowing that it couldn't according to the laws of probability go sixteen rounds without even a cherry payout, but it was doing it, and so she coaxed it and said, "Come on, now," and tried a few experiments, punching the buttons gently and then forcefully, but the machine seemed to have folded its arms and begun sneering, until she ran out of quarters and, inflamed and in the heat of battle, demanded of the change lady several more rolls of coins, and now she had enough ammunition for a titanic battle of wills between her and the machine, she would force it to pay out, the son of a bitch was fixed but she would ride it out, ride it out, ride it out. . . .

Her hand scrabbled in the change bin. She was out

of quarters, and sixty bucks down. The man next to her
gave her a sideways glance and then looked hurriedly
away, and she felt the intense humiliation of the loser
with an empty purse. No one must see that there wasn't
a single quarter left in her change bucket. She picked it
up and, remembering that "slot machines" was an anagram for "cash lost in 'em," ditched the bucket between
a couple of Genie's Treasure slots a few rows away.

As she slunk out, she happened to look over toward
the escalators leading toward the Race and Sports Book
area on the second floor. Mrs. Geiger and another lady
were gliding up toward it, talking animatedly, with the
same bewitched expression on their faces that she had
felt on her own face coming in.

And it was Mrs. Geiger in the waiting room on
Monday morning, her purse in her lap and her bird-
like darting eyes bright with anticipation, when Nina
came in.

"The check came in on Saturday," Sandy explained.
"And you said to let her know right away."

"Great! I'll be right with you, Mrs. Geiger."

She grabbed her messages and went into her office.
Ginger and Tony wanted to talk to her. Jim had called.
So had three other clients, two opposing counsels, and
an insurance adjustor in a pear tree. She resigned herself
to that kind of day.

Sandy escorted Mrs. Geiger in and laid some papers
on the desk along with the insurance company's check
in the amount of two hundred and forty thousand dollars and no cents.

Nina explained the paperwork point by point while
Mrs. Geiger sat and listened, her bright-eyed expression
never changing.

When Nina said, "Do you have any questions?"

She piped up, "I have to pay sixty thousand dollars for my legal fee to you? That's a lot, hon."

"It's right here in the contract between us, if you'll recall. My fee is twenty-five percent of the gross recovery."

"That's a lot. Considering there was no trial."

"It is a lot. But if you had lost your case, which was definitely a possibility, I would have recovered nothing. Partly the fee is a reflection of the fact that I was right there with you taking the risk, Mrs. Geiger."

"Just like on Friday night."

"I beg your pardon?"

"There we were at Harrah's, taking the risk together. I saw you down on the main floor as I was going up. You win anything, hon?"

"Well, I don't think—"

"Me neither. But my sister and I, we had a whale of a time. We won the first race. Too bad about the rest of them." Mrs. Geiger sighed. "Well, all right, hon. You take your fee. And this other eighteen thousand I'm not getting?"

"Medical bills you haven't paid yet, costs of deposition, your doctors' reports, filing fees."

"That's a lot, too."

"It's a good recovery," Nina said. "You seemed quite satisfied with it before."

"Oh, I am, hon. It's enough to buy a little house in my sister's neighborhood and buy some stock. I'll be all right. In a couple years I'll be getting sosh-security and I'll be just fine."

"How's it going with Mr. Geiger?" Nina asked.

"Oh, he hauled his tired old carcass back to Oklahoma, hon."

"I'm sorry to hear that. Really. I hoped it was a temporary problem."

"He was the problem. Skinflint. Didn't know how to have a good time. Thirty-one years sitting in his dad-blamed fishing boat. Bored me silly. My sister and me, we're going to get out there now and raise hell."

"So—I take it you still want a divorce?"

"ASAP. Just point me where to sign."

Nina took some more notes so that she could prepare the petition for dissolution. At length, Mrs. Geiger hopped up to leave. "You take care, now, hon," she said. She folded up her check thoughtfully and stashed it in her wallet. With a wink, she was gone.

Nina got on the phone and sprayed extinguisher on a few minor wildfires while Sandy tapped on the keyboard outside. Due to the new hot-milk whipper Nina had purchased at the Raley's when she finally made it there on Sunday afternoon, the coffee tasted superb. Botelho crooned in the background. The fig in the corner seemed to be enjoying the new fertilizer she was putting on it.

A semblance of calm and control reigned over the office. Mrs. Geiger had her check, and Nina had her own big fee to fatten up the skeletal bank account and pay off some recent heavy bills. Maybe the geologist and Ginger could convince Judge Flaherty at the prelim that Jim shouldn't be bound over for trial. Maybe she would buy one of those Apple G3 laptops like Ginger had. One might almost imagine, at this moment, that practicing law could be satisfying, even enjoyable.

From her office she watched a uniformed cop walk into the outer office. "Mrs. Reilly here?" he asked Sandy.

"What's it about, Vern?" Sandy said.

"A delivery. Papers from Mr. Hallowell. Additional discovery in the Strong case."

"Well, what are you waiting for? Hand it over."

"You have to sign for it, Sandy," he said.

"I know that. Here." A manila envelope passed from hand to hand. Sandy's chair screeched faintly in relief as she left it. There came the sound of jingling from silver bracelets. Her face loomed in the doorway, the envelope flapping in her hand. She brought it to Nina's desk and turned to go.

"And how do you know Vern?" Nina said as she picked it up.

"Vern?"

"The policeman who just came in."

"He's my other next-door neighbor," said Sandy.

Nina tore the envelope open, removed the cover letter, and looked at the interview summary that Collier was providing to her under the Rules of Court requiring that he share his evidence with her.

Somebody named Gene Malavoy. Something about Jim firing him. Something about an argument between Jim and his father.

Something that smelled like more fresh, steaming trouble.

"Tell me about Gene Malavoy, Jim."

"He was a night host at the lodge. We had to let him go."

"Why?"

"I suspected he was doing drugs in the bathroom on his breaks. He's a complete loser. He's a good-looking kid and the customers like him, that's why he lasted as long as he did. What's this about?" She had caught Jim at a busy time at the lodge. He looked impatient, even angry to see her. Sun poured through the windows onto the down- and polyester-filled jackets of the skiers crowding the tables.

"He's given a statement to the D.A.'s office claiming that you fired him wrongfully."

"Figures. To be expected. Look, I'm very busy."

"There's more. Somebody else, a girl named Gina Beloit, told Mr. Hallowell that you and your father had a fight about it, and that your father wanted to replace you with Alex as the lodge manager."

"See? I know Gina. She quit the other day. They're getting their whole backstabbing game together. She said that?"

"She's resisting giving a sworn statement. The phone call is probably inadmissible as hearsay, but I still need to check with you on it."

"Both of them, big losers." He caught her response to that line and he dropped the angry expression. "When am I supposed to have had this argument?"

"Two days before Alex died."

"So what would it mean, if my father did want to replace me?"

"Well, it might be inferred from that that you had a motive to harm Alex."

"But we're going to prove it was an accident!"

"No, Jim," Nina said. "We can't prove that at this point. We do have people working on proving it. I have to check on things like this with you as they come up."

"Well, it never happened," Jim said, his face set. "It's a plot against me by the staff. My father let them get completely out of control, and they don't like my efforts to shape them up. And they want to think I killed my brother. They want me out."

"The summary says that during this alleged conversation Gina heard your father say, 'Marianne won't like it.' In reference to your firing Malavoy."

Jim said, "She's an accomplished liar. Good detail. Because, see, Marianne knows him from somewhere. He's French. She got him the job. Gina would know that."

"Really." Nina made a mental note to confirm that. She had flashed to the Dalbello boots outside Marianne's door in Zephyr Cove—Malavoy's? "His name isn't French," she went on, puzzled.

"Yeah, it is. Gene. Spelled 'Jean.' You know, like 'Zhaungh,'" Jim said. "He tells everybody it's the American spelling, because he's embarrassed at having a girl's name. That reminds me. I forgot to tell you this. Forgot it myself, until now. Gene gave Alex a black eye. I saw it on the mountain, the day he died. Alex said Malavoy jumped him."

"Why would he do that?"

"You've got me. Alex didn't have a clue. He didn't even report it. I mean, I'm the one who fired the kid."

This brought up another point in Gina Beloit's statement. According to that statement, Jim had bragged about telling Gene Malavoy that Alex was the one who had made the decision to fire him. If true, it would explain perfectly why Malavoy would attack Alex the day before his death. It gave Malavoy a grudge against Alex, maybe even a motive to kill him. But would Jim admit he'd done something so malicious? He was denying that there had even been a conversation.

How to approach this?

"Are you positive you're not mistaken? Are you sure there was no conversation about Malavoy with your father?" she asked.

"No! I'm telling you, there wasn't!"

She gave up, but she didn't believe him.

"How long have you been the manager at the lodge?" she asked instead.

"What difference does it make?"

"How long?" Nina said, resisting the pressure to slack off.

"Three months!"

"And what did you do before that?"

"Operations manager outside."

"And Alex was working—where?"

"At the lodge. He'd been doing it for years. We did a switch. I wanted to be in the lodge. He didn't mind."

"Your father must have had a lot of trust in you, to put you into that job."

"Trust? I don't know if that's the word. But I'm trying. Alex was too soft with the staff and I'm handling that problem. And I better get back to it. I'm trying to keep everything together until my father gets back. There's another mess happening too. It's Marianne."

"What about her?"

"It's the stock shares. She's got one third of the company now. She's hinting around at selling out if I'm not nice to her. She knows my father and I can't afford to buy her out right away. She could blow the company wide open. We'd have to go public. It wouldn't be the Strong family operation anymore."

"So be nice to her."

"You don't get it," Jim said. "You don't get what being nice to her means. I'm not going to fuck her for money. Or marry her. She's a cobra."

"I didn't mean that!" Nina said, shocked.

"Oh, let's drop it," Jim said. He was getting more and more agitated.

"Sure. I'm sorry to have interrupted you, but it was important to tell you about this and get your reaction."

"What's happening, huh? I get up this morning thinking, it's all right, I'm gonna be okay, we're getting a geologist and this whole thing will blow by next week in court. Then you show up with your questions. Do you know how hard it is for me to keep going with all this? And nobody to help me? They've all let me down. Alex and Heidi and my father. They don't care about me or the resort."

"Your father cares about both you and the business, I'm sure, Jim," Nina said, trying to calm him down.

"Then where is he? Let me tell you where he is. He's off grieving over Alex while I go to hell. You know why he's not here? He can't stand to look at me!" Jim was shouting. He looked around him, at the shocked face of the cashier nearby.

"Whaddaya think you're looking at?" he demanded, and she looked down nervously. Nina was kicking herself for trying to talk to him at work. He had warned her before to call him at home because he didn't trust his reactions. She ought to know by now that he was impulsive.

"I'm sorry, Jim," she said. "We should have met at my office."

"It's true about my father. He called me and told me to take some time off when he gets back. I think he's going to kick me out of the only thing I've got left."

"I'll talk to him."

"You will? Change his mind?"

"I'll talk to him. Go back to work. Sorry I disturbed you."

"It's okay. Sometimes it feels as though everyone is against me but you—"

"I know."

"I just want things back to normal. I want to do my job and be left alone. It'll be over soon. Right?"

"Good-bye, Jim."

14

Jim Strong's arrest had been reported at great length in the *Tahoe Mirror*. The San Francisco papers and all the suburban dailies had by now picked up the story and resurrected old photographs of Jim and Alex on the slopes together. Nina found one photo, printed in color by the San Jose paper, particularly poignant. It featured all four of them, Alex and Marianne, Jim and Heidi, all smiles, arms around each other, frozen images of health, happiness, and family fealty.

Fortunately, the explosive forensics findings either hadn't found their way into the insatiable maw of the reporting machine, or the papers were taking a cautious course and waiting for the prelim, which would be public and hard news.

Anyway, another story shared billing with Jim's case in Tahoe that fall—the weather report. Not since the ghastly winter of 1846, when the snows began in October and continued until April, had so much snow been predicted in the Sierra. Every night, the people in town turned on their TVs to watch the weather lady cheerfully predict another wave of storms.

All day trucks lumbered along the streets with loads of wood, propane, and extra supplies for the grocery stores. Matt had all his tow trucks, now comprising a small fleet, tuned up and ready to go, with extra drivers ready on call. The bears were rumored to be coming into town at night to forage, and the ski resorts were pausing in their money-counting to wonder if they were in for too much of a good thing, and the traffic would come to a screeching halt, buried under the weight of all that snow.

A quiet frenzy of preparation gripped everyone, including Nina and Bob. They had stacked several cords of wood under the porch now, all they could stuff under there. The dial on the propane tank along the side of the house registered full.

The question was not if there would be a power outage, but when. The frontier culture had always underlain the modern town, and the locals returned to it almost gladly.

The town had become so beautiful in this new season, not dirty around the edges as it would be in the spring, but glorious and fresh, like an extended Christmas. Or was it being in love that gave her this buoyant energy, that made the world glorious and let her carry her loads lightly?

Collier came over for dinner every couple of nights. She fixed something simple like spaghetti and the three of them sacked out in front of the fireplace on the rug and played board games. Collier taught Bob to play pinochle and Bob soon beat him.

The Monopoly game was dusted off and, like a Rorschach blot, brought out their core personalities—Bob, headstrong and erratic, buying indiscriminately and sometimes having to sell for ready cash; Collier, the slow and steady empire builder, cautious and implacable; and Nina, propertyless except for the hotels on Park Place and Broadway that she always managed to erect, all her hopes resting on the red plastic traps on the board that sometimes caught the other two.

Nina thought—hoped, prayed—that they liked each other. Bob was struggling with it, she could see that, and she felt the familiar guilt at putting him through another change.

And on those same evenings, after Bob had gone to bed, at first they would go out for an hour, drive to the top of Ski Run Boulevard or Kingsbury Grade, and park the car like teenagers. But that was intolerable, cold and uncomfortable, and what if a cop on patrol shined in his flashlight and rousted them?

So they started driving straight to Collier's and took their single hour on his bed with its black sheets and gray comforter. Then Nina would jump up and throw on her coat and drive the four miles home along Pioneer Trail alone, in complete disarray, worrying about leaving Bob alone at night, worrying about hitting a tree on the lonely icy road and having to go to the hospital with no underwear on, worrying about the files waiting for her attention on her own bed, worrying because it was all getting too complicated too fast.

But not worrying enough to slow down. They were riding a tsunami. Nothing could slow them down.

At the office, the Strong case ate up more and more of her time as the prelim approached, and yet she coasted through the difficult juggling act required to keep her caseload balanced. The fee from Mrs. Geiger's case stabilized her wildly swinging finances, and Jim had also paid his monthly bill.

The question at the preliminary hearing would be whether there was enough evidence to hold Jim for trial, and Collier didn't have to show much. He would meet his burden of going forward using Doc Clauson and the fiber findings even without Heidi's statement, unless she put on a defense that offered a compelling innocent explanation.

She thought she could do that. She had Tony Ramirez, and Ginger, and a geologist named Tim Seisz from the University of Nevada all getting ready to testify. Tim had already called to tell her he thought the patterns on the skin in the autopsy photos were as likely to be natural as man-made.

She wanted a dismissal badly. She wasn't sure, but she thought she might be able to pull it off. She knew from experience how Collier would put on his case. He would build it fact by fact, just like he played Monopoly, until he had staked a claim to just about the whole board. But he wouldn't have the big blue properties, those would be hers, and she would try to take him there, to where her big hotels waited to bankrupt him.

She repeated the names of her hotels to herself. Gene Malavoy. Marianne Strong.

She would have made a lousy prosecutor, but she was perfectly suited for the defense attorney's role of spoiler.

She thought these thoughts during the day, but her mind kept sliding away from the fact that she and Collier were in a critically important competition—surrealistic, as though Mike Tyson and Evander Holyfield had been secret lovers who fought for the championship and then went home to each other. Would Tyson have given Holyfield a little squeeze and said, sorry about the earlobe, baby; you know it's all part of the game?

Collier was acting as a co-counsel with Barbara Banning on a robbery and assault case at the moment, and Nina would glimpse him coming and going in the courthouse hall, or see him talking in a knot of people on the pathway to his office. Always, their eyes met, and she would see in those eyes his swift, violent embrace.

Twice, she had to talk to him on the phone. She pretended—he pretended—they stayed within their roles, models of professionalism. But when she hung up she would pace around the office like a dingo in heat, the timbre of his voice bringing her right back to his bed in her thoughts. How should she treat him at the prelim?

About ten days after Jim's arrest, on Friday night, Nina left work early. At the house, they had a quick dinner. She packed herself and Bob into coats and mittens.

"Where are we going?" Bob asked as they started up the road to Paradise.

"Ever heard of the Festival of Lights?" asked Nina, who had not, until she met Marianne. She wanted to do something with Bob before he left, but as usual she had more than one purpose. She wanted to have another look at Marianne, maybe catch her off guard. Marianne had told Tony she didn't want to talk to him.

"The Festival of Lights? Uh uh."

"It's a snowboard exhibition," said Nina.

"All right! Like the one at Sierra-at-Tahoe?"

"Um. I don't know. What do they do there?"

"It's in March. The G-Shock North American Championships. It's part of a three-event tour that starts in Colorado next month."

"And how do you know that?"

"Taylor. He's getting a snowboard for Christmas. He's gonna let me borrow it. Unless I get really lucky and Santa brings me one." He gave Nina a hopeful look.

"I think this is more like . . . a fun local event than

a competition." She pulled out a brochure she had picked up at the grocery store and handed it to him.

Bob sat back against the seat to read it, twisting his muffler. Flipping it over he read out loud, " 'Featuring multiple disciplines, including big-air, snowboard cross, and half-pipe.' "

"They're doing all that tonight?"

"It says so right here!"

"So what is a half-pipe?"

"You have this machine called a Pipe Dragon that chisels out a U-shaped launching pad. It really cuts. People can make a lot of money riding, y'know," Bob said, studying the pictures.

"Oh?" said Nina. "How is that?"

"They give out prizes. Over three hundred thousand dollars for all the events at the G-Shock. Taylor wants to go professional. We're gonna learn switchstance frontside three sixty's. By the end of this winter, we'll be whompin'."

"Is that so "

The parking lot brimmed with cars. They parked at the far end and used flashlights to guide the way until the lighting picked up as they approached the lodge.

"Oh, this is great," Nina said. Soft yellow bulbs looped in tree limbs shimmered like candles. On both sides of a slope near the lodge, grandstands had been set up. White spotlights lit a ramp on one side. Already, people dressed as colorfully as tropical birds swooped and spilled down the slope.

Up high in the bleachers, they found a good vantage point. Piped-in music began playing, the slopes cleared, and a woman announcer sputtered through the loudspeakers, announcing names and events.

First, a series of young men did stunts off the ramp,

which resembled the kind pro ski jumpers used. However, there were no tight tucks and long graceful rides for these guys. According to Bob, who talked continually in his excitement, they landed fakie, took hits, and rode goofy foot, in addition to fly swatting, getting good air and patting the dog, which involved stooping down to touch the ground with one hand. One spectacular fall rated a terse whistle from Bob and an epitaph. "He spanked off too soon. Ooh. Egg beater time."

Marianne showed up in the second group, and it was clear that these people were far more experienced than the preceding performers. There were no more egg beaters churning up snow in this bunch. Even Bob held his tongue to behold the stars of the snow.

Marianne went last, taking three runs, each one individual, each one more death-defying than the last. Her body shot the board through the half-pipe, and in a tightly choreographed series featuring controlled acts of wizardry, she danced like a fairy just slightly above the snow, all the way down the hill. After the final run, she kicked up powder just inches shy of the grandstands, gave a wave, and shot off into the night, while the crowd cheered wildly, standing to give her the biggest applause of the evening.

"What an athlete," said Nina, standing and stretching, thinking she was such a powerful young woman, agile, fast . . .

"Bob, stay here for a minute." She climbed down the bleachers and set off through the snow to the crowd of people who had gathered around Marianne. But the crowd was already dissipating, and Marianne had slipped away. The announcer was saying good night and the people in the stands were beginning the long hike back to the parking lot.

Then Nina saw her arguing with someone in the darkness under the farthest grandstand, still holding her helmet, feet apart, her free hand making swift downward stabs in the air. Who was with her? She let a chattering group sweep her close and then stopped at the other end. It was freezing and dark under there, slats of light shining through the gaps in the seats.

"Tais-toi!" They were speaking French, practically shouting, which didn't matter as no one else was around. Nina lurked behind them, trying to remember her high school French in the torrent of words. Marianne's companion was so tall he was stooping a little. Nina could see the outline of a long angular face, long hair. In spite of his size he sounded like a teenager.

She heard the word "Jim." She could only pick up a word here and there. The young man was accusing Marianne of something having to do with Jim and kept saying, "It's mine, too! For when we go back to France!"

Suddenly Marianne put her hands up on his chest and pushed him, actually knocking him backward a step or two. "Shut up!" she said again, switching to English. "You're only here because of me! Look at the trouble you've caused! You're drunk right now! Don't lie about it, I know! Why should I go back with you? Go into business with you? Hah! Listen, I'm in charge now!"

For a moment the boy just stood where he'd been pushed.

"No, Jean—look, I'm sorry," Marianne said, putting her arms up. His head jutted forward on his neck, and although Nina couldn't see his face, she read blind rage in the way his fists came up.

"No!" Marianne cried. He jumped at her and started pummeling her, socking her in the body like a little kid might go at his mother. She was so small compared to him that his body blocked all view of her.

Nina started to run forward, but then the boy emitted a sharp cry and jumped away, clutching his arm.

"You cut me!" he yelped.

Marianne slipped something into her pocket. Nina hung back again, hardly breathing. While the boy took off his parka and examined his arm, Marianne calmly began dusting herself off.

"Let me see that," she said. "Idiot." She took his arm and their voices lowered to a murmur and switched back to French. His voice had taken on a whimpering tone, while Marianne's tone had become soothing.

The show was over. Nina edged away and went looking for Bob.

The boy was Gene Malavoy, she was sure of that. He wanted to "go into business" with Marianne, but he seemed a lot closer to Marianne than a prospective business partner.

Tony could find out more. Nina waved at Bob and walked toward the lights. For some reason, she was smiling, shaking her head.

It was Marianne, the way she had treated the boy. She was definitely the boss. Like Mrs. Geiger, she was as tough as rawhide when it came to defending herself.

Nina's moment of amusement faded away. They were violent, impulsive, dangerous people, both of them, and they had powerful reasons for wanting control of Alex's shares in the resort.

"Let's go," she told Bob. She put her arm around him and they walked past the groups of laughing, carefree people toward the Bronco.

———

Sandy came in late on Monday with a self-satisfied look on her face, carrying a paper bag with a lot of envelopes in it. Clearly, something good had happened.

"So what's new?" Nina said. She was in the conference room, pouring freshly foamed milk into the soup bowl she called a coffee cup, getting buzzed for a deposition in a medical malpractice case that was scheduled for nine A.M. Her mind wasn't on it. She was still mulling over the significance of the argument she had overheard at the Festival of Lights. She had already called Tony.

Sandy continued the ritual of putting away her coat, pulling out her chair with the lumbar pillow just so, and descending as slowly as a bathysphere into it.

"I've been wondering about Joseph," said Nina.

"Were you now?"

"You said you used to live with him." These promptings had yielded no information in the past, but today Sandy seemed ready to talk.

"I was married to him. For fifteen years."

"Is—he—Wish's father?"

"Yep."

"What happened?"

"Irreconcilable differences," said Sandy. There was something wickedly satirical about Sandy's use of this vague legal phrase used as the grounds for almost all divorces in California. It was her way of answering, none of your business.

"So you're moving in together?"

"Uh huh." Sandy turned on the computer. "You checked the answering machine yet?" she said, keeping her eyes on the blue screen with its smiling apple.

"Sure did. So how's it going? Your relationship?"

"The depo still on?"

"Yes, the depo's on."

"Because I put the file on your desk."

"That's fine. What about Joseph?"

"What about him?"

"My question exactly."

Now the CD player went on. A few tentative guitar chords, the Rio audience yelling, *"Mas forte!"* Louder! Botelho went into his first samba number for the ten-thousandth time, and then . . .

"Ah," Sandy said. She began to sing along with the music. "Love takes its rhythm from the sea, seeking and leaving eternally." Her voice sounded like fingernails on a chalkboard, but Nina appreciated the sentiment.

"It's love, huh?"

"It better be. Since we were moving back in together, we decided we might as well get married next week. Again."

"Well! Congratulations!" Nina said when she had found her tongue.

Sandy reached in the bag and handed her one of the envelopes. "You can come if you want," she said. Inside, a white card announced the wedding of Sandy and Joseph at a home near Markleeville on Thanksgiving Day. It was such a plain little card, plain and simple and really quite dignified, like Sandy.

Nina felt herself getting all choked up. Sandy was getting married—to Wish's father—it was all so romantic . . .

"Look, I'm not gonna quit," Sandy said. "So get hold of yourself."

"Well, that's great. Great news. I'd love to come. Oh, shoot. Bob will be in Germany."

"Bring along the boyfriend if you want."

"Can I help with anything? You know, the arrangements?"

"Just show up."

"I really wish you—and Joseph—all the best, Sandy."

"He's a good old man. He'll do me fine. Now we better get to work."

Only when the day was over, and Sandy was turning off the lights as they headed out into yet another snow fall, did Nina think to ask, "Why did you decide to get married on Thanksgiving, Sandy?"

"We thought it would be about right. It's a big Native American holiday, after all," Sandy said.

"Hmm . . . I never thought about Thanksgiving that way."

"Oh, yeah. It marks a very special day in Native American history. Remember, the Pilgrims were starving, so the Indians gave them seed and taught them how to plant. So at harvest time the Pilgrims had plenty of food and survived the winter."

"I remember. From fourth grade."

"Yeah. The Indians still talk about the day of the big feast. We even have our own name for it. We call it the Hey You Guys Day."

"I never knew that."

"Mmm-hmm . . . The Indians came, bearing gifts, and they sat down with the Puritans and everybody ate plenty of corn and turkey, and after dinner the Puritan governor belched and took another pull on the peace pipe and turned to Chief Massasoit and said—" Sandy paused.

"What? He thanked them? What?"

"He said, 'Hey you guys, you can get started clearing the table now.' "

15

"I did a thorough examination the first time around. Went to the site, performed the autopsy, spoke with the defendant about what happened. Looked like an accident to me."

Doc Clauson's testimony so far had more holes in it than a Moscow theater curtain. He had shown up at the courthouse visibly nervous in his trademark red bow tie and Nina had caught him smoking in the sun outside the courthouse. Collier was questioning him right now, trying to explain away that first report that called Alex's death an accident.

To the left of the witness box, Judge Flaherty took notes, pinched his pouchy cheeks thoughtfully, and stared out into space, communing with the spirits. He would decide in the next day or two if the charges against Jim would stand.

"And then what happened?" In his navy jacket and gray pants, Collier had the look and resolute attitude of a military man on a mission, like a true officer of the court. He had come in early like Nina and set up his files, stopping only to say Hi with utter impersonality, never letting so much as a change in the rhythm of his breathing indicate that he felt any different about her than any other defense attorney.

Due to the sunny weather, the conviction that she had a defense, or the dreamless sleep of the night before, Nina felt less nervous than usual herself. She felt more like predator than prey, reckless, almost high spirited.

"I received additional information," Clauson was answering.

"Go on."

"A statement by the defendant's wife."

Jim, sitting beside Nina, nudged her. She nudged back, saying, "Objection," at the same time. "The contents of any such statement are hearsay and inadmissible."

"I haven't asked him the contents yet, Judge," Collier protested.

"You will," Nina said.

"As a matter of fact, I *would* like to put the statement in evidence, Judge, so we might as well argue it," Collier went on. He handed Nina and the judge's clerk copies of Heidi Strong's statement.

"If the Court reads the statement, since the Court is deciding the facts without a jury, the damage is done," Nina said. "The information has entered the judicial, uh, sphere. Therefore, I request that the Court decide the defense's objection without reading the statement."

"Now how can I do that, counsel?" Judge Flaherty said.

"I will stipulate that a statement was made to the South Lake Tahoe police on or about October 24th, that the statement was made by Heidi Strong, and that it deals with an alleged conversation between Heidi Strong and her husband, the defendant herein. Under the rules of evidence, Your Honor, Doc Clauson can't testify about her statements. It's hearsay."

"As to the hearsay argument, Judge, this statement

can still come in because of the exception which applies
if the witness is unavailable." Collier handed out more
paperwork. "This is a declaration prepared by the investigator assigned to work with me on the Strong matter,
Sean Voorhies, indicating that the witness appears to
have fled the jurisdiction. Basically, she has disappeared."

Nina read it quickly. Heidi Strong had provided a
confidential address on the North Shore to the district
attorney, to be kept confidential, but she had left that
address and could not be located.

"The witness seems to have absconded, Ms. Reilly.
Under the circumstances, this statement is all we have
and it can come in, I would think," said Judge Flaherty.

"I would like to question the investigator about
whether all efforts have really been made to find Mrs.
Strong," Nina said.

"Oh, this isn't a full-fledged trial, counsel," Judge
Flaherty said, frowning. "The investigator's statement
will do."

"Very well. But there's another very clear ground for
objection. Because the person giving the statement is
married to the defendant, the spousal communications
privilege is applicable. The conversation cannot be admitted under Evidence Code section 980."

"Mr. Hallowell, will you stipulate that the parties
were married at the time of the conversation alluded to
in this statement?" said the judge. He still had not
looked down at Heidi's statement.

"I have no information to the contrary," Collier
said. "But as the Court knows, the strict rules of evidence don't apply in a preliminary hearing—"

"But this is precisely the kind of situation where

they should be applied in the Court's discretion, Your Honor—" interrupted Nina.

"The statement makes a strong showing of malice of the defendant toward—" Collier threw in.

"Objection! Objection! He's leaking the contents! This is a blatant attempt to prejudice the Court!" Nina shouted. "I request sanctions be applied to Mr. Hallowell for pulling that trick! He knows he's got no chance of getting this statement in at a trial. We can't cross-examine this lady, Your Honor. How can the Court judge her credibility—"

"Pipe down, Ms. Reilly," said the judge. "Both of you, let me think for a minute." He shuffled the two sheets of Heidi's statement in his hands as though he had a great blackjack hand, playing with it, and Nina thought, he really wants to read it and if he does, Jim will definitely be bound over. But she knew Flaherty to be scrupulously fair, and he wouldn't like the way Collier had deliberately brought in the malice bit.

"Here's the thing," Flaherty finally said. "It sounds like section 980 is going to knock this statement out at trial, so why should I make a decision regarding the necessity of a trial based on it? It's one thing to relax the rules of evidence, Mr. Hallowell. It's another to relax them into nonexistence. Call it my great respect for marriage. Now you continue questioning the witness and keep away from the contents of the statement."

"Very well, Your Honor," Collier said. Nina totted up the score mentally. Statement not read, a goal for Jim. Judge knows Jim told Heidi something that indicated malice toward Alex, goal for the prosecution. Score: one to one.

She glanced toward the chair beside her. Jim was looking pleased. He didn't quite realize it was only a tie.

Doc Clauson had been forgotten during this exchange. Now Collier turned back to him and Nina saw him tense.

"When did you receive this statement by Heidi Strong?" Collier asked him.

"Three days after the death of Alex Strong. The body had already been released and cremated."

"And after receiving a copy of this statement, what did you do, if anything, in response to the information contained therein?" Flaherty's ruling necessitated the klutzy form of this question.

"I reopened the investigation. Now, how can I give my reasons for reopening if I can't talk about this statement?" Clauson asked the judge, folding his bony arms in their short sleeves.

"I'm afraid you'll have to restrain yourself, Doc," said the judge.

"It's not right," Clauson said.

Collier coughed, shifting attention back to him. "What new investigation did you perform?" he asked.

Clauson unbent his arms. Nina could almost hear the creaking of the bones as they repositioned. He was getting old, fragile even, she realized to her surprise. She remembered her first case against him—how frightening it all had been, including him. Now, she saw through the thin skin to his vulnerabilities.

"First," Clauson replied, "I went over the autopsy photos, my notes, and my report again. Got interested in the photos that showed some patterning on the epidermis above the mid-torso area that I had originally attributed to the fall."

He pulled out a group of photographs, which Nina had already received but which Flaherty would be seeing for the first time. Collier had them marked, and Flaherty studied them intently.

"We have some blowups," Clauson said. He nodded and a uniformed policeman began projecting slides on the screen in the corner of the courtroom. Several views of the faint striped pattern on skin appeared.

"I looked at these again, and I knew we might have a problem," Clauson said. "Didn't look natural to me. So I examined the clothes again." This time, the courtroom was treated to a gory frontal view of Alex Strong, naked except for the black shirt.

Nina glanced over at her client, who sat quietly with his hands folded, studying the photographs, just following the action, seeming unmoved, or else keeping any emotional response to the photographs private.

"Clothing was all wrong," Clauson said. "Injuries to internal organs, but some tearing and damage to the front of the shirt worn against the skin. Since the back of the parka was all torn up from the fall, and even the back of the bibs which covered that area ripped pretty good—" He showed pictures of the bibs and parka. "How come, I ask myself, the fronts of the parka and bibs weren't torn up? So I looked again at the patterns and I started thinking about what weapon might cause such patterning."

"And did you find such a weapon?"

"Yup. Delivers foot-pounds with sufficient pressure to crush and tear the liver in half, common object worn while skiing—" He paused for dramatic effect, then said—"person in ski boots."

"Did you subsequently test any ski boots to determine if there might be similar patterning found?"

"We got the defendant's ski boots, the ones he was

wearing the day of the incident. Tecnica Explosion 10s. Checked 'em out. Have a look, Judge."

A blowup of the soles of Jim's Tecnicas. Short striped patterns.

"We have the boots, already marked," Collier said, and handed them over.

"Seen these?" said the judge to Nina.

"Yes."

The clerk handed up the dirty boots one by one, wrapped in plastic, and Flaherty turned one of them over and studied the sole.

"Didn't trust myself, so I brought in a guy from the forensics lab in Sac for a second examination and report," Clauson continued. Nina objected without success, and he passed along that report to the judge.

Flaherty read the damning conclusion that the patterns matched.

"Anybody can see it," Clauson said, pointing to the screen.

Jim's emotions could no longer be contained. He squirmed in his chair, whispering, "Do something!"

"Objection. Nonresponsive. Move to strike that last sentence," Nina said.

"Overruled." Flaherty never lifted his head. He was rereading the report.

Having made his point about the patterning, Collier started in on the black fibers found on the soles. They, too, had been double-checked in Sacramento. An evidence bag containing the fibers was introduced. Collier led him smoothly through the scientific testimony.

"A perfect match to the shirt," Clauson concluded.

The lunch hour had arrived, and with it Clauson's big moment. Collier read his question from his notes, which, legalese aside, was: Based on your experience, based on the autopsy findings, based on the fibers, the skin markings, the state of the clothing, what was the amended finding of the Office of the Coroner?

"Homicide," Clauson said. "Turned over to the police for further investigation."

"Hello, Doctor Clauson," said Nina after lunch. She used the formal address intentionally. He preferred "Doc" because it entrenched him firmly in the old-boy network here. She did not want to propagate the impression that his authority should have a lick more import than the testimony Ginger was going to give.

Her mood hadn't changed. She felt ruthless, like a lioness stalking almost invisibly in the shadowy bush, eyes locked on a pale wildebeest in a red bow tie.

"Hello." The wildebeest gave her a testy hand wave.

"Your testimony is that you made a major mistake the first time around as to cause of death?"

"Understandable. As I've been trying to explain—"

"You originally thought it was an accident?"

"Correct. But—"

"You had the autopsy photos and the clothing the first time around?"

"Yes."

"You found nothing suspicious about the photos or clothing the first time around, did you?"

"Further evidence came to my attention. Mrs. Strong's statement—"

"Did you ever talk to Mrs. Strong?"

"No. She didn't want to talk to anybody."

"So anybody can write down anything and you'll jump up and change your findings and call it a homicide?"

"Objection. Argumentative."

"Sustained. No need for posturing, Mrs. Reilly. There's no jury present."

The judge did not like her hardass pose. Fine, she would relax her shoulders ever so slightly. "Now, I'm going to show you some blowups of some patterns, sir, and ask you which if any of the patterns also seem to you to match the marks on Alex Strong's skin."

That drew a storm of argument from Collier which went on for almost fifteen minutes. In the end, Judge Flaherty's curiosity got the best of him and he ordered Clauson to go ahead.

"But I can't see the blowups well," Clauson said.

"Here," Nina said, handing him five eight by tens. "You can see these, can't you?"

"Certainly." He muttered to himself as he looked at the pictures which had been shot with rulers included for scale, in the same sharply contrasting black and white as the skin photos.

"You want some sort of preliminary opinion?" he said.

"That's right," Nina said.

"They all look like the bottoms of ski boots. They all could match the photos of the skin markings."

"Thank you," Nina said. "Now please turn the first four pictures over, sir, and read to us what they represent. I will represent to the Court that our forensics expert, Ginger Hirabayashi, took these photos and identified them and is available today to testify to that effect if the court deems it necessary."

"Okay, then, turn the first four over, Doc," said the judge.

Clauson turned them over one by one and read, "Dalbello ski boots, men's size eleven. Lange ski boots, men's size nine and a half. Nordica ski boots, women's size eleven. Dolomite VXR ski boots, size ten." He looked up. "I'd have to look at these photos in the lab, with better equipment, and I'd want a better look."

"But isn't it true that you first thought the markings were natural, and now find that they might match almost anybody's ski boots?" Nina asked, and Collier objected, and off they careened into more argument. Finally Flaherty told them he'd heard enough and that he would take the demonstration for what it was worth.

Nina said then, "I guess we ought to turn the last photo over, then, Your Honor, before I move on. Which, the Court will recall, also seems to the coroner to be similar to the skin markings."

"Preliminarily," Clauson added.

"Preliminarily." Flaherty nodded, and Clauson turned over the last picture. "Quartz mixed with granite, taken from rubbings of rocks at location of body," he read. "What's that supposed to mean?"

"The rocks where Alex Strong landed," Nina explained to the judge, not bothering with Clauson anymore.

"What's she talking about?" Clauson said, looking toward Collier. Flaherty wasn't having any trouble understanding it.

Nina turned to Collier too. If he wanted more argument, she was ready.

Collier's mouth moved, and she was sure he was saying, "Same old shit," to her. Offended, she turned to the judge.

Collier was already talking. "I have to renew my objection. This demonstration is completely worthless. I could have balled up my dirty sock in a picture in just such a way that it would look similar. Similar, Your Honor. Not the same. Request permission to bring Doc Clauson back tomorrow after he's had a real chance to compare these pictures in a scientific setting."

"No problem, Your Honor," Nina said. "We have already conducted our own review in a scientific setting, and will have our own expert witness ready to testify that the fifth picture, of quartz in granite, was taken personally by her at the site of Alex Strong's death, and that it is just as likely to produce a pattern similar to that in the autopsy photo."

"All right," Judge Flaherty said. "Are you finished with your cross-examination of this witness for today?"

"Not quite," Nina said. "I have a second demonstration for the Court." She went to the brown Raley's grocery bag on her counsel table, ignoring the disguised groan from the other table.

"I'm not doing any more courtroom comparisons," Clauson said hurriedly from the witness stand.

"Absolutely not, Your Honor," Collier said. "Absolutely not! Anything else she wants compared, he'll take it back to the lab and compare it. That's it! No way."

"That might save time, so I have no objection," Nina said. She removed five labeled plastic Baggies which contained swatches of black material. Clauson saw them and mouthed the word "fibers" to Collier.

"That's right," Nina said. "Fibers. I wouldn't want to surprise you or anything, Doctor, since you don't seem to like surprises. For the record, these are swatches of black cotton material taken from, let's see: Exhibit twelve a: black cotton socks, men's, Miller's Outpost; twelve b, black cotton T-shirt from Macy's in Sacramento; twelve c, black cotton purse lining from Cecil's

Market, Stateline; twelve d, black cotton socks found in Alex Strong's sock drawer, dirty socks as referred to earlier.

"And last but not least, twelve e, black cotton boxer shorts belonging to Philip Strong. I'd like you to compare them to the cotton fibers found in the grooves of the Tecnicas as per your report."

"Very funny, Judge," Collier said. He had evidently decided to go further. Now he didn't want Clauson touching Nina's samples in the lab, either. "I'm not about to turn the State's crime lab into a tool of the defense. She can get her own experts and put on her defense and the defendant can pay for all the fishing he can afford, but we're not going to do it. The photos, okay, we'll have a look at them. But chemical analyses—no."

"I have to agree with that," Flaherty said. "I see no reason for such forensics work to be carried out while the prosecution is presenting its case. However, Mr. Hallowell, Ms. Reilly has stated that she intends to present her own set of results at the time she puts on a defense. It might indeed save time for you to take the swatches and have a look at them now, to avoid a motion to continue the prelim when we get to the defense case."

"But there isn't time!" Collier said.

"I will take the lack of due notice into account, I assure you," Flaherty said. "Now. Doc, you may step down and I direct you to return for further testimony at nine A.M. tomorrow morning. We'll take a ten-minute recess, and then you can call the next witness, Mr. Hallowell."

Doc Clauson stuffed the swatches and photos into his

briefcase and stood down. As he walked past Nina he
gave her a hunted look, and she gave him the yellow
lioness eye. He was going to work all night, and she was
glad, because he had done enough harm and he never
would again.

16

"CALL GINA BELOIT." A long day was about to get longer, as a wholesome-looking young woman with short blond hair that looked a little like Heidi Strong's was called into the courtroom and marched to the witness stand.

"State your full name for the record," Collier said.

"Gina May Beloit." A soprano voice. "I got a subpoena and I'm here under duress."

"That does say it all, Judge," Collier said. "Request the witness be considered a hostile witness under Evidence Code section 776."

"So stipulated," Nina said. Collier could now lead the witness, impeach her, and generally have more latitude in his questioning.

"Where do you work, Miss Beloit?"

"I'm unemployed. Until a week ago I worked at Paradise Ski Resort. The lodge."

"What were your duties there?"

"I was the day hostess. I led customers to their tables, took reservations, made sure they had their menus. Sometimes I took their orders, served food, poured water, cleaned off the tables, that sort of thing. I had to quit due to my boss, Mr. Jim Strong."

"Little bitch," Jim whispered to Nina at the counsel table.

"Move to strike that last phrase," Nina said. "Nonresponsive."

"Overruled."

"During what period of time did you know the defendant?"

"About three months."

"And during this time did you overhear a conversation occurring regarding the employment status of Gene Malavoy, the night host?"

"Yes."

"And what were the circumstances of your overhearing this conversation?"

"I eavesdropped," said the girl defiantly. "The coat room was right next to the office, and I could hear them from in there."

"Who did you hear?"

"Mr. Strong senior—Philip Strong, and Jim Strong."

"Anybody else?"

"No."

"And how did you know whose voices you were hearing?"

"I've talked to Philip several times. I also knew his office adjoined the place I was standing. And Jim Strong was my boss. I knew his voice very well."

"What did you hear?"

"Well, it was about Gene. Jim had told him he was fired. Mr. Strong wanted Jim to back off, but Jim was stubborn. He said Gene was a loser and he wanted a girl. Mr. Strong didn't like that, and Jim just told him to butt out, that he was the manager of the lodge and . . ." The girl went through the conversation, bit by bit, that had been covered in the interview summary in Nina's possession.

"What else was said in this conversation?" Collier asked finally.

"That was about it. Then they were interrupted and that was it for the conversation."

Collier paused for effect. Then asked, "And when did you say these events took place?"

"I didn't. Between one-thirty and two o'clock on October twenty-first, two days before Alex died."

"Cross-examine," said Collier. He sat down.

"Hello, Miss Beloit," Nina said, giving the girl a hard stare.

"Hello."

"You say you quit because of Jim Strong, the man sitting beside me?"

"Uh huh."

"In what specific way did Mr Strong cause you to quit?"

"He made my job miserable. He was continually in the restaurant, watching every move any of the employees made. He shouted at me and called me incompetent. I don't have to put up with that. The money wasn't worth it."

"So you didn't like the way Jim supervised you or the other employees?"

"To say the least."

"And how does that make you feel about Jim Strong here?"

"It seemed like a good job at first. I thought I had the whole winter planned out, but I couldn't stay with him as my boss."

.

"How did that make you feel about Mr. Strong?" Nina said again.

"Upset, of course."

"Angry?"

"I suppose."

"Oh, come on. You're furious at him, aren't you?"

"I wouldn't send him a valentine."

"You'd like to see him suffer like you've suffered, am I right?"

Miss Beloit actually seemed to think that one over. She was a forthright girl, and Nina thought for a moment she would agree, but she thought better of it. "No," she said. "I'm not vindictive like you're trying to make out."

"Isn't it true that you were so angry that when you heard that Jim had been charged with a crime involving his brother, you called Mr. Hallowell here and told him a lot of lies about this whole incident?"

"No."

"You wouldn't even tell him your name, would you?"

"I didn't want to end up testifying like this, but I thought he ought to know—"

"You didn't dare say under penalty of perjury the things you told him?"

"I thought the information might help him understand why Jim would want to kill Alex."

Flaherty lifted his head at this and gave the witness a keen look. Her statement unfortunately cut through all the legal smoke Nina had been blowing. Trying again, Nina said, "Move that the witness's response be stricken as nonresponsive and speculative, Your Honor."

"She has a right to explain why she called me," Collier said.

"I'll allow it," said Flaherty.

Nina decided she'd better meet the statement head-on. "All right," she said. "You say that Mr. Strong suggested to Jim that he might be replaced by Alex at the lodge?"

"It was stronger than that, like Mr. Strong had made up his mind."

"Both men were angry? Saying things they hadn't really had time to think about?"

"Mr. Strong kept his temper the whole time. He was very calm, considering."

"Did Jim say anything like, this job is so important to me I'll kill anyone you try to replace me with?"

"No. I told you what was said."

"Did Jim threaten Alex at any time in this conversation?"

"I thought his tone was rather threatening."

"But all he said was, 'It's always Alex . . . well, not this time'? That was the sum total of his reaction?"

"Yes."

Nina turned to the judge. "Your Honor, I'm going to move that all testimony of this witness be stricken. There's not a shred of evidence that goes to any element of the case, just a lot of prejudicial fluff by a disgruntled employee. All the testimony is incompetent, irrelevant, and immaterial."

"Mr. Hallowell?" said the judge.

"It goes to intent, Judge. Malice. The testimony is that the defendant had a reason to commit a murder. Jim Strong was going to remove the man who would take his place as manager."

"That's not the testimony," Nina said. "The testimony is that in the course of an argument about something else, Philip Strong essentially said something critical of the way the defendant had handled a business matter. In all fairness, this conversation between Philip Strong and the defendant does not have any probative value as to motive. It should be stricken."

"Well," Flaherty said, "I'm not going to strike the testimony. I suppose it could be said to have relevance to the issue of criminal intent. Your argument goes to how much weight should be accorded the testimony, Mrs. Reilly. I have to say, I'm not too impressed with this testimony but I will weigh it along with the rest of the testimony at the conclusion of this hearing. Any more cross-examination?"

"No, Your Honor."

"Any redirect?"

"No, Judge."

"The witness may step down."

On her way past Jim, Miss Beloit moved her lips into a loud mock kiss. "Creep!" she said in a low voice.

Jim lunged up and Nina grabbed him.

"Order! Order! We'll take the afternoon break."

"Call Gene Malavoy."

He had been waiting out in the hall, with every court clerk under the age of forty taking a peek at him. Gene Malavoy was barely twenty years old, but he was well aware of the stir he caused. Six foot four or more, angular and broad-shouldered, with a strong face, a jutting man's nose and long hair casually brushed back, he strode to the stand and sat down, legs stretched out. He wore an old tweed jacket with his jeans and a thin gold chain around his neck, the kind that makes a woman imagine it on a bare chest. Nina would have been as impressed as everybody else if she hadn't seen him whimpering like a baby under the bleachers.

"As night host, I greeted people as they came in and escorted them to the tables, gave them menus, watched the waiters, kept people cheerful when there were long waits," he said as Collier led him through the preliminaries. His French accent, more pronounced than Marianne's, added to the overall effect.

"And are you acquainted with the defendant, Mr. Strong, sitting over there at the counsel table?"

"Not any more," he said. "Not since the day he fired me."

"And what was the date of that termination?"

"October twenty-second."

"Please explain for the Court the circumstances of your termination."

"The circumstances? Oh, yes. I had worked at Paradise seasonally for two years. Alex Strong had been my supervisor the whole time, and we got along great. My performance ratings were always excellent. Then, this year, Alex went into Operations and Jim came in. Within two weeks after the opening, Jim called me in and said that Alex had told him to let me go."

"He said Alex Strong had demanded your termination?"

"Yes. He said that Alex had warned him about me. I couldn't find out any more. I kept asking him what I'd done wrong. I couldn't believe it. He called security. I was escorted to my car."

"What did you do?"

"I went home and tried to call Alex. I wasn't feeling too happy about any of the Strongs right then. I felt that Alex must have had something against me that he was too chicken to tell me. I felt that Alex had treated me in a sneaky way. When I couldn't reach Alex, I called Mr.

Strong. The owner. I told him what Alex had done and I said, 'Philippe, you can't be doing this to me.'"

"What was Mr. Strong's reaction?"

"He said he'd look into it."

"Did you subsequently have a conversation with Philip Strong?"

"He called me the next morning and said—I don't remember how he said it—I think that I was better off to move on. Things weren't going so well at the lodge. That was it. He was my final hope."

"Your witness," Collier said to Nina. He had used Gene Malavoy to corroborate Gina in an indirect but very effective way. It was clear that at least some of what Gina had testified to was true, unless he and Gina were conspiring to perjure themselves with the same lie. The notion that Alex had been murdered because he was going to take Jim's job wasn't that compelling, but it was all Collier had. Although Flaherty didn't need to know why a murder had occurred in order to bind Jim over, he was a judge who preferred to have what he called "a sense of the case." So Collier had given him a motive of sorts.

Of course, Malavoy's testimony could twist another way.

"Mr. Malavoy?" Nina remained seated at the defense table, conspicuously not bothering to get up. "Things have been tough for you since you were terminated, haven't they?"

"I'm getting evicted from my apartment, so I guess you could say that."

"Do you blame Mr. Strong here for that?"

"Absolutely."

"Tell the Court about your relationship with Gina Beloit."

"Objection," Collier said. "Outside the scope of direct."

"Overruled. You may answer."

"There was no relationship," the young man said.

"You worked together, didn't you? Didn't you talk about your problems at work?"

"No. I knew who Gina was, but we never socialized. She might have had ideas, but I wasn't interested in her."

"You have never discussed this case with her?"

"No."

She wasn't getting anywhere with that, so Nina moved into her flank attacks.

"You have heard Gina Beloit's testimony here today? In which she says that Jim Strong told his father that he, not Alex Strong, made the decision to fire you?"

"Yes." He stuck his chin out and the muscles of his jaw worked picturesquely "I have known for several days."

"But you believed Alex Strong had done this to you as of October twenty-second, didn't you?"

"Yes."

"Did you act on your belief?"

"Objection. Vague, speculative, irrelevant, immaterial."

"Can you rephrase that, counsel?" Flaherty said.

"Sure, Your Honor. Isn't it true, Mr. Malavoy, that you waited for Alex Strong to get off work on the night of the twenty-second of October and isn't it true that you challenged him to a fight and when he refused to fight you, that you knocked him down before leaving the Paradise parking lot?"

He looked surprised. "How did you know that? It's true, I admit it."

"Why did you do that?"

"Like I said, because of Jim. Jim lied to me and told me it was Alex getting me fired. I never should have believed him, but—who would imagine he would blame his brother like that? It was a dirty trick on Alex to turn my anger toward him. It worked. I was boiling about Alex all day and drinking too much and I went at it with Alex without giving him a chance to explain. I just took a wild swing and took off. I didn't hurt him."

"You were outraged, infuriated at Alex on that day, would that be fair to say?"

"Of course. I don't mind saying it. It's true." His hand smoothed back a stray lock of hair.

"That was the afternoon of the twenty-second?"

"Ye-ees."

"Marianne Strong, the victim's wife, is your half-sister, isn't she?" Flaherty's eyebrows went up at this revelation, and Nina heard a sharp intake of breath from Collier. So he hadn't known! Tony hadn't had an easy time finding it out.

"Yes, she is. She helped me come over from Chamonix two years ago. We have the same father."

"You very much enjoyed working at the ski resort, wouldn't that be fair to say?"

In a tight voice, Collier said, "Is there a point to this, or are we just going to jump all over the place like fleas in a flea circus?"

"There's a point," Nina told Flaherty.

"Make it then," Flaherty said. Turning to Malavoy, he said, "Answer the question."

Shrugging, Malavoy said, "Yes, I liked it very much. I love skiing, being around the resort atmosphere. Of

course, I didn't belong in such menial work there. I'm
not just a waiter."

"No? What's your ambition in life then, Mr.
Malavoy?"

Collier rolled his eyes, but Flaherty indulged her.

"My ambition? To meet many lovely girls." A dash-
ing smile.

"I mean, in terms of work."

"Well. To own my own resort."

"You've talked about this ambition with some of
those lovely girls, and —"

"I talk to everyone about it—"

"And you've talked about it with your stepsister."

"All the time."

"Now, Marianne Strong inherited Alex Strong's interest in Paradise Ski Resort, didn't she, upon his
death?"

"She told me she did." Collier stood up to complain
but Flaherty just raised a hand and said, "I know it's
hearsay. Let's just get on with this."

The moment had arrived. "Now. Isn't it true that
from the day of Alex Strong's death you have repeatedly
urged Marianne Strong to sell out this interest and to
use the money to return to Europe with you to invest in
a ski resort there?"

Malavoy thought about this. So did Collier. So did
Flaherty.

At length, Malavoy said, "Yes, it's an idea I have
talked over with her." He had become very still, as
though he realized that a blow was about to be administered.

Nina administered it.

"All right," Nina said. "All right. Let's see if I

understand your situation on October twenty-third correctly. Please note that I am talking now about the day of Alex Strong's death. You were in a rage at Alex Strong and you had attacked him the previous day. Furthermore, you knew that if Alex was dead your stepsister would inherit a considerable property, and you have very strong ideas on the subject of what she should do with it.

"Isn't it true that on the twenty-third of October you followed Alex Strong off-trail, watched him have an accident as he was skiing with his brother, and took advantage of his helplessness by stomping him to death?"

"God! No! I never saw him the next day!"

"Oh, brother," Collier said for all to hear.

"How well do you know the mountain at Paradise? In terms of skiing?" Nina went on.

"Everybody knows the mountain."

"Where were you on the afternoon of the twenty-third of October?"

"At my place, unemployed, getting drunk! I didn't kill him. I was— I wouldn't do anything like that. You're just trying to get your client some breathing room, that's what it is."

"He's denied it," Collier said. He had been listening with an angry frown. "There isn't a shred of evidence Mr. Malavoy had anything to do with Alex Strong's death. I object to any further testimony being taken on this line of questioning."

"I'm merely demonstrating that Mr. Malavoy is just as likely to have killed Alex Strong as the defendant," Nina said evenly.

"Gather ye motives as ye may," Flaherty said.

"You'd need more than that to make such an accusation at trial. Now let's move along."

"Certainly, Your Honor. I just have one last question. If I may?"

"If you must."

"What brand and size of ski boot do you wear, Mr. Malavoy?"

"What brand? Dalbello."

"What size?"

"Size eleven. I hit him the day before, that's all! I swear it!"

"The record will show that this witness wears ski boots previously identified as having bottoms which could match the patterns on Alex Strong's skin." Nina said. And Collier jumped up to raise some hell, but Flaherty was staring at Malavoy's clenched fists and pale face, and Nina knew she'd made her point.

Later, Jim said, "Oh, man, you laid into him like—like—he was cringing. Even though I knew you were going to do it to him, I didn't realize how bad it would look. You almost had me convinced. But he couldn't do anything like that. He hasn't got the guts, no matter how much he drinks or shoots up. He thinks he's such a hot shot. I can outski his ass anytime, any place. He thinks every woman on earth would like to climb into his bed—what did you think of him, Nina?"

"Me? I didn't pay attention to his looks." That was one huge humdinger of a lie, but Jim's dark face called for it.

"Twice, the week before I fired him, he was late. I talked to him about it. The day I fired him, he had left his post. I didn't know where he was. Shooting crystal in the bathroom was my guess. So I took over his job until he showed up again. Then I took him into my office and terminated him."

"Did you blame it on Alex?"

"Why do you keep asking the same question? I've told you over and over. Of course not. Gina's lying. She's got Gene madder than before. Now Gene will be waiting outside the courtroom for me. Gina would like that. He better not try anything. I'll—"

"It just doesn't make sense, though," Nina said. "If you never told Malavoy that, why did he attack Alex in the parking lot on the twenty-second? You know? It's just a very strange thing."

"Yeah. It's strange. That kid has a lot he's hiding."

"It's just inexplicable."

"Life is inexplicable," Jim said.

"And your father never threatened to remove you as manager of the lodge?"

"How many times do we have to go over this? She made that up."

"Would your father testify to that?"

She saw again that resentful look Jim had whenever she mentioned his father. "My father? You'd have to ask him if he wants to do anything for me. I think he's going to stay out of it."

"He could help you on this point. What's going on between you?"

"Nothing." She asked him several more questions about his father, but Jim wouldn't add to that.

Nina pushed back her chair and said, "Keep your chin up. We're doing well. I think Collier—Mr. Hallowell's in trouble. Clauson didn't do well today, and don't think the judge is going to pay much attention to the two ex-employees. They don't want to bring in your father, as I told you before."

"Alex died in an accident," Jim said. "My father shouldn't be dragged into this too. God, I hope it ends here."

"It might. It might not. The judge is only looking for probable cause to bind you over for trial. That doesn't take a whole lot of evidence. But I think— Ginger's really going to go after the forensic work, and Tim Seisz, our geologist, is going to say that it could have been patterning from the rock striations. He went to grad school at USC, where Flaherty went to law school. Flaherty will listen to him about the patterning evidence."

"And the fibers?"

"Ginger's ready to testify that they're indistinguishable from dozens of shirts of that type sold at Miller's Outpost."

"That's where we always bought 'em," Jim said. "I'm glad you called and asked me."

"We should get back." They climbed the staircase. Even though they were running late, no witnesses awaited in the hall, only the usual crowd of news reporters and photographers. The bailiff cleared a way through them into the courtroom.

"Where are the witnesses?" Nina asked Flaherty's clerk.

"Mr. Hallowell said he'd be a few minutes late. We couldn't find you to tell you."

Nina raised an eyebrow at this. Back at the counsel table she doodled on her yellow pad, gathering her thoughts. They'd talked to the cops, the paramedics, the coroner, Beloit, and Malavoy . . . Collier wouldn't bring in Philip Strong because he wouldn't trust Strong to back up Gina Beloit. He was Jim's father, after all. Who else should they worry about?

Collier might have to rest his case now. He knew she had a couple of big scientific guns to pick Clauson apart. She had him on the run.

Gradually, the reckless high she'd been feeling all day had deflated. Clauson had been a sitting duck, and Collier deserved better witnesses.

She looked down at the pad where she had been drawing. She had doodled an enormous animal. You could only see the back of it. It had a head on its tail, and its tail was a ski. It was her defective memory of the surrealist painting she kept thinking about.

The Elephant Celebes, she thought. What are you doing in my case?

Collier walked in, his face grim. "Call in the judge," he told the clerk.

When Flaherty had seated himself on the bench, Collier said, "I must report to the Court that there has been a change of circumstances which requires me to request a continuance herein."

"A continuance?" said Flaherty. "What's going on?"

"I received a phone call from Boulder Hospital about ten minutes ago," Collier said. "Doc Clauson has suffered a stroke. While driving back to his office, he felt sick. He drove on to the hospital. His physician advises that he's been admitted. He won't be able to testify tomorrow."

"Do you have any other witnesses scheduled for tomorrow? Maybe he could get back in the next day," Flaherty said.

"I have no other witnesses, but even so, it sounds to me as if his illness may incapacitate him for some time."

"Hmm. Well. Under the circumstances, Mrs. Reilly, I suppose I should find out your position on this," said the judge.

"We will not agree to any continuance, Your Honor. The statute plainly says that the defendant has a right to have a preliminary hearing within ten days of the filing of the charges, and for that hearing to continue uninterrupted until completed."

"Yes, yes, of course, but if you don't choose to extend this minimal professional courtesy to Mr. Hallowell, I will be compelled to dismiss the charges without prejudice, and he'll be free to refile the charges at his convenience, and we'll have to start all over again."

"That's exactly what I will do," Collier said.

"We've gotten this far," Flaherty said, frowning. "I don't see why you can't give it a couple of days until we see how the Doc's doing. Avoid repetition, waste of judicial resources, that sort of thing."

"I'm sorry, Your Honor, but we will stand on the statute." She was doing what was best for Jim, but she wasn't proud of herself.

"And we will refile the charges, at a time convenient to us," Collier said stiffly.

"Perhaps, upon the further review necessitated by this unfortunate event, the district attorney's office will change its mind about refiling," said Nina.

"Not gonna happen," Collier said, without looking at her. "Your Honor, the prosecution is unable to proceed at this time."

"You could rest your case, let Mrs. Reilly put on her case, and see how I rule," said Flaherty.

"I can't go ahead without being able to be in close consultation with the county coroner," Collier said. He was right, he would be lost without Clauson, and he was too experienced to sail on without help.

"Then I suppose we'll have to bow to the inevitable. You request a dismissal without prejudice at this time?"

"Yes, Your Honor," Collier said.

"Very well. So ruled." Court adjourned. Flaherty left and the clerk handed out the Minute Order confirming that the case of *People v. Strong* had been dismissed in its entirety.

Until next time.

Collier left without comment, four or five reporters with clipboards and notebooks in hand, trailing behind him.

"Am I free?" Jim said. While Nina finished up her notes on what had just happened, he and Nina were still sitting in the courtroom.

"That's right. All charges have been dismissed. You can even get your bail back. But you might want to wait until we see if Collier refiles the charges within a week. I thought Clauson looked wiped out in court, but— I'd better try to find out how ill he is." Nina wanted time to think about this turn of events. Unsmiling, she packed up her briefcase.

Jim was beaming. "You won! You beat them!"

"This round only, Jim. And it was a TKO. We haven't convinced the D.A.'s office to drop this matter. I think you should assume that they will refile, and we'll have another prelim in a few weeks."

"That's the future. It might never happen. You've been great, Nina. Great." He leaned in and gave her a big hug. Though she wanted to feel good for his sake, his closeness reminded her unpleasantly of the day on the mountain at Paradise. She pulled away quickly.

"Let's go out and celebrate. Drink champagne," he said.

"Can't. Sorry. I'll talk to you soon."

"You are so fucking good," he said, as if he couldn't believe it. He was still shaking his head as she practically ran out the door of the courtroom and headed toward the bathroom, where she waited until she was sure Jim was gone.

She didn't feel good. She felt nauseated, disgusted, at the whole half-assed proceeding, at her arrogant treatment of the witnesses, particularly Clauson, and at how artificial her defense had seemed to her even as she was pushing it. Granite striations, indeed. She didn't want to talk to Jim anymore.

The case against him had fallen apart, and she had done what she could to speed up that process, but there had been no trial of the facts by a disinterested third party Clauson had not marched back into court to do his damnedest to refute her theories about rocks and fibers. Collier had not had any chance to cross-examine the geologist, or to go after Ginger.

If there had been a fair fight and Flaherty had dismissed the case, she would have relaxed and said to herself, yes, thank God, he's probably innocent, Flaherty thinks so too. Or even if Flaherty had bound Jim over, she would have been able to gauge how realistic the defense theories were, to form her own opinion.

She hadn't been good. She had been lucky. Too lucky, in a way. So lucky she felt more uneasy than ever.

She washed her hands, combed her hair, and left, alone. Then, feeling like a phony, she gave the shivering reporters who were waiting by the Bronco a couple of posed smiles and selected word bites for tomorrow's papers, muttering something about vindication.

17

"I'M HERE FOR a consultation," Nina told the spectacles at the desk. It was late, past six o'clock. She had already called Bob to remind him to work on his homework and to put frozen fish sticks into the oven.

"I'd like to help you, but he's about to go home. We could get you in tomorrow morning."

"I'm tied up tomorrow. Have to see him now."

"Nina?" The white-haired man had been walking past her, toward the exit, carrying the usual heavy case.

"Artie, have you got just a minute?" Nina said. She must have looked really needy at that moment, because Artie Wilson didn't even stop walking, he just swiveled and reversed his direction, saying over his shoulder, "Follow me."

In the shuttered conference room of Artie's law office, surrounded by the familiar law books and his comforting presence pulling out a chair for her and bringing her a cup of water, she realized just how bad she felt.

"How can I help you?" he said, as he must say to the criminal clients he represented.

Artie, a criminal defense attorney with forty years of experience, had just retired to Tahoe from San Francisco a few months before. At least, he had expected to retire, but he quickly wearied of playing golf and drinking with his fellow retirees at the Chart House, so he had opened up an office in the Starlake Building just above Nina's on the second floor. He loved Mexican food and talking law, and they had fallen into the habit of eating lunch together several times a week.

"It's a case I have. I need to consult you," she said.

"Sure."

"I'll pay you."

"No need."

"So there won't be any confidentiality problem down the road. You know."

"Okay. Pay me. I'm listening."

"Well, I just got all the charges against Jim Strong dismissed today."

"Nice work!"

"Thanks, but I have to tell you, I'm very unsure about this case. For one thing, I'm sure the prosecutor will refile."

Artie liked to skip the anesthetic preludes and go directly for the root, however painful the operation. "You think he killed his brother."

"I don't know. That's what's bothering me. If I thought he was innocent, I could defend him whole-heartedly. If I thought he was guilty, I'd do the same, to make sure he got a fair trial. But I want to know which it is. I can't figure it out. It could have been an accident. If it was a murder, someone else could have done it. It's all tangled up. I have to know if he's lying."

Artie pondered this. "Are you ever going to have a clear answer to that question?"

"I don't see how. He's not going to change his story, if he's lying."

"Why won't you defend a lying killer? You'll defend a killer, you just said so."

"Because—because you see, we're a team. He turns me into a liar if he's a liar. The whole thing turns false, into a charade of justice. I look for exculpatory evidence that doesn't exist, and I assert theories that are hooey—I construct this whole edifice of lies without even knowing it. I—"

"He uses you to defeat justice."

"Yes, that's it. I use all my skills, my smarts, everything, in the service of a lie."

"But that's our job sometimes, isn't it?" Artie went to the credenza and withdrew an untouched bottle of liquor and two very small silver-rimmed glasses. "What difference does it make, except that maybe you do a little better job if you think he's innocent?"

She took the glass. "Bottoms up," he said, and they both tossed theirs down.

"Uh . . . uh . . ." Nina's esophagus was afire and her eyes were bulging out of her head. A wildfire swept through her body. "What is that stuff?" she sputtered.

"Mezcal. Premium Oaxacan. Made from the agave plant. No worms in the expensive mezcal, don't worry."

She set the glass down carefully. Slowly, her insides began the first phase of repairs, damping down into a contained burn.

"So what do you care if he fools you?" Artie said.

"Artie, this is a first for me," Nina said. "With my guilty clients, the evidence against them is usually overwhelming. They don't have to lie to me or make excuses. It's easier. I explain that even if they have done what they are accused of doing, I can help with the process, make sure every mitigating factor is considered."

"You've never gone to trial with a client you knew was guilty?"

"Not knowingly," Nina said. "I've handled quite a few appeals where I thought the client was guilty, but the client was sitting in prison in San Quentin or Soledad or someplace and it was all intellectual arguments and filing papers. I did my best, but I always felt confident that the system would work at that level—the attorney general's office would put up a fight and the court would make a reasoned decision. There had already been a trial. I didn't have to make up facts—"

"You just had to massage them within an inch of their lives," Artie said. "Are you making up facts in this case? Is that what you think you're doing?"

"No! I don't mean to say that. I'm . . ." She thought about it. "Making up explanations for facts. And the prosecution isn't fighting back like it should." She explained about the time squeeze she had put on Collier, the late revision to the autopsy report, Doc Clauson's sudden illness, and Heidi's disappearance.

"It's like you put the hex on them," Artie said. "I see your problem. The balance of power isn't working."

"Yes, that's it."

"You feel uncomfortable and want your fetters. You don't want to be allowed to run amok."

"Correct."

"Have another tot. Bottoms up." They drank. The liquor stoked the fire. A shudder ran through Nina's body. Artie coughed a couple of times. "Good stuff," he said, wiping his eyes.

"Y'know, Nina," he went on thoughtfully, "we lawyers tend to get too self-important sometimes. We're very good at taking on responsibilities, and sometimes we imagine that we have a whole lot more responsibility than we actually have. Take your situation. You're worrying about all sorts of things that aren't in your bailiwick. You're just a lowly defense attorney, and your duty is to defend. That's all. It's very simple. You're an advocate, and not for justice, but for your client. If you start taking on other roles like judge and jury you're not doing your job. Quit worrying. Quit trying to see all sides. Defend your client."

"I know that's my duty. I am loyal to the client. I believe in what I do. I like my place in the system. But if other parts of the system are breaking down all around, I have too much power," Nina said. "I'm just a cog in the machine, but if the machine is shaky, and I just keep blindly doing my cog thing, I could corrupt it."

"What is a cog, anyway?"

"No idea."

"So you're scared, eh?"

"No, I never said that."

"Then you're nuts. I've been afraid for forty years. After all, we're closer than mothers to some people whose lot in life is to lay waste to other people."

"That's something else. I don't want to think about that part of the job right now."

"Listen. Don't worry. The system has its ways, and some of them aren't quite straightforward. If Strong did it, he'll be caught one way or the other no matter how brilliant the defense."

"I hope you're right. But—what if he's guilty? And I get him off?"

Artie shrugged. "Then one guy out of a thousand slipped by," he said. "It's the conflict at the heart of our work. Now and then he's guilty but you can't get a deal and you have to go to trial, and you find yourself saying things to the jury that are intended to mislead, and that's the way it goes."

"I just can't accept that."

"It's not up to you to accept it or not accept it. It's up to you to defend him like hell. And if he gets off, he gets off."

"I won't be used like that," Nina said stubbornly. "Unwittingly."

"Aha! It's the unwitting part you object to. Look, if you can't stand the ethical dilemma, unload him," Artie said. "But I warn you, it'll come up again and again. Most of your clients are gonna be guilty."

"I know that! It's this particular case, this situation—"

"So— unload him."

"But—he depends on me. He thinks we have a great relationship. He's got a lot of issues with abandonment. I think it would cause him harm, and that's not ethical, either."

"Is this some kind of male-female thing, Nina?" Artie said, his keen if somewhat bloodshot eyes boring into her. "Something between you two?"

"No. But he—he relies on me. He begs me not to desert him like his wife did, and his father."

"Sounds like a master manipulator to me," said Artie.

"I don't know if he is, or if he's utterly sincere," Nina said. "God, Artie, don't give me any more. And put the bottle away, or we'll both get pulled over on the way home." While Artie was doing that, she watched his bowed back and the two tufts of white hair around his hard-headed skull, and she had an idea.

"Artie?"

"Uh huh."

"Would you work with me on the Strong case?" That made him turn around, hitch up his pants, and give her a good look. "You've been having a good time defending purse snatchers and drunk drivers and klepto-maniacs during the three months you've been here. I've watched you in court. You're fiendish. You're so good, you don't even have to think."

"I'm retired. I'm just fooling around, keeping my hand in. It's my gambling money. Keeps my wife happy since I'm not home bothering her all day."

"Bull. You're as good as ever, and you must be bored."

Artie adjusted his glasses and said, "Boredom can be quite entertaining if it's a new experience. I've been in the game a long time, Nina, and I'm happy to get out of the stormy sea and just dabble my fingers in it from the safety of my dock."

"Are you going to tell me you can resist my offer? Think of it. Murder One, Artie. Prominent family. Lots of media exposure. That will bring in more clients, if you want them. And you know, he just may be in-nocent."

"Too much work."

"Please . . . I'd really appreciate it."

"Stop batting your eyelashes at me, young lady. You're too attractive for your own good."

"Please?"

"You do all the paperwork," Artie said. "I'll only do court work."

"Deal."

"My knees are bad. I complain a lot, and take long lunches. I don't hear out of my left ear. I'm sixty-four years old."

"In your prime."

"Apparently not too old to be twisted around your dainty finger."

"Thank God."

They shook hands, and Nina went home to Bob.

Who had packed up his baseball cards. And a bunch of Chinese movies. And his precious stuffed animal, the purple dragon that still went with him everywhere. But no clothes yet, although he was leaving in two days.

And he hadn't made a fire, but the heat blasting through the vents gave the cabin the fierce climate of midsummer Texas. "Did you put dinner in the oven?" she asked, throwing off her coat and leaping out of Hitchcock's way. At least the dog was enthusiastic about her return, wagging his tail, his entire body wagging in fact.

Bob, on the other hand, sprawled insensate in his blue beanbag, eyes fused to the new laptop on which VCD star Chow Yun-Fat, God of Gamblers, was blowing away a few dozen Hong Kong triad members with an infinite-shot Magnum.

"Are you a good boy? A fine fellow? Yes, you are," she crooned, letting Hitchcock jump up and put his paws on her shoulders. The dog gave it up, tail, back, ears, furry chest, his jaws open in a toothy grimace, while Bob basked in his electronic ecstasy, impervious to ordinary human contact.

"Bob! Well? Did you?"

A stir at this disruption. One eye cocked her way, like the eye of the tyrannosaurus in *Jurassic Park*. "Of course I did. You asked me to, didn't you? You never remember the good stuff I do. Remember this video?"

"We watched it last night. How could I forget?"

"The good part's next. Want to watch it with me?"

"No thanks. I'll go check the oven." The oily breaded fish sticks, slightly blackened, lay in perfect rows, an aesthetic universe apart from actual fresh fish, just the way Bob liked them. She pulled a prepackaged salad mix from the fridge and poured some nonfat dressing on it. Finding a slightly shriveling lemon in the refrigerator drawer, she cut it into wedges, placing it neatly on a plate in the middle of the table. "Bob, wash your hands," she called, and dished everything up, the fish and the salad and some sliced apple. And all, as Sandy would say.

They ate at the dining room table. Nina felt that was important for family life. However, the laptop, unconcerned with family values, had also made its way to the table. Chow Yun-Fat seemed no longer to recognize his spunky sidekick. It was no wonder, since Chow had suffered brain damage in an accident and had capered through the entire movie with a mental age of about five and a half. The sidekick crept off, sad and unappreciated.

"Eat some of that salad. Man does not live on grease alone. When you're in Germany, I want you to eat a piece of fruit, a banana or something, every day. Now where's the to-do list? Okay, tonight we do laundry and sew up your green sweatshirt." Chow suddenly recovered his brains and remembered everything after all. He surprised his buddy and promoted him from sidekick to partner. The God of Gamblers was back! Chow and his happy posse headed out for another night of gunplay and mah-jongg.

The End.

"Aw," Nina said. "I liked him better when he was brain-damaged."

"You don't have to be sarcastic, Mom. You're not in court anymore."

"Now turn that thing off. Let's get to work."

The moment came. Bob boarded an American Airlines flight at the airport in Reno at seven-thirty P.M. on Sunday night.

"Call me as soon as you get in."

"I know, I know."

"Call me at the airport in Denver if you have any trouble at all."

"I can handle it."

Her brave face was crumbling. "If Kurt isn't at the gate in Frankfurt . . ."

"I remember."

"Love you."

"Love you, too. See ya, Mom." He shouldered the backpack and went through the door. She watched it, waiting for him to come back out and tell her he was just a frightened boy who couldn't go through with it, but soon the door was locked.

Through the cloudy window, she saw his plane taxiing down the icy runway outside, taking with it his childhood, while she remained behind, still puzzled at how it could have slipped by her and gotten away.

"You're a good lawyer," Henry McFarland, the D.A., said. "We've known each other for a long time, and I've always respected you, Collier. But this is a fuckup of major proportions. The investigation, the missing wife, Clauson and his report . . . How is he?"

"Paralyzed on his right side. I don't think he'll be back," Collier said. They were eating lunch on a busy

Monday at Henry's desk in his big new office in the corner, where the best windows were.

McFarland looked sorry to hear that. He probably was sorry, but you never could tell, because he was such a good actor. He'd been a drama major at UC Davis before going into law, and it got him great reviews with the juries. His real expression, on the few occasions when he was caught unaware, was inert but watchful, like a lizard waiting for a fly to drop by. "That was a bad break, but even so, it was too early for an arrest. You let yourself get pushed into a prelim you couldn't handle."

"You're probably right." No use making excuses, Collier thought to himself. There weren't any. He was there to take his medicine, and the new D.A. was playing doctor today.

The previous year, just before his breakdown, Collier had been running against Henry for the office Henry occupied now. They had both been deputies, but Collier had the seniority and the reputation, and nobody had been more surprised than Henry when Collier dropped out of the race, leaving it to him.

Henry was doing an okay job dealing with the board of supervisors, shuffling the work reasonably fairly. There shouldn't be any hard feelings, but there was an awkwardness between them, and maybe some paranoia on Henry's part. Henry was younger by a few years, and less experienced. That stung, now that he was the boss.

Henry had okayed Collier's return from his leave of absence. There were administrative reasons for that, most urgent among them the fact that the office was chronically short-staffed and Collier's return from leave didn't count as a new hire. Collier knew the ground under him was earthquake prone.

Henry said, "Look at this news article in the Sacramento paper. They're making comparisons to the investigation in the Jon-Benet Ramsey case. It's affecting my reputation, and the office's reputation. First we say it's an accident. Then we arrest the brother and call it a murder. Then the whole thing dissolves into chaos. Get me?"

A nod. Yeah, he got that he was in deep shit.

"And . . ."

"And?"

"Barb says you're seeing the defense attorney. She didn't tattle, it just came out while we were talking about something else at lunch."

"I'm not throwing the case so she'll sleep with me, Henry," Collier said. "Just in case you'd be stupid enough to think that."

"No, 'cuz you're already sleeping with her. That's the word. Is it true?"

"She and I—we don't talk about work. We're professionals. It's a small town, and you meet who you meet. I mean, I seem to recall you having a flaming thing with the wife of a witness in that triple murder last year—"

"That's none of your goddamn business!" Henry's fist hit the desk.

"Exactly," Collier said. He finished his sandwich and drank some of his Coke while Henry collected himself.

In a softer voice, Henry said, "I'm getting the feeling that you're not ready to come back, Collier. You've changed. I was depending on you. You said you were ready to charge him."

"I can handle this, Henry," Collier said calmly. "And it's not over yet."

"We only get one more prelim. If Flaherty doesn't bind him over next time, we may be done. Now here's the big question. Should we drop it right now, before the fallout gets any worse? I mean, are we gonna win a second prelim? 'Cuz if we don't win, it's gonna hurt, Collier. It's gonna hurt me, and I'm going to pass the hurt along."

"I hear you, Henry, and I assure you, you can count on me to make it stick, if we go that far. I'll let you know whether I think we should go forward in a few days."

"If we go forward, you have to have the evidence, get me?"

"Of course."

"I want you to review what you have with Barb before you go ahead. I'd sit with you myself, but I'm tied up from here to kingdom come with the casino bomb threat case. Don't blow it next time, I mean that."

"Okay."

"Okay." They got up, avoiding each others' eyes.

Sean Voorhies was waiting in the office. Sean said, "You all finished getting reamed? The secretary told me."

"Hey, Sean. You find the girl?"

"Not Heidi. But I talked to the little sister, Kelly Strong."

Collier dropped into his chair. He could tell by the bright eyes and nervous hands and loud puffing, Sean was excited. He seemed to have run all the way in from the parking lot.

"Ready?" he said.

"Go for it."

"Kelly's twenty-five. She's a student at the University of Nevada. Level-headed girl, though it was a bitch getting her talking. Also, she wouldn't even let me in. We had to stand there in the doorway. Turns out her father's inside."

"Philip Strong?"

"She says he's not doing so good. Mourning and all that. That was frustrating. I tried everything to get in and I tried to talk to him, but she held her ground. Said he's under a doctor's care, so I got the number."

"I wasn't really looking for him," Collier said. "I didn't think he'd help at the prelim. Interesting he's there, though."

"But that's not all. So she says a few things, like she's busy at school and doesn't know anything and hopes everything turns out all right, and I nod my head and take a note. We start talking about skiing. She says she doesn't ski now, but it used to be the biggest thing in her life.

"I ask, funny you don't ski with everybody else in the family being big on that. I go on about how come she's not involved with the resort. She gets a funny look on her face and says Jim's responsible for that. She really wants to talk, but her father's somewhere back there."

"Jim's responsible . . ." Collier said.

"She's down on him. I don't know why. She has something to tell us. She's getting ready to say bye and close the door, but then she has a change of heart. She firms up, stands up straight, you know? Says she'll talk to you right now if you promise to keep it confidential. I guess the dad's about to leave Kelly's place."

"Impossible," said Collier. "I'm completely booked."

"Unbook yourself. Can you?"

"What does Jim Strong's sister have to say that's such a damn emergency?"

"I don't think it's an emergency. I just think this is the moment she's ready to unload something. Maybe something really good for us."

Collier ran his hand through his hair. "It might be a break. We could use a break."

"I drove all the way here to get you. Come on, I got a county car." Collier flipped open the appointment book, eyed it briefly, and slapped it shut.

"Let's go."

They walked out to the main room, affectionately known as the pit, from which all the other offices branched, and Sean waited while Collier knocked on Barbara's door. She was sitting with a cop, going over some testimony. "Excuse me, Barb. Any chance you could handle the afternoon felony calendar for me? The files are on my desk. It's light today."

Barbara looked surprised. "Are you kidding?" she said. "I can't juggle that and the prelim I've got this afternoon."

"Sure you can. Just tell Flaherty you'll need to start an hour late, and go upstairs and take care of it for me. I've got an emergency."

"What kind of emergency?"

"The Strong case. Are you going to help me or not?"

"This time, Collier," Barbara said, "but it will cost you."

Everything always did.

18

"COLLIER?" SEAN WHIPPED around a left curve in the road around the lake. Just past Cave Rock in Nevada, they trundled along behind a lumber truck doing about thirty. Narrow because of the snowbanks on either side, the highway looked like a sleigh trail. The car smelled of stale cigar smoke.

"Collier? You still with me?"

"Sorry. I was picturing Doc Clauson drooling out of one side of his mouth onto the sheets. A shame, a real shame. His sister is a nurse and seems willing to take care of him. That's about the only good thing about any of it."

"Must be worse when you're a medico yourself. You know exactly how bad it is."

"He's not that old."

"It was the smoking."

"Or quitting smoking. The pressure, years of attacks in court. I don't know."

"You think his mind was affected?"

"Probably. He's been having some trouble. Like with the Strong autopsy."

"We'll come up with something from these people in Incline. We'll work around it."

"He said something to me," Collier said. "Earlier, before the stroke. I can't get it out of my mind."

"What?"

"He said Strong is a monster. He was talking about the crime."

"You'd have to be."

"I'm going to be very unhappy if I can't barbecue this guy."

They went on in silence. Collier had things to think about, and Sean didn't seem to mind the lack of chit-chat.

Incline Village, the most expensive of the North Shore resort towns, had one casino-hotel, three fine restaurants, a giant condo development or two, and a couple of hundred vacation homes, all clustered in deep forest along the lake. They pulled alongside a five-foot-high snowbank and climbed out. The deep windless shade made the day bone cold.

The girl who answered the door wore a blue denim jacket, metal-rimmed glasses, and red-rimmed eyes. "Come in," she said. "It's a long story."

"Those are the best kind," Collier said matter-of-factly.

Nina had just returned from the airport and was on the phone when Collier exploded through the office door. He grabbed her and pulled her out in the hall while Sandy and Mrs. Geiger, who had just arrived, watched openmouthed. The door shut behind them.

In the dimly lit hall, his warm mouth found hers and they leaned against the wall. As if she had been missing a part of herself, his touch relieved her. He kissed her neck, hunching down to reach her though she was on her toes already, his hands moving up and down her back, continually gathering her closer into the rough material of his open coat until she was engulfed in it.

This went on for quite a while. The real-estate ladies down the hall came out of their offices and turned around and went back in again.

"Oh, baby, I missed you so much this weekend."

"Me, too."

"I don't ever want to be separated from you again."

"It's three o'clock in the afternoon," Sandy said from the doorway. "Just thought you might want to know."

"I'll be—right in, Sandy."

"Hmph." The door shut.

"Why are you here?" She brought his head up, made him look at her.

"I want you to get out of the Strong case," Collier said. "Please do that for me. And don't ask any questions. I promise you, I'll never ask you to do anything like this again."

Dismayed, Nina stepped back.

"Why?" she said.

"I can't tell you."

"You have some new information?"

"Don't ask. Other people are involved. I can't explain. Just trust me."

"Tell me why. You have to! What did you find out?"

"I found out," Collier said, his mouth at her ear, whispering, "just how dangerous and vindictive he is. You're in danger. Hear me?"

Now she was frightened. But she couldn't just say, "All right, sure, whatever you say." Of course Collier was prejudiced against Jim. She had to be able to assess—

"You have to tell me. What's he done?"

"Do what I say. Go back in there and call him and say you're through. Return whatever money he's given you."

"It's not that simple."

"Make it simple."

"I have to think about it."

"Don't think long."

"Can I see you tonight?"

"Your place?"

"I'll be off at six. I'll cook dinner."

"Six. Please. Go in there and call him. Do it." Collier was gone.

Nina went back in, somewhat dazed, and said, "Sandy, call Artie's office and see if I can run in and see him as soon as Mrs. Geiger and I finish up. And call Jim Strong and see if he can come down this afternoon. I have to talk to him. Hi, Mrs. Geiger. How are you?"

"Not so good, hon."

"Well, come on in."

They went into the inner office and shut the door. Nina's face was still warm from Collier's heat, and his alarm had rubbed off too. She calmed herself. Mrs. Geiger waited patiently, perched on the edge of her chair because her feet didn't reach the ground otherwise.

"Sorry," Nina said. She was a little brusque, not at all recovered from the intensity of that brief meeting.

"No problem. You're in love with that fellow, I see."

"Yes. I suppose I am."

"That's nice. I haven't been in love since 1967, but remember the feeling well."

"What can I do for you today? Uh, I think we had everything all taken care of . . ." Nina opened the file, scanned it, and went on, "Yes, we've sent out the last of the medical bills. Sandy was just going to put this file in the closed cases. We just filed the divorce petition for you."

She took a good look at Mrs. Geiger, who still wore the same somewhat threadbare navy coat and the same black purse. Her mouth was set in a permanent smile, the one her mother had undoubtedly taught her to wear no matter how bad it got.

"So you're not doing well? What's wrong?" Nina said, her tone softening.

"Well, I was just wondering if we could change our minds," Mrs. Geiger said.

"Change our minds?"

"Get more money for the injuries."

"I'm very sorry, but no, we can't do that, Mrs. Geiger. You've signed a release of all claims against the parties. We've accepted a settlement check. It's all over."

Mrs. Geiger took that in. "But you know, hon, my back's really acting up."

"Oh. I see. Okay, no problem. We got you future medical expenses, so long as your orthopedist agrees the treatment is related to your preexisting condition. You just call up and—"

"I went back to the Honeybee Restaurant, where I always worked, and asked for a part-time job. I know I wasn't supposed to, but I did. My boss, Mr. Hendrickson, he's a fine boy. He said sure and started me next day. And I found out—I found out I can't do it anymore. I mean, my back was plain killing me. I had to lay down all day the next day."

"But your doctor has explained to you that you can't do that anymore. You can't work. That's what the settlement is for."

"But I *always* worked. I like to work. I don't want to sit home with nothing to do. I thought as soon as the case was over I'd be right back there and able to earn my living. Why, I've been working since I was twelve years old."

Nina smiled at her and said, "It's time to take a rest now. Visit some friends, travel around, enjoy life. You can afford it."

"I need to *work*. But my back won't let me."

Her eyes grew big and saucer shaped as she said this, and Nina thought, it's finally hit her, that she really is disabled. She must have thought that she could collect the money and go back to her old job. She thought it was all some kind of wonderful break that she wouldn't have to pay for. "I need more money," she persisted. Her smile trembled a little.

"But there's nothing I can do, Mrs. Geiger. There is no more money."

Without a word, Mrs. Geiger pulled out her check register and spread it open in front of Nina. It showed the deposit of her settlement money, followed by a daily series of large withdrawals, five to fifteen thousand dollars a day.

The balance was forty-six dollars and thirty-two cents.

"Where's your money, Mrs. Geiger?" Nina asked, puzzled.

"We-e-ell, I lost it, hon."

"How?"

"Playing the horses at the Race and Sports Club at Harrah's." This took a minute to settle in. Casinos didn't give money back. Ever. The money was gone. Unbelievable!

"You lost a hundred and sixty thousand dollars in a—a—week?"

"Twelve days. Twelve days of finishing out of the

running. The worst bad luck. I kept getting these hunches, and I kept being so close, then I was losing a lot of money and I figured my horse was bound to come up now, so I kept betting more and more. It was my turn. But my turn didn't come. They make it so easy!"

So Mrs. Geiger was a compulsive gambler, a common problem at the lake. Nina thought back to the madness that had seized her too on her last visit to that slot machine, the one with which she had the relationship.

"I used to hand my paycheck over to my husband every Friday," her client went on. "And I knew I ought to be careful. I even talked to my minister, Reverend Minor, about putting the settlement away for me. We had it all set up for him to give me some of it each week. But I never did make it over to the church."

"Oh, I'm so sorry," Nina said, shaking her head. She could hardly believe it. "How about your husband? Could he help you?"

"He's not coming back. I told you, he's gone back to Oklahoma. I don't ever want to see that man again anyway."

"But what will you do?"

"My sister says I can live with her, but I have to pay groceries and everything until the sosh-security starts coming. That's still two years. So I came in today thinking maybe you could help me. Since we did share the risk."

"Wait a minute," said Nina. "Share the risk?"

"Well, we thought we had the crow in the hand. But that darn thing flew off. With the money. Not all the money, though."

"I suppose you're talking about my fee?"

"Sixty thousand dollars worth of fee. That's a lot, hon."

"I'm not going to return the fee, Mrs. Geiger. I have a family. We have a contract. I did the work."

"Oh, I don't want all of it. I thought we ought to split it. It's *my* back, after all, hon. You're not going to let me starve, are you?"

Nina sat back in her chair and thought about it. Mrs. Geiger's game smile was still hanging on her face, though it was mighty wobbly. Nina had the feeling that, once that smile was gone, it would never come again.

How many hours had she actually put in on the case? A hundred, maybe. She'd been paid fantastically well, but she'd taken the chance of being paid nothing. She'd fronted all the expenses, saved the day. She'd only done what any lawyer does. Why was she feeling so guilty? Artie would have ushered the woman out with many a fine word about contracts. After all, Mrs. Geiger had done it to herself.

But she was a client. Nina had taken on Mrs. Geiger's problems, all of them. She wasn't prepared to see her panhandling in the snow.

She opened her bottom drawer and brought out the office checkbook. Mrs. Geiger sat there solemnly. Nina wrote out a check from the office checking account and handed it to her.

"Hon, you are a peach. Thirty thousand dollars. Why, it's made out to Reverend Minor!"

"In trust for you. Have him call me if he has any questions about setting up an account. Take this, too." It was a business card with the phone number for Gambler's Anonymous. "Go to a few meetings. You need to talk about what just happened to you."

"Good girl," said Mrs. Geiger. "You're a peach, hon. A real lady." The smile had gotten a lot wider.

It almost made it worth it.

"I'll send you a corrected fee agreement. Good luck. Take care of yourself."

Sandy was just hanging up as Nina walked Mrs. Geiger to the door. "Artie says to come ahead."

Nina climbed the stairs to the second floor. Artie was sitting in his conference room at the computer, looking up some cases on Lexis.

"One second," he said, not looking up. Nina went to the window. Artie had a good town view, the slushy street out front with its solid line of traffic, the convenience store and Mexican restaurant across the street. Behind them, mountains. Behind them, far-flung sky. And behind that? What was behind it all? Was there some ordering principle? Some all-seeing power which would one day explain why she had just calmly given away thirty thousand dollars?

"Ah, shit," she mumbled to herself. She knew it had been the right thing to do. She didn't even have time to worry about it now.

When Artie swiveled around to face her, she said, still standing at the window, "I've come to ask you a question. Would you be willing to take over the defense for Jim Strong?"

"Without you?"

"Without me."

"No. No, I wouldn't do that." Artie spoke gently.

"I thought not. But I wanted to ask."

"Why?"

"Because I'm thinking about getting out of this case, and before I talked to Jim I wanted to have someone else I trusted lined up for him."

"I've gone through too much to get my blood pressure down. Sorry, but the stress would—"

"You don't have to apologize, Artie. The opposite. I apologize for busting in on you like this."

"I'm kind of disappointed. I thought we were going to work together. Did something come up?"

"Yes, something came up. Or no, it's just an ongoing feeling that I don't want this. I want out."

"Still thinking that he's lying, eh?"

"I suppose."

"The going's getting tough?"

"Yes."

"What about loyalty to the client? All that? He done anything like bounce a check on you?"

"No, no."

"Then he's done his duty by you."

"Someone I trust, who ought to know, says he's dangerous. To me personally."

"Any specifics?"

"No."

"This person who you trust—has he or she got any axes to grind?"

"Yes, but—"

"We've got a duty, Nina," Artie said. "Our nerves may be shot, we may stop sleeping, our kids may be neglected, we may hate the crook whose hand we're holding. But we've got a duty. Even when we have a failure of nerve."

"It's not a failure of nerve! It's a failure of trust. I don't trust him."

Artie said, "I still don't see what that has to do with it. Nothing says you have to trust him. Defendants aren't trustworthy, in general. But he has to be able to trust you, because that's your duty. And I see he can't trust you." Artie turned back around and acted like he was very interested in the case on the screen. She felt that she had lost a lot of luster in his eyes.

"Well, thanks anyway," she said.

As she was walking out the door, Artie said, his eyes still on the screen, "I'll still work with you, if you change your mind."

19

WHEN SANDY BROUGHT Jim into the inner office late
that afternoon, Nina was sitting upright behind the
desk, her hands folded in front of her, all business.

"Thank you for coming," she said as he threw himself into the chair. He looked like he had run all the way
from the resort. He must have been working outside—
sweating and hatless, he wore only a red wool shirt
above his jeans, though it was in the thirties today.

"I was coming anyway," he said, the words rushing
out before she could get her mouth open. "My father
finally did it. He fired me. I knew it was coming. It's
been hanging over me. It's almost a relief. No, it's not a
relief, it's another hellish hit, is what it is." He looked so
disheveled and agitated, his news was so bad, that Nina
decided her own agenda would have to wait a few minutes while she tried to help him absorb it.

"It's final? He didn't ask you to do something else?"

"No. He came back from his trip and things were
kind of in a mess—what did he expect? I'm the one
facing a murder charge . . . but I've tried to keep
things together, deal with the lodge employees and the
equipment breakdowns and the Ski Patrol people, all of
it, and this hearing was coming up. I mean, there's an
actual possibility I'll go to jail! So what does he do? He

leaves and dumps everything on my shoulders. He came in about six o'clock in the morning, and when I showed up at eight he called me in and said he wanted me off the property."

"I don't understand," Nina said. "I really don't. I take it that you feel his reason for firing you was a pretext, and it sure sounds like one. But if it's got to do with your brother's death, why go off and leave you in charge in the first place?"

"I don't know either. He's never been an easy person. Now we're like strangers." He paused, thinking. "Someone has poisoned his mind against me since he left. He wouldn't even tell me where he's been. But unfortunately for me, he has the power. He's the managing partner. I'm out."

"Was there—did the conversation get heated?" Nina asked.

"No, no. I tell you, Nina, I just didn't even have the heart to argue with him about it. I just turned around and left. I went home and tried to sleep. I did finally drop off, about noon, but only for an hour. I'm so tired."

"After things calm down," Nina said, "your father may change his mind."

Jim got up and paced. "He seems to hate me now. If I can't convince him that I had nothing to do with Alex's death, I don't think he'll ever have anything more to do with me. After everything I've done to make him . . ."

"To make him what?" Nina said. Then she thought, to make him love me. That was what Jim was choking back.

"Give it a few days," was all she could think of to

say. She wasn't going to suggest any of several legal remedies that had come to mind. This dilemma wasn't a legal one, and the law couldn't solve it.

"I need you more than ever, Nina."

"Well, let's talk about what's happening with your case. First, I'm sorry to tell you that there's still no word on Heidi."

Sitting down again, Jim bowed his head, effectively hiding his expression, but the humility of the gesture suggested to Nina that he had come to grips with Heidi's absence.

"At the moment, you're free, but as you know, you can be rearrested and another hearing can be held on whether there's probable cause to bind you over for trial."

"Whatever happened to double jeopardy, anyhow?" Jim asked.

"Let's just say it's been whittled away so much, there's just a microscopic twig of that doctrine left," Nina said. "However, if they lose two prelims, you'll be home free."

"This is too much! It's eating up my money. It's ruining my life!"

"I know. I know. But you have to prepare yourself. The police forensics lab is running more tests on those fibers found on your boots. They're even looking for Alex's DNA. They have the idea that if Alex sweated enough they might be able to link the fibers to his particular shirt."

"They can find stuff like that?"

"Oh, they live in a science fiction world. Look at the navy blue dress that nailed Clinton."

"If they don't find anything, will that clear me?"

Now that was a very good question, the kind of

question an innocent man asks. "Not really," she told him reluctantly. "Ginger says there are a number of reasons why no DNA would be found even if Alex was wearing the shirt, with the current state of testing."

"I wonder what I should do. Being accused like this, and never completely cleared, it's like having plague or leprosy in the old days. The only thing left for me to do is go hide. It's true, isn't it? There's no way to prove a negative. I didn't do anything wrong, but I'm marked for life."

"Don't— Try not to be bitter, Jim. It'll just hurt more." Jim turned away from her. He stared out the window at the mountain beyond. She hoped he could find comfort there, since she didn't seem to be much use in that department.

During the silence that followed, Nina let herself tune into her own interior struggle. Collier had scared her, maybe stampeded her. What facts had he given her? She was a defense attorney. Her job was to fight for her client, not to allow these constant doubts to shake her up. And Jim seemed to be genuinely suffering.

He might be innocent! What about the scene between Marianne and her stepbrother that she'd witnessed at the Festival of Lights? Did she really believe Malavoy was that dangerous? Yes, she did. They were both viable suspects.

"I almost forgot. You called me in. Why did you want me to come over?" Jim asked.

"Because—because I want to bring in another attorney that we can consult with, who'll be available to help with any trial, if it should come to that—"

"But you're doing great!"

"Thanks, but I do recommend we bring in Artie

Wilson. He's got tremendous experience. He's outstanding. You'll like him, Jim."

But Jim was shaking his head violently. "No! Let's just keep on like we have been."

"But can't you just—"

"I don't want to meet him—I don't want to deal with somebody else. I don't want to pay two sets of lawyers. No!"

His vehemence surprised her, but did not deflect her. She wanted Artie. She needed him. Without Paul . . . she stopped that line of thought. Artie would provide a very necessary role as a sounding board in this case. She couldn't discuss the case with Collier or anybody else, but Artie, as co-counsel, could know everything. In her last big civil case, she had discovered both the virtues and drawbacks to collaboration. This time, she could imagine nothing but good coming out of the association.

She hated thinking in a vacuum. Every once in a while, the nagging thought intruded that maybe she had constructed something so faulty in her own mind that the entire edifice would crumble under the least scrutiny. Artie would keep her on track and keep her thinking sturdy. Nothing Jim said would sway her from that determination.

"Look, Jim. I don't feel able to advise you, handle all these complications, alone. I want Artie to join the team. I can't keep on myself if you won't allow me to bring in a co-counsel. Artie isn't going to need a separate retainer. We'll just call him in if and when we need him. Let me assure you, he's very good."

"Will you quit if I don't hire this guy?"

"I didn't say that," Nina waffled.

"What—who's got you thinking this way?"

"C'mon. Let's go upstairs and meet him. Then you can decide."

They climbed the stairs together in silence, Nina in the lead, Jim clomping up behind her.

Artie's receptionist was out, but he already had clients in his office. Nina and Jim waited in the reception area, allowing plenty of time for Jim's already dark mood to turn to black. Nina leafed through a glossy magazine about travel to remote islands, one eye on Jim, totally unable to concentrate on anything except her agitated client.

After ten tense minutes, Jim stood, preparing to leave. As if listening behind his closed door, a busy lawyer heeding the call of the totally disgruntled at the last possible moment, Artie suddenly appeared. A couple of rough-looking characters drifted out behind him, ignored Nina and Jim, shook hands with Artie, and left.

"Into the conference room." Artie nodded in that direction.

As soon as the three of them were together, Nina knew she had done the right thing. She felt much less anxious with Artie involved.

So, of course, Jim couldn't stand him. He didn't like him at the beginning of the conversation, and he seemed to like him less toward the end. Artie tried to jolly him along, asking questions thoughtfully and gently, but Jim answered monosyllabically. To him, young and fit and interested in nothing better than rushing down a mountain as fast as was humanly possible, Artie must have looked like an old fool who couldn't ski his way out of a paper bag.

And Artie, to be honest, was tired, not at his best. He had a perfunctory air, which Jim clearly sensed.

So when they had said polite good-byes and were

back out in the second-floor hall, Jim said only, "I have to take him if I'm going to keep you?"

"I'd feel better with Artie on board. Yes."

"Then I guess he's on board."

"Thanks, Jim. It's for the best. Now try to get some rest tonight."

"I couldn't do without you, Nina. Can I—that is—"

"Yes?"

"Could I just—give you a hug? To thank you for everything? I'd like to." He took a step forward.

She felt prudish, or was it prudent? Anyway, she said only, "I don't think that would be a great idea."

"What's the matter? I let you bring him in. Don't I get a reward?"

"Drive safely."

They were locked tight on Nina's bed. Candles flickered on the bureau.

Downstairs, a chicken roasted in the oven. The half-eaten appetizers, some olives and havarti with crackers, and two glasses of wine, lay neglected on the bedside chest.

They had proceeded to the first course, urgently communicating in the new way between them. As Collier moved on her and she gave back, he said, without using words: I need you; I want you forever. I'll never leave you. And Nina answered: I can't stand being away from you; I don't care about anything but you.

He rocked her, his face buried in her hair. I love you . . . Yes, go ahead, do it, yes, I'm greedy but I don't care, I don't care . . .

She held him tight. And up they went, into the new and timeless place they had found, up and up and then shuddering back down into the world and time.

Collier fell on her. She accepted his weight. They didn't move.

Hitchcock whined at the door, grouchy at being locked out. Collier had said, "No witnesses."

After a long while had passed, and their breaths had synchronized into a peaceful doze, Nina said, "Let me up, Collier. I have to go check on dinner." She climbed down and went into the bathroom. When she came back and saw him sleeping on the bed, breathing heavily, the sheets covering one leg, his head hidden under his arm, she smiled.

He could have an hour. He could have the night.

At nine o'clock he came down, looking surprised and still sleepy. Nina was reading on the couch in her bathrobe. His plate still lay on the table; hers had long since been taken to the kitchen.

Smiling, she motioned to the table and said, "Sorry. Couldn't wait."

"I ought to be the one apologizing."

"Don't. I loved the idea that you were upstairs."

He smiled back. His hair was damp and he was wearing a pair of boxers. He seemed very dear to her.

"Your dinner's in the oven," she said.

"Thanks." He wolfed down a big plate of chicken and fettuccine at the table and then joined her in front of the fire. They talked, as usual, about nothing much. A lot of the time they didn't say anything, just held hands while Nina's head lay on his shoulder.

"Let's go back to bed," she said at eleven. "You're staying the night, aren't you?"

"I wouldn't miss it for the world."

The four-poster seemed to be waiting for them. Hitchcock lay on his blanket at the foot of the bed, twitching now and then in his dreams. And now they did talk in the darkness, in total safety.

"Did you take my advice?" Collier said. "I'm sorry to have to ask."

"It's all right. Not exactly, but I did associate in Artie Wilson."

Collier breathed in sharply. Her hand on his chest witnessed its rise and fall. "You said you would!"

"I—I—"

"I've already lost someone I loved. I don't want to lose you!"

"Give me some facts! I have a duty to my client, and you want me to ignore that just because you say so?"

"Yes!"

"You can't tell me any more about what has you so alarmed?"

"No!"

"Are you going to arrest him again?"

"I hope so," Collier said. "I don't want you representing him. Why won't you take the benefit of what I know, even if I can't tell you the precise facts?"

"I can't."

"God damn it!" He got up and paced around the cold bedroom in the dark.

"Collier, come back to bed. Please. I can't abandon this client just because you're worried. We're going to have to live with a lot of worry because of our work. You have to accept that."

He sat on the edge of the bed, and she pulled him gently down.

"Let's not talk about this," she said.

"I'll try."

"Let's not talk about this either."

"This? Or this?"

"Ohhh. Let's—"

"Let's."

On Thanksgiving Day they went to Sandy's wedding.

Running south from Tahoe, the Luther Pass Highway led through forests which burst out in spectacular displays of color in fall. Now the many deciduous trees thrust skeletal branches to the sky, very Currier and Ives, as specks of cross-country skiers, hikers, even bikers, brightened the white with their rainbow parkas.

"Let's go snowshoeing soon," Collier said. He was driving.

"I always wanted to try that. You know, if the Donner Party people had known how to make snowshoes, they could have walked over the last pass easily. But they were mostly Missouri farmers. It was the snow depth that did them in."

"Yes, that's a hell of a story. Stuck just below a seven thousand foot pass that would have led them straight down and out of the snow."

"It is. I think about them when winter comes here, imagine the mothers trying to feed their kids . . . you know, the Irish family never resorted to cannibalism because they were the only ones who could manage to eat the cattle hides they had used for roofs."

"Pretty grim to think of them coming to America to escape the potato famine, only to starve here."

"The luck of the Irish—I always wondered in what way we were so lucky," Nina said. "What luck? We're just above the Sudanese on the luck scale. But at least the Irish have one talent to keep us going."

"And what might that be?" Collier asked, somewhat warily.

"We're famous bullshitters," Nina said. She looked at him from the corner of her eye. "It's no secret. And did you know that it was an Irishman named Thomas Maguire who invented snowshoes?"

"No, I didn't know that."

"Yep, he made the first set, and then he called in his family and said, 'See what I've made.' And his wife says, 'Well, Thomas, what're they for?' And he says, 'They're for trampling down the grass on the trail down to the pub.' And trample it he did, for the next twenty-four years until he passed away, and the rest of the world had to wait until somebody else reinvented them."

"You just made all that up on the spot."

"Never! I can prove it."

"How?"

"Okay, I can't prove it," Nina said.

They were in Alpine County, the least populated county in California. They passed through the forests into open meadows, and passed the quaint settlement at Sorenson's Resort through Woodfords, where the main event was a small general store. In another few minutes they had arrived at Markleeville, the county seat, little changed in a hundred years.

Nina, holding the wedding present and the map, said, "Take a left here. Sandy's friend lives near Indian Creek."

"The reservation?"

"No," she said, studying the map. "She's between Indian Creek and the Carson River, right before you get to the reservation."

"Wait. I have to put it in four-wheel-drive." In summer, the road would be dirt. Now, slush and snow covered it, and two wavering grooves led the way for wheels to follow. As they pulled off to make sure they weren't heading off into complete wilderness, a pickup truck full of Native American men whooshed by, sending up a rooster tail of snow.

After some time, they came to a large, rustic ranch-style cabin on a wooded knoll, completely surrounded by a classic car dealer's dream of trucks and cars, some battered and just old, others spiffed-up and gleaming. Small groups of people were still arriving—elderly ladies with covered baskets, small children in snowsuits and mittens, young men in cowboy hats. The sky glowed high-altitude blue, with a few clouds on the eastern horizon.

A wide-planked porch surrounded three sides of the house, and colored lanterns had been strung and lit. Bunches of pinecones, pine branches, and red berries tied with ribbons decorated the railings.

At the green front door, surrounded by the smell of white gardenias from a wreath hanging behind them, Sandy and Joseph stood together, receiving their guests. For the first time Nina could remember, Sandy looked nervous.

She wore a fitted blue suede jacket with a thousand small beads sewn on it and long fringe along the arms and across the shoulders, a long skirt, and her turquoise earrings. Handing her the present, Nina said, "Happy Hey You Guys Day. I'm so happy for you, Sandy." Sandy nodded. Nina reached up to shake Joseph White-feather's hand. He looked upright and handsome in his white cowboy hat. Close up, she saw where Wish had gotten his long jaw and benevolent expression.

The house framed a large interior courtyard, paved in stone and swept clear of snow. In spite of the cold weather, somebody put on recorded music and the kids got into a circle and started dancing out there, a simple one-two step in unison, while the grown-ups stood on the sidelines, some from behind the warmth of plate glass, looking on and drinking punch.

A few of the kids, up to about age thirteen, were dressed in full regalia, with headbands and feathers that stuck straight up on their heads like elaborate punk hairdos, or drooped down their backs like raccoon tails. Their clothes were long sweeps of fabric in blue, yellow, red, and white decorated with diamond patterns.

The youngest, about two years old, wore what appeared to be an oversized, fringed bib with a large yellow star centered with a smaller red one. Watching an older dancer, he lifted his tiny feet solemnly, staring first at the ground, then back at the other dancer's feet, then at his own.

Nina watched him. God, he was cute. Maybe someday soon . . .

The guests talked to each other in low tones, formal sounding and subdued. A few men wore suits, and Nina noticed Hal Cole, the current mayor of South Lake Tahoe, and Cathy DiCamillo, the city attorney, earnestly explaining something to Sandy. From the kitchen in back the smell of roasting turkey emanated, and Nina could see the backs of the men and women crowded in there. A big red cooler sat against the wall. Wish was handing out sodas.

"I'll bet that's got something for me in it," Collier said, heading for it. Nina leaned against the wall watching the children dance, sipping her punch and feeling quite content.

A shadow fell over her.

Looking up, she felt a weird sense of displacement. What was he doing here?

"But you're supposed to be in Washington!" she said. She touched his arm. "Of all the places . . ."

"I got an invitation to a good friend's wedding, so I flew out," Paul Van Wagoner said, grinning. "I figured you'd show up."

With his blond hair and white sweater, he seemed to attract all the light in the room.

"You do get around," Nina said.

"Told you I was getting bored. I have to go back tonight and be back on duty at eight A.M."

"It's good to see you."

"It's been a while."

"Remarkable. You flew all the way out here."

"Why not? She's my friend."

"Why not?" Nina echoed.

"So Sandy's broken down and decided to make it official with Joseph. I never thought they would do it."

"You knew about them?"

"I know more than you think. About everything."

How Paul loved double entendres. "It's so sudden," she said, not ready to open the conversation they would have to have too soon.

"You have to go for it while you're hot together, or it never happens," Paul said.

"To be honest," Nina said, ignoring his suggestiveness, "Sandy was the last person I expected to remarry. She's so independent. She's lived alone so long."

"At three A.M., when the traffic shuts up and the birds go to sleep and the only sound is the noise of your own damn thoughts, even the strong get lonely," Paul said, and gave her a look that reminded her of the many occasions that they had kept the loneliness at bay with each other. "You look terrific," he went on.

"Remember the dance at the Elks Lodge, that spring

—what was it, two years ago? When we met each other again. I had just moved to Tahoe."

"We had some drinks. You wore red wine on your sweater. I wore beer on my shirt."

Nina laughed. She had missed him. Tony Ramirez was a good investigator and a good man, but Paul would always be the best.

If only—she wished again that he was working with her on the Strong case. Paul could find out anything, charm anyone, and he was infinitely curious, to the point that he would continue to work on things everyone else thought were hopeless.

Of course, there was also Paul the problem, Paul the unpredictable. He never lost his temper, exactly. He simply trusted his instincts, even when they took him outside the usually constraining influences of law and morality.

He seemed to be following her thoughts. Reaching out, he ruffled her hair. "Too bad it got so complicated."

"Sandy almost quit the day I fired you."

For a moment, he stood contemplating her, and had the grace not to mention that it was he, not she, who had ultimately called for an end to their relationship. Then he looked toward Sandy. "She looks happy, doesn't she?"

"How can you tell?"

"One corner of her mouth is turned up a millimeter."

"Oh, yes. I see now."

"I gave them a hell of a wedding present," Paul said. "I know she's been pining for one. Every time I talk to her, it's the same thing. So I picked up a used one in Reno. It's being delivered tomorrow."

"Oh, really? She never told me she was pining for anything. What is it?"

"A small tractor."

"No kidding!"

"You have to see it sometime. Twenty horsepower, attachments for everything from plowing a field to harvesting the alfalfa. Joseph has twenty acres near Woodfords. I'm just sorry I won't be here when it arrives."

"I never knew you and Sandy were so close."

"Once a friend always a friend," he said lightly. "Listen. Grover Hot Springs isn't far from here. We could have a soak after the party."

"I didn't bring a suit. Paul, I'm in love."

Paul didn't move a muscle. They were pressed together in the crush, so she would have known.

"Anyone I know?" he said.

"Collier Hallowell."

"The D.A.? He's back?"

"He's different, Paul. He's fine. He's been back for a couple of months. We started seeing each other and—it's gone very fast."

"Is he here?"

"He's over there somewhere, trying to land a beer." She scanned the group again, but couldn't see his head.

"You're sure about this?"

"Very sure."

"I'm surprised."

"Yes."

"Someone finally got through to you."

Nina said simply, "Yes. He did."

"And he's—"

"He's in love, too."

"Well." There was a pause. Then he rested his hand

on her shoulder lightly, bestowing a benediction. "I wish you the best, you know that."

"Thanks."

He looked into her eyes with the same old warmth, the same old twinkle. "I'm still here for you. If you need me, I'll come take care of it."

He removed his hand from her shoulder, and Nina turned away from him, touched. There was a sweetness in the words that made her smile and ache at the same time. "You can count on me too," she said.

The kids had gradually stopped dancing, almost imperceptibly slowing and fading off into the kitchen or out front. A handsome young woman with curly black hair that fell below her shoulders, wearing a blue vest with a long black skirt, held up a big book. She spoke, and the room hushed.

"Let's perform the ceremony," she said. Nina saw now that the book in her hands was a Bible. Where was Collier? Outside? But Sandy and Joseph were walking through the crowd, which parted for them, making their way to the young woman. Wish trailed behind, along with an assortment of other close relatives, a few Nina recognized. And just like that, the marriage ceremony began.

"As it says in Psalms, God has tested us," the minister said. "Sandy and Joseph know all about this test." She smiled and began to read from the book, " 'Thou hast tried us as silver is tried. Thou didst bring us into the net . . .' "

Except for the occasional babbling of one of the toddlers, the room, the whole cabin, fell silent and listened. " 'We went through fire and through water; yet thou hast brought us forth to a spacious place . . .' " the minister read.

Nina, at first listening with half an ear, felt herself drawn in. " 'Sing praises to the Lord, O ye his saints, and give thanks to his holy name. For his anger is but for a moment, and his favor is for a lifetime . . .' "

Sandy held Joseph's hand. All Nina could see of her was her long black hair, held loosely by a silver pin, spilling down her back.

" 'Weeping may tarry for the night, but joy comes with the morning.' " She closed the book.

"Sandy and Joseph, I'm so happy today to see you together again in this 'spacious place,' full of harmony and love. We don't often get two chances to make things right in this lifetime. You're blessed, and I believe you know that you are blessed.

"You know, I used to see you when I was a kid, walking together twenty years ago along the road by Woodfords, and it pleases my soul to think you might do it again. Anything's possible when you love each other. And I know this time you're going to love, honor, and cherish each other for the long haul. This morning, your joy has come.

"Let's have you take the vows."

In five minutes, it was over. Sandy and Joseph didn't exactly kiss, they just sort of brushed cheeks. People surrounded them, and Paul and Nina watched from their corner.

"It takes a lot of guts to do that," Paul said. "Extra guts to do it with the same person twice."

Nina, who had completely choked up during the ceremony, wiped her eyes. "Maybe they never really broke up," she said. "Where's Collier? Do you see him anywhere? He missed the whole thing."

"Let's go find him."

A procession had begun from the kitchen. Everyone

was bringing out the potluck dishes to the linen-covered tables that had been arranged in the main room. Nina and Paul made their way slowly past the parade toward the front door, until at last they could negotiate their way outside. "Let's check the car," Nina said, and they trekked through the snow to the tree that shielded Collier's Subaru.

Which appeared, like Collier, to be missing.

"Hey!" They turned back toward the house. Sandy was waving at them, so they headed back. "I was trying to talk to you, but I had to get married first. Collier had to go in a hurry. He got paged. There were a lot of people in that room and he couldn't find you, so he told me to tell you he was sorry to take the car."

"No problem," Paul said. "I've got to go right through town to get back to the Reno Airport. I'll take her."

"He could have found me," Nina said. "I didn't go anywhere. It must have something to do with—" He had been afraid to drive back with her, afraid he might say something he shouldn't.

"You better get used to it," Sandy said.

"Well, at least I know where he is. Sandy, that was a beautiful ceremony. Thank you for inviting us."

"It's not over yet. Come on in. First, we dance and eat. Then I'm going to cut the cake and there's coffee."

Paul held out his arm. "Shall we?" he said.

Inside on the patio, everyone had joined hands in a circle. The older children, feet moving lightly as feathers over the stone floor, demonstrated the steps. A Shoshone woman began to sing, and everyone was expected to join in.

"You have to get in the circle and dance," Sandy

said. "Linda's singing. She's all the way up from Death Valley. A big circle means big luck for the singer."

"And she's going to need that tonight at the casino," said Joseph, who had appeared beside her. Then occurred one of the most astounding things Nina had ever witnessed.

Joseph gave Sandy's waist a tickle. And Sandy squirmed and was heard to make a high-pitched giggle!

Paul had rented a car, a red Neon which, in spite of being an economy model, drove like a sports car. He whipped around corners like a teenager. Clutching the handle on the door, Nina told him more about herself and Collier, which he took stoically, and he told her about a woman he had been seeing in D.C., which she attempted to take stoically. Although she had no claim on him, she discovered in herself a tiny touch of possessiveness which she had absolutely no business feeling.

Wasn't it strange that, even in the midst of the dizzying depth of her love and her complete attachment to Collier, she could feel so close to another man? She knew what she felt was not disloyal—she had simply known Paul for too long and gone through too much with him to make a complete break. She wasn't sure she ever would, although any feelings for him would stay separate, removed and remote from Collier.

"Paul, could you please slow down?" Nina asked. "Today shook me up enough. And I might think you can't wait to get rid of me."

"You know that's not so, Nina," he said, slowing down to a nice cruising speed. "Anyway, to prove my undying love of your company, we're making a quick stop on the way home."

"What?"

"The day is young," he said mysteriously. In Mark-leeville, he turned left.

"Where are we going?"

"Grover Hot Springs."

"But I told you I don't have a suit!"

"Sandy's friend had an old tank suit that should fit you," he said.

They reached the park in the late afternoon. The long shadows of trees fell around the two green pools, one very hot and one warm. A few ruddy-looking people lounged around the edges. In the middle of the warm pool, a small girl in a Mickey Mouse swimsuit splashed. Her father held her up by her stomach and lectured her on swimming safety.

In the wood shacks that passed for changing rooms they put on swimsuits, meeting on the concrete outside. "Hot," they said, shivering in unison, heading for the smaller pool.

They sank out of winter's chill into the hot pool.

Nina shivered again, this time with pleasure. "I'm reminded of a recent evening with Andrea in a hot tub," she said, "although I have to say, this beats your basic backyard setting." The trees were black and emerald and dappled with snow, and the mountains turned purple in the distance.

They lolled a good long while in the water, until their toes shriveled and the lights came on in the pool. Nina swam laps in the colder pool while Paul shot the breeze with two cross-country skiers who had spent the day at Paradise. When Paul got hungry, they dressed and returned to the car.

At Markleeville, they went into the saloon on the corner. Nina had a sandwich and Paul ordered a burger. The crowd inside was sparse but rowdy. After they had

been there for only a few minutes, two locals who had
been drinking quietly in a corner suddenly stood up,
their chairs scraping. The man in the black cowboy hat
took out a large-caliber gun, letting it hang loosely from
his hand.

"Now you're makin' me damn mad, Cody," he said.

His erstwhile friend held his hands at his sides. The
two of them stood across from each other, both listing
slightly to the side.

Paul got up, seeming entirely ignorant of the action
that had instantly blanketed the room in quiet. He saun-
tered over to the bar and ordered a beer. The lady bartender slipped a beer on the counter and disappeared
without taking the proffered bills. Several other patrons
edged toward the door and made quick escapes.

Nina, in the center of the room, froze. Cody's pockets hung heavy on him. She imagined handguns and
buck knives. If she got up, she would be involved, and
that was the last thing she wanted.

On the other hand, there was the distressing reality
to consider that she, aligned only one table away from
Cody, was directly in the line of fire.

"She ain't worth it," Cody answered.

"I told you before, don't talk about Beth like that!"
Black Hat raised the gun but before he could do anything with it Paul slammed into him, grabbed his gun
hand, whipped him around, and took the weapon.

"I'm glad you didn't kill him, pal," Paul said,
" 'cause then I might have to kill you." He gave Black
Hat's arm a good hard twist for emphasis.

"Ow!" Black Hat howled. "What's your business in
this?" he cried, struggling. "We got a sheriff here, and it
ain't you."

"Ah, but I have an interest in the overall safety of this room," said Paul, letting him go. He pocketed the gun.

"Gimme my gun back!" Black Hat yelled.

"You go on outside with your disputes," said the bartender, reappearing from behind the bar. "This is the last time you drink in here, Billy Boy."

"Aw, no, don't say that, Rochelle. I bring you plenty of business," said Billy, but the bartender had him by the scruff and was leading him out the front door.

"And don't come back!" she shouted, wiping her hands against her apron as she came back inside. "You go on with your fun, folks," she said. "He's gone for tonight, anyways."

Cody, completely unembarrassed by the preceding scene and set at ease by Billy's departure, came up to Paul and said, "Thanks."

Paul said, "Better not talk about his wife like that any more."

"Lemme buy you a beer."

Paul returned to Nina holding two fresh beers.

"Whoa," said Nina. "It's the wild, wild West here. You were good, Paul."

"I'm surprised to hear you say that," Paul said. "You being an officer of the court."

"I could have got up and argued with him," Nina said. "Tried to make him see that shooting would result in a felony conviction. But then he would have been even more riled up and he would have shot me."

Paul laughed. "True," he said.

"Paul?"

"Yeah?"

"Back there at Grover's, remember how I told you

Andrea's been talking a lot about codes of honor. How would you describe your code of honor?"

"I never put it into words," Paul said. "But if I had to, I'd say, 'Make love, but when the war starts, make war.' "

Now it was Nina's turn to laugh.

"And yours?" Paul asked.

"I've been thinking about that. Maybe just, 'Do your duty.' That covers just about everything for me."

"What if there's a conflict among your duties?"

"Then, like Andrea says, family first. It's pretty simple, really."

"So simple to say, so hard to carry out," Paul said.

"Yes." She set her beer down on the table, reminded of all the complications.

"I sense a duty coming on," Paul said. His mood, too, had changed.

"I need to go home, Paul."

"Why?" He had a stubborn expression. He didn't want to go anywhere, he wanted to pretend things hadn't gone wrong between them, that she wasn't with someone else now. Nina felt that she had made a mistake going off with him.

"Because it won't do either of us any good to sit here and get drunk together, and then maybe do something we'd regret," she said.

"You'd regret. Maybe."

"I'm sorry, Paul."

"I should have let him shoot you," Paul said.

20

"THEY ARRESTED JIM again. He was arraigned this morning and I called the bail bondsman. He won't be out until tomorrow morning," Nina said. She hadn't enjoyed the late-night call from the jail, and she was yawning from the subsequent night of worry.

"I expected it," Tony Ramirez said. Sandy and Wish nodded their heads in eerie unison as the investigator spoke.

Sandy had taken a three-day honeymoon and had shown up as usual on Monday morning. She looked well fed, well rested, and, if it was possible, even more smug than usual. Wish looked happy, too. Having his father at home must agree with him.

Tony continued. "I contacted Kelly, the youngest sister. She refused to talk to anybody for a long time, but for some reason she's decided to come forward now. She was hostile but she told me a few things, including a weird story about the client. She's been subpoenaed. Nina, she could cause trouble."

"What does she know, Tony?" Nina said. They were in the conference room. The file in the Strong case filled three boxes on the long table; pleadings, background, transcripts. Artie came in, and Nina introduced him to the others.

"Pleased to meetcha," he said to them all and sat down and opened his notebook.

"Kelly is twenty-five years old," said Tony. "She looks younger than her age, no makeup, coltish if you know what I mean. Okay. She's going to testify that our boy has a long history of violence. It's an old family thing. Listen up." He didn't need to say that. He had their attention. "Timewarp back fourteen years. Jim's sixteen, Alex is thirteen, Kelly's eleven. Kelly says Jim's doing things to the neighborhood cats."

"Like what?" Nina said it, but there were interested looks all around.

"Like hurting them. He likes to stomp them."

"Uh oh," Artie said. Nina's breath caught. It was such a chilling detail.

"According to Kelly," Tony went on, "something's wrong with Jim. He needs lots of attention. He's jealous of Alex and Kelly—he thinks Kelly gets all the parental attention because she's the baby. One day, Kelly is skiing with him and she swears he runs her right into a tree. She has a concussion and breaks her leg in several places and spends three days in the hospital. The hospital records have been subpoenaed."

"Too remote in time," Nina said, and Artie nodded. "At most, it shows a propensity," he said. "Flaherty's not going to admit evidence of bad character as a teenager. Did Jim confess that he did it?"

"Denied everything. It was her word against his. No charges were filed, nothing like that."

"Maybe Kelly's the liar. Who knows? It won't come in." Artie was thinking like a lawyer, looking for the impact on the case. Nina tried to do the same.

"Kelly claims she hasn't skied since. Bad leg," Tony

said. "Their mother started having problems. Her nerves, whatever that means. Anyway, she decided she couldn't take it any longer. She wanted Jim sent to a clinic for disturbed adolescents. Philip opposed the idea. He thought Jim would grow out of it."

"Out of what?" Wish said.

"Out of being a teenaged Satan," Tony said. "Anyway, there was a huge family fight."

"This was all fourteen years ago, supposedly?" Nina asked.

"Right. While all this is going on, Alex is walking home from school one day and gets hit by a car. No witnesses, he didn't see it coming. He has a concussion, but no permanent damage."

"So?" Artie said.

"So Jim just got his driver's license the month before."

"So what?"

"You could say that. But the mother didn't. She says, I've had enough. The mother blames Jim, takes Alex and Kelly, and leaves Tahoe. The family's torn apart. She goes to Colorado and doesn't come back. She and Alex and Kelly stay for several years, and there's a divorce.

"Meantime, Philip tries to keep Jim on an even keel. Jim's furious at his mother and the brother and sister. He thinks they all ran away from him."

"Which they did," Sandy said.

"More years go by. Jim goes to work at Paradise for his father. Meanwhile, Dad's sneaking away when he can to Colorado, a place high up there in the Rockies called Breckenridge. That's where he visits with the rest of them. He and Mrs. Strong still have a thing going, divorced or not. But Mrs. Strong still doesn't want to ever see Jim again, doesn't want Jim to know where she is. Kelly claims the mother's still afraid of him."

"Did Kelly offer any proof about this alleged propensity for harming animals and breaking people's legs?" Artie asked.

"I'm lucky she's talked to me at all, Artie. I don't worry about proof at this stage. Okay. Now, Alex has turned into a good skier. He and his father decide it's all under control, Jim's grown up and straightened out and seems cured of whatever his problem was. The father invites Alex to come back and work at Paradise. Alex moves back to Tahoe, and Jim seems fine with it. Jim doesn't show any interest in seeing his mother or sister.

"Several more years go by. Mrs. Strong dies—a heart attack—Jim marries Heidi, and Alex marries Marianne. All is calm, all is bright, right? So far as Kelly knows."

"I don't like this story," Artie said. He'd given up the pretense of taking notes and was leaning back in the chair, just listening.

"Kelly moves to North Shore so she can go to the University of Nevada, and Philip's supporting her. But she still doesn't want to have anything to do with Jim. He knows she's around somewhere on North Shore, but that's it. They don't communicate. They are estranged. That's the word, I think."

"If Kelly thinks her brother ran her into a tree, whether he did it or not, she's got a whale of a bias. When's the last time she saw Jim?" Artie asked.

"Ten years ago, until a few weeks ago. She did go to Alex's funeral. She and Jim spoke briefly," Tony said. His beeper went off and he got up and left the conference room.

"Then she knows nothing relevant," Artie concluded. "All she knows is background. This whole regrettable story has nothing to do with Alex Strong's death. That's my opinion."

"It is sad," Wish said. "Nina? Do you think he did bad stuff to animals? And to his sister and brother?"

"I have no idea, Wish." Wish looked troubled that she couldn't reassure him. Nina continued, "You know, Wish, this young lady's told a shocking story that makes Jim look really bad. You often hear shocking stories in a law office. It doesn't mean they are true."

"Yeah, but all this stuff is from a few Ice Ages ago— no problem," Artie said. "Let's do a Motion in Limine and get an order that Hallowell can't even begin to bring up that ancient history."

"I agree. Alex's death was an accident," Nina said. "Nobody's been able to prove otherwise. This case isn't going to trial. We're going to dispose of it again at the second prelim, and that will be it. They can't do a third prelim. Kelly's story is pretty flamboyant, but I agree with you, Artie, true or not, it's ancient history. We ought to be able to get an order excluding it at the prelim."

"So what else has the prosecution got? I mean, they rearrested Jim, there must be something else," Sandy said.

"If there is, Collier will have to disclose it within the next couple of days. I know the DNA results still aren't in," Nina said. "They have a forensics expert from Sacramento coming up to testify. Ed Dorf. I have his report. He still can't prove the fibers came from Alex's shirt. He doesn't add anything about the skin markings, so he's not much of a help for the prosecution."

"How can they hope to win this one?" Artie said. "Why are they pursuing it?"

Tony came back in and took his seat. He looked excited about something.

Nina chose her words carefully. "I believe that Collier has a personal belief that Jim killed his brother. I believe he's pushing it even though he knows the evidence is weak."

"He's not in a position to push losing cases," Artie said. "I've heard about him, though I haven't had him on a case yet. He used to be good, but he lost it. He's a flake."

He looked around at the grimacing faces in the room. Wish was doing a strange dance with his hands, waving something away. "Hey, what'd I say?"

"He's not a flake, Artie," said Nina.

"Okay, he's not a flake. He's just stupid."

"He's not stupid. He just believes in what he's doing."

"Fine. I have no problem with that," Artie said. "Just so he loses."

She changed the subject. "Sandy, pull up some form Motions in Limine for me. I'll start working on that tomorrow. Tony, I want you to keep working on Marianne Strong. She's on the subpoena list and I need to know if she's going to add anything."

"Which brings up a point," Tony said. "The half-brother who gave Alex a black eye. The ex–night host."

"Gene Malavoy."

"Yeah. I just got a call. Malavoy was picked up this morning. Possession of crystal meth. Looks like they're going to charge him. He went for the arresting officer and had to be subdued. He's in big trouble."

Nina said, "So Jim was right. He is a druggie." So

Jim had told her the truth about Malavoy! She stored that up to use against her doubts on her next sleepless night.

"Let me know the prelim date," Artie said. "I'll be there."

"Okay. And, Wish, would you be able to go up to Incline to see Kelly Strong with me this afternoon? I have to talk to her, obviously."

"You bet!" Wish said.

They left about three. Kelly hadn't answered the phone, but Nina couldn't wait. She felt a sense of urgency about the girl. She was kicking herself for not talking to Kelly earlier, but Jim's sister hadn't seemed to be involved with the events in South Lake Tahoe. Marianne and Malavoy had taken up her attention, rightly or wrongly, and the forensics problems had been so thorny . . .

Collier had obviously just talked to Kelly, that day he had come back to grab Nina and insist she get out of the case. Kelly must be believable.

Nina didn't like the sensation that she was following Collier around. She needed to move faster. The problem was, she was dog-tired, this afternoon especially. One problem was, she had no Paul to keep ahead of the case. Tony was great at carrying out orders, but Paul had always taken the initiative.

Wish, buckling up in the passenger seat of the Bronco, said, "Look." They could see Paradise, looming off to the right. Only the upper part of the mountain was visible, vertically striped with white runs. "It looks so smooth until you're at the top of the run and looking down. Then it looks like corrugated cardboard covered with ice."

"I take it you don't like skiing, Wish."

"I tried it once. I snowplowed all day. My legs were so sore I spent the next two days in bed. Do you like it?"

"Sometimes better than other times," she said, thinking of her day with Jim.

They drove slowly, stopping at the series of traffic lights at Stateline, then left the town and got stuck behind a loud snowplow chugging along at about twenty-five. There were no detours, and there was no other lane. Nina bit her fingernails and chatted with Wish about the wedding, and at Spooner Junction the plow turned right. After that the road lay clear ahead, and they pulled into Incline by four-thirty.

The town was so hidden in thick forest they should have left a trail of crumbs as they turned onto Country Club Drive. Only a block or so from the lake, there was no snow on the lawn in front of the condominiums where Kelly Strong lived. They went to number twenty and waited.

No one home.

Back to the car. It was getting dark.

"We could go take a look at the lake," Wish said. She would have preferred to doze in the car, but they walked down and watched the stars coming out one by one, reflected in the burnished water. Nina was tired of talk. She just wanted to get on with it, get a personal impression of Kelly so she'd know how to attack her at the prelim . . . Her shoes were full of sand. She pulled them off and touched the ice-cold water with her toe.

She felt ice cold too. She'd have to be that way to get through another hearing. She felt a pressure building inside. She was holding something back from herself. The combination of fatigue and anxiety wasn't good.

The lights came on just as they drove up. "On second thought," Nina said, "this is a young girl. She's going to be hard to talk to. I might do better alone, okay, Wish? It won't be as threatening."

"Whatever you say. I'll wait." She got out of the car, leaving her briefcase behind, and walked along the asphalt path and up the stairs. "Hi," she said when Kelly Strong opened the door.

"Yes?"

"I'm Nina Reilly."

"Oh."

"Your brother's attorney."

"I know."

"I'd just like a minute to talk to you. Please?"

Kelly hesitated. Then she stepped out onto the landing, closing the door.

After the ultra-athleticism of all the other Strongs, Kelly was a relief. No suntan, no muscles, just a small, rather frail-looking student in a UN baseball cap. She looked like a washed-out, watered-down version of Jim, with sloping shoulders and freckled hands. A kid.

Nina looked at her, hard.

Kelly took the look. "Talk away," she said, her voice sounding just like a kid's, too. "Mr. Ramirez told me you might come."

"I understand you've agreed to testify at your brother's preliminary hearing."

"Yes."

"I was wondering, why now? Why didn't you come forward the first time around, if you had something to say?"

She crossed her arms over her chest. "Because it has to stop somewhere," she said. "You know, I'm not going to go through the whole story with you again. I'm tired, and I have to work on a term paper tonight."

"What are you studying?"

"Poli Sci."

"Great. Want to teach?"

"No. I'm going on to law school, if things work out." She gave Nina a curious look, vulnerable, as if Nina was the first woman lawyer she had ever seen.

She was one of those kids who dream of the law, of being respected and doing some good in the world and making pots of money. Nina was always surprised to come across such old-fashioned attitudes in these jaded times. "Good luck," she said. Kelly would need it.

"Whatever. So what do you want to know?"

Nina had come to cross-examine Kelly, if Kelly would let her. But she was off-key tonight. She wasn't up to it.

"I suppose—I'll be honest with you, Kelly. I came to meet you. That's about it. I need to see people who are coming to court. I wanted to get a feeling as to whether you'll be a credible witness. I don't really need to talk with you for a long time. It's just a feeling that I get right away."

"I won't tell anything but the truth."

"No, I believe you won't." Nina hadn't meant to say this. She felt again that something was wrong with her.

Kelly relaxed somewhat on hearing this.

Meeting her, seeing the big innocent eyes behind the wire-rimmed glasses really had been enough. Feeling defeated, she thought about leaving, but Kelly said, "You can come in for a minute if you want."

Inside, a student's room, a room full of books from floor to ceiling, a few scruffy chairs and tables. No TV.

Nina walked over to look at the books. Twentieth century French writers, books on Dadaism and Surrealism, poetry, psychology—nary a book on political science or law in sight. "I'd really rather be reading anything but," Kelly said with a nervous laugh.

"Could I take a look?" Nina pulled out a heavy volume on twentieth century art and checked the index for Max Ernst. "If you don't mind. There's a painting that's been on my mind, and—here it is."

Such a hideous painting! Dreary industrial sky, sharp shadows. The sky had a crack in it, and the plantlike structure on the right was collapsing. In the center was the Elephant Celebes, a dream monster like a crude elephant, its back to the viewer, shaped like a boiler with a pipe for its tail, a fake misshapen horned head growing from that tail. You couldn't see the real head, and you didn't want to see it, you really didn't. Enough to see that the long tusks were just turning toward you, turning in spite of the artist's struggle to keep the real head hidden because it was too awful to see . . .

In the forefront of the picture, a naked classical woman's torso running away. Headless, charred around the neck.

Nina stared at the painting, fascinated. It had been at the back of her mind for weeks. It seemed to her to encapsulate her current position, but in some nightmarish way, indescribable in words.

When she had first seen it, years ago, she had thought the picture was funny. It had never been funny, but she had been too inexperienced to see the horror in it.

Her heart pounding, she closed the book and propped herself against the bookshelf, gasping. "Sorry," she said. She was hyperventilating. Panic seemed to have a grip around her middle—she was going to fall down—she couldn't breathe at all—she had never been so frightened in her life—was she about to die? She was, she was going to die now, and it was going to be bad, terrible, awful—

"Are you all right? What's wrong? Here, let me help you sit down."

Kelly brought her a glass of water, then sat down in the chair opposite. Slowly, Nina brought herself under control. She counted mentally, bringing her breath back to normal and relaxing the tense muscles.

"You had an anxiety attack," Kelly said. "I know a bit about that myself."

"I'm embarrassed. One minute I was looking at that picture, and the next—I imagine that's what a heart attack feels like. I'm afraid it'll come back."

"It's over now. You know," Kelly said slowly, "I make my judgment right off the bat, too. I believe you are a decent person. And because of that, I'm going to tell you something you better pay attention to."

"I'm not sure I want to hear it."

"I have to say it anyway. You're right to be afraid."

"Of what?"

"Of my brother."

"I'm not afraid of Jim."

"Sure," Kelly said.

Nina drank some more water. "Feeling better?" Kelly said.

"Yes."

"Could I ask you a question, then?"

"Go ahead."

"Where is Heidi? Jim's wife? You know, she called me."

"When?"

"A couple of weeks ago. I met her at the funeral, and we talked, and exchanged phone numbers. I was very surprised to hear from her. She was right next door in King's Beach, staying at a motel. She wanted to talk to me, so we agreed to meet at the casino. But she didn't come."

"Did she leave any number where you could reach her?"

"Just the old number of the place where she was staying. I called it, but it was just some place in King's Beach. She took off and left all her stuff. They were gonna keep it to pay her bill. Is Jim after her?"

"No. Not in the way I think you mean. He's worried about her too."

"So you don't know where she is either?"

"No."

Kelly said, "Good, then."

"What's that supposed to mean?"

"Just that people are safe," Kelly said. "Except my father. I worry about him now."

"Kelly, I don't understand you, all of you. Your family."

"Don't include Jim in that word."

"You act like Jim's some kind of Ebola virus. Couldn't you be mistaken? I know him, I've talked to him many times. He's lost his brother, his wife's left him, you all hate him. Now he's lost his job. He's facing a murder charge."

"All true," Kelly said. "Except for one thing you said. You don't know him."

"You know, the case against Jim is very weak," Nina said. Kelly tensed, and Nina went on, "No matter what the D.A. or his investigator told you. Your testimony is peripheral, and the forensic evidence is weak."

"Is that so?"

"That's so. Most of what you have to say will never be admitted as evidence. That's the truth."

"But—But—"

"No matter what they told you."

This upset her. "I think you'd better go. If you're feeling better."

"Where was Heidi staying in King's Beach?"

"I don't remember."

"Do you still have the number somewhere?"

"No."

"I see. Well, thanks for talking with me."

"You're welcome." Kelly saw her to the door. She stopped just outside, and said to Nina, "What made you decide to become a lawyer?"

"My mother died. Some things connected with that."

"Hmm. But why do you do this sort of work? You know, defend people like Jim?"

Nina thought about that. "I guess I identify more with the guy who's got the least power in any given legal situation. The criminal defendant—he or she often has no one. He's been pulled into a machine he doesn't understand, that will crush him whether he's guilty or innocent, if he doesn't get help. I feel that it's important to stand in the way of that process."

Kelly nodded.

"And why do you want to go to law school?" Nina asked.

"I don't know. It's something I've wanted ever since I was a kid. Of course, that may not happen now."

"Why not?"

"Because someone who claimed to work at my old high school in Colorado called the dean of the School of Social Sciences and said that I faked the transcripts I sent in when I applied. There's going to be an investigation." She looked down, and Nina could see how much this had hurt her.

"Did you? Fake something?" she said gently.

"No. But it won't be easy to clear up. It's just like him. He's on me now, but I don't care, because like I said, this has to stop. He said to me, when I was in the hospital—I wasn't sure what had happened at that point, I had a short-term memory loss from the concussion—he was talking about my skiing—I really loved to ski then—he said . . ."

"He said?"

"I take the thing you love the most," Kelly said. "He said that. I never forgot it."

"Wish! Wish! Wake up!"

"Huh?"

"Open the door!"

"Yeah! You bet!"

Nina slammed the door, and said, "Head for King's Beach."

"Sure. And get some supper there? There's a Kentucky Fried Chicken, a Taco Bell, a Subway . . ."

Once they left the forest, the highway became a solid strip of vacation houses, road construction, and half-defunct casinos. King's Beach wasn't far, but it was a very different community from upscale Incline. Cheap motels lined the road, with college kids spilling out of the fast-food places and wall-to-wall traffic, every car with its rack of skis on top. From here, on the north side of the lake, you could ski Mount Rose, joining the Reno people coming up from the other side, or Squaw, if you followed the lake west. They stopped at a place called Wave's to order burgers.

While Wish stood in line, Nina found the pay phone with its phone book and started calling every motel in town. She was looking for a friend of a friend, a pretty blond skier . . . the police had been around to ask about her . . . it only took three calls because the manager remembered the police. "As I already explained," the manager of the Five Pines Motel told her in a pronounced accent, "the lady left quite some time ago. And that is all I know."

"I'll be right there." Wish came out with a bag stuffed with junk food. They ate french fries oily enough to kill seabirds while Nina steered with one hand.

The Five Pines Motel, on Bear Street, had nary a treetop on its small property. Maybe it was named for five pines it had displaced. Nina and Wish marched in and rang the bell.

The manager came through a half-open door, through which a scene of warm domesticity was displayed—the TV, of course, a cat curled up on top of it, a woman in a sari sewing in a chair, a diapered tyke standing up in his playpen. The manager frowned when he asked again about Heidi Strong. "I don't know where she went. She left on October twenty-sixth, I can tell you that. She didn't pay her bill either."

"That's why I'm here," Nina said. "I came to pay her bill."

"You did?" His face broke into a smile.

"And to collect her things."

"Her things? What things?"

"The things she left for me," Nina said. "You did have them, didn't you?" Clearly, he hadn't mentioned

Heidi's possessions to the police. He had taken them because he hadn't been paid. She couldn't blame him. "Her Tioga camper and her personal items. My friend will take them out to the car," Nina said, extracting her checkbook and opening it.

"But she took her truck! You are very mistaken about that. And I don't have those other things anymore! Oh my gosh, I didn't know you were coming! I only have the sack for the Goodwill! And the cat! Tell her I am sorry!"

"Oh, no!" Nina said. "What's happened to her jewelry, her clothes?"

"I sold everything to pay the bill. But I still have one sack!" He called in an excited voice to his wife, and she appeared in a moment with a large grocery bag packed with mostly clothes.

"This is all you have? Absolutely all?"

"But how could I know? And I didn't make my room rate, not by a long shot." He looked at his wife looked back at Nina. "You can't blame me."

"She will be very disappointed when I tell her."

"Tell her next time to pay the bill!" shouted his wife A discussion between the manager and his wife in rapid-fire foreign language ensued. The woman bega pointing back into her living room and shaking her hea violently. Nina reached out for the bag but the woma snatched it back.

"I am sorry, but I must have the difference of twent dollars to make up for the room rate," the manager sai apologetically. "And she gave us the cat."

"Keep the cat. As for the money, you're kidding right? That's a joke," said Nina.

"Ten dollars then?"

"Only because I'm in a hurry." She handed him

ten-dollar bill and received the grocery bag in turn. Out they went to the car with their find.

"It's evidence," Wish said dubiously as she turned on the interior car lights and began emptying the bag.

"Only after a thorough examination will I know that, Wish. And if it is, I will transport it to the police at the first available opportunity."

Not much was left—old makeup and a brush, a torn *Ski World* magazine, a couple of books, a stained sweatshirt, a curling iron—things the manager's family couldn't sell or use. "She left without her makeup?" Nina said. "Well, maybe this is old."

"What's this?" Wish said. "A map of Nevada." It was crumpled, torn, useless even to a thrift store. Wish already was unfolding it. "Hey, X marks the spot," he said. Nina saw the penciled circle.

"Pyramid Lake," she said.

"Nobody goes there in winter," Wish said. "Except natives."

"Well, we're going there. Right now. Can you?"

"Sure. But I have to call my mom. Nothing will be open this time of night. There's only the general store and some trailers, a few houses. It's probably all closed up. She can't be there."

"Seat belt. We'll take the Mount Rose Highway, then pick up Highway Eighty toward Reno. How far is it past Reno?"

"A ways. Nina? This is important, huh?"

"I have to find that woman again," Nina said. "You drive, please, Wish."

21

"So why did your parents break up?" Nina asked Wish. She had dozed for a while and awakened feeling a lessening of that pressure inside her.

They were winding over the last pass, north of Sparks, on the road to Pyramid Lake. They had left the snow and the Sierra and were driving the high desert now. Darkness lay all around, except above, where the stars were shards of shattered glass. In their long descent they had moved back into autumn; the air felt positively balmy.

Wish fingered his incipient mustache. "I dunno. My mom threw him out. I didn't expect it. They always got along. My daddy is a good man."

"That must have been hard for you. How old were you?"

"Oh, seven I think. He went away for a few years, but then he came back. He didn't like the rest of America, he said. But my mom wouldn't talk to him. Then he started sending her presents, things she would never buy. He has a good job now, and he likes to share his money. That got her worried, so she started handling his finances for him. She put it in the stock market pharmaceuticals I think."

Nina listened to Wish ramble on about the enigmatic Sandy.

"I guess they fell back in love, is all I can say," Wish was saying. "They like to sit outside on the porch and watch the sunset. It's good."

"You look awfully happy about it."

"Sure. She's not going to be lonely when I move out. She's been trying to keep me at home, but now she's got my daddy. That's how it goes. People leave, but new people come. If you're lucky."

"You're leaving home?"

"I'm nearly twenty. My mom has a big thumb, you know? And a man needs his freedom. Hey, hear the coyote out there?" He pulled over for a minute and they listened to the long and lonely wails.

Somewhere out there was the huge shallow lake, bounded by scrub and rock, too dark to see. Pyramid Lake was the remnant of an ancient inland sea that during the Ice Ages had covered a third of Nevada. It was known for the many prehistoric settlements in the rocks along its edges, and for the fishing.

John Fremont had seen the lake in 1844 on one of his expeditions and named it for its pyramid-shaped island. In 1860, all the land surrounding it had been made into a Paiute reservation. The Paiute, who didn't agree with this plan, had fought several major battles with the whites here.

The Paiute, relatives of the Washoe, and the white man still weren't exactly friendly out here.

The road pointed straight through the desert, moving up a long incline now.

Just before nine, they came around a bend and pulled into Sutcliffe, a tiny settlement amid what felt like total desolation. The lake must be a few hundred feet away.

They could smell it to the east as they got out of the car, an atavistic sense telling them that the water was in that direction.

The name of the store was Crosby's. It was closed, but the gas station with its minimart next door was open.

The lit sign and the cars parked out front meant someone was around to answer questions. Nina wished she had a picture of Heidi.

"I'll go in," she said.

As he turned the car off, Wish asked, "What do we do if we find her?"

"Just talk to her."

Inside, a couple of unshaven types were lounging at the counter, watching a TV set high on the wall. Ignoring them, Nina gave her Mastercard to the boy behind the counter and said, "Twenty dollars."

"Regular?"

"Yeah." Wish, who had ambled in behind her and set a pint carton of milk down on the counter, said, "I'll go pump it."

"Thanks."

"You want the milk?" said the boy. One eye was trained on the TV.

"Yes. You want a twenty-buck tip?" Nina said. Both slightly bloodshot eyes focused quickly on her.

"How do I get that? You want me to wash your windows? I can't leave the register."

"No. Just help me find a friend."

"What kind of friend?"

"A girl who came here a few weeks ago. She migh still be around. Her name was Heidi."

His mouth turned down. In a disappointed voice, he said, "I don't know any Heidi."

"Sometimes she uses her middle name, but I can't remember it. She's very pretty. Very tall, with short blond hair and pale skin, very athletic."

"I might've seen her. Let me think." He was trying.

"Kind of nervous. In her early twenties," Nina said.

"You know, man," said one of the regulars who had been listening in. "The stuck-up skier." Nina jumped and turned toward him.

"That's her," she said.

"I would've thought of her, if I just had another second, Marvin, you jerk," said the employee.

"Well, I thought of her, so I get the money," said the regular. His low-hanging jeans had been worn too many days, and he wasn't wearing his shorts. "I don't know her name, but she was staying over at the trailers out there, in Dick and Dottie's trailer."

"Is she still there?"

Simultaneously, they said no. "We'd know, because this is the only place to get gas, unless she's staying in the trailer all day. We'd a noticed her. Big girl. She sat outside waxing her skis one day, that's why Marvin called her the skier," said the employee.

Wish came in for his milk. "All set," he said. Nina signed the form and took her receipt.

"So how about the twenty?" said the unsavory Marvin, who had first spoken up.

"Show me Dick and Dottie's and you've got it," Nina said.

A dirt track led to some mostly dark trailers, surrounded by large tufa rock formations and a few scraggly trees. A few lights shone from a few windows, but for the most part the place seemed deserted. Nina was glad Wish was with her.

"Here we are." Set well back in a stubbled yard, a

broken-down Silverstream on blocks, white maybe, not very big, no lights at all.

Nina handed her guide the twenty. "For another twenty I'll go on in with you," he told her, folding it into eighths and jamming it into his watch pocket.

"No thanks, your job is done," Wish said. He came up and stood beside Nina. He was tall, if not intimidating.

"Right then." Marvin went back down the path toward the gas station a few hundred feet distant.

Nina pushed open the gate. No lights came on in the trailer.

"Anybody home?" she called.

Nothing. Before she could set foot into the yard the Silverstream's nearest neighbor came out, a bearded man carrying a baseball bat.

"What do you want?"

"We're looking for Dick and Dottie," Nina said.

"Well, they ain't here."

"So it appears." He was slapping the end of the bat into the palm of his other hand.

"What about their friend? The skier?" Nina said.

"Dottie's niece? She's gone."

"Where?"

"Wouldn't know. I watch the trailer when they go. Now, you asked your questions. And I been polite. So. G'wan. Get."

"I've got twenty bucks for you if you have any information that might help me locate her," Nina said. She held out another twenty.

"What are you? Bill collectors? Not cops. Beat it, I said." The bat stepped up its rhythm. Thwack! Thwack

"But if you'd just—" Wish took Nina's elbow and

steered her onto the path. "We're gone, man, no trouble," he said, but he didn't get an answer, just that rhythmic slapping.

Back in the Bronco, Wish said, "What now? A stakeout?" He was still excited. He would lie out there on the sand braving snakes and baseball bats and flying beer cans all night if she asked him to.

"Home. I've had enough." She was looking through the glass into the bizarrely bright and modern interior of the Sutcliffe gas station, a beacon in the darkness, where the three yokels were emptying a six-pack, an Edward Hopper painting redefined for the nineties.

"What happens now?"

"I don't know. Tony can come back out here. Maybe Heidi was here. Maybe he can find something out."

She had tried and found nothing. That was all she could do tonight.

Tony went out to the desert the next day. About four o'clock he reported back that he also had not made it into the front yard but he had found Dick and Dottie's home address in Las Vegas. Nina had Sandy book him a flight down there. She wanted Heidi. Heidi seemed to her to be the only chance. Logic wasn't driving that thought. She had to know! Was Jim innocent or not? She couldn't stand the constant shifts of thought — guilty, innocent—innocent, guilty—

She didn't tell Jim about the trail she had found on Heidi. Logic had nothing to do with that thought either.

She spent a day at the modest law library on the second floor of the courthouse researching a Motion to Exclude Evidence. Usually, such a motion was heard after the prelim, when the actual testimony could be cited, but she planned a preemptive strike. By Friday, the papers were on file and a hearing had been set on the motion for eight-thirty on the day of the prelim.

December blew in with more snow. When the storm cleared, they had to contend with two more feet of it.

Because she was angry that he had rearrested Jim and because she was so busy, she had not tried to contact Collier, but she missed him badly. By Friday, between the pressure of the case and missing him, she felt slightly nuts. She called him at his office.

"It's me," she said.

"I'm glad you called."

"Why didn't you call me?"

"You told me not to. Last time I pestered you at your office."

"You should have ignored that."

"You said we were moving too fast."

"I take it back. Let's move fast."

"Tonight? I can't get there until eight."

"See you then."

She had time to shop and whip up some frozen pre-sauced shrimp in the pan and make noodles. She even had time to take a bath. By seven-thirty she had started on the wine. She began to think, always a danger sign.

By eight-thirty, when Collier knocked on the door, she had talked herself into calling it quits with him. Poor guy, he had no idea she'd been conversing with him in her mind for an hour before he arrived with a potted evergreen and another bottle of wine. That was fine, they would soon all be potted.

He held out the presents, smiling. "In honor of December third," he said. "I believe it may be a holiday in the Azores." He wore his Norwegian sweater and corduroy slacks. With his beard, he looked like a European writer with irresistibly important things to say. She tried to ignore the impact this had on her.

Without a word, she led him to the table set in front of the fire and poured out what was left of the first bottle. "We need to talk," she said.

He drank deeply from the glass, exhaled, and leaned back. "Eventually," he said. "Sit down. Drink with me. It's Friday and we've made it through another week. Reason to celebrate. Hear anything from Bob?"

"I called last night and talked to him. Kurt took him to Paris for the weekend. Imagine! Kurt got on the phone afterwards and I could tell how much he's enjoying Bob."

"Bob's living it up," Collier said.

"He's growing up too fast!"

"He'll be home soon."

"The sooner the better."

"How was your week?" Collier said.

"I can't talk about my work with you, as you well know."

"Let me just say one thing. I got your motion. It's very well written. As for the specifics, I can't comment until next week."

"No comment, no comment, no comment. It's driving me crazy! We can't go on like this!"

Collier looked sharply at her. Then he said, "I'm going to open this bottle I brought now. And I'm going to drink another glass of wine. Then I want you to come over here and sit on my lap."

"No. Not until we talk."

"Come on, now," Collier said in a wheedling tone which made her laugh and come over to him and park her bottom on his lap.

"That's my girl," he said. "Put your arms around my neck. Like this. My goodness, you smell good. Herb-y. Shampoo-ey." He nuzzled at her.

"But we have—to talk!"

"Very soon, very soon the talking time will come. Now, up you go. I'd like to carry you up to bed, but those stairs are mighty steep, so you'll have to be content with me following behind and pushing."

They went upstairs, Collier herding her like a sheepdog. In her attic bedroom, Collier said softly, "And now I'm going to undress you, my pretty. Very slowly. Resistance is futile." He pulled her sweater off, said, "Breathtaking. I like lace. Take it off. Take it all off. Ah."

They got into bed and he began kissing her. The kisses were a balm on her troubled soul. She began kissing him back, and it became clear that the talking time wouldn't come just then.

Midnight. They ate reheated shrimp at the coffee table. Collier looked rakish in Nina's green silk kimono, his knees and elbows sticking out. He had adopted a pedantic expression. "So what did you want to talk about?" he asked her, licking his fingers.

"Oh, about—you know."

"About how we're on opposite sides of the fence and have to fight in court?"

"Yes."

"About how we have fundamentally different viewpoints on the role of prison as a deterrent and as a punitive measure? Not to mention our divergent views on the death penalty."

"Correct."

"About how our home life would be full of strange pauses as we tried to remember if we were about to divulge confidential information?"

"Precisely."

"It's a lousy career move, as well," Collier said. "Complications everywhere."

"That's what we need to talk about."

"Well, then, it's settled."

"What's settled?"

"We want to be together, don't we?"

"Y-Yes."

"We do not wish to return to our previous lonely and loveless existences?"

Nina laughed. "No," she said.

"We need to present a united front, to strengthen our position. Am I making myself clear?"

"No."

"Oh, yes I am."

"You can't be saying—that."

"Oh, yes I can."

A pause. "Get down on your knees, then," Nina said.

Instead, he got up and rifled through his jacket pocket, which was hanging on a kitchen chair.

He came back and knelt in front of her. "Nina, will you marry me? I love you and I want to be with you forever." He popped open a black silk box. Inside, sparkling orange in the firelight, was the largest diamond solitaire Nina had ever seen.

She raised her head up and looked into his gray eyes. There was a lot of hope there.

"But I'm afraid!" she said.

"I'm terrified." But very gently, he took her hand and slipped the ring on her finger. "A perfect fit," he said. "We were meant for each other. So what's it to be?"

"Yes! The answer is yes!" She threw her arms around him. "And Collier—why, this ring is magnificent! You're magnificent! You planned all this?"

"From the minute I saw you again, I hoped for it." He pulled her into a long kiss.

Eventually, they ended up on the couch, sitting close together. He covered Nina's bare legs with a soft afghan. "Now, the logistics," he said. "Think anyone's open at this hour?"

"Are you serious? I mean, it's past midnight. And we just got engaged."

"I hate long engagements, don't you?"

"You're right. What are we waiting for?" Nina twisted her hand, slipping the ring up and down, watching it shoot glitter around the room. "We could go to Reno and just do it. The registrar is open twenty-four hours a day, every day, including Christmas."

"You checked?"

"A client told me." Misty Patterson had told her that. Misty and her ill-fated husband had been married at a chapel at the Reno Hilton. "We could do it at the Reno Hilton," she said aloud.

"I think I have one clean suit in the closet. And have a collection of silver dollars I've been saving for a lucky day."

"Wear your sweater," Nina said. "I like it."

"But—Bob?"

"He's not here, and the time is now. He likes you. He'll be relieved at not having to go to a wedding."

"You should call him."

"Good idea. It's about nine A.M. there, I think." She got out the phone and called Germany. Kurt's answering machine came on again. Bob was the only one who could have talked her out of it.

"No luck," she said. "What about your mother?"

"Afterwards," he said. "First thing in the morning, then? No more talk?"

"You ever noticed how talking takes the life out of things?" Nina said.

They got up late. "Now you've slept," Collier said. He was drying off in the bathroom. "You're sane again. So?"

"So, I'm still crazy."

"You're sure?"

"Very sure."

"Let's get going, then, before another storm hits."

"You will have to wait just a minute while I try on everything in my wardrobe." She hurried him out of the room and began to pick through her closet, settling on a soft cream wool dress that floated down from her hips. She had bought it once in the midst of an amnesia attack about the fact that that sort of dress did not belong in her sort of office. She was very glad she had hung on to it, thinking someday she would wear it to a wedding. Humming, she brushed her hair, tried a few ways of pinning it, and decided to let it float, too, which it did, all the way down her back in one big fluff.

He stood at the bottom of the stairs, waiting patiently.

They took Collier's Subaru. Stopping at the florist shop near Nina's office, they picked out white and red roses, which the florist deftly fashioned into a bouquet.

In Reno, they stopped at the county clerk's office and registered and paid a fee to the indifferent clerks. They escaped with their piece of paper.

"You can still turn back," Collier said as they walked into the shopping mall under the hotel.

"Do *you* want to turn back?"

"No. It was only a rhetorical question. Covering my bases in case you regret it someday. I can say that I gave you every chance."

"Stop, then. Come on, it's around the corner."

In the basement, just as Misty had described, a store-front studio advertised that it was the Celebration Wedding Chapel. A young lady with stiff hair sat in a small office in front.

"Chapel fee, sixty dollars, plus thirty for the minister's fee, payable in cash," she said. "Will you be needing witnesses?"

They looked at each other. "We forgot those," Collier said.

"Thirty dollars apiece. Myself and the photographer. Would you like pictures?"

They arranged for some pictures. Fifty dollars.

"Flowers? A ring?"

"Nope. We're all set," Collier said, looking at Nina. They sat down together and held hands while the lady fetched the minister and the photographer. Forever after, Nina thought, taking a deep breath, she would remember that moment and her mad happiness when she smelled roses.

"It's not just because of Sandy and Joseph?" Collier whispered. "A copycat crime?"

"No. And it's not because I'm lonely. It's because of you that I'm getting married," Nina said, and he patted her hand. "I'm starting to feel a bit emotional," she added. "This is a big deal, Collier."

"I'll never leave you," he said.

A CD started up and began playing "Here Comes the Bride." They walked past the empty pews to the minister, a white-haired gentleman in a blue suit holding a Bible. Behind them, the young lady and the young photographer sat down.

"We are gathered here to—what's your name again, honey?" He had a pronounced Southern accent. Behind him a yellow and blue stained glass panel made it seem like church.

Some stray thought, about church, or her childhood, or her mother, had uncorked Nina and she started to weep. She just couldn't stay cool. Her mascara was coming down in torrents.

"Nina Fox Reilly," Collier said.

"To join this man, Collier John Hallowell, and this woman, Nina Fix Reilly, in holy matrimony . . ."

She couldn't stop bawling. The minister offered his handkerchief. His embarrassed pink face was only inches from hers. "Do you, Nina, take Collier to be your lawful wedded husband, to have and to hold . . . in sickness and in health, until death do you part?"

"I—I . . ." she blubbered. Floods of tears were punctuated by the occasional loud gasping sob. All she could think of was how she had promised herself never to say the "obey" part. Had the minister said it? She was making so much noise it was impossible to tell.

They were waiting, but she couldn't catch her breath to say the words. "Would you like me to say it for you, honey?" the minister whispered.

"I do!" she wailed.

"And you, Collier, do you take this woman, Nina Fix Reilly—"

"Fox!"

"Nina Fox Reilly, to be your lawful wedded wife . . ."

"I do," Collier said, quite cool-headed, considering the circumstances.

"The ring?"

Nina began to wiggle the ring off her finger but Collier put up a hand to stop her. A second box, this one in velvet, appeared in his hand. He opened it. Inside, curled together like lovers, two slim gold bands nestled. "One for me," he whispered. He was looking at her to see if she liked them. She liked them so much that it brought on more joyful sobbing.

"Put it on her finger," the minister finally suggested.

Collier lifted her limp left hand and slipped the gold ring on right beside the diamond. He handed her the other ring, and helped her to put it on his hand, clasping her hands in his, steadying her.

"Ah now pronounce you man and wife," the minister said as soon as he safely could. On an invisible cue the CD broke into the triumphant Dah da dadada da da da–dada da DAH song. The minister beamed. Collier held her up and she wiped her eyes on the handkerchief. "I'm s-so happy," she said brokenly.

The lady came up and gave her a tape cassette. "Congratulations and here's your precious memory," she said.

"Thank you," said Nina, her voice quavering.

"I'm afraid we have to clear out, now folks. There another couple waiting." The photographer took photo of the four of them, the lady and the minister st beaming in back, Nina smiling tremulously, feeling th makeup smearing on her face but not caring at all, standing with Collier in front.

On the way out, she dumped the cassette in the nearest trash can. The only sound would be sobbing, anyway. Collier carefully folded up the marriage certificate and put it in his wallet. The instant photos he carried in one hand. "Feeling better?" he asked her.

"Yes." She removed the last of her mascara with a long wipe.

"You like the rings?"

"You know I do."

"We can always go together and choose something else."

"No," she said, looking at the two rings that fit so snugly together on her finger, and then admiring the gold band that now encircled his. "I love them. And Collier, you are an amazing man. I never expected this, any of this. Being married to you is going to be a real adventure."

"Can I kiss the bride? It didn't seem like such a good idea in there." He put his arms around her and she murmured into his shoulder, "I'm sorry I cried. I'm such an idiot. I always cry when I feel really happy."

"Let's go have a drink and drop a few hundred," Collier said. "It's a casino, after all. You don't feel sorry? About not having a party like Sandy?"

"This is our party, Collier," Nina said. "A private wedding, an intimate one, for just the two of us. Nothing else matters now, except that we are together." She slipped her arm through his, absorbing the strength that the two of them had.

"Feel like a winner?"

"Roulette," Nina said. "That's how good I feel."

"Red and odd."

"Number three." They went up the elevator.

They spent the night at the Reno Hilton on a round bed, enjoying the kitsch and the champagne provided by the management. Nina finally got home around four in the afternoon and invited herself and Hitchcock over to Matt's for dinner.

"So we went to Reno and did it," she finished. "I called Dad before I came over. He's fine with it." Matt didn't bat an eyelid. He got up, went into the kitchen, and came back with another Coors. He popped it, poured some down his gullet, and set it on the table.

"So what do you think?" Nina said, spooning a second helping of peas onto her plate.

"Can he chop wood? Can he shovel snow and put on his own tire chains? Can he unfreeze the pipes and most importantly, can he play stud poker?" said Matt.

"I'm sure he can."

Andrea said, "My turn. Can he pick up his own socks, cook something besides frozen pizza, and keep the TV off when guests come over?"

"Absolutely."

"Then bring him on over, and we promise we won't tell him about your teenage years," Matt said. That was it. They were so accepting, so kind.

"I bet you were nervous about calling Bob," Andrea said.

"Oh, he knew. He'd been around us quite a bit. I've talked to him before. He's having such a good time with Kurt that I doubt it sank in right away. We'll do some adjusting when he gets back. The thing is, though—Collier is great with him. He really loves kids."

"How about Jack?"

"Jack?"

"You know, the guy you were married to for five years. I bet he'd want to know."

When Jack walked out on her only a few years before, she had thought she would never recover. She could look back on that now and realize she'd passed through it, passed through the shock and grief and loss and come out the other side. As Wish had said, people leave, but if you're lucky, new people come.

"I'll be darned," she said. "I forgot about Jack. I'll call him tomorrow."

"I guess Collier will move in with you," Andrea said. "Since he's renting." She started gathering up the plates. Matt got up to help. Hitchcock followed them, hoping a crumb would fall. Troy had already left to work on his homework. Even little Brianna had some sort of project that required many sheets of construction paper.

"In the next month or two. There's no hurry. He likes our cabin a lot," Nina said.

"Have you told him about your cooking disability yet?"

"Very funny. Don't worry. He knows I cook like Julia Child practices law."

Matt stopped on his way to the kitchen. He looked thoughtful. "I can't keep up with you, Sis. I never have been able to. You've always had this way of pushing right through everything when you decide to do it. You move in a blur, too fast to follow."

"It wasn't too fast this time, Matt. There were a lot of obstacles, challenges, you know? We couldn't let the pressure separate us. We knew there would be a whole —I guess the word is, realignment of those challenges if we were married. Everyone can see that separation isn't an option now. It changes things for Collier at work."

"I was wondering about that," Andrea said.

"It'll just have to work itself out. That's what I mean. We're married now and the machine's going to have to burp and absorb the new configuration and move on."

"You are fearless, Nina."

"That's not it. I just feel like you have to make your life, not just let it happen."

22

On Monday morning after court, Nina told Sandy, Artie, and Wish about her marriage at the same time, since Artie had stopped in to talk about the motion to exclude evidence anyway.

She told them in an underhanded way. They had assembled in the conference room that nippy morning with their coffee mugs. Artie had just finished telling her that the motion looked good. She had just finished telling him and Sandy about her trip to Pyramid Lake and Tony's Las Vegas lead on Heidi. Wish had a pad of paper and seemed to be assiduously taking notes.

"We do want to find her?" Sandy was asking, dubious.

"Oh, yes. If Heidi would just recant her story, the prosecution case would look like London after the blitz. Henry McFarland would put a stop to the whole thing. There would be no hearing, and that's exactly what I want, to have all charges against Jim dropped without a hearing."

"You don't think the judge would find probable cause?" asked Artie.

"A judge can find probable cause in a can of beets, if he wants to. There's always that risk. Better to keep it away from him altogether."

"Sounds good to me," said Artie. He noticed Wish scribbling away. "Don't tell me you're writing down that stuff about the beets," he said to the boy.

Wish blushed to his roots. "No."

"What is it then?"

Wish tried to whisk the paper away, but Artie showed he still had some speed left in him. He lunged and tore the page from Wish's hand. He unfolded and smoothed it, then held it up for all to see. There, in the middle, with the beginning of excellent detail, was a picture of a tin can with "Beets" marked on it.

"Nice work, Michelangelo," Artie said.

"Glad to see you're paying attention, Wish," said Sandy.

Wish took his paper back and moved farther down the table, out of Artie's reach.

"Judge Flaherty's going to feel some heat because this is the second time around," Nina went on. "If he gives in to it, then the whole trial sequence begins. Jim can't afford it, financially or emotionally. It would cost a fortune to fight."

"You're an ambitious young lady," Artie said. "It's not enough to win the hearing, you want to prevent it from even taking place. But what if you find her and she doesn't change a word?"

"Then we're no worse off, because she can't testify since they're married. Speaking of being married, I am."

Sandy, who was also taking notes, jotted on for a minute. Artie seemed not to have heard.

Wish put down his pencil very slowly and stared at her.

"We could take his shares of stock as security, so

we're sure we get paid," Sandy said. "Or did you marry a millionaire?"

"Huh?" Artie said. "What?"

"No, he's not a millionaire. I married Collier Hallo-well."

Artie said, "You're kidding, right? This is a big joke on me for coming in late, is that it?"

"In Reno. On Saturday."

"Paul's gonna love this," Sandy said, shaking her head

"Whoa," said Wish admiringly. "Now that's a move I bet the police never expected! Smart thinking!"

"But—Nina, really. How's this going to impact the case?" Artie said. "I mean, congratulations!"

"I'm not so sure it's a smart move, it's just the one I wanted to make," Nina said to Wish, smiling. "And Artie, I don't know how it's going to affect the case. It's more than the case. It's my whole life, you know? A whole new perspective."

"You really did get married? We gotta celebrate," Artie said. "Great news." He gave her a big smacking kiss on the cheek.

Sandy began gathering up her notes. "I'll go call Jim and have him come in," she said. "And I'm gonna have a hair appointment at that time."

"You do that. I'll disclose it to him, and then I've done what's required. There's no conflict problem if he agrees he wants me to stay on."

Sandy went into the outer office and began clicking on her keyboard.

"She didn't even congratulate you," Artie said. "She's damn rude."

"She'll come around," Nina said, looking after her. "She was rooting for somebody else."

As the time for Jim's appointment rolled around, Nina began feeling an uncomfortable mixture of defiance, embarrassment, and distaste. She had no idea how he might react to her news. Maybe he would feel that it gave him an edge.

The one thing that she didn't want was for Jim to fire her in anger. The prelim was coming up again and he needed her, and it would hurt his case for him to fire her. Even if he did the firing, it would be as a result of her action, and she would feel that she had abandoned him. She felt her duty even more strongly since she actually wanted out of the case in many ways.

She worked on a motion in her purse-snatching case until three o'clock and was just handing Sandy the tape for transcription when Jim came into the outer office.

"Your three o'clock," Sandy said on the intercom. Nina had closed the door to the outer office.

"Sandy, are you really going to leave?" Nina said into the phone.

"Come to think of it, I can get my hair done tomorrow. Or next month."

"Thanks. I'd feel better if you stay in the outer office." She didn't say why she might feel better.

A knock. Sandy opened the door and ushered Jim in. Wearing the Tommy Hilfiger jacket again, he looked more like an ad in *Esquire* than an unemployed murder suspect. Sitting down in the right-hand chair, he pulled it up to the side of the desk, as always edging ever so slightly too close.

"So?" he said. "News?"

"Thanks for coming down today, Jim." In response to this mass of masculinity sitting so damn close to her that she could feel his breath brushing the hair on her arm, she pushed her chair back from the desk.

"I wanted to talk to you about some personal news. Something that's happened . . . in my life," Nina continued.

He looked apprehensive. She had never before mentioned her personal life, and he must know any talk of it was bound to mean bad news for him. "Like what?"

"Well, uh, I guess I'll just say it. I got married this weekend." She kept her face cordial, professional.

He cocked his head at this, as though he didn't trust his ears. Then he tortured his lips into a smile. "Now that's disappointing," he said. "I was going to marry you myself. Ha, ha."

Now that was a truly weird statement. If it was a joke, it was an alarming one. "As you probably know," Nina said, more formally than she'd intended, "if something comes up that has even the appearance of a possible conflict of interest, an attorney has to discuss it with the client so that the client has full knowledge of it."

"Huh," he said. "Well. Although I'm very, very disappointed in you, Nina, I don't think that makes for a conflict of interest, does it?" He still wore that strange, lopsided smile. Suddenly she recognized the expression. He looked like a man caught doing something squalid, something despicable. With increasing unease, Nina said, "Why are you disappointed, Jim?"

"Oh, I suppose I thought . . ." He let the sentence dangle.

She decided she didn't want to know after all and left it dangling. "I need to tell you this because the person I married happens to be the deputy district attorney prosecuting your case." Feeling stifled, she got up to open the door to the outer office, bracing herself for his response. As she passed him, Jim reached out and caught her arm.

"What in the hell were you thinking! He's our enemy, Nina! You married our enemy? What does that make you?" She took her arm away and opened the door, then returned to her desk, wondering how to handle his reaction.

"It doesn't change me at all, Jim, or our relationship. I'm still your lawyer, still totally committed to helping you. I'm telling you this because I have an ethical responsibility to tell you. But I want you to understand very clearly. I'm a professional, and I keep my home life separate from my personal life."

"That's impossible," he said flatly.

"I don't agree."

"How long has this been going on?" he asked.

He made her feel like a perfidious wife. "We've known each other quite some time."

"All this time you were seeing him. You never even mentioned it to me. Don't you think I had a right to know you were sleeping with the enemy?"

Nina sighed. "It was only a friendship for a long time. Then rather suddenly we found we were—"

"Did you talk to him about my case?"

"I would never, never talk to him about anything confidential, Jim. Never. Do you understand? I never have and I never will."

"How do I know that?"

"Because I'm telling you."

"It's completely unacceptable."

"What's unacceptable?"

"You marrying him."

"Well, it's a done deal. If it really is completely unacceptable to you, I'll ask the judge for a continuance on the hearing to give you time to find another lawyer. But I hope you don't do that."

He clapped his hand to his forehead. "I'm screwed!" he cried. "Completely screwed. You screwed me. I can't believe it. Things were going along so well."

"No, Jim, I—"

"How could you do this to me?" He was shouting. Sandy appeared in the doorway.

"Calm down, Jim. Sit down and let's talk about this. I'm quite shocked at your—"

"You're shocked? *You're* shocked? What about me!"

"Stop that shouting!" Sandy said, her deepest, loudest voice roiling into the room over his.

Jim whirled around to face her. "Get out of my face!" he shouted. Sandy stood her ground, solid as a tank in tennis shoes.

"I leave when you twiddle the volume down to low," she said.

Nina said, "Look, Jim, take some time. Think about it, and then call me. I'm sorry I surprised you with this, but I had to tell you. I hope you can realize it's not as bad as you think. It doesn't really change a thing between us."

He looked at her over his shoulder. She didn't like the look. "I'll say only one thing," he told her. "You're my lawyer. You're staying my lawyer. You're not passing me off on that worn-out turkey in a cheap suit." He picked up his jacket from the back of the chair and took a step toward Sandy.

She stepped aside, holding the door for him.

Exit irate client.

Nina held on to the side of the desk. "Oh boy, oh

boy, oh boy," she said. "Check down the hall, will you?"

Sandy moved to the outer door and opened it. "No sign of him." She locked it, came back in, and sat down in the chair Jim had just vacated. "You okay?" she said.

Nina rubbed her cheek. "I never dreamed he'd take it so hard. He acts as if I stabbed him in the back."

The phone rang. They looked at it. "If that's Jim calling me from around the corner or something," Nina said, "tell him I am indisposed."

Sandy picked up the receiver and held it as if a jelly-fish lived in there. "Oh, hello, Tony," she said. "Yeah, she's right here. Most of her." She handed Nina the phone.

"Nina? Hey, I talked to Dick and Dottie here in Vegas. Heidi is Dick's niece. They hadn't heard from her in fifteen years, since she was a kid. She called about three weeks ago and said could she borrow the trailer, and they told her where the key was. They thought she was still there. She hasn't called them since."

"Is there a phone in the trailer?" Nina asked.

"No. They use the gas station when they're up there."

"They think she's still there? That's all they know?"

"That's it. What now?"

"Did you check the trailer?"

"I tried. I still couldn't get in the yard because You Know Who never leaves his place next door. But I don't believe Heidi's around. I staked it out until four in the morning. No lights, no sign of the Tioga she was supposed to be driving."

She let out a breath she seemed to have been holding since Jim first arrived. "Better come on back, Tony. Can you stop in tomorrow?"

"Sure. About eleven?"

"See you then."

She heard Sandy's fingers clacking on the keys out-side, trying to finish some paperwork that was due at five. There was never enough time to absorb anything—anger, fear, dread. The scene with Jim had seemed so out of control, but they were all being swept forward so fast, she'd have forgotten it in five more minutes.

And now came the news that Heidi's trail had gone cold. Wild stories, baseball bats, vague hints that led nowhere . . . Might as well chase a real wild goose. Okay, forget her. Onward to the next move, the next crisis.

Nina put her hands behind her head and stretched, looking out the window at the mountains. She was sick of it, all of it.

She really wanted this case to be over. She wanted to get on with her life with Collier, and until this thing was resolved their relationship could not start up prop-erly.

That was a selfish thought. She felt guilty about be-ing so selfish and about the conversation with Jim. Without meaning to, she had harmed the relationship between them. How would she react, if she were the one charged with murder and her lawyer had married the man prosecuting her? She might well have shouted. She might even have cried. At least he hadn't cried.

The Strong file sat in the middle of her desk directly in front of her. She put her hands down on it and picked up, then thumbed through the pages, one by one.

What had she missed? What more could she do?

The government-issue clock on the wall said three-thirty. Collier had been told to sit on the antique green settee which Henry McFarland had brought in to add some class, as he described it, to the corner office.

The settee was hideously uncomfortable. Collier wondered how much this had entered into Henry's calculations. Certainly, it made Collier eager to keep their meeting brief.

"I don't believe we've ever had a situation like this before, Collier," Henry said, once he had raised his nose above his notes. "I have to say, I don't feel good about having her opposite you."

"My marriage makes no difference to our case."

"Pillow talk. That's what everyone will be thinking about. This case was already fraught with problems. I've been reading the file. You don't have anything new."

"Ed Dorf will make a much better witness than poor Doc Clauson," Collier said. "We all know he was in bad shape during the first prelim. Now, we've got clean, compelling forensic testimony. I believe Flaherty will bind Jim over when he hears what Ed has to say."

"And then there'll be a trial. And if we, by some miracle, convict Jim Strong, he'll appeal on grounds that his lawyer was incompetent. She was drawing hearts on her legal pad and slipping them to the prosecutor. That's what the *Mirror* will say. And the *Chronicle* and the *Examiner* and the . . ."

"Who reads those rags anyway?" asked Collier.

"Heh, heh," said Henry. "Millions read them cover to cover, feeble comics included, as you well know. Now, here's my question for you. Can you persuade her to get out?"

"Get out?"

"Resign as his lawyer."

"Oh, I don't think so."

"Something has to give, Collier."

"She would never do that," Collier told him. "She has a strong sense of duty. She's not going to abandon him on the eve of a prelim when she's in such a strong position."

"Maybe we could file a motion. She's got a conflict."

"That's a bizarre notion. Think of the publicity *that* would attract. No, if her client knows we're married and decides he wants her to stay on, she has every right to continue representing him."

Henry made his pen spin like a miniature baton. When he dropped it, he picked it up and twirled again.

"Henry, just—take the information about Nina and me and file it away in some compartment in your head and don't worry about it. I'll do my job, she'll do hers. The newspapers don't have to know anything. We'll keep the situation quiet. Because she is insisting, which is her right, we have to have the prelim within ten days, as you know. Nobody else is up to speed on this case. So why don't you let me handle this my own way?"

"I guess you didn't hear me. Something has to give. I'm not saying you can't handle it. I'm not saying you can't go up against her in the future. But this one is already as jiggly as gelatin. Your judgment—forgive me—your judgment doesn't seem to be as sound as I would like to see."

The phone rang, and Henry picked it up, still intent upon his pen exercises.

Collier hoped the phone call would distract him. He needed the win in the Strong case because he didn't feel solid in the job yet. But it wasn't just that. He believed Clauson. Strong had to be put away. Henry wasn't convinced of that like Collier was. He had to be there, to see it through. . . .

Henry could seize his marriage to Nina and use it as an excuse to take him off the case, or even decide the evidence was too paltry and the whole thing a no go, if Collier didn't act quickly.

"Tell her to come on in," said Henry. He set his toy down. "Barb's outside," he told Collier. "The P.D.'s office took the plea bargain in her case."

"That's great!"

"Isn't it?" said Henry.

Barbara opened the door saying, "I don't want to disturb you."

"Are you kidding? You just saved the People of the State of California a million bucks and you don't want to disturb me?" Henry came around the desk and gave Barbara a kiss on the cheek.

She accepted it with a smile. "I am so pumped up," she said.

Collier had stood up. He held out his hand. "Fantastic," he said. "Great work."

"Thank you."

"Tell us all about it," Henry said, and she sat down next to Collier on the settee to regale them with the story, managing to look both hard-charging and winsome at the same time. She had unkind words for her opponents. They had made the foolish mistake of underestimating her. She had played with them like a cat playing with balls of yarn, clawing at them with one maneuver after another until they unraveled.

Her excitement at the win was contagious. As she talked on, leaning forward, using her long, slim fingers for emphasis, they basked in her confidence and power. Henry's eyes lit up and stayed lit up.

While Collier listened, nodding his head now and again, a plan began taking shape in his mind. Henry was not going to let him off the hook on this conflict of interest. And along came Barb, smart, effective in court, just finding her wings. She had worked under Collier for a while, saw him as a sort of mentor, even seemed to have a soft spot for him. With her as a figurehead, he could maintain some influence and a role in seeing that bastard Jim Strong put away for a long, long time. . . .

"Let's go out and have a drink after work. Everybody in the office," Henry said when she had finished. "My God, it's the kind of day every prosecutor dreams of having."

"Henry, I'm so sorry, but I can't," Barbara said. "I've got my aerobics class. Then I have my piano lesson. Maybe tomorrow."

Disappointed, Henry said, "Sure, sure."

Collier spoke. "You do love a challenge, don't you, Barb? Ready for a new assignment?"

"I have plenty of back burners waiting. It'll be good to get back to them."

"Such a busy lady," said Henry, stuck on the wasted evening.

"How about you take over the Strong prelim?" Collier said.

"What?" said both Barbara and Henry.

"Ah, Henry." Collier turned to face him. "You sound dog. I know where you are taking us with this, bringing her into the meeting, making such a fuss. You don't have to convince me. She's just right for the job."

Henry stared at him with growing interest.

"You said yourself, it's jiggly as gelatin. Turning a case like this over to a less effective prosecutor will doom our chances. You need Barbara. You want the best for this case, and I appreciate that."

"Wait a minute! I don't want that piece of—" Barbara said.

"See," Henry said, now completely with the program, his voice rising only slightly, but asserting its rank in the room's hierarchy with every carefully enunciated syllable, "Collier just married the defense counsel. We're in a bind."

"Collier! You didn't!"

There was real pain in her voice.

"So I've decided," Henry said. "The Strong case is yours." He cleared his throat. "Okay, we've got that thorny problem out of the way. Now come on, Barb, let's move." He walked over and stood in front of her until she also stood. "First thing we do is to tell everybody you're in charge." He put his hand on her back and steered her toward the door.

She folded her arms and stopped in her tracks. "I don't think you two are listening to me."

Jumping in before Henry got too assertive with her and made her dig in her heels further, Collier said hurriedly, "Of course, I can appreciate how hard it is to jump into a big case like this. There's a lot of publicity, a lot of pressure . . ."

"That isn't it . . ." Barbara began.

"And then, you'd be going up against one of the strongest defense attorneys in town. She's more experienced than you, and has a reputation for winning weak cases . . ."

"Are you implying I can't beat Nina Reilly?" asked Barbara, pulling away from Henry to face Collier.

"Not at all."

"Yes," she said, looking astonished and angry. "I believe that's exactly what you are implying."

"Or maybe you're thinking," Collier steamrolled on

"that Henry's putting you in too late because he knows if we make it past the prelim it will be a tough case to win."

"I . . ." she said.

"Or even that Henry doesn't have the nuts to go after a man who coldbloodedly stomped his own brother to death. Why? Because he doesn't want a loss on his record."

Henry, standing back from the fray, his arms folded like Barb's, a smile frozen at the corners of his mouth, looked content to let Collier smear him, if it got them what they both wanted.

Barbara stepped between them, facing Collier. "You know, Collier, you've just insulted me deeply. Even so, you should know better than to think dime-store psychology will make me do something I don't choose to do. But hey, I'm going to do you a favor. I'm going to rescue you from this flimsy case and bag that prelim. That ought to convince you that you are wrong about Henry's motives. And maybe when you see all that, you will also see that maybe you don't belong here anymore. It's a shame. You used to be so good."

Henry cocked his eyebrows at him. "That's her real strength in or out of court, Collier, wouldn't you say? She's not too squeamish to cut through the bullshit. I know I have trouble being so forthcoming. I for one find it very refreshing. Ready, Barb?"

Collier waited for them to leave the room before allowing himself a sigh of relief. He had done what he could to preserve his position. Too bad the news about his marriage had provoked Barb, but she was a pro. He could work on her, bring her around. Together, they could take Jim Strong down.

Collier smiled at the maitre d' and let his eyes roam the dining room of the Christiania Inn searching for Nina. He found her knocking back a glass of wine and looking at a picture on the wall. "Over there in the corner," he told the guy, and made his way through the packed room toward her.

Skiers, skiers everywhere, all sunburned, young, and well heeled. And tipsy on their choices from the superb wine list. The Christiania pulled in the Heavenly crowd with its atmosphere of Scandinavia and sleigh rides. Crystal chandeliers glittered over the laughing faces of the girls.

Nina wore work clothes, but she had taken off her jacket. Her lavender silk blouse hugged her curves, and her hair fell down her back. He didn't see a briefcase. She must have left it behind in the Bronco for once.

He liked the way she brightened when she saw him. He saw that seeing him could make her happy, and he brightened too.

"And here you are."

"Hungry as a bear on the day after trash collection." He bent over to kiss her. She put her arms around him unselfconsciously.

"How are you?"

"Great, now that I'm with you." He sat down. "And how are you?"

"The same. This house sauvignon blanc is great. Want to try some?" He nodded, and she motioned to a nearby waiter. "The same for the gentleman," she said.

"I had no idea how much I would enjoy you ordering for me."

"I missed you today," Nina said. "Whenever I go over to the courthouse, I find myself looking around for you, just to catch a glimpse. I remember a girlfriend of mine haunting the neighborhood when she had a crush on a boy, and I finally understand what that was all about. It's wonderful to know you're close by. Did you have a fruitful day?"

Collier loosened his tie, reminding himself that he mustn't loosen his tongue. "Same old shit," he said. "And you?"

"The same. Actually, today was tough."

"Tell me what you can." His eyes moved down the menu. When he looked back at her, he was surprised to note how troubled she looked.

"It's so hard not to be able to talk to you. I mean, to tell you everything. Not everything, but—having to watch myself every second to make sure I don't accidentally say something."

"It's like that with lawyers," Collier said. "We're so used to keeping secrets that we even get cagey about what brand of toothpaste we prefer. But I know it's specially hard between you and me."

"Well, let's try to forget about it tonight," Nina said. "Let's talk about the moon and the stars and the snow." he smiled. "Okay?"

"For a while," Collier said. "While we have our dinner. Then there is something I'd like to talk about. No, don't worry. It won't wreck your evening, I promise."

"I didn't mean that."

They ordered and drank, speaking about things that were as far as possible from their profession. During the meal, they took every opportunity to touch, touching hands, touching feet. At some point, each reached out the other person to flick off imaginary lint or push a hair back into place. Each landed a kiss on an unoccupied hand.

The salad came, made of unpronounceable greens that tasted of fennel or even anise, and then grilled fish with fresh zucchini and mushrooms. They finished everything and asked for more bread. Their appetites were unfettered with each other.

Collier felt that he had never been so free. He was more and more sure that what he was about to say was right.

Glasses clinked. The voices around them moved like waves, murmuring, then rising, then falling.

The waiter took his time clearing, sweeping crumbs and stacking fussily. He showed them a dessert menu full of scrumptious offerings, which they shook their heads over in dismay.

"Where are we sleeping tonight?" Collier said after the waiter had left, clucking over their failure to stuff in a final sweet bite.

"You left a clean shirt at the cabin," Nina said.

"And your bed is so much better."

"Yes, but you have the great water pressure in your shower."

"It's just an apartment," Collier said. "You've made the cabin a real home."

"You just haven't had time—"

"We're going to live in the cabin, aren't we?" There it was out. He had started the ball rolling into what was really on his mind.

"I hoped you would want to."

"Of course I do. It's Bob's home, too." He forged on, noting the heightened flush of her cheeks, and the way she looked up at him, and he filled up with love for her. He tried to sound casual, so that if she took issue with anything he proposed, she would never guess that she was ripping his heart out. "Why don't we do the move in January? It'll take that long to wrap up some loose ends I have lying around. I'll give notice on the apartment tomorrow. If that sounds okay."

"Yes, please, Collier!" she said. She had two thumbs under her chin and was resting her elbows on the table. "You were right. It's all so simple now."

The time had come. He adjusted himself at the table. "I have something to say."

"I knew there was something else. The Strong case?"

"Good news on that front," he said, and then kicked himself as he saw the eagerness in her eyes. She thought he meant they were dismissing charges against Jim. "I mean, it isn't a sore point anymore," he said quickly, rushing to mitigate the damage. "I can't go into the details, but I believe Barbara's taking over that case."

She listened to him. "You're joking." She had withdrawn very slightly as they began to talk about the case. Well, she had to be as careful as he did, but he was sorry to see it.

"I'm not."

"Oh, Collier, I—I want to talk to you about this. Tell me you didn't give it up to help me—"

"Nina, it wasn't like that. It was strictly an administrative matter. I can't say anything else."

"Because I was thinking of trying to bail out myself. I was having some— Oh, what's the use. I can't say anything, not a thing."

"You wanted to bail? I'm surprised if that's so, because I had the impression from our heated discussions in my office that this case meant a lot to you."

"Never mind," Nina said, shaking her head. "We

have to stop talking about it. I'm just floored. I know I'll never get to sleep tonight."

Collier consulted his watch. "Speaking of sleep, it's late, and I saw on the docket on my way out of the office that we both have court at eight-thirty tomorrow morning."

He chased down the waiter, who had run off with his credit card and failed to return, while Nina stopped in the rest room. In the anteroom, they picked up their coats, and he helped Nina put on her long down-filled parka. Pulling on her red mittens, she suddenly said in a halting voice, "Before we go—I just want to say—I love you so much—our future together—it's going to be beautiful. A new life . . ."

He put his arm around her and brought her close. The top of her head came up to his chin. They went out like that, into the pure and freezing night.

23

"ALL RIGHT," SAID Judge Flaherty, "the motion be-
re the Court is to exclude any and all testimony at the
eliminary hearing relating to alleged prior acts of mal-
e perpetrated by the defendant." He was reading the
ading on Nina's brief.

"Let's see," he went on. "The primary concern
ems to be expected testimony from Kelly Strong, sister
the defendant. The prior acts of malice include caus-
g Miss Strong to have a skiing accident some fourteen
ars ago, engaging in various acts of cruelty toward
imals some fifteen years ago, and other instances. So
you don't want any of this to come in, counsel?"

"Correct. Basically, we seek to exclude any testi-
ony which purports to show prior bad character, or a
disposition to commit a crime, Your Honor," said
na, who was still wearing her coat as she stood at the
unsel table summoning up her arguments.

Eight-thirty in the morning, with the second prelim
eduled for nine. Outside the courtroom the lights
re still on, because the winter had closed Tahoe into
dark fist of a storm. Artie hadn't even made it, but
would certainly be around by nine. The courtroom
s deserted, except for the two attorneys and the court

personnel, and Collier, sitting a few seats behind Bar
bara, arms folded, deceptively at ease.

Even Jim wouldn't be arriving until shortly befor
nine. With its yellow lights hardly breaking through th
black morning, the courtroom felt as cold and remot
from the world outside as one of the prehistoric caves
Pyramid Lake, a feeling reinforced by the scrawled stic
figures on the blackboard left by a cop in some earli(
hearing.

"I've read the papers," Flaherty said in his warnir
tone. He didn't want to waste any time this mornir
hearing a rehash of cases and points Nina and Barba
had already made much more efficiently in writin
"Go ahead, counsel."

Nina said, "Let me be brief, Your Honor. Kel
Strong hasn't seen her brother, except for a few minut
at the funeral of the victim, for a number of years. T
subject matter is stale. It's so old, Your Honor, that
don't even need to go into the second argument we'
made, which is that the subject matter itself has limit
or no probative value, is incredible, and would be intr
duced only to show bad character, which is impermis
ble pursuant to section 1101(a) of the Evidence Code

"I've got that. That's how you lay it out," Flahe
said. "Miss Banning, how do you respond to the co
tention that the testimony you'd like to adduce is t
old to do us any good?"

Barbara stood up in a suit as red as a cardinal's rob
However, a cardinal's robes would not have ended
mid-thigh as her skirt did. She wore fabulous gold je
elry on her wrists and neck. Even her files were aligi
in an elegant fan pattern on her table.

In spite of the bold duds, she was all business. "It

pattern from childhood to adolescence to early adulthood that sheds important light on the modus operandi of this defendant," she said. "The evidence isn't of some trivial childhood transgression, Your Honor. The testimony doesn't involve a few isolated incidents. What the testimony *will* show is at least twelve instances in which the defendant has demonstrated a lifelong pattern of terrorizing people around him.

"And what is his method? He attacks in a very specific, yet devious manner, Your Honor. He destroys something that the object of his attack cares about more than anything else. For example, the testimony will show that he destroyed his sister's professional skiing career, the thing she wanted the most. A beloved pet, the pet his mother loved. The list goes on and on. To commit these acts of malice amounts to a compulsion, Your Honor.

"The last incident, in which Kelly Strong was almost killed, is fourteen years old. But the first incident is twenty years old. We're talking about a period of several years. There is ample reason to infer that this same pattern has reasserted itself. So we're not asking the Court to allow such evidence because it shows the defendant's disposition to commit violent acts against family members, or to show bad character generally. The prosecution understands that such evidence is inadmissible.

"What we are saying is that the method of killing Alex Strong was the same method used when the defendant became angry at other family members. Violence, Your Honor, a particularly ugly violence with a particularly malicious flavor, recognizable throughout the defendant's life."

Flaherty scratched his cheek with his pencil eraser. It is true that the exclusionary rules may be relaxed in a preliminary hearing," he said as if to himself, but making sure that the whole courtroom could hear him. "Mrs. Reilly, your objections are all technical. In a preliminary examination perhaps we should allow this, in a condensed form perhaps."

Nina said, "If I may respond?" and Flaherty nodded.

"Ms. Banning's central point is that all the alleged acts fit a certain pattern. And what is this pattern? I wrote down the crucial sentence in the argument that's just been made, Your Honor." Nina read from her legal pad. "I quote: 'He destroys something that the object of his attack cares about more than anything else.'

"If that is the pattern, I ask counsel: how does it fit here? Let's assume for the moment that the defendant does demonstrate such a devious pattern. So what did he destroy that Alex cared about more than anything else? His life? Give me a break. That's not devious. They don't claim that he broke Alex's legs, or killed his cat, or even hurt his wife or something. He's supposed to have killed Alex, a direct act if I ever heard of one. The so-called method or pattern of indirect malicious acts, even if there were one, doesn't fit, Your Honor!

"Furthermore, this pattern only is supposed to come into play when the defendant is angry at a family member. If so, there has to be some foundationary evidence that the defendant was angry at his brother! In the witness summaries I've read, there's no evidence like that. In fact, the statement the defendant gave to the police, which will come in, indicates that Jim Strong held his brother's head as he died in a tragic accident—"

"Wait!" Barbara said. "We do have a witness who overheard the defendant's father tell the defendant that his job was going to be taken by the victim."

"You mean Gina Beloit?" Nina loaded her voice

with incredulity. "We have an eavesdropper with an agenda, that's all we have," Nina said. "Did the father make one move to replace him? Would Alex have accepted? Why blame Alex? Why not kill his father? No, Gina Beloit's testimony will not a motive make. Without motive, a solid reason Jim Strong might have wanted to harm his brother, there is no trigger for this alleged pattern.

"You can ferret out a hundred bad things any of us did as kids, but that doesn't prove he perpetrated a heinous crime out of the blue against a family member."

Nina was using an old technique to humanize her client by identifying herself and others in the courtroom with him, while at the same time casting aspersions on the prosecution for acting like small, vicious animals. The judge was too savvy to fall for the obvious ploys, but she trusted unconscious influences to sneak into the decision-making process.

She shook her head, saying emphatically, "It's just that the prosecution doesn't have anything else to work with, Your Honor. What they really want to do with this evidence is to persuade the Court that Alex Strong was murdered. If the defendant looks like a bad enough guy, maybe that will make up for the fact that there's no direct evidence of a murder and that the forensic work was lousy."

Flaherty was getting her real point: that Kelly Strong's testimony would lead to frequent objections, lengthy argument, corroborative witnesses, and rebuttal witnesses. The hearing would get messy and would be significantly protracted.

Flaherty's face lengthened.

Collier fidgeted in his seat, obviously itching to jump

"We can finish her direct testimony in half an hour," said Barbara, just as instantly responsive to the judge's mood.

"More like two extra days," Nina said. She smiled at the younger attorney. Barbara fingered her gold and smiled back. She wore the composure as well as the color of a cardinal, Nina had to admit.

"If I may—" Barbara began, but it was too late.

"I'm not going to allow the testimony," Flaherty said. "It doesn't have much probative value. It's old, and it just doesn't seem to me to assist in demonstrating modus operandi."

"But—"

"So ordered. We'll start the hearing at nine."

They went up to the clerk together to pick up the minute order. Barbara showed no sign that she had been bested. "What perfume are you wearing?" the clerk asked her.

"Oh, do you like it? White Linen. It's old-fashioned but I love it."

"And I dabbed on some Tom's Natural Toothpaste before I left," Nina said. They ignored her. The chat turned to fingernail polish, which Nina was not wearing. She left, having no hope of competing in that arena.

She passed Collier in the hallway. He shot her a glance, then swept past her, completely focused on Barbara.

So he was out, but not completely. Barbara had him lurking in the court for backbone, not that she seemed to need another one. Or was he still in charge?

Outside in the hall at the bank of phones, Nina called Artie's office. She often left her cell phone in her car, and Sandy had been on her about using it frivolously, a finger's distance from a pay phone.

His answering machine came on at the first beep.

"This is the Law Office of Arthur Wilson. I have been called out of town and will not be able to return messages for some time. Please feel free to leave a message which I will return as soon as possible." Artie's voice sounded far away already.

She put in some more change. "Sandy? I just called Artie. His message says he's left town! He's due here in court! What's going on?"

Sandy said, "He left us a message too, but before eight o'clock so I didn't get to talk to him. He says," Nina heard the shuffling of paper, "there's been a change of plan and he won't be able to sit in with you."

"Where did he go? What change of plan?"

"That's all he said."

"What's his number?" Nina pulled a small notebook out of her bag and clicked a pen. "I'll give that rat a piece of my . . ."

"He didn't leave a number."

Nina clicked her pen uselessly. "Okay, Sandy, do me favor. Go upstairs to his office and see what you can find out. Call me right back. I'll be waiting."

She waited impatiently, the pleasure of winning her motion evaporating by the second. She had been depending on Artie to defuse her relationship with Jim, to ke it back to a more even emotional and professional eel. Artie knew that she was depending on him for at, and to help her through the prelim. Where the hell as he? Should she ask for a continuance?

The pay phone rang once, a sharp sound in the mpty hall. She grabbed it . . . "Sandy?"

"That's what they call me."

"What's the story?"

"You aren't going to like this."

Nina looked at her watch. "Just tell me."

"I moseyed up there. The door was locked but the landlord was just opening it. I asked him what happened to Artie. He said he didn't know, just that Artie had cleared out. He said Artie's secretary just left with her things and is gonna file a claim against him."

"What?" said Nina, dumbfounded. "But—he had a lease!" she said, and hearing herself, felt foolish. As if that guaranteed his stability.

"He broke his lease. The landlord wants to know if he can retain you to sue Artie."

Nina said, "I can't believe he would do this! He made a commitment!"

"The landlord let me scope the place out. Looks like Artie left all his books and furnishings, but the personal stuff is gone."

"But what about the files?"

"Gone wherever Arties go."

"He's gone? For good?"

"He's down the road."

"Okay. I'll call later. See what else you can find out."

"Kick butt, now."

She hung up. It was a blow, a particularly galling low blow that had found a vulnerable place and pounded her. Artie had been a friend, but he had also become her support in this case. She would never have done that to a fellow attorney, and had never anticipated such a possibility. He'd abandoned her!

What the hell had happened to him over the weekend? She tried to remember some hint she had overlooked—if he'd ever mentioned some ongoing problem in his life, but he always seemed so happy. He loved h wife; he had some money socked away; he was enjoying his modest office.

A health problem? He wasn't young, and she assumed his wife wasn't either. Her mood wavered between anger and concern.

Jim appeared at the top of the staircase. He walked over to her, jaunty in his parka, his hair slicked back, carefree and healthy as a young man about to hit the slopes or make time with a fresh new babe. He pointed at his watch and said, "Eight forty-five. Right on time. You look good."

"Thanks." Her expression must have warned him, because he said abruptly, "How did the motion go?"

"We won."

"Thank God!" Jim said. "All right!" His face expressed pure pleasure. "So we're past this hurdle."

"But there has been a change in plans. Artie's been—called out of town. Suddenly. He won't be able to join us."

"Oh. Okay then."

"I was relying on his experience, Jim. I think we ought to ask for a continuance."

"You mean, wait to get this over with?"

"Yes, at least a few days, until Artie—until I can talk Artie."

"Wait a minute. We're the ones that insisted on having the second hearing right away, like we did with the first. You said it was a good strategy."

"I still think that. But I don't feel comfortable without Artie. We'd already decided which witnesses he could take, and he was going to be a big help with the coroner's office especially."

"But you were brilliant before, dealing with them.

You've already been over the testimony. What's the problem?"

"Jim, I wanted Artie. I don't think I—"

"He was useless," Jim said. "I mean, I hate to say it, but you're fine on your own, Nina. Where's your confidence? I don't think Artie believed in me, to be honest with you. Maybe that's why he left. Maybe he felt you'd pushed him into something he didn't want to do."

Nina thought about that. She had pushed Artie. He hadn't really wanted to come in.

If that was his problem, he had sure picked a moment to leave which would inflict maximum damage.

"It's five of," Jim said. "Please, Nina. Let's go ahead. I have to put this behind me. I can't stand to wait any longer. I want to start putting my life back together."

Nina, who had many of the same feelings rioting at the moment within her, shrugged. "All right. I guess I can handle it. I've already been through most of it once, as you say, and I have all the files. It's just—"

"What?"

"I can't believe he ran out on me." The place was filling up with the buzz of people. A man gabbing into a cell phone strode by, looking important.

She turned away from the phone and walked with Jim toward the courtroom, thinking. She could go in there, make a scene, destroy any progress she had made, and stall for time. She could forfeit any advantage the tight time frame imposed upon the prosecution.

No. She couldn't take the chance that the case might be compromised. She'd just have to do it without Artie.

Because of the blizzard outside, the prelim started twenty minutes late, and even so, some of the subpoenaed witnesses still hadn't arrived. Marianne Stro-

called to say she couldn't get out of her driveway, which seemed pretty funny; the trailblazing snowboard champ was marooned at home due to snow. Philip Strong, too, called and received permission to report the next day.

They wouldn't have been called to the stand today anyway, since the entire morning and afternoon were taken up with a tedious rehash of the first prelim. Barbara laid her groundwork impeccably. It was just that there was so little groundwork to lay. The same "amendment" to the original coroner's report was covered; the same descriptions of the rescue effort and Alex's death at the hospital were entered into the record.

In the afternoon when Ed Dorf, Doc Clauson's replacement, got to the later forensic findings of the pattern on Alex's skin and the black cotton fibers, he flashed a state-of-the-art laser pointer and professional-looking exhibits, but the slickness and high-tech doodads were not enough to demolish the defense. Nina had had a few extra weeks to shape her cross-examination.

When the dust cleared, two things were obvious: that the presence of the fibers on the bottom of the Tecnicas was suspicious, but might have occurred when the boots came into contact with clothing in the back seat of Philip Strong's car that night; and second, that the pattern on Alex's skin was too faint to convince a jury that a ski boot had caused it, especially after Nina finished grilling Dorf with her own photos of the rock striations where Alex had fallen.

Barbara's uncanny composure never wavered. She was magnificently clinical. Nina's respect for her increased by a hundredfold as she administered blow after blow and Barbara fought back steadfastly. No rolling of eyes, no outbursts, no anger, just the facts, elegantly presented.

When Barbara had more to work with, no one would be able to beat her. She must have been angry to be handed this case at the last minute, and Collier had hinted once that her interest in him had been personal. If that were true, her confident presentation was all the more remarkable.

Inspired by Barbara's performance and mellowed by this calm, academic atmosphere, Nina, too, found herself in top form. As the stronger party, she wielded a scalpel, not an axe, vivisecting official witnesses so neatly that they didn't realize their limbs were being lopped off. They started off whole, normal, credible. When she finished, they were like cartoon figures run through a chain saw, arms and legs dropping away as they stood up.

At four o'clock, as they were all tiring, the lights dimmed in the courthouse. The storm had taken down a line somewhere. Flaherty gave the usual admonishments to the witnesses and adjourned in the light of a couple of emergency lanterns.

In her time at Tahoe Nina had greatly enjoyed the weather, the heat and piney scents of summer and the sunny snowfields of winter, but this was the worst blizzard she could remember. The Bronco was about a hundred feet away in the parking lot, but the storm presented a few problems she, along with the other people in the courthouse who wanted to leave, didn't quite know how to handle.

First of all, the main doors to the outside had frozen. She waited along with everyone else for the back door to be dug out, almost half an hour, she and Jim off one side of the hall, and the prosecutors and court personnel on the other. Then, the rarely used back path was two feet deep in the white stuff. As soon as the doors were opened, the wind tore her hat off and whipped her scarf around so she was again blind.

Led by a grim, chin-jutting deputy, they struggled like pitiful refugees toward vehicles buried up to the hoods in snow which had hardened into ice due to previous plowing. People scattered in all directions. Collier came over and helped Nina shovel out the Bronco. Through the snow, Nina could make out Jim twenty feet away doing the same thing on his car. Even Flaherty was out there with the deputy, trying to get the frozen door open on his Land Rover.

At last, they got the front door open partway and climbed into the compartment together. She turned on the windshield wipers and ripped off her hat, then turned the heater to full blast.

"I've got to get to Matt's," she told Collier.

"I'll take you to the Reno airport."

"He has a tow truck. If anybody can make it off the mountain, he can. He's waiting for me."

"Are you sure? I could—"

"No, really. I'll be there in five minutes."

"Call me from Reno so I know you mean it."

He kissed her and said, "Be safe," then got out to go dig out his own car. She pulled out her cell phone.

"I'm on my way," she told Matt. "What's the weather in Reno? Are they canceling Bob's flight?"

"I just called," Matt said. "Reno's having some rain, nothing severe, and the planes are on time. Can you get here? I've got the tow truck gassed up and ready. I can come get you."

"Let me get out onto the road and see." Bob's flight

arrived in Reno at seven-thirty. She had thought she had plenty of time. Now she was starting to wonder.

Steering through the lot with her brights on, she picked up occasional silhouettes still digging out. Jim seemed to be gone. Barbara was just getting into her SUV, bedraggled and hatless.

So this was the mountains! She finally felt like a local. And her thoughts went back again a hundred and fifty years to the Donner Party, struggling up the Sierra in wagons amid a constant series of blizzards. What super-human strength had brought them, mostly on foot, to seven thousand feet before giving up? How dreadful to see the summit but be stopped forever just below!

She got behind a snowplow as it progressed slowly along Pioneer Trail, avoiding the splash of snow it spit out as it went. Soon, the Bronco led a convoy of trucks and SUVs behind the plow. She hoped the guy at the wheel of the plow could see better than she could. If it fell into the sewer pond at Cold Creek, they would all cheerfully follow.

After another ten minutes of this, she saw the famil-iar turnoff for Pony Express and left her position on the trail, honking out a thanks to the plow.

The short side street where Matt lived had a slight uphill angle and was unplowed. At the end Matt had turned on his floodlight. Like any self-respecting local he had an emergency generator. Turning the Bronco on the right side of the road, she wrapped up as best she could and climbed out into the street, then slowly trudged toward that beacon while the storm raged around her in the dark.

At the warm house she was greeted with open arms. Andrea gave her a hug and lurched back, wiping w hands on her slacks. She pushed Nina into the bedroom, saying, "Don't come out until you're stone dry."

When Nina emerged some minutes later in Andrea's jeans and sweater, the family was finishing dinner. Matt was primed for action, wearing his striped ski hat with the tassel.

"Ready?" he said. "It's five-thirty. We'll hustle."

"Hustle? In this?"

"You're with the King of Snow, Mr. Ten Cylinders, here. I'm the guy they call to dig everybody else out."

"What's that mean? Ten cylinders," asked Nina.

"It means, he wishes he had that many on his truck," said Andrea. "Matt slept all day, so he's very frisky now, but when he gets back, he's going to work all night. We'll see how masterful he's feeling about four A.M." She flipped the tassel on his hat as he passed by.

While Nina put on a spare parka, gloves, hat, and boots, Andrea went into the kitchen. "Here," Andrea said when she returned, handing Nina a plastic grocery bag. "Supper."

"You are the best."

"How true." She went over to Matt, unrecognizable in his warm duds, and said, "Don't fall off Spooner Summit."

Matt said, "Keep the lamp lit and burnin'. "

He went first and started up the ignition and heater, holding the door for Nina a few minutes later. They put on their seat belts and settled in for the ride.

Nina had thought the Bronco was a good snow vehicle, but the tow truck was a complete snow hound. With the chains on its massive radials, the load of tools in the back, the sheer weight of the thing, she felt like they might actually make it. And they had to make it.

What could Bob do at night in the airport if they didn't? Call a taxi and find a hotel at his age?

"See, this is why I didn't want him to go," Nina said, her mouth full of dinner as they bounced over a branch in the road. "He could cope with an average flight, but not an emergency like me not coming at all."

"Hush up," Matt said. "You eat, I'll drive. No sweat."

It was ghostly. The truck shook from the furious gusts and the traffic lights were dark. The good news was, nobody was insane enough to be out except emergency personnel. The snowplow attached to the front of the truck did its job as needed, and they moved slowly through the white, torn landscape of fallen trees and red emergency lights along the invisible lake to the Spooner Pass turnoff, then over the summit, sliding on new ice, to the dry side of the Sierra.

"Feeling better?" Matt said.

"The food helps."

"Is all this tension radiating out of you, about Bob? Or is it that case? The Strong case? Are you having problems?"

"Sorry I'm so preoccupied. No, it's going very well. I'm wiping the floor with the prosecution," Nina said.

"Is that why you look so haunted?"

"You're too damn smart, Matt." It's the Elephant Celebes, she thought, it's turning its awful head, I just know it, and I'm afraid I won't be able to stand it when I finally see its real face. She shook her head sharply to get the image out of it and tried to see ahead of the snow which seemed to be coming right at them onto the windshield.

"You ought to be happy and carefree," Matt said.

"You just got married. Why don't you take a honey-moon?"

"Already had it. The weekend in Hawaii."

"That's not a honeymoon! A honeymoon comes af-ter"—he saw her expression, and finished—"after I shut my big mouth and drive. But, and this is a big but, a big whale of a but, a great big huge ugly but"—now he was making her laugh—"I'm worrying about you again. Keep your chin up and your eyes peeled, okay?"

"Okay."

They left the blizzard behind and emerged into rain on clear roads, riding down the mountain at fifty toward Reno.

"See?" Matt said. "Nothing to it."

Nina looked back. A plume of snow blew off the roof. They were alone on the road. Below, Carson Val-ley twinkled.

She looked at her watch and was surprised to dis-cover it was only six-thirty. They would make it.

And they did, with twenty minutes to spare. Aside from a few airport personnel and the ubiquitous slot machine players the airport was almost empty.

At the American Airlines gate they hung their wet outer clothing on chairs. "Coffee," Matt said, and went off to hunt for some.

Nina sat down and got out her cell phone.

"We made it," she told Collier. He was staying at her cabin. "How is it up there?"

"Very romantic with all these candles and the emer-gency broadcast station lady crooning weather forecasts. I'm going out every hour to clear the driveway. The plows came by on the street a couple of hours ago. I've filled the front closet with wood. The only thing miss-ing is you. Oh. Tony's trying to get in touch with you.

It's amazing that the phone lines are still working, isn't it?"

"What did he say?"

"He said it was urgent. He was calling from Reno." Collier told her the number.

"Okay, I'll call him."

"When do you think you'll be back?"

"Ten or so. Matt's working tonight. He'll take us to the cabin."

"Call me if you'll be late."

She looked out the window. No sign of the plane, no announcement yet.

"Hi, Tony."

"Nina! Where are you?" Tony's voice sounded slightly demented. She could hear the br-r-ring of the slots behind him.

"Well, I know where you are," she said. "I'm at the airport."

"Perfect! Listen, I'll be there in ten minutes to pick you up."

"Oh, no, you won't. I'm picking up my son here. He's coming home after three weeks in Europe."

"When will you be free?"

"I won't be. There's a blizzard going on up in the mountains, Tony. We have to get home as soon as we can."

"Are you alone?"

"No. My brother's with me."

"Great. You stay over in Reno tonight. I'll book you a room. Meet your kid, send him home, and come out and meet me in front of the— What airline are you at?"

"What's going on, Tony?"

"I think I found Heidi."

"Where?"

"Pyramid Lake. But I'm not going out there alone. You need to be there. I want a lawyer with me. Just a minute." He left her to a rhythmic clanking punctuated by bells and laughter.

She listened to the sounds, thinking about what he had said, liking it less and less. After a minute, Tony returned, saying, "I just won seven hundred bucks in the dollar slots and I don't even care. That's how freaked out I am."

"Talk to me," Nina said.

"Aunt Dottie," Tony said. "Remember Dick and Dottie with the trailer? We got on pretty well when I went to Vegas to see them. Now Aunt Dottie gave me a call this afternoon and said the guy that lives next door to the trailer called her."

"The baseball bat man?"

"Right. He said the trailer's starting to stink."

"Oh, God!"

"He won't go in there, and they can't get up there, Dottie's about to have cataract surgery. She wanted to know, should she call the police."

"Jesus!"

"Just what I said. Who knows? It could be rotting garbage! Anyway, the neighbor has a key. Dottie called him and said he should give it to me. Did I do wrong? Should I call Dottie back and have her call the cops?"

Loudspeakers were reporting that Bob's plane was landing. Matt ran up with a couple of big paper cups full of coffee. Smiling, he motioned with his head toward the doorway where in a few seconds, Bob would be coming out.

Nina couldn't muster up a smile back. "Okay, Tony," she said into the phone. "Pick me up in half an hour." She told him where to meet her and hung up.

Dribbles of passengers, then a flood, came through the doorway. Bob came out, holding his mouth as if to keep a big smile from breaking out, a heavy backpack on his back, wearing heavy cords and a new windbreaker. He looked several years older.

"Hey," Matt said, punching him and making him put up his hands to defend himself. Bob lost it and broke into a smile.

"Hey, Mom," he said.

"Hey, handsome."

"Don't kiss me. Later."

Nevertheless, all the way to the baggage claim, she held his hand.

24

THE SKY WAS falling. Rain fell in a solid sheet outside. Tony Ramirez pulled into a loading zone and Nina ran to the car.

His eyes were wild. He gunned the motor and they sped north. "Don't worry, I'm sober," he said. "I never drink when I gamble. I booked you a room at Circus Circus."

"Well, that fits," Nina said, rummaging in her bag for something to dry her face with. "It's only about half an hour to Pyramid Lake, isn't it?"

"In this rain—could be an hour, hour and a half. What do you suppose we'll find up there?" Tony rubbed off the windshield.

"I just don't know. I hope we're all wrong. I hope I wake up early in the morning with all this behind me and go home to my family." She remembered that the second prelim in the Strong case started at nine A.M. the next morning. "And that court gets canceled because of the weather," she added.

"I don't have a family to go home to," Tony said. "But I have the cats. Right now I'd like to be sitting in my chair smoking a cigar with a cat on my lap."

"You live in Reno?"

"Biggest Little City Inna World. I love it. The glitz

of Vegas, but four thousand feet higher up so you can go
outside in the summer. And Tahoe up the hill. So, uh,
what happens if Heidi's in the trailer after all?"

"I don't know yet. I don't want to speculate."

"We have to call the cops if she's there."

"I suppose."

"The neighbor could be wrong."

"That's what we're going to find out."

"Thanks for coming with me," Tony said. "Hones
to God, I couldn't go there on my own."

They left the Reno–Sparks lights and entered th
desert. The rain lessened, then stopped. She hated imag
ining Bob and Matt stuck in a blinding snowstorm righ
now, but the thought of Matt's tough, heavy truck reas
sured her.

At Pyramid Lake, the gas station blazed bluish ligh
out into the darkness. They drove past it to the mobi
home park. Night covered up the rusting and peelin
trailers, but emphasized the edgy, insecure feeling Nir
had felt on her previous visit. All the people living her
were one paycheck away from the streets. A trailer in th
desert was fine for a winter vacation for a rock hound
a hunter, but she wagered a lot of these folk wou
rather be watching TV in some modern apartment
Reno.

They pulled up in front of Dick and Dottie's ya
and sat in the car, getting their courage up.

"I'll go get the key," Tony said heavily. He walk
over to the neighboring trailer, each step more relucta
than the last.

She thought she could smell it with the car do
shut. How had they missed it before? She remember
that she and Wish had been chased off before they cou
even get into the yard. She wondered if the neighb

had checked inside before calling Dottie and decided to forget whatever he had seen.

The neighbor appeared at his door, said a few words, handed Tony the key, and shut his metal door with a hands-off slam. Tony walked back to the car and opened her door. He held a flashlight.

"It's strong," he said. "You sure you want to—"

She got out, clutching her ski hat. They walked the hundred feet to the trailer. Two forlorn wooden steps led to the door. Tony climbed them, opened the torn screen door, and knocked desultorily.

No response.

"Miz Strong?"

No answer. He shrugged, got out a handkerchief, and turned the key in the lock. A wave of sick-making air came out. "I'm going in," he said over his shoulder.

"I'm right behind you," Nina said. She held the damp ski hat over her nose and mouth.

Tony cast the flashlight around the entrance, but Nina's gloved hand found the light switch right away.

They were in the middle of a nightmare.

Heidi Strong lay spread-eagled on red sheets, her throat slashed so savagely her head had almost been cut off. Her eyes, staring at them, were moving.

Ants, or worse.

The smell was overpowering.

Nina gripped Tony's arm. "Don't go any farther," she said through the wool hat. "Take a good hard look around, Tony. Remember what you've seen."

"I'm—I'm gonna throw up." He pushed around her and rushed down the steps. She heard him out front.

She breathed through her mouth, through the hat, and thanked heaven for the strong smell of wet wool. Her eyes raked the freezing room. Heidi on the bed on the right, dressed in boxers and a camisole—her nightwear. Bruises still visible on the arm hanging off the bed. Broken glass on the floor, the bedspread half on the floor. One of her skis lying on the bed as if she had tried to use it to fight back. She hadn't been caught completely unawares. She had fought for her life.

Nina was looking for the knife. No knife was visible, and she couldn't go inside and mess up the murder scene for the forensics team to come. No knife, no other sign of a weapon. Heidi's purse was gone. That was a smart touch, make it look like a robbery . . .

Her eyes went back to Heidi. The ants go in, the ants go out . . .

She felt her equilibrium going. She was going to pass out.

She brushed at the wall with her elbow and the light went out. Backing out, she closed the door firmly, stumbled down the stairs and back to Tony's car. He sat in the driver's seat, motor running, right foot hovering over the accelerator.

"Go," Nina said. "Go!"

They putt-putted decorously to the edge of the trailer park and then roared out some side road, stopping only when they came to some picnic tables at the end of the road. In the headlights, they could see a rock beach. The ancient lake lay ahead in the darkness. The air smelled dank. Nina breathed in deeply.

"Well, we found her," Tony said, throwing his door open. "I'll be right back. I just need some air."

Nina was grateful to be left alone for a minute. She should call the sheriff's office or whoever was in charge here. Were they on reservation land? Probably not. She had to call someone.

She closed her eyes, but the image of Heidi on the

bed opened them. To slow the staccato of her heart, she
scanned the scene in her mind for information, moving
the energy from her heart to her mind, where she could
handle it better. No knife. Heidi's purse gone. The bedspread pulled down.

It would take a lot of work to sort it out. Oh, Jim
would be questioned. But much information would be
lost after so long a time.

Why, Heidi must have been dead for weeks. The
cold air had preserved her so well, even the bruises, but
the ants had found her anyway.

Jim had stopped asking about Heidi, she realized that
now. At first, Heidi had been the main topic of conversation. Then, it was as if he had forgotten about her.

Forgotten about her? Or found her himself? They
were husband and wife. Maybe Heidi had forgotten she
had mentioned the trailer to Jim years ago.

Biting her lip, Nina tried to back up, to think of
some way it wasn't Jim. Why was she so sure?

The scene returned in full color. Broken glass. Heidi
had struggled with her assailant. A nightstand, the drawers closed, a book with a page marked. She saw Heidi's
body, her hand dangling over the side of the bed.

Something had been missing.

She was staring blindly at her own hand, looking at
the nails and ridges and the new diamond that seemed
to glitter even in the dark on her finger.

It had probably been the only item in the trailer
worth more than a few dollars. No thief would bother
with the most beat-up trailer in the park, all for the sake
of Heidi's gold chased wedding band, the one she'd
continued to wear because she liked it, even if she didn't
like Jim.

Now Nina was sickeningly sure.

She tried to think through the next steps. She would call the police. All night long, she'd be making statements. She couldn't—she had to be careful about implicating Jim. She didn't really know anything.

She just felt it, right in the solar plexus.

25

"GOOD MORNING, COUNSELOR," Jim said. "Three feet of snow in one night! Wonderful skiing weather!"

She had been up until two-thirty the night before talking to the cops about Heidi and thinking about what to do. She had slept until five in a room on the twelfth floor of Circus Circus in Reno, met Tony downstairs, and driven for two hours along barely plowed highways back up into the mountains to the cabin. She had changed clothes, eaten, called Bob at Matt's, and shown up at court.

She had been waiting in the courthouse hall for him since eight-thirty.

She was on the brink.

"Let's go down the hall where it's more private." She led him around the corner and stopped him.

"You look tired today," Jim said. "Whereas I feel great. It'll all be over today."

"There's something I've been meaning to ask you," Nina said.

"What?"

"Would you mind taking off that parka you live in?"

Surprised, laughing a little, Jim took it off. Underneath, he wore a blue long-sleeved cotton shirt.

"Now, how about your shirt?" Nina said.

"This is hardly the place for that, is it? What's this all about?"

"Take your shirt off, Jim. Nobody's around. I want to see your arms. All the way up to the shoulder."

"Why?"

"Because several weeks ago Heidi told me that you cut yourself on that bathroom mirror."

"I told you I didn't break the mirror. Heidi did that."

"I want to see for myself."

He mashed his parka between his hands. "Let's not go there," he said softly, then turned the full force of his gaze on her.

She tried to ignore the sensation, the threat she felt emanating from those eyes, but she couldn't. "I have to see or . . ."

"Or what?" He was taunting her.

"Or everything changes between us right now."

"We have a deal, and so far, it's worked very well. So maybe you want to think twice before you mess with it."

"Let me see your arms." She didn't pause between words intentionally. The sentence just came out that way, full of portent.

He continued to mash his jacket, as if he could make it very very tiny by pressing hard enough. "Now she believes me, now she don't," he said.

"Show me!" she cried.

"Fuck you!"

"I saw Heidi last night, Jim."

"You—you found her?" All hand action ceased. The handful of parka unfurled and dropped down.

"She wasn't looking too good. She's dead, Jim. you know. I went to the trailer and found her there.

"What are you talking about?" he said. "What trailer? Heidi wouldn't be caught dead in a trailer."

And then she saw it, a telltale flickering at the corner of his mouth.

He thought it was funny!

"You're a psychopath," she said, backing away from him.

Jim pretended to think about this. "I don't believe so," he said. "I loved Heidi. Psychopaths don't feel anything. I read up on them. I feel so much love, so much hate."

"Okay, I've had enough!" She held up her hand. "Don't bother to deny it."

Jim took this in, and she watched the click, click, ticking in his blue eyes as he tried to decide how to handle her, and her information. "Do the cops know?"

"Of course. I called them right away. They arrived Pyramid Lake before ten o'clock. I was questioned half the night."

"And," he said, "what did you tell them?"

"Masks off now, right, Jim?"

"Whatever you say," Jim said. "You're my lawyer."

"I told them why I was there. I didn't break the attorney-client privilege, if that's what you're wondering. I didn't help them at your expense. It's a different state, so you probably won't be brought in for questioning until Monday."

"There's no evidence," Jim said. "I guarantee that. Nobody's going to get me for cutting Heidi."

Jabbing like the knife she had never mentioned, his comment took her breath away. "Why, Jim?"

"This is still a privileged conversation?"

"I haven't looked it up," Nina said. "But I believe it's protected."

"Then I'm going to take your word for it," he said
"You're an ethical lawyer, Nina. I rely on that. And
you're full of surprises, which is why this whole proces
has been a real Ferris wheel ride. Don't ask, don't tel
right? You didn't really want to know the truth.

"Hmm. So, speaking hypothetically, just in case th
conversation is not privileged," he said with a sma
smile, "why would I kill her? I loved her, right? M
guess is, she made the mistake of saying something un
forgivable."

"Such as?" said Nina.

"That she preferred my father to me. To me!"

"Your father!"

"It wasn't Alex she was in love with," Jim said. "
was my father."

Nina tried to take that in.

"She told me some crap about how she turned to n
father because she was unhappy with me. Bullshit abo
never knowing love until she met him. She was disloy
and she left me, Nina, but I would have forgiven h
almost anything. Under those circumstances, in this l
tle fiction I'm telling you," he said, looking up at h
from the window he had been staring out of, remer
bering his game, "I would probably even offer to ta
her back."

"But she wouldn't come," Nina said.

"No, she wouldn't. That shouldn't have come a
shock to me, but it did. Her loyalty meant someth
once. I really thought, if we could just talk, she mi
have a change of heart, see how I loved her. And ther
got very, very angry . . ."

"I see." She hung her head and exhaled.

"I hate to ruin your fantasy world," Jim said. ""

ried so hard to believe I didn't do a thing. I loved every loophole."

Nina said, "You are such a practiced liar. It was hard to believe you could do something so—so—"

"So just. So right."

"But why? Why Alex?"

"Because my father slept with my wife," Jim said.

Nina stepped back again. His hatred pushed her back, though it wasn't directed at her.

"My mother left me. I spent years dealing with that betrayal, Nina. I found Heidi and thought I'd be all right. I worked hard at Paradise. For so long I was such a good boy."

He paused.

"Then my father—slept—with my wife."

Nina held her hand up to her eyes as if to shield them.

"Marianne told me Heidi was sleeping with somebody. I went to ask her, not believing it, and Heidi said was true. It was my father. Can you believe the extent the betrayal?"

Nina's hand went to her mouth. She stared at him.

"So—I took Alex away. My father's a broken man now. He'll never get over it. That's the way it should be. I, so now you hate the sight of me. But nothing's changed! You never believed I was innocent. You just wanted to pretend, so you could feel self-righteous out defending me."

"I did believe you were innocent! For a long time."

"No. You always held back. You weren't totally al, like you should have been."

"You tried to use me to find Heidi."

"Well, pat yourself on the back for not finding her in e. I had to do that myself. Come on. This shouldn't

affect our relationship, except that there are no lies between us now. Now get me off and send me on my
way."

"No," Nina said slowly. "No, I don't think I'll do
that, Jim."

"Why?"

"Why? Because you make me sick."

"So what?"

"I can't continue."

"Now settle down. We'll finish up this hearing today
and we both know the judge won't bind me over. And
you and I will be quits."

"God! Artie! Did you hurt Artie?"

"The shyster in the office upstairs from yours? The
one that's so crazy about that bag of a wife of his?"

"You threatened to hurt his wife?"

"Certainly not." Jim smiled. "So. Don't worry. Artie's been around. He got the message. Discussion
closed. We go in there and finish up, and—"

"No, we don't," Nina said. "I'm asking for a continuance. I'm going to withdraw. You can see how you do
with somebody else."

"Now, wait a minute," Jim said. He seemed sincerely surprised. "We already talked about this. We need
to get this over with today, so they don't have time to
get it all together. And you can't withdraw, you're my
lawyer, you know the case, you're bound to take care
of it."

"No. I'll say I'm sick or something. You won't be
prejudiced. But I'm not going forward today."

"Sure you are," Jim said. "You're just dying to spend
some time with that new blended family of yours, aren't
you? I heard your kid just got in from a trip last night

ut it's still a lonely little place you live in, for a big shot
wyer."

She stood there, swallowing. He was threatening her
mily.

"I'm only making sure you do your job. Finish the
elim, then they can't come at me again on Alex. I'm
t worried about the Heidi thing. My guess is they'll
d evidence that points to my father in that case. So
u just go in there and finish the prelim. If you don't,
be terribly disappointed. I'll be violently disap-
inted."

She closed her eyes.

"Well? Are we still in business?"

"Okay," she said, because she had no choice.

"That's my good ethical counselor at law," he said.
o your duty. No mistakes now."

She turned to leave.

"Oh, Nina. One more thing to show you how much
ust you never to reveal our secrets . . ."

He pushed the sleeve up on his arm all the way to his
ulder.

Scars.

Barbara approached Nina just before Flaherty came
court and said, "We heard about Heidi Strong this
ning, just before I came in. You found the body,
't you?"

"We'd been looking for her, too," Nina said, with-
a glance toward Jim, who was standing beside her.

"If he doesn't go down for this one, he'll go down
her," Barbara said, jerking her head toward him.

im sighed and looked hurt.

"That's the thought that will get me through the
" Barbara said, ignoring him.

"Her death won't help you," Nina said. "You st can't get her statement in."

"Well, I'm going to try. You can't stop me fro trying. Flaherty deserves to know she's dead."

"It won't help you," Nina repeated. "The mari privilege still applies after her death."

Barbara said contemptuously, "You people are t' lowest of the low." She turned her back and went to h counsel table.

"Them's fightin' words," Jim said. He seemed have enjoyed the interchange. But she felt the tension him as intensely as the blue scrutiny of his eyes. I would be watching her every move until the day v over.

All morning, Nina did her job. Flaherty glanced riously at her a couple of times as if bothered by son thing, but she cross-examined the police witne: thoroughly and carefully. Concentrating was easy w her family at stake.

All she had to do was her job.

Collier came in to watch and sat in the back. Barl stayed angry, although this anger was expressed by more than a titanium glint in her eye. She tried ev thing she could think of to convince Flaherty of position, but every thrust she made, Nina counte Flaherty knew which way it was going. They all di

At the break, Nina said, "We aren't going to pu a defense, Jim. We'll win without Ginger and the ers."

Jim said, "But aren't they added insurance?"

"No, they're risks. Barbara's good, and she's thr ing about like a wounded eel right now. She could

the wrong question to them, and they're not going to lie. You don't need them is what I'm saying."

"You're not trying to pull anything, are you, Nina?"

"No!" She forced herself to be calm. "Can't you see I'm doing the best that I can?"

"You're kind of halfhearted," he said in a light, teasing tone that wasn't meant to fool her. "I'm willing to overlook that," he continued, "because you know you have to win. How you do it is your business. All right. Now, let's get back in there and finish it."

Just before the noon hour, Barbara came to the end of her testimony. Her job had been to show probable cause that a murder was committed and Jim was the perpetrator. She hadn't met that burden.

Her greatest problem was the complete lack of evidence that Jim would want to kill his brother. Although he did not have to prove motive, all her experts' talk about patterns and fibers was unconvincing, because there was no evidence that Jim might want to hurt Alex.

Not that Barbara hadn't tried. But Kelly's testimony was out. Gina Beloit, the disgruntled employee who had heard the conversation with Jim's father about Gene Malavoy, had been neutralized, and nobody else had anything to say. Philip Strong hadn't been called, because Barbara was afraid he'd support his son, and Marianne wasn't going to help the prosecution.

Collier hadn't stirred in the back all this time, and gradually an idea had formed in Nina's mind. Her idea depended on Collier, with his intimate knowledge of the law in the case.

"I have no further testimony to present, Your Honor," Barbara said at ten minutes to twelve. "At this time, I move that the Court admit a statement made to

the South Lake Tahoe police one day after the death of
Alex Strong." Flaherty pulled out the papers.

"Old business," Nina whispered to Jim. The moment she had waited for all morning had come.

She glanced at the prosecutor's counsel table. Collier
was leaning over Barbara's shoulder, whispering in her
ear. Then he turned and walked out of the courtroom.

Why now? What was he doing? Nina wondered.

Barbara said, "The Court should be made aware that
Heidi Strong, who has been missing ever since she made
this statement, was found last night, her throat cut, in a
trailer at Pyramid Lake—"

Nina stood up. "I object to any such representation,
Your Honor! It's not relevant to this case inasmuch as
the statement is still clearly inadmissible. The marital
privilege continues even after the death of the spouse."
She cited a case. "There's no need to get into this."

"But the Court wants to get at the truth," Barbara
said. "This is a fact-finding hearing. The Court can
relax the technical rules in the interests of justice."

"There are good reasons for technical rules, Your
Honor," Nina interrupted. "And the Court can't relax
the rule relating to marital privilege. We claim the privilege. The communication was made in confidence between the husband and wife. Even in the less formal
preliminary hearing the privileges of confidentiality
hold. Why? Because once the privilege is broken, you
can't repair the break.

"As section 985 of the Evidence Code states, the
only exception is when the spouse who holds the privilege, waives it. Then the other spouse may testify. In this
case, Your Honor, we have never and will never waive
that privilege. Let me make myself clear on that point.

She glanced at Jim. He was nodding, pleased. She held her breath. It was up to Barbara now.

Had she heard what Nina had said? Everything that he had said? Had she heard Nina discuss an exception to the marital privilege? Had she heard Nina's slight misstatement?

Had Nina reminded her that there were in fact other exceptions?

Collier would have picked up on it immediately. Barbara didn't know the law of the case well yet.

A fine line appeared between Barbara's stenciled brows. Nina saw that fine line, willed it to deepen, willed her to open her mouth and say the right thing . . .

Barbara looked at the clock and said, "Your Honor, I wonder if we could finish this argument after the lunch break. I have a telephone conference at twelve sharp back in my office."

Flaherty said, "Mrs. Reilly?"

"We object to stopping now, Your Honor. Miss Manning is on the run and she's hoping she'll think something up over the lunch hour. Really, there is no reason to continue. We don't intend to put on a defense and we are ready to submit this matter for the Court's decision now. Let's not drag it out." Now she prayed, let him be as good as I think he is . . . let him over-rule me . . .

"Well," Flaherty said. "I guess we can spare ten more minutes on this after lunch. After all, it's the second go-round in a murder case. I'm going to adjourn until one-thirty."

Barbara left immediately. Out in the hall again, Jim said sullenly, "She's really hanging this up. We should be done by now."

"I want it over too. I'm doing everything I can. Now, I'm leaving until one-thirty."

"We could have lunch together. That would be a good idea."

She stuck her chin out and said, "I'll do the prelim. But don't expect me to smile at you, you son of a bitch."

"You shouldn't talk to me that way."

"You shouldn't have threatened my family."

He watched her go.

She drove to the lake, which was mogulled with whitecaps left from yesterday's storm.

She had done what she could.

It was all up to Barbara, from here on out. The deputy D.A. was new to criminal law, she had been thrown into the case, and she hadn't done the legal research herself. She had used Collier's old briefs on the marital privilege question.

But she was very bright. How bright? Nina was about to find out. If Nina had read things right, Barbara had frowned and had manufactured an excuse to allow her time to go back to her office and read the Evidence Code.

Jim had had no idea what was going on, of that Nina was sure.

She sat in the Bronco, looking at the lake, sick with fear.

One-thirty. They were all there. Barbara had come marching in, not deigning to look at them. Collier had returned. This time, he sat down in the second chair at the counsel table with Barbara. Nina hoped they had spent the whole lunch hour together. She made herself look serene, even bored. Jim sat beside her, scowling, anxious to be set free.

"Where were we?" Flaherty said. "Oh, yes, ten more minutes arguing about this statement of Heidi Strong."

Barbara was already on her feet. "If I may continue?"

"Proceed."

"As I was saying, the death of Heidi Strong casts a whole new light on the admissibility of her declaration." Actually, Barbara hadn't said that, but she was saying it now. "Let's look at this declaration in an entirely new way. There is an exception to the marital privilege that was not previously applicable to this matter. But it is now." She paused to look at some scribbled notes.

"There is no confidentiality privilege when the testimony is relevant to a crime against the spouse," she continued. "For example, in the case of *People v. Michaels,* the husband threatened the wife numerous times prior to beating her severely a month after the threats began. No one overheard these threats. Only the wife could testify about them. She was able to do so, because the crime involved was against her. The privilege doesn't apply in such a case."

It was Barbara's finest moment, but Nina would never be able to congratulate her on it. Now, if she could just keep it up.

"What relevance does that have here?" Nina asked. "The defendant isn't charged here with murdering his wife. Mrs. Strong couldn't have been a witness in this proceeding because of the privilege, so the declaration can't come in as evidence of retaliation against a witness. She's just blowing smoke, Your Honor." Some of her desperation unintentionally seeped into her voice. Fine. Maybe Jim would mistake it for sincerity.

"Let me take this one step further, Your Honor," Barbara said. "We have established that the privilege is waived insofar as the declaration is offered to show a crime against the spouse. My point is, whether Mr. Strong killed his wife is relevant in this case, *not* because she might have been a witness, but because it is evidence of other similar crimes."

She had gotten it out. Other similar crimes was the right theory. Heidi's declaration, like the live thing i was, had evolved into something else.

Barbara went on, "If the Court will remember, yesterday we argued the defendant's motion to exclude evidence of prior malicious acts of the defendant. The People lost that motion. The alleged malicious acts had occurred too far in the past."

Flaherty nodded his head, looking puzzled. Nina made her face look puzzled too.

"I now move that the declaration of Heidi Strong be admitted on grounds that it is evidence of a *subsequent* act of malice. It couldn't be more recent. It is relevant to show, not the bad character or predisposition of the defendant, but his commission of another, similar crime in the same time frame. Look at the similarities, Your Honor. A close family member. Look at the brutality evident in both crimes." She paused. Flaherty was thinking hard. Nina managed to look astonished.

Work it, Barb, she thought.

"Let me see if I follow this argument," Flaherty interrupted. "You're piggybacking. You're saying that the marital privilege is no longer a problem, since the declaration is now evidence that Mr. Strong may have murdered his wife. And second, you are saying that wheth

Mr. Strong committed this other alleged crime is relevant to the charge in this Court because it is evidence of other similar crimes. It is my recollection that evidence of other similar crimes may be admitted in the Court's discretion, whether or not there has been a conviction or even a trial of the other crimes."

"That is correct, Your Honor."

"Your Honor," Nina said. "The defense has been surprised by this oral motion which it has not had time to study. It should not be raised at this time. I strongly object to the motion on that ground." She went into a harangue about how there were no similarities, about how the prosecution was trying to sneak in something that was inadmissible, and on and on, saying all the right things and hoping Flaherty wasn't listening, until Flaherty raised a hand and cut her off.

"Do you wish to request a continuance to respond to counsel? You seem to be well versed on the issue and many of these matters are already touched on in your brief."

Jim shook his head vigorously. Nina said, "We do not want a continuance. The defendant has been through enough already. We want the matter decided today."

"Well, if you don't want to continue the matter, I'm going to decide this oral motion, then," Flaherty said.

Nina remained standing. She didn't want to have to sit down next to Jim.

"I think the prosecution raises a compelling argument," Flaherty said. "One of the interesting things about it is that if the marital privilege is out of the way, the Court has broad discretion to rule on the relevancy question."

"This is an inquiry into a murder!" Nina said. "This is no time to relax the rules!"

"All right, I've heard enough," Flaherty said. "Both of you, sit down. I'm going to take a ten-minute break and read the Evidence Code and the annotated cases."

"But Your Honor!" Nina said loudly.

"Sit down, counsel!"

She sat down. The judge disappeared. Barbara disappeared into the hall with Collier. The clerk whittled at her fingernails. The clock ticked. "Nina?" Jim whispered. Nina shrugged, hoping he did not look at her hands, which were almost bleeding as she dug her fingernails into them.

The ten minutes stretched to fifteen.

Flaherty came back in and took his place on the bench. "All right, we're back on the record. Now then I read some of the cases having to do with subsequent acts of malice. Don't jump up, Mrs. Reilly, they're on cases already cited in both parties' briefs in connection with the motion to exclude we heard yesterday. You've both read and cited them.

"Now. Yesterday I was disinclined to bring in Kevin Strong's testimony about prior acts of malice. The acts were more than ten years old and none of them included a murder.

"This is different. A murder of someone close to the defendant has been committed within weeks of the death of the victim in this case, also someone close to the defendant. The evidence tends to show a similar course of conduct—that the defendant may seek to retaliate violently against those family members who aggrieve him in some way.

"The Court will exercise its discretion to admit the

declaration, which tends to show probable cause to believe a crime was committed against defendant's wife by defendant, which in turn tends to show a similar course of conduct on the part of defendant in this case. Now, we've gotten past the preliminaries. Let's have a look at his declaration."

Nina shook her head and looked unhappy and beaten. Barbara cast her a triumphant and contemptuous look. Collier leaned back in his chair with a look of grim satisfaction on his face. Jim sat biting his lip while Flaherty read.

"I KNOW WHAT YOU DID." Nina was remembering Heidi's Post-it note. Jim had destroyed that. But her declaration was right here in Flaherty's face, telling about the bathroom mirror and Jim's rage against his mother.

It was the connection Flaherty had been looking for. That was clear a minute later as he said brusquely, "The court will now render its decision." He read the boilerate speech he gave at the end of each preliminary hearing, then said, "The Court finds that there is probable cause to believe that the crime of murder has been committed in this matter, and further, that there is probable cause to believe that the defendant committed the said crime."

The clerk smiled at Barbara. "She wasn't supposed to do that." Nina whispered to Jim. "He's bound you over for trial."

"What?"

"We'll set a trial date next week," Flaherty said. "Anything else, Miss Banning?"

And now Nina was trying to still the trembling all over, trying to stay still so Jim wouldn't know, rooting for Barbara to stand up and say—

"The People move that the defendant be immediately remanded into custody," Barbara said. "Probable cause has now been found in this brutal crime. The defendant faces a trial. And furthermore, another murder has occurred and there is probable cause to believe the defendant may be involved in it."

"There's no such probable cause, Judge!" Nina cried, standing up and putting a pleading tone into her voice, praying Flaherty would pay no attention to her.

"Maybe not, but there's an investigation going on right now and plenty of reason to believe the defendant may be a flight risk," Barbara said.

She was doing so well, just fantastically well, and Jim was about to be led away—Nina was jabbering something so it would sound like she was opposing a remand . . .

But Flaherty wasn't as smart as Barbara. At the very last moment, when Jim was about to be safely neutralized, Flaherty made a mistake.

"I think we'll have to schedule a formal bail hearing on that," Flaherty said.

Collier jumped to his feet. "He's a danger! The Court should remand him to custody immediately!"

Flaherty said dryly, "Sit down, counselor. I'll hear your motion on Monday morning at eight A.M. So ordered." He wiped his brow and took his leave, while Nina stood there, stunned.

"It was Heidi," Jim said. "Coming back to haunt me. Lousy rotten timing! But I've got until Monday. What will happen then?"

"I don't know."

"Don't give me that!"

"I'll try to arrange bail for you, but—there's Heidi. t was hard enough keeping you out the first time."

"You're telling me they're going to put me away?" It vas finally his turn to look terrified.

"I've come this far," Nina said. "I'll do that hearing or you."

Jim wasn't thinking about Monday. He looked off to he side, calculating.

She thought, yes, the son of a bitch is going to run.

Run, run, you son of a bitch, she said to herself, but ook care to keep her hope out of her expression. "I did verything I could for you, Jim. You saw for yourself. ou're not going to blame me for what happened in ere, are you?"

He gave her a chilling look. "But you didn't win."

"I did the best I could. Don't come near me or ine," Nina said. "I'll be protected. Do you under- nd?" He'd watched and listened to her fight for him, d he couldn't have noticed the way she had steered rbara toward that second exception.

He didn't answer. He was thinking about his escape. e reached out and took her hand and pressed it almost sent-mindedly, as if they were just ordinary people ring good-bye, and she let him. She knew for sure he s going to run when he did that.

"Good-bye, Nina." He gave her that lopsided smile t concealed so much, and watched her go.

In the truck, she hugged herself for a long minute, d down on her chest. It had been the most horrible rtroom scene in her life.

She had sworn to defend him.

But when he threatened her family, when she saw he was the monster in the painting, not the system, when she saw his real face turning toward her, she had betrayed him.

She had thrown the case.

It was over, and he hadn't guessed.

Collier called Sandy about two-thirty. "Seen Nina?"

"She's on her way over to see you," Sandy said. "She's off for the afternoon."

"Well, don't work too hard. It's Friday."

Barb passed by the open door of his office, on her way to Henry to report on her win. He didn't feel like sitting on Henry's sofa and dealing with those two right now, so he grabbed a *California Appellate Decisions* volume and walked out to the courtyard toward the law library.

No sign of Nina coming in from the parking lot. He went into the main courtroom building and on up to the second floor.

Strong was standing in the stacks, reading the Evidence Code. When he saw Collier at the door, he jumped up and came toward him.

Collier tensed for the action he expected, but Strong didn't go for him. He paused in front of him and said, "I was just leaving."

"Feel free," Collier said, thinking, for two more days, anyway, thanks to Flaherty being such a bonehead.

The two men brushed by each other, and Collier really saw him, saw the cruelty and misery and the corrosive self-pity in him. He shrank from it. Strong seemed to smile.

Then he was gone.

26

IT WAS OVER. Jim knew a window of opportunity when he saw one. Nina was quite sure she'd never see him again.

Which didn't mean she didn't intend to protect herself. She picked up Bob, called Sandy to say she was gone for the week, and went directly back to Collier's office. While Bob waited in the secretarial area, she sat down with Collier.

They looked at each other for a long moment.

"You were right," she said. "I'm afraid of him. I can't say any more."

That was all she said, and he didn't press her for details. Before they left together, Collier arranged for a patrolman to be assigned to them for the weekend.

"I'll be there," he said. "We'll be careful. But what happens Monday?"

"I'm not concerned," Nina said.

"Well, you should be—ah! He's going to run, isn't he? Did he tell you that?"

"No."

"I don't care what Flaherty ruled. I don't give a shit what Henry says, either, at this point. I'm going to call Nevada and offer to have our guys pick him up for questioning in the Heidi Strong matter. They're moving too slowly." He spoke to someone in Reno, then told her that Jim would be picked up as soon as he could be located.

Before dinner, Nina cornered Bob on the couch in front of the fire, where, jet-lagged, he had curled up and fallen asleep.

She woke him up and unleashed a torrent of groggy talk that she listened to eagerly, knowing he would only enjoy telling his adventures abroad once.

While they talked, Collier kibitzed from the kitchen inserting a word here or there, hanging back when the subject turned to Bob's dad, Kurt. He was making dinner.

Nina stroked Bob's spiky hair, overwhelmed with relief to be through with Jim Strong.

On Saturday morning, snow began to fall mor gently. The drifts piled high in the doorways, sneakin under cars, inside of coats, into ears. Bob and his tw buddies in the neighborhood dashed outside for a swif harsh snow battle somewhere in the area of the burie backyard fort. Officer Floyd Drummond, who wa spending the weekend with them, kept an eye on ther outside.

Collier had taken up the duties of sentry at th wooden table next to the kitchen. "Did you see that? he asked, laughing when Bob smashed a big one. "He got an arm on him."

In honor of a day at home, she was actually cookir —a recipe she called accident soup, made of cabbag carrots, onions, squash, and tomato chunks in a sau made mostly out of cream of chicken soup. Collier s

over his yellow pad chewing on a piece of paper, studying the boys through the blurry window. He really enjoyed them. They hadn't said a word to each other
about the Strong case. Nina's only thought was, someday we'll have a child . . . she went to him.

"It's been weird weather, hasn't it?" Collier was say-
ng. "So much snow. Then more snow."

She bent down to kiss his forehead. His arms went
round her waist and he leaned his head against her
stomach.

They stayed like that for a long time. Finally Collier
looked up and said, "I believe that your stomach is tell-
ng you it's hungry."

"True." She moved away and took a taste from the
pot. He was still looking out the window, his strong
profile outlined in the light. The Strong case had been a
vindication for him professionally. Now no one could
doubt that he was back in the top of his form. She
watched him and wanted him and thought of all the
nights to come.

She threw a scoop of mashed garlic into the bubbling
sauce. The cabin was light and peaceful and warm.

After a few minutes, Bob banged on the door to be
let inside, soaked and jubilant. He changed clothes and
added his heavy wet clothes into the washing machine.

Collier took the bread out of the oven and Bob
brought in the napkins. Officer Drummond ate lunch
with them.

The afternoon passed, and the evening. They stayed
in the cabin. Collier made some calls and reported that
Jim had cleaned out his bank account and hadn't come
home at all on Friday night. There was an arrest warrant
out for him now. Barbara had come into the office and

convinced Flaherty that Jim was on the run. Jim belonged to her now, and that was just fine.

They all watched a Jackie Chan video, Officer Drummond in the chair beside the couch.

That night, the house rattled and shook with wind and snow piled up over the front door, making it impassable. Upstairs, underneath the Hudson blanket, they murmured to each other.

She woke up to the sound of a pinecone hitting the window.

"Open up!" Bob shouted, "and bring a shovel! It's five feet deep out here!"

Collier continued to snore. Searching the cold floor with her toe for her slippers, Nina lifted herself off the bed and pulled on a thick robe. Padding over to the window, she lifted back the curtain.

Morning sun lit the scene below like an Andersen fairy tale.

Fresh deep snow in drifts, white and regal, reached up to the sky like miniature Alps. No wind stirred the trees. The yard was a still life in white and green and sapphire, every shadow focused and crisp.

"Get up!" she said to Collier, bending over to let him grab for her and kiss her once before she flew down the stairs. "And dress warm! Today's the day we bust out of this place and break in those funny-looking snow shoes you brought over."

"Are you sure, Nina?" he called down. She stopped at the foot of the stairs.

"Floyd will be with us. He's armed," she said. "What do you think?"

"Bob would love it," Collier said. "We'll be fine. I'll call Barb and let her know where we are."

They took the Bronco on Highway 89 along
the west side of the lake, Drummond following in his
four-wheel-drive police car. The highway had been
groomed, probably early in the morning, but the white
of the hillsides made Bob jump with excitement in the
back seat. Every spot looked better than the last one.
Collier finally pulled over into some National Forest
land.

A wide valley spread before them with a series of
gentle slopes. At the far end, a mountain angled up
steeply, rising so precipitately that Nina had to bend her
head back to see the top. The only marks in the ocean
of white were deer prints.

"Sunglasses," Nina said to Bob.

"Check." He put them on.

"Sunscreen." She slathered some on all three faces.

Bob squirmed with impatience as Collier methodically stacked the snowshoes beside the car and began to
dig below some blankets for Bob's new snowboard. As
soon as the snowboard emerged, Bob headed for the
nearest hill.

"Stay close," Nina called. "And stay off the mountain slope with that thing."

"Oh, Mom," he called back cheerfully. "Nothing I
can't handle."

"No way," she said.

"Fine," he said with practiced disgust. He went off
and she watched him trudging up a rise across from the
mountain. "I'll hang around the truck," Floyd Drummond said. "This way I'll be able to keep an eye on all
three of you." He was sitting in the Bronco with the
heater going.

"He's getting strong," Nina said, watching Bob take

his first run down the slope across the way, as Collier fastened his snowshoes.

"He's growing up. Here. I'll help you."

With dismay she noted a few other cars had pulled up behind them and across the road. Oh, well, she thought. The snow is big enough to hold all of us.

Why, here they were on the cusp of the wilderness, with miles and miles to go in any direction. Sure enough, within minutes the cars had emptied and the people disappeared into the forests all around.

"It's a beautiful day," she said, straining to put her boot into the snowshoe. "We're going to have a blast."

They set off across the snow-covered meadow. Collier led them up a pathway that traversed the valley. From where they were hiking, Nina could watch Bob, who seemed content to snowboard up and down the same hill over and over under Floyd Drummond's watchful gaze. Drummond could see them, too, as they moved among the trees of the lower elevation of the mountain.

For an hour, they shoed along what might be a snowed-in trail through blazing sun and into the cold dark swatches cast by tall trees away from the road and into the valley, until they stood in the mountain shadow. Collier saw so many things she didn't notice, the tracks of animals, plants still flourishing in the high bare rocks, sounds of nature.

Finally, Nina sat down on a log, puffing. "You didn't tell me how much work it is to walk around in these things."

Collier pulled out a bottle of water and handed it to her. "Should I tell you a secret?" he asked while she sipped.

"What?" She wiped the water off her mouth with he rough fabric of her sleeve.

"I've never done this before."

"No! But . . . what was that all about back there?" he nodded toward their footprints. "Oh, here's an ex-ellent spot for schussing. And let's slog it down this hill. thought you knew all kinds of lingo. I thought you ere such an expert."

He was shaking his head, laughing. "Just playing it y ear," he said.

"Why, you little . . . !" She reached down for a ndful of snow, balled it up, and smacked him with it a the shoulder.

"Don't get all worked up, now. You had fun, didn't u?"

"My legs are rubber," she said. "We came a long ay uphill," she added, looking around. It was true. 1ey had climbed quite a bit up the lower, most gentle pe of the mountain. She looked through the trees for b, and caught a flash of his yellow hat across the eadow. Good boy, she thought.

She took off her shoe and shook off the accumulated w.

"Let's go," Collier said. "It's cold in the shade."

"What's that?" Nina asked, cocking her head. They ked around, but couldn't see anyone, but it was clear ugh what they were hearing. A snowmobile.

"Damn," Collier said. "I hate the noise those things ke."

Nina put her shoe on and stood up. "Which way k?"

He led her out of the trees toward the big valley. ey were high up the side of the mountain, almost in middle of the steep slope rising behind them. Here the ground was much steeper. "Let's go back the other way," Nina said nervously. "I'll fall here."

"Let's just cross to the other side. Then we can come through a new way back to the road."

"Mom! Collier!" Bob shouted, spotting them far above him. "Watch this!"

He snowboarded rapidly down a hill in the direction facing the mountain, sliding to a stop at the bottom Floyd met him there. He looked up and waved.

"Wow!" they shouted. And that's when she heard it the sound of the snowmobile approaching from the far side of the mountain, higher still. It roared into view close enough for Nina to see the driver's red and white and black ski parka.

"Oh, no," she said. "C'mon. Let's go down Quickly."

Collier looked intently at the snowmobile, which had stopped at the edge of the snowfield above them, if the man on it was studying them. "You know wh that is?" he asked.

"Jim Strong."

"How sure are you?"

"I know that parka." They turned around and beg to go back as swiftly as they could the way they h come, clumsy on the snowshoes.

The snowmobile took off. Angling straight up t mountain, it peaked parallel with the mountain alm directly above them, and roared down the other side the trees they were heading toward.

Collier stopped. "What do you want to do? N he's that way. We can't avoid him, so we'll confr him. I'm with you. I'll watch him."

"Floyd!" Nina shouted down the mounta "Floyd!" Drummond saw her waving to him and s the snowmobile. He began climbing toward them, but he had a long way to go.

"Okay," Nina said, suddenly very, very tired. Her feet felt heavy and awkward as bowling balls and she remembered the mountain climbing books she had read all of one winter, how climbers at very high altitudes took eight breaths to make one step. She didn't want to go toward that revving motor in the trees. But Jim was much faster and could cut them off easily no matter which way they went. She took sharp shallow breaths and tried to prepare herself as they trudged forward.

Jim Strong gunned the snowmobile and roared away from them, up the mountain.

"Thank God," Nina gasped. "He's going away."

"He's high-marking," Collier remarked, watching him zigzag up the face. Jim handled the snowmobile expertly. It was as if he was showing off for them just how good he was in the snow.

"High-marking? Is that more made-up language?" Nina asked.

"No. It's when they try to go as high as they can on a mountain without tipping over. What's he up to now?"

Jim had gone higher than she would have thought possible. He was about two hundred feet above them, still sitting on the snowmobile. Suddenly, there was silence.

"Maybe he stalled," Collier said. "Anyway, he's cut the motor."

Anxiously, she scanned the hills below and found Wyd still climbing, far below and to the side.

Collier was looking up and her eyes too were irresistibly drawn back. "Collier," she said, pulling at his jacket, feeling very close to tears. "We have to get out of here quickly!"

She felt the cold creeping into the gaps between her gloves, up the legs of her pants. She felt the nose on her face harden and hurt with it.

Panting with exertion, barely balanced on her snowshoes, she turned once more to look up.

With a mighty roar, the machine lurched to life. It began cutting back and forth above them as they turned and began struggling down the mountain as fast as they could. They both knew what he was doing now. All that snow, the tons and tons that had dropped from the sky . . .

The mountain came alive.

They were moving even though they stood still, Nina's hand at her throat, Collier reaching toward her, moving downhill, faster and faster.

They were moving because the huge slab of snow that they were standing on had broken loose above them and was sliding down the mountain toward the valley below.

For a second that took forever she watched the snow above them break into massive, bricklike slabs accelerating at different speeds down the mountain. They were right in the middle of the face, traveling down with with nowhere to go. She saw Jim take off, racing for the side of the mountain.

They changed direction and began traversing frantically, trying to sidestep it somehow.

Below, she saw Bob on his snowboard.

He sees it, she thought, because he was racing for the side of the mountain, racing for the trees at the edge the slide.

Jim knew all about snow, she thought. The

round her darkened with snow crystals. Her hair
whipped around her face. Something hit her in the
back. They were moving faster! She threw herself at
Collier, held him desperately, braced herself.

No sound. No air. She was knocked forward by a
all of snow. She went somersaulting down the moun-
ain, wiping out in a tidal wave.

She slammed into something, a rock or tree, slid past
and continued her free fall, completely out of control,
ruck over and over by rocks, conscious in spite of the
ain. Just like in the ocean, she tried to swim up, get her
ead up so she could breathe . . . but the snow was as
ep as the sky, and she was drowning. . . .

27

SHE AWOKE TO blackness and a dark so smothering
not a glimmer of light penetrated. She remembered
blows to her head—something hitting her over and
over, until, dazed but relieved, she had slipped into un
consciousness.

So something had hit her. Good. That was a start

The damage to her head must account for th
strange confusion of mind. She did not know where s
was. A crushing weight pressed down on her chest.

Pressed on all sides, enclosed and immobilized, s
did not know where she was or why she was there.

But—why was she so cold? She tried to reach for t
covers, but she was not in bed. She knew that. She v
crouching, suspended somehow in this icy blackne
Her body was inert, a lump of ice in a frosty cave.

She tried to breathe. Freezing air sliced into
throat, stale and moist at the same time. Her hands w
cupped a few inches from her face, and a pocket of
made it possible for her to take in breaths in slow ga
which she tried to warm in her mouth before tak
into her lungs.

Because her lungs hurt.

That was good, wasn't it, that she could feel
lungs? Somehow, this reality check slowed the risin

er panic. She tried to move, but she could not move.
Jedged, she had only the pocket of space in front of her
ce that contained her air and was formed by her own
pped hands. She licked her lips, tried to shout. Her
vn voice came back to her, soft, muffled, distant.

She opened her eyes to the blackness again, but ice
izzled in, so she covered them again like a blanket over
r cold pupils. She tried to get a better sense of her
dy. She wiggled her toes. They were somewhere be-
w her, encased in something, stiffening.

Snow, not white but black.

Snow surrounded her. Snow melted in the cracks of
r clothing. Snow oozed over and froze on her lips as
e breathed in the air that seemed so thin and used up.

She knew where she was. She remembered her free
under a great wall of snow, and the surge of fear
en she realized they all might die.

But she wasn't dead yet. Instead, she seemed to be
wly suffocating.

Frantic, she began to push with her hands. If she
ld enlarge her breathing space, get more oxygen. If
could think . . .

Nothing budged.

Weakly, feeling tears freezing on her cheeks, she
ed. Again her soft mewing voice surrounded her.
elp!" She took a deep breath to call louder, but the
ssure on her chest made her cough.

"Help!" she cried as loudly as she could.

No use. She could hear nothing from above, no
s, no rescuers, no voices.

No wind or soft sliding sound of skis. Only her rag-
breaths, and the thumping of her own heart.

Underneath her eyelids, inside her mind, her vision
rned. Above her, she watched a man cartwheel

down the mountain, and below, a snowboard as fragil
as a matchstick making a frenzied rush for the trees.

She had been struggling mindlessly for some tim
when the thought came that she was using up all h
oxygen. She stopped instantly. Yet the panting didn
stop, but continued and continued, because her hea
was overcome with fear. All she could think about w
running out of air. Her chest moved up and down.

After a while she remembered the trick she used
go to sleep on stress-ridden nights, to count her brea
down into slowness.

One two three four five six one two three fo
five six . . . one . . . two . . . threefourfivesix .
one . . . two . . . three . . . fourfive . . . six . . .

She could feel her legs tangled together, immoval
in snow. Her right elbow had a couple of inches, a
her right hand over her head gave her face four incl
or so. The fingers of her left arm could twitch, but
arm itself seemed encased in ice. The air wasn't clean
was full of ice crystals. She was coughing intermitten
But she had air.

She opened her ice-encrusted eyelashes, her eyes,
the terrifying darkness.

Buried alive.

She counted to six over and over, thought only
the numbers. And she thought of the Elephant Cele
the figure of the woman in the painting running par
stricken from the monster . . .

Directly above, it seemed to her, the blackness
came less black.

She called again, conserving her energy and
voice. If Bob or Collier had made it, they would
help. "Hey-y-y! Hey-y-y!" It was more of a moanin

ening sound she made, trying to be sharp and high
d clear.

While she called, she thought about her own death.
wouldn't matter to her. She would be gone. The
ing part would hurt, but it would be over at some
int, and she would know while it was happening that
 would be relieved soon. She thought of how quiet
tchcock became when his muzzle was wrapped at the
's, of how the gazelle caught in the jaws of the tiger
ets and endures. She, too, was quieting in the face of
 much stronger thing that had her in its jaws.

She kept calling, thinking, Bob would be all right
h Matt. She had given him enough love over the
rs to manage. He would not be destroyed by losing
. Collier—was he buried somewhere near, calling?
 stopped and listened.

A faint voice, calling from far away. Had she really
rd it?

'Collier . . . Collier . . ." she called. Louder
es. The snow above her shifted slightly. Terrified,
screamed, "No!" The movement was causing the
v to press down harder. Ice crystals filled her mouth.
v she couldn't call, or breathe.

Voices.

The snow came down and now she was truly buried
 she knew the complete quietness of impending
h as her nose and mouth filled with snow.

 shovel struck her foot. She was sliding down. It
 't so bad. She could endure it.

ut now there was pain as desperate hands yanked
 y the hair, the shoulders, trying to get a purchase
 e she suffocated, not caring.

he was being pulled from her burial place, so
 ly, choking and coughing . . .

Breathing. Someone was holding her in a crouc
beating on her back and making her cough it up, her i
hair clinging to the ground.

She breathed, mouth open. She turned her head, s
crouching, blind in the sunlight.

Bob was crouched in front of her. She grabbed h
and pulled him to her.

"Mom," he said. She held him hard enough to bre
his ribs.

"Collier?" she said, her voice gritty. She turned
face Floyd Drummond and two other men she h
never seen before. Bob was brushing snow off her.

"Bob. Where's Collier?"

"They're looking for him, Mom."

"Oh, no! No!"

"Can you stand up?" said one of the men. He
Bob each took an arm. Slowly, she got up.

"Incredible," said one of the men. "She's
banged up a little."

"My husband," she whispered, leaning on Bob.
snowshoes were long gone. The smooth soft snow
been replaced by a field of blocks of snow, many t
than she was. She had fallen almost to the valley fl

"I can see the rescue squad coming across the
ley," one of the men said. "They'll find him."

"There was a snowmobile. A man set it off," I
said clumsily through frozen lips.

"I told them," Floyd said.

"He's long gone," said the man. "I saw him n
off to the side. I don't know where he went. I saw
whole thing from the other side of the valley. You
down there less than ten minutes."

She shook her head dumbly. "Bob? Did you
where Collier fell?" He stroked her hair.

"No. I couldn't see him." The snow on her hair was
elting, soaking her. Bob helped her take off her jacket
d gave her his to wear.

A few minutes later, many people came. She was
apped in a blanket. The mountain crawled with peo-
:.

Two hours later they found Collier about two hun-
:d yards away from where she had been buried. Floyd
led from the mountain to the Bronco, where she was
l sitting, refusing to go anywhere.

"I'm so sorry," he said. "I blame myself."

"Don't let him die! Work on him! Do something!"

"They are. But—"

"No! No!" She clutched at Bob. "Work on him!"
He was frozen, ice-coated, broken and hurt. She re-
:d to believe he was gone.

They tried to revive him long past the time they
uld have quit, and then they brought him down and
led him to Boulder Hospital.

She waited in the hall, disbelieving, huddled in the
.ket, shaking her head and protesting that he
ldn't be dead, he could come back. She kept order-
them to do something, until an ER doctor came out
gave her a shot.

ater, she would be told that he had died long before
ame to rest.

oon after that, Andrea and Matt took her away from
er, and put her to bed in the room with the yellow
d where she had spent her first night at Tahoe.

/hen they had all gone to bed, when she was lying
: with her eyes open looking at the ceiling, a wind
: into her room, to the bed, and entered through
op of her head and traveled down her spine so that

she shivered deeply. She felt that he had come, that h
was still with her.

She began talking to him, asking again, how cou
you leave me? How could you go? Am I responsible?
seemed to her that he was above her, looking dow
Her center of gravity moved up, uncertainly, towa
him. Now it seemed to her that he was there with h
mother.

Grief shook her. She spread her arms wide on t
bed, and begged them to take her. She wanted to
drawn up to them and be reunited with them.

She was aware of the solemnity of her decision. S
was asking to die. She meant it. She gave up and
there.

But death did not take her. Her heart did not stop
she had thought it would. Collier and her mother fa
away. She was left alone.

No one ever to love her again. No one to call her
darling. No one beside her when she woke up.

One tear came after another then, stately, slow te
tears of surrender.

She slept.

The next day, leaden, she told the police about J
Not everything, just the part about the threats and
distinctive parka. They said that Jim had definitely
the lake, driven to Reno and flown to New York C
where his track, so far, had evaporated.

Time passed. Andrea helped her make funeral
rangements. Collier's mother would be flying up to
his body back to the family plot in San Diego. Coll
ring would stay on his finger forever, just like hers

She would never remember much of the funeral
vice. Her heart had frozen. She moved like a zomb

After the service, many people came to Collier's
ırtment. Floyd Drummond cried, and everyone from
police department and the D.A.'s office came. Barb
ked drawn, as if she'd been crying too. She came up
Nina and said, "I wish he'd never met you." Henry
Farland, beside her, said quickly, "She doesn't mean
Nina. No one blames you." He led Barbara away.
Her father came up from Monterey, and Collier's
school friends from San Diego. Paul flew back again
the funeral, but he only talked to her briefly, his face
stone.

People seemed to need to touch her. She suffered
because it gave them comfort. Collier had so many
ıds she'd never met. He had been loved and appreci-
by many.

Philip Strong came up to her as she was saying good-
to Floyd.

He had lost a lot of weight and looked emaciated,
y year of his age now weighing heavily on him. It
hard to believe that this was the man who had stolen
on's wife and precipitated so much terror.

May I speak to you?" he said humbly. She let him
her aside.

I came to tell you that I recognize my fault in what
ened. I am deeply sorry. I'll never be able to make
r any of it, or—or show you how much I regret

don't blame you, Mr. Strong."

won't rest until Jim is stopped. If he ever comes
to Paradise, I will turn him in. But he'll never dare
here again. He's gone forever, and I pity the
with him roaming in it. But still—forgive me—
ill his father—I can't help but pity him too. He

must be suffering like a wolf in a spring trap where he is. He can't be so far gone that he doesn't realize h failed completely, that there's no hope left. Please do be angry. I know—it must seem incredible to you th can say I pity him. You hate him, of course."

When she didn't answer, or turn her back on h Strong seemed to take courage. "It struck me that tween Jim's lies and my silence, you might not re understand some of the things that happened. I'd lik explain."

She sighed.

"Or perhaps I'm wrong. I would understand it if never wanted to hear Jim's name again."

"Go ahead. I want to hear what you have to sa

Looking at his shoes, Strong said quietly, "He wa aberration, even as a young child, so different from other children. An aberration—that's a cruel word, I've never used it until now, but that's what he even as a baby in diapers, with those blue eyes that some frightening light in them.

"He was always aggressive, pushing things out o way, smashing things—my wife tried to talk to about the things he did, but I found an excuse for ev thing—his cruelties, his lying, his truancies. Alex the only person Jim could tolerate, I suppose be Alex looked up to him. Alex was happy. Jim was a from the start.

"When he entered his teens, my wife became alarmed and took Jim to several psychologists. Jim them and complained to me. I took his side. I w champion in the family, you might say.

"Then our dog died. Alex told my wife that Jir boasted that he ran him over. I chose to believe denials. I just felt that he would come out of it someday, if we could just hold on." Strong looked at Nina. "He was my son. I wanted to protect him.

"Then something very frightening happened. Kelly, who loved to ski more than any of us, had an accident on the mountain. She was seriously injured. And she said that Jim had come up behind her and pushed her into a tree."

"And you believed Jim over Kelly. I know how well Jim lies, Mr. Strong."

"Yes." He hung his head again. "My wife insisted that we institutionalize Jim, and he begged me not to. I couldn't do it to him—couldn't believe he was capable of such a thing. Other events occurred. Over a period of years, the family cracked up, you might say. Like a car wreck in slow motion. My wife moved with Alex and Kelly to Colorado and divorced me. I stayed at Paradise and tried to control Jim.

"I think, when the family left, Jim became frightened of himself. He took the loss of his mother very badly. She had cut off all contact with him, and this affected him so deeply that he seemed to start to turn around completely. He graduated from high school, got some college in, and started working with me at Paradise.

"My wife died just before Alex finished college, and he wanted to come here and work. He and Jim were both on the Ski Patrol, and they started up again as if they'd never been apart. Alex put up with Jim's moods. They went around together, double-dated—I thought Jim was going to make it.

"Alex took over the lodge and Jim ran the ski operations for a few years. They both got married. Jim was completely taken with Heidi, and for the first time in his life he seemed happy.

"But about a year ago, Jim came into my office and accused me of favoring Alex. He had that old look on his face. I was very concerned.

"He wanted Alex's job. Eventually I gave it to him. He was no good at it. He was no good with people, with details, with paperwork. He kept at it, but there were incidents, and I knew I was going to have to do something soon.

"Heidi began coming to me, knowing how well I knew Jim. She told me that Jim had become so abusive to her that she was planning to leave him. I was very alarmed for her safety, for Jim's stability—I wasn't sure what to do. I tried to talk to her, to try to persuade her to stay, and somehow, we—we—"

"Fell in love," Nina said. She was listening intently, looking for understanding even if there was to be no comfort for her.

"I will carry the guilt for the rest of my life." He closed his eyes.

"Go on, Mr. Strong."

"I'm not sure how Marianne found out."

Nina said, "She overheard Heidi calling you from the equipment rental room one day. She didn't know who Heidi was talking to."

"Marianne had dated Jim before Heidi and was still interested in him. I have thought sometimes that she married Alex just to stay close to Jim."

"I wouldn't be surprised."

"So, of course, she told Jim about Heidi. She wanted Heidi to leave him. Out of spite, or because she thought she could turn him toward her—she's a—a—"

Nina nodded.

"When Heidi got home he made her tell him who it as. He threatened her and bullied her into staying with im. And he made her promise not to tell me that he new. He was deciding what revenge to take, I suppose. knew nothing except that Heidi suddenly wouldn't en talk to me. Jim acted perfectly normal. Can you lieve anyone could do that?"

"Jim could."

"Alex died a few days later, and I thought it was an cident. I thought it was an accident! Why on earth uld Jim hurt Alex? What did Alex have to do with eidi and me? Then Heidi ran away. She thought that n had killed Alex. But I had my head in the sand one t time. I told her we would wait and see what came t of the police investigation. I looked into Jim's eyes, d I couldn't tell. I thought I was going crazy myself. I d to get out, but I was afraid to go to Heidi.

"I could have saved her. And Alex."

"How?" Nina said.

"I could have. I could have sent Jim away when he s sixteen."

"I doubt you could have," Nina said softly. "I ldn't save my husband. I tried, just like you tried, to trol someone who was completely out of control. n if—if you and Heidi hadn't fallen in love, Jim was ng to kill someone eventually."

Strong's shoulders slumped. He looked old. "Please 't be so kind," he said. "I don't deserve your kind- s. It's just another blow. Why don't you despise me? n when Jim was arrested for Alex's murder and I w there was evidence of it, I looked the other way. truth was too horrible for me to face. And so my ht beautiful Heidi was lost too."

Nina put her hand on Strong's shoulder.

"Thank you for listening to me," he said. "I realiz[e]
now I did even this for myself, subjected you to thi[s]
selfish and maudlin confession. You're a fine lawyer an[d]
fine person, and I am so sorry for what my family h[as]
done to you."

Nina nodded.

"If there is anything I can do for you at any time—[?]

She nodded again. He took her hand. He frowne[d]
as though he hadn't been able to say what he mea[nt]
at all.

Something deep and sad passed between them.

"So sorry," Philip Strong mumbled as he mov[ed]
away.

Collier was gone forever from contact, but in t[he]
sense of an impenetrable wall between them, not in t[he]
sense that his spirit was finally extinguished. The wi[nd]
and the shivering came every night. She left her wind[ow]
open to make it easy for him.

> Maybe our spirits can intertwine
> Til there's no more of yours and no more of
>   mine

Her spirit shrank from the world. It felt as tho[ugh]
she was looking at it through a keyhole. None o[f it]
mattered. She was still clinging to him.

The grotesque became normal. The day after [the]
funeral she went back to work. Collier's body still la[y in]
the snow of her mind while she looked at her ph[one]
messages and spoke to the court clerk on the ph[one.]
Sandy held most of the incoming calls while she [?]

hrough the cards and letters. Ginger wrote, "Don't give
p. We need you."

She opened a card from Mrs. Geiger. Inside was a
heck for thirty thousand dollars. Her note said, "I got a
b doing the accounts at Cecil's market. That's what I
ally needed, a job. It wasn't right of me to take your
oney. God bless you for what you did."

"Send it back to her, Sandy," she said.

"But—"

"Just send it back."

An investigator named Sean something called to say
was coordinating the search for Jim. There had been
possible sighting in Miami. He told her that they fig-
ed Jim had left the jurisdiction before Collier had
en been found.

The newspaper lay on her desk. The buyout of Para-
e Ski Resort by a German corporation had attracted a
of attention.

So Marianne and her stepbrother had forced Philip
open the family business, and Philip must have given
and sold out completely. Marianne and Gene would
on their way to the Alps with a million dollars in
ir pockets. Paradise would never be the same.

Toward five o'clock, Sandy came in and said, "Time
go."

"Okay." She put on her coat, picked up her bag and
ked outside, following Sandy.

It was already growing dark. She could see Christmas
orations in the trailer park behind the parking lot. It
very cold.

"The wind's gonna let loose tonight," Sandy said.
u watch yourself." She turned to go, but then came
k to where Nina stood alone in the lot and said,
u gotta be brave."

"I know. I'm trying."

"Okay then. See you tomorrow." Sandy stood be side her car, watching until Nina turned the Bronco o and drove out of the parking lot. The stars were comin out one by one, and the cold was deepening.

28

Snow falls upon this dream of mine
This dream we had together
Oh why can't happiness endure . . .

THE WIND STARTED with a soft hush, then acceler-
ed into many small whirlwinds. Cold began to grip
e night and everything in it, a chilling hand.

Driving on Pioneer Trail, completely unexpectedly,
na began to have another panic attack. She felt again
e terror spiraling up in her from the place she had
ed to hide it. It was like a pressure against her heart.

And still the wind increased in intensity, until the sky
ed with the snowless gale, cold and clean and pure
d deadly, penetrating every crevice. The killing cold,
rciless, rode with it.

As she drove, her mind fighting its own whirlwind of
ck and fear and loss, she could barely keep the car on
road. The gusts pushed the Bronco around on the
d like a toy.

She finally remembered to turn on the heater, but
cold had already infiltrated and she began to shiver.
the same moment, Jim came into her mind again,
ehow mixed up with Bob.

At last she had it, what Kelly and Marianne and

Heidi had been telling her if she'd only been able t understand.

He takes the thing you love the most, she though Panic made her weave over the center line.

He'd already taken Collier. He should be long gor by now, to Belize or some other faraway place where l could hide. He'd taken her love.

Had it been enough for him?

What did she know about his mind? She grabbed tl car phone and called home, heard the useless buzz.

"Oh, my God," she said aloud. Oh please God, n She gunned the car to race home.

In the clear night, she felt she could see all the way heaven, the stars so close you could almost hear the sizzle. Wind tore across the lake, creating cresting da currents, picking up moisture.

I'm so cold, thought Nina. I can't believe how col am. She swung around the corner of Natoma t quickly, nearly sliding into an old green Travelall hide in the darkness under some trees.

He's got to be all right. He has to. She couldn't b to think any other way. The shivering became unce trollable. Clenching the wheel, she turned onto Kul Street and pulled into the driveway.

No lights. A stillness that looked like death to l She jumped out, hair slapping at her face, almost falli and pounded on the door. No answer. The bo numbing wind blasted her. She called, "Bot Bobby!" But her voice trailed off in the wind.

Trembling, she fumbled the key into the lock, fee an awful fear of what she might find and a new sens danger.

As if something were behind her . . .

She threw open the door and yelled, "Are yo

ere?" Then, overcome with terror, she ran down the ll to Bob's room.

Nothing, no one, just his bare bed. Into the kitchen, mping into things, the light—

And then she saw a note on the kitchen table.

"Hi, Mom. Aunt Andrea picked me up so I ouldn't be alone. Come over if you want, she says."

A heart drawn hastily at the bottom. He was all ht! She sat down at the kitchen table, and sobbed th relief. A few minutes passed before the flood re-ded.

Finally, feeling very shaky, she got up to get the fire ng. Damn! Only one small log. She was going to e to go outside to get more wood. She closed her s for a minute, steeling herself, then put her coat and pping boots back on. Grabbing the flashlight, she ned the door.

The wind hit her in the face, nearly knocking her r. It must be a front for a hell of a storm. She would k the place up tight, call Andrea, drink some whis-, and go to bed. The panic attack had left her so ry . . . she didn't want to go to Matt's tonight. en she woke in the early morning, she didn't want n all to hear the sound of her grieving.

As she bent down to fill her arms with logs, she ight she saw something moving in the trees on the e of the yard. It reminded her of the day at Paradise Philip Strong when he talked about seeing Alex nd every corner. She peered into the howling wind a long moment, and the creepy feeling of menace ned. Would it always be there? How could she it? Quickly, she gathered the wood and went back e, slamming the door and locking and bolting it as as she could.

She had thought she smelled almonds. She was imag
ining things.

Stacking the wood by the fireplace, she crumpl
some newspaper and lit the fire. The bright color an
heat made her feel better. Then she went into th
kitchen and put on the teapot. She dug around in th
front closet for her mukluks and pulled out an afghan
the same time, returning to the kitchen just as the ket
began to whine.

Pouring the hot water over some Swiss Miss choc
late, she added a shot of Old Bushmills to the m
turned on the stereo to the oldies channel, and sat b
fore the fire, arranging the red blanket around her. T
one Collier had put over her legs that night . . .

Then she called Bob on the cordless phone, a
talked to Andrea who said Bob was fine and who urg
her to come over. "Not tonight," Nina said. "I'd rat
be home."

"Call if you need us," Andrea said. "Matt will co
get you, you know that."

"No. Thanks for taking Bob."

"I don't feel right letting you stay alone."

"I have to get used to it."

She hung up and sat huddled in the blanket. The
slowly warmed the cabin, even as the wind roared
the fireplace flue, until finally she stopped trembl
She drank the chocolate slowly, the mug warming
hands.

At last the taut, frightened muscles surrendered
by one to the warmth of the blanket and the drink,
all the horror of the last month dulled for a few min
Safe, she thought. He's long gone. Bob is safe. I'm
and sound and home.

The wind clattered against the locked cabin. Nina
ugged the blanket to her. Exhausted, she fell asleep.

I'll make you pay, bitch.

I'll make you beg me to kill you.

Hooded in his parka, hands in thick ski gloves, Jim
atched the house. He watched the smoke billowing
it of the chimney against a black sky, imagining her
side. The kid had been driving away with a woman
st as he arrived, and the woman had looked back at his
r just once, but he was wearing his parka and drove
ght by the house.

When the two of them were gone, he had parked
e car up a street called Hunkpapa and pushed his way
ough the blasts of wind back to the back yard. And
ited.

Bad weather didn't bother him. He found it invigo-
ng.

He hadn't quite paid her back for pulling that trick
court. The enormity of her betrayal had taken time to
in. She was the worst traitor of them all, worse than
idi, worse than his father. She had even thought she
ld fool him. As if he couldn't read her.

None of it was his fault.

They had all left him now, and he had nothing but
mpty gnawing hole in his soul. Hole in my soul, he
ated to himself, hole in my soul, slayer of betrayers,
the one you love the most and take you be-
s . . .

The gnawing was in his gut right now, cramping and
tening and making him sick. Christ, he was being
n alive!

He'd begged Heidi to come back to him, but she

wouldn't understand. He hadn't wanted to use the kni[f]
on her. It was his father's fault.

He'd have to get out after he killed Nina, but h[e]
wasn't finished. Next year for Kelly, who had testifi[ed]
against him. And of course, his father.

No one would escape. And the night-gnawin[g]
would end.

An hour or so went by while he froze outside h[er]
house. Enough time had passed for her to put on h[er]
robe, sit down for a meal, do whatever she was going [to]
do, just so her guard was down.

He was sensitive to women. He had a feeling she w[as]
asleep.

He moved silently through the trees near the woo[d]
pile, then stopped there under cover of blowing blac[k]
ness. The snowfield next door reflected just enou[gh]
starlight. Goddamn cold! He looked for a way into [the]
house.

She made it so simple, he almost felt insulted. [She]
had forgotten to bolt the back door. Noiselessly, m[e]
thodically, he jimmied the lock. What a cinch.

Prepare to die, bitch, he thought. His rage surged
in him again, warming him.

She would beg, damn her.

He turned the knob.

Something hard and sharp struck him on the bas[e of]
his spine through the parka. He figured a branch [had]
blown into him, but as his hand tightened on the k[nob]
he felt the sharpness deepen, taking his breath a[way.]
Turning his head just far enough to see behind him [he]
saw a stranger, a big blond man, his head ringed [with]
stars, his face terrible. He tried to scream but no so[und]
came out. The man had clamped a hand like iron

is mouth. And then, incredibly, he felt another, crush-
ng pain, like a spear, like an arrow, like a dagger. He
felt appalling pain as a blade drove into his body, into his
pine, and tears in his eyes, and the cold, my God, the
old—

"Rhapsody on a windy night, motherfucker," the
man whispered. "The last twist of the knife."

He felt the pain tear him apart, and he wanted to
scream but he had no breath left. He wanted to end the
ony that corkscrewed through him but there was no
ay back to the wind and the stars and the night.

"Ah—!"

He was sucked down to the still and silent hell that
aited him.

The phone jangled Nina back to the firelit living
om. Still dazed from her deep sleep, she put it to her

"Hi. It's Paul. I wanted to let you know I was think-
of you."

Paul's voice was so reassuring. She started jabbering,
ing him things. Paul listened patiently on the line.

"I know, honey, I know," he kept saying.

"They say—the police are sure Jim's gone. There
n't been a trace of him. But I'm still—I had a real
ic attack tonight on the way home. I thought Bob
ht be in trouble and he's fine. I keep doing that,
ig along and then—it's just—"

There was a silence on the other end. Then Paul
, "Don't worry about him anymore, Nina."

"But I can't be sure. I don't know if I can live with
fear, Paul. I can live with the grief, but not constant
I don't know what to do."

"He won't be back, Nina. I guarantee it."

She didn't answer him. She thought, I want to be lieve that, but how can I?

"Listen to me, Nina," Paul said in a peculiar, insis tent way. "You'll never see or hear from him again."

"You sound so sure," Nina said. "Do you kno where he is?"

The line crackled, and she thought how far aw; Paul was, on the other side of the country, and how sl missed him terribly.

"Paul? Are you still there?"

"Yeah, I'm here."

"Do you know where he is?"

"I'll be damned if I know," said Paul.

And that night, alone in her bed in the cabin, Ni turned her head on her wet pillow.

Perhaps her heart couldn't take any more pain. P haps the mountain god had finally taken her into arms, soothing her, sending her back to a moment lc ago when she had been happy.

In her dream she was a child again, running in Pacific surf on a sunny day, her parents behind her. was a little girl full of joy, a joy which had come bef and which would come again, in time.

Turn the page for a preview of
Perri O'Shaughnessy's new hardcover
Nina Reilly novel

MOVE TO STRIKE

Available from Delacorte Press in August 2000

Moist night wind swept the skin on her arms and icked sharp points of hair into her eyes. Pulling her weatshirt tight against the gusts, Nikki tucked her air inside the hood and splashed the oars into the ep black water of Lake Tahoe. A hundred years o, under the same slim crescent moon, a Washoe dian in a kayak would have known how to dip the rs silently, secretly, but no matter how she tipped em, they sucked water into the air, leaving a trail of und.

Silvery snow tipped the mountain peaks that circled e clouds around the lake. She stayed close enough to shoreline—flat black trees against a glinting navy sky to track her progress, but far enough out to remain identifiable to anyone nosy enough to observe her. e could not be seen. She could not be caught, be- se tonight . . .

Tonight, she was going on a raid! And for the first e, she was going alone.

She felt high on the strength of her arms and the ness of her legs as she rowed, as high as she had felt New Year's Eve when her mom had let her drink mpagne. So even though she didn't like being out e all alone, floating above a deep, dark immensity she didn't want to think about, she wasn't about to turn back.

Scott would have come with her if she had told him about it, but tonight—tonight was personal. She was not just skulking and peeking in windows for a joke, or scrounging a few leftover Heinekens out of an outside cooler. Not that she didn't miss having him along. She wouldn't mind a warm body beside her floating into the dark moonlit haze.

As a steady breeze blew over the lake, the water churned, pushing her out farther than she liked. But it wasn't far now.

She knew what she was doing was wrong. But a while back, being bad had stopped feeling bad. Scott had helped her with that. So many rules were stupid. He had shown her a whole new way of thinking. You had to make your own way.

Tonight was about making something really wrong right again.

She stretched. Her arms ached. She wasn't used to rowing so much, but then, her original plans for the year hadn't included breaking into someone's house. She hadn't exactly trained for this. She had been forced into it. Three days before, her mother had received a letter from a law office. That scared her. Her mother wasn't around, so she'd opened it. A so-far nice day turned real bad right then. The letter said they were about to be evicted. The landlord wanted his money and he wanted it right now. Only money, right away, could save them.

When her mom came home Nikki held the letter in her face, making her read it. "What is this?"

"Don't worry, honey," Daria had said in that dr

way she had. As if everything took care of itself some-
ow. As if they weren't going to have to pack their
elongings in boxes in about two weeks and go squat in
condemned building. Nikki sat her down, tried to
ave a practical conversation with her. Where was her
st paycheck?

Gone. They had a lot of back bills to pay.

Not worth screaming about. The bills never got paid
util the third notice because they weren't Daria's pri-
ity. At least this time she hadn't gotten rooked by
me guy who was off to make his mark as an artist or a
usician in Vegas.

What about her job? Nikki had asked, Where were
e paychecks? Oh, she had lost that job a few weeks
o. She didn't want Nikki to worry and had planned to
l her just as soon as she had another one, which
uld be any day now.

Nikki had decided. They would resort to the un-
nkable. They would borrow money, using Grandpa
gan's land in Nevada for collateral. That was when
mom got nervous and darted around the living
m rearranging trinkets.

Finally, Daria had admitted it. She had sold the land
Nikki's Uncle Bill for twelve hundred stinkin' dollars.
Forty acres!

Her mom shrugged, saying what was done was done.
at land is in the middle of nowhere and it's basically
thless. He did us a favor."

"Where's the money?" Nikki had asked, guessing
answer but hopeful still. Maybe Grandpa's land
ld perform a heroic rescue. Maybe it would save
home. But no. Her mom had already spent that
paying a few other late bills. The money was gone,
like everything else. Like her dad. Like the security

she had once had, that she would have lunch money c
new shoes in the fall.

Her mom had never grown up. She trusted every
body, even Uncle Bill. He had never helped them ou
before and he hadn't helped them out this time. Nikl
knew darn good and well that land was worth mor
than he had paid. All you had to do was to check o
the *Reno Gazette*. Land in Nevada was going up, eve
scrub desert in the foothills. You couldn't buy land f
thirty bucks an acre. You couldn't buy anything f
thirty bucks, period. He had taken advantage of h
mom's totally inept sense of business.

All of which she had told her mom.

"Oh, honey. Your uncle's a very savvy businessma
Believe me, he knows how much that land is worth

Duh! He knew, all right, but he was smart enou
not to pay it.

Her next thought was, okay, she would talk to hi
maybe just ask him to pay a fairer price for Grandp
acres. But that was dreaming. He couldn't stand her
Daria, because they were poor and he was rich. Son
times Nikki even thought Uncle Bill was afraid of h
maybe because of her smart mouth.

But they were really in the pits this time, so
thought, they'd ask him for a loan. But any time she
Daria had been hurting in the past, he had made sur
joke about how stupid it was to loan money to relati
rubbing his clean surgeon's hands together and watcl
to make sure they got it.

That made up her mind. She would go to his ho
find money and take it. She had studied the newsp.
classified. She figured the land as, rock-bottom m
mum, worth twice what he paid. She was sure he
cash around the house. She would take no more

hat he should have paid them in the first place. To-
orrow, before he had time to call the police or some-
ing dumb like that, she would 'fess up.

Because, let's face it. He owed them.

If he got really ugly about it, they could promise to
y him back when they could. He would just have to
mp it and accept that the money was gone. Ultra-
spectable Uncle Bill would never tell anyone his niece
me and had to steal money from him to save herself
d her mother from being evicted. He would never
ow a public scandal that might reflect badly on him.
s surgical practice depended too much on people ad-
ring him and thinking he was so brilliant and such a
nt. Nobody wanted a mean, stingy guy cutting them

Did she hear splashing? Turning her head, she looked
hind her. If there was another boat or something out
e, she couldn't see it. When she was young, she be-
ed that monsters roamed this lake. Bedtime stories,
knew, but still . . . she was alone, shivering in a
v rush of wind. The lake felt powerful and alive un-
her. For a moment, fear took over. She fought the
e to turn around and go home.

Tears welled in her eyes. For some reason, her dad's
, the one in the picture of him and her and her
n, appeared in her mind. Maybe it was a blessing on
ight, him coming around. She was off to fight. He
ld approve of that, wouldn't he? Thinking about the
ng that had been done to her and her mom allowed
r to heat her up and burn away the fear.

"Payback time," she said to the black sky. She was
Gibson in *Ransom,* out to get even. Her voice
ded high and scared, so she said it again, growling.
hrough a clump of trees she saw a low wood cabin,

classic old Tahoe, looking like something tossed to
gether from recycled crates. Rich people had this tric
of trying to look poor on the outside so thiev
wouldn't rob them. Scott had taught her about that. B
Nikki already knew this place was like a mansion insic
and filled with expensive junk. She and her mom ha
visited there many times.

Letting the kayak wash in on a miniature wave, sl
managed to get out without swamping and pulled
behind a bush. Water sloshed around her feet on t'
brief beach, the wind making the leaves blow and sig

Wishing the wind away, she moved commando-sty
toward the house, keeping low behind the plants th
made a privacy border. He had a swimming pool, s
knew. At the same moment she saw the kno
lacework of reflections from the pool water flicker l
the light from a TV on the fence. Her first problem v
the gate, but it was unlocked, easy. She stopped j
inside.

Four deep breaths, in and out. Her hands came u
clenched and she could open her eyes to the surrou
ings without feeling like a bear might jump out and
her. Nobody should be home. Aunt Beth and Cl
were in LA and her mom had mentioned more t
once that Saturdays were Uncle Bill's night to
poker at Caesars.

Remembering the Washoe, she moved slo
through the bushes near the pool, toward the do
glassed-in doors that led to his study. He would l
anything important there.

No sign of anyone around. She crouched down f
moment, intending to creep out into the open an
the door. Just as she straightened up, the door
open. Shit! She ducked back fast behind the d

rush, stumbling, holding her hands out to keep the
ushes back.

Uncle Bill stepped out onto the concrete patio, so
ose to her she could smell the brandy on his breath
d soap on his nude skin. So much for freakin' poker.

Wow! she thought, checking him out. He was butt-
ked, his dick swinging like a pendulum under his
lly as he moved past her. Tight buns and legs showed
worked out all the time. He looked so young, very
fferent from the famous Doctor Bill she remembered
eing in a starched white coat and glasses at his clinic.
obably it would give her a complex that her first good
ok at a naked man was her uncle.

Her heart stepped up the beat and anger took over
in. That lying, cheating bastard! Just seeing him out
e enjoying himself on a spring night, not a care in
world, made her so mad she wanted to throw some-
ng at him, slug him or something. He was too big;
d catch her for sure. The thought of him catching
in the bushes made her sick. That would blow ev-
thing.

Holding the brandy bottle in one hand, he padded
ard the steaming pool, put his feet in and plunked
butt down on the highest step where the water was
y a few inches deep. He took a swig.

"Goddamn!" he said, shaking his head. He took an-
r drink.

Nikki managed to sit down in the pine needles and
e a little viewing place for herself through the fronds
ne of those dinosaur-era ferns that grew under the
. Just when she was getting used to the whole
e, he started to jabber. "Not like I had any choice,"
aid. The sound of his own voice seemed to startle
and he looked around sharply. Like an idiot, Nikki

closed her eyes. As if he wouldn't be able to see her her eyes were closed! The fronds rustled. Had he sense someone spying? She couldn't look, but in her mind h moved swiftly toward her, pulled her out of the bush and . . . she was breathing loud enough to lead hi right to her.

He mumbled something. What was that? "Nik?" soft, she wasn't sure if he said it or if she dreamed it, b the sound was so chilling she froze.

Nothing happened. His hand didn't reach over a yank her out. She heard a splash. When she dared open her eyes again, he was gone . . . no, he v swimming away from her, toward the deep end of t pool, where the underwater light was.

He swam to the far wall, dove down deep and ca up inhaling and coughing, then dove again. Nil pushed open the branches so she could watch. He v doing something with his hands down in the water the deep-end wall. Nikki had been in that pool wl she was little. She knew it was nine feet deep. Here was, most likely drunk, acting crazy at the bottom of pool. Was he trying to drown himself? Should she m a run for the house while he was down there?

No. He might come out and see her.

Kneeling, she pushed the ferns back and stared. stayed down for almost a minute.

She was bad at waiting. Waiting gave her time think and thinking had a way of contaminating the p ing minutes with doubts. The smell of chlorine m like toxic gas with the smell of the fir trees, making feel sick. None of this was supposed to happen. shouldn't even be home, and here he was acting so pid!

He surfaced, took a breath, and dived again.

Swallowing the acid in her mouth, Nikki steeled
rself and sneaked toward the study. He came up again,
ashing, but he still had his back to her. In one hand
held a box made of metal. While he swam to the side
the pool, holding the dripping box up above the
ter with one hand, Nikki slipped back into the
hes.

Hauling himself out at the deep end, grunting, he set
box on the concrete deck. After he caught his
ath, he sat cross-legged at the edge, twisting some-
g on the box. The lid came off and he took some-
g out.

What freakin' luck! So that was where he hid his
ney. In the freakin' pool!

The wind had finally eased. Now Nikki faced a new
d, the complete silence. Except for the pool pump,
le Bill's harsh breathing, and the rasp of the box lid
e opened it, there was nothing except the noise of
clacking teeth and whomping heart. Not even the
kets were singing.

He was holding something wrapped in a cloth. Bills,
igured. Maybe some rare coins, since the cloth was
ic at the top, sewn like a pouch. Light filtering up
the pool pocked his face with ghoulish shadows.
looked like Jason in a slasher movie. The whole
was like a nightmare, the pool with its blue light,
larkness closing in, Uncle Bill, squatting like an evil
lha, drunk, fondling his secret stash . . .

fter a few moments, he put the pouch back into
ox, screwed the lid closed, dove into the pool, and
ned it to some hiding place in the deep end. This
he got out immediately and trotted to the study.
aking from the cold and scared to death he would
er at any second, she watched him wrap a towel

around himself. As he slid his feet into rubber sandals the door to the study, the doorbell rang. Shocked by t sound, she let out a little yelp. He jerked, turni around to face her, scouring the bushes, looking direc at her! He took a step forward, scaring her so bad s practically screamed, but the doorbell rang again. He tating for a second, he finally went back into the hou

Tossing off her sweatshirt, Nikki ran for the po The water curled over her body, silky like one of mom's costumes, much warmer than the air. She d Toward the bottom, directly below the pool light, gr ing, she finally felt a plastic ring in the wall, just enough to slide the tip of her finger underneath. Tw ing the ring back and forth, pulling, she discovered hiding place worked just like a drawer. Chlorine st her eyes as she reached through the milky light, pu out the heavy box, pushed the empty drawer closed, shot to the surface, gulping air, trying to see through strings of her hair.

She pulled herself out of the deep end. Holding box, she started to run for the boat. A phone rang ir the house. Good, more to keep him busy. She got as the gate before she remembered. Her godd sweatshirt! She'd left it by the pool! Stuffing the under the waistband of her drenched sweatpants, sh back toward the house, staying close to the wall away from the windows, really cold now, soaking Where had she thrown it?

Through the glass, she saw Uncle Bill talking o phone in the study, sounding happy in there, way d ent than when he had mumbled by the pool. With she realized he had no clue she was right outside lu around in the night, watching him. Unable to Nikki came a little closer and peered in.

He held the cordless phone to his ear with one hand
_d the towel around his waist with the other. He was
_iling, talking, saying "How's it going?" and "Gee,
_'s great." In that instant, Nikki felt the sweet rush of
_tory. She had done it, stolen it from under his nose.
_: was certain now she had what she had come to get.

Just as she was turning away, a change in her uncle's
_ression brought her back to the glass. His face
_ged, melting downward. His mouth dropped open
_ his eyes bulged. Like someone blinded by a bright
_t, he groped around as if hunting for some stable
_g to keep him from falling down. He staggered,
_ fell against the desk.

"No! Please God, no!" he shouted over and over,
_ into the phone, then, pressing a hand against the
_thpiece, away from it.

_he watched him stare into the receiver, then drop
_phone to the ground. He collapsed onto the floor
_curled up and cried like a baby. Now all she could
_vas the back of his neck, his muscles ropy and tense
_noose. She could hear the heaving sobs.

_ shadow ran in and bent toward him. Someone else
_here! Well, of course someone else was there. The
_bell had rung, hadn't it! She caught a glimpse,
_d, and slammed herself back against the cabin. A
_splinter pierced the skin of her palm, but she didn't
_t, even when blood began to flow onto the wood
_ house.

_er pocket sagging with his treasure, her sweatshirt
_tten, she pressed back against the wall, paralyzed.

ABOUT THE AUTHOR

O'Shaughnessy is the pen name for two sisters,
la and Mary O'Shaughnessy, who live in Hawaii
California, respectively. Pamela graduated from
rd Law School and was a trial lawyer for sixteen
Mary is a former editor and writer for multi-
projects. They have jointly written *Motion to*
ss, *Invasion of Privacy*, *Obstruction of Justice*, and
of Promise, as well as their upcoming Nina Reilly
Move to Strike. Readers can contact Perri
ughnessy at perrio@hotbot.com.